MORN

Nameless

The Destiny Trilogy
Part One

A.C. Williams

STEEL RIGG
AN IMPRINT OF CROSSHAIR PRESS

This is a work of fiction. The characters, incidents, and dialogues are products of the author's imagination and are not to be construed as real. Any resemblance to actual events or persons, living or dead, is entirely coincidental.

NAMELESS
Published by Steel Rigg, an imprint of Crosshair Press.

Copyright © 2014 by A.C. Williams

ISBN-13: 978-0692204764
ISBN: 0692204768

Cover design by Rachel McDonald
Photography by Katie Morford, featuring the Old Cowtown Museum in Wichita, Kansas

ALL RIGHTS RESERVED.
No part of this publication may be reproduced, stored in a retrieval system, or transmitted, in any form or by any means—electronic, mechanical, photocopying, recording, or otherwise—without prior written permission.

For information:
www.CrosshairPress.com | morningstar@crosshairpress.com

For Katie,
the other half of my brain,
who knows the real me
and loves me anyway

"You can't see yourself....
Out there in the world, as you move
among your fellow human beings,
whether strangers or friends
or the most intimate beloveds,
your own face is invisible to you....
We are all aliens to ourselves,
and if we have any sense of who we are,
it is only because
we live inside the eyes of others."

— Paul Auster
Winter Journal

CHAPTER 1

Mean drunks are overrated. It's the clingy ones you have to watch out for.

The loser at table four had thrown back one too many shots and mistaken Xander's arm for a teddy bear.

Again.

The more she struggled to escape the grip of his bony fingers, the more desperately he clutched, whispering obscene nothings against the soft inside of her elbow. And he was drooling.

Fantastic.

With her luck, he'd have some kind of dreaded mouth fungus. Because, let's face it, the nightmare of living life with no memory and waiting tables at the Oasis wasn't enough of a character building experience. No. Dreaded mouth fungus from a clingy, drooling drunk had to rot her arms off too.

Xander snatched one of table four's half-filled shot glasses, ignoring its spit-encrusted texture. When Cuddles turned his head to continue slobbering against her skin, she dumped the contents into his ear.

She'd heard Himalian whiskey could scour the radioactive sludge out of a hyperdrive engine wall, so it was no wonder Cuddles shrieked and flung himself backward like a possessed man in the throes of exorcism. He clawed at the side of his head and wailed, an eerie noise somewhere between braying donkey and emphysemic cow.

His gyrations tipped his chair over, and he crashed into the filthy floorboards, twitching and gasping until he began to snore.

Typical.

He'd have a heck of a goose egg when he came to, and nobody deserved it more.

"Xander!" Cedric howled from the bar. "I need glassware!"

She rolled her eyes and piled her serving tray high with the remaining shot glasses, stepping over Cuddles as he sawed logs at her feet. At one point in their lives, the shot glasses had to have been clear, but the Oasis took everything clean and smeared it with an impenetrable layer of spit, blood, and other bodily fluids.

Xander wiped her hand on her apron, though it was dirtier than the glasses. Not for the first time, she longed for hand sanitizer. A lovely aqua-clear gallon jug of sharp isopropyl-scented gel. But no one here had ever heard of it. No one anywhere had ever heard of it. So either it had never existed or it was like her name, a memory lost in the broken shadows of her mind.

Once she had all the grimy shot glasses, she pocketed the credits left as tips and stepped over the other unconscious men on the floor as she walked back to the bar, ignoring the ones who were only pretending so they could look up her skirt.

She hated that skirt.

"About time." Cedric snatched the tray from her and dumped its contents into the sink. "Old man at seven's still there. Is he dead?"

The old man had come in hours earlier, muttering to himself, staring at nothing. All he'd ordered was a gingerroot soda, the only non-alcoholic beverage they sold. His vibrant red scarf draped noose-like from his wrinkled neck. The accessory popped in the dingy light of the dirty illuminators, set at a level somewhere between dark cave and den of iniquity.

"I think he's still breathing." Xander handed Cedric the tips from table four, which he fed into the safe.

"Well, go get the old coot's creds before he bites the big one." Cedric scraped at a hardened speck on a shot glass. "If he keels over, someone'll clean him out before we get paid."

Xander took her tray back and headed toward the old man.

He was the oldest person in the bar by decades. So much for age bestowing wisdom. The old fool should have known better than to buy anything at a place like the Oasis. Then again, if he'd had any sense, he wouldn't have been on a shoddy, rundown moon like Callisto to begin with. Maybe he was just an old pusher who'd helped himself to too much of his own product.

The old man's hazel eyes pierced her. The cloudy, dull expression she'd seen before was gone, replaced with a penetrating stare that stripped away her confidence.

In a single glance, the old man knew how lost she really felt inside; he had to know. Why else would he look at her like that?

Forget the clingy drunks. The old man was worse by far.

"Can I get you something else, mister?" Unexpected emotion choked her voice.

No one could see the real her. No one knew the real her. Not even her. But the old man did. That's what his eyes whispered: *I see you. I know you.*

He cocked his head, face like dry leather, hair like cobwebs, eyes like daggers, clear, cold, and calm. "I don't drink."

She started to respond, but the words died on her lips. In the space of a blink, the clarity in his eyes vanished like it had never been there. His expression became a child's, innocent and wandering and confused. And he had no idea who she was.

Had she imagined the whole thing? Was she so desperate to

remember herself that she'd even consider asking a crazy old man sitting in the shoddiest whorehouse on the dirtiest of Jupiter's moons?

One of his twisted hands twitched on the table, spinning a daisy between his fingertips.

How could the old loon have found a daisy on Callisto? Nothing grew on Callisto but bacteria. Somehow the daisy was pristine; it glowed brighter than the old coot's scarf.

She tore her eyes away from the daisy. "Sir, can I get you something?"

"Water."

"Water? Sir, we don't serve water here." She grimaced. "Even if we did, I wouldn't suggest drinking it."

"Coffee, then."

Her fingers tightened on the tray. "We don't serve coffee, sir."

"Tea. How about sweet tea?"

"Sweet tea?"

His gaze dim and distant, tears welled behind his weathered eyelids until they spilled down his cheeks.

"I remember sweet tea," he whispered. "It's been so long since I've had it."

Sweet tea. Something else familiar. The memory of its taste tingled on the back of her tongue, bitter and sweet and cold and refreshing and like nothing that existed on Callisto. Just the thought of tasting something so pure again made her want to cry.

"I'm sorry, sir." Her voice stuck to the back of her throat. "We don't have sweet tea either."

"Oh, I see. That's too bad."

He was an old man, all alone and lost, wandering and

helpless. That's what he looked like. Maybe he wasn't really. Maybe he was a con man, but it didn't matter because he remembered sweet tea.

Maybe he had some hand sanitizer.

"I can get you another gingerroot, sir."

The old man stared at her, not the same way the other men in the bar did. His sharp hazel eyes held her steady in the depth of their clarity. Strange when moments earlier they'd been as murky as Cedric's dishwater.

"Gingerroot."

"You have to pay for the first one. Then, I can get you a second one."

The man looked confused until he glanced at the empty bottle on the table. Still twisting the daisy between the fingers of one hand, he reached into his shirt pocket and pulled out a single cred card.

Tray under her arm, Xander accepted the card and marched back to the bar. Cedric whistled off-key beside her as she swiped the card through the reader. But the reader didn't process the card as it normally did. It flashed an error and restarted. She tried again without success.

So much for technology.

"Cedric?"

"What?"

"Something's wrong with the card reader."

Cedric hovered over her shoulder. "No, there's not." He pulled the cred card from her fingers. "This is a total balance card. You can't debit."

"Why not?"

"To stop folks from using so much plastic. How the hell should I know?" He turned the card over. "This has two-hundred creds on it." He shoved it back at her. "Go tell him to pay some other way because we can't give change for that."

A fist fight erupted in the furthest corner of the bar. One more mess she didn't have time to clean up. The noise level rattled her ear drums, but it didn't seem to bother the old man, all his attention focused on the daisy between his gnarled fingers. But he noticed when she approached and smiled at her, his expression half-vacant.

"Sir," Xander said, "there's a problem with this card. Do you have another one?"

"No." Unconcerned, unhearing, he spun the daisy so its bright petals flared.

"This is all you have?"

"Yes. You can just take the card and give me change."

Xander pressed her lips together.

"Unless—unless there's only enough on the card to pay for what I've purchased, of course." His smile sparkled. "Then, you can take the card."

"You don't know how much is on the card?"

"No. Is there enough on it to pay for my drink?"

Something dark surged deep inside her.

The old man didn't know how much was on the card. He probably didn't know how much the gingerroot had cost to begin with. Maybe what he didn't know wouldn't hurt him. Having two hundred credits to add to her escape fund certainly wouldn't hurt her.

But it's wrong. The singular thought stopped her cold. *I shouldn't take this from him. What if it's all he has?*

The man stroked the daisy with gentle fingers. And hummed.

What was she thinking? The man was a crackpot. Likely he'd stolen the card himself.

Oscar pays me dirt. I've been here for months, and I can

barely afford a ride to the shuttle station, let alone a ticket to NUSaxony. She glared at the card as though it could tell her what to do. *No one else would hesitate. It wouldn't bother anyone else. I need it more than he does.*

She clenched the card between her fingers.

But he's just an old man. It's not right.

Never mind that no one knew what was right and what wasn't. Why did she care what was right and what was wrong when no one else did? Why was this a hard choice? She needed to get to NUSaxony, and this was the easiest way. The more time she spent at the Oasis, the greater risk that Oscar would find something more profitable for her to do, whether she wanted to do it or not.

It's wrong. She ground her molars until her head throbbed. *Everything is wrong.*

"Oh, are you back already?" the old man asked.

"I didn't leave, sir."

"Oh." He held the daisy out to her. "Isn't this a beautiful flower?"

Xander struggled to speak clearly through her clenched teeth. "Yes, sir. It's lovely. Where did you find it?"

"Where?" He stroked the daisy's petals. "I don't know where. Maybe it found me." The man blinked forcefully, and his eyes zoned in on the card she held. "Is there something wrong with my card?"

"You can't use this card to pay for what you bought." How many times did she have to say it?

"I can't?"

"No."

"Oh. I don't have anything else. Why won't it work?"

His eyes held her with such innocent concern.

When was the last time anyone in this bar had looked at her

like that? Every customer in the Oasis groped her, pulled her into their laps, ran fingers up the back of her thigh as she took orders. Every customer except this crazy old man.

Who was this fool, and why had he come here? To make her life miserable? Was this some kind of a test? Something in the back of her broken mind told her that she liked tests, liked to show she knew all the answers.

What a crock.

She thrust the card at him. "There's two hundred credits on that, sir. The soda cost ten, and I can't give you change." She took a deep breath. "So we'll just say the one is on the house, and you can go about your business."

The man stared at the card, perplexed.

Didn't he understand? Didn't he know what she was sacrificing? Two hundred credits would go a long way to buying a visa, and she was giving it up.

The old man smiled at her again, this time differently than before. A smile like the sunrises her broken mind remembered, bright and warm and filling the sky, not the piteous pinprick of light in the polluted Callisto sky.

"You're a good girl."

It was her turn to look confused. The quiet statement—a compliment, no less—was the last thing she had expected.

"Do you like daisies, little girl?"

The daisy sparkled in the dimness. Xander liked the daisy now, but had she liked daisies before? "I don't know."

The old man leaned back in the chair and sagged like a sandbag left to gravity's pull. "Funny. I don't know either."

"Xander!" Cedric barked from the bar.

The old man's gaze clouded, a shadow of what it had been

moments before.

"Keep the card, little girl," he mumbled. "You can keep it."

She gaped at him. Was he serious? He couldn't just give her two hundred credits for no reason. Could he?

The old man's gaze softened, drool running from his mouth as his dull eyes slanted almost shut. What was he staring at off in the corner?

"Xander!" Cedric snapped, eying Oscar's office door. "Now!"

Keeping Cedric happy came first. She wanted to thank the old man, but she couldn't stand and wait for him to wake up from whatever dream had stolen his attention. Xander turned on her heel and tucked the card in the back pocket of her skirt.

She yanked on the skirt as she walked, trying to get it to cover more of her backside than was actually possible. She *hated* that skirt.

She stopped at the bar. "What, Cedric?" He always made everything so complicated.

"I got people need serving, carrots." Cedric dumped another tray of glasses into the foul dishwater. "Did the old fart pay?"

"No. He didn't have anything else."

"What about the card?"

"He gave it to me."

"He what?" Cedric squeaked like a mouse someone had stepped on.

"He gave it to me." Xander glared at him. "I tried to give it back."

"You—what?" His jaw hung open. If a fish could gasp for air, that's what he looked like.

"It wouldn't have been right to take it."

Cedric gawked at her until his greasy glasses slid down his hawk-like nose. "It wouldn't have been right? What the hell is wrong with you? Just—go—work. And that soda is coming out of your tips today."

"Fine."

"Fine." He flapped his hands. "Fine, Cedric. Fine." He threw a collins glass into the murky dishwater with a plop. "Nine's done. Go take care of them."

Xander didn't answer and passed the old man on the way to table nine. The least she could do was thank him for his kindness. But she stopped before she reached him and wished she hadn't tried.

He hunched in the chair, eyes empty, plucking petals from the daisy. The soft bits of pure white fluttered to the grimy, stained tabletop like ruined snowflakes.

It was just a flower. But to watch the slobbering lunatic tear something so clean and untouched apart felt obscene.

Stomach twisting, she fled to table nine, collecting the scattered tips, trying to block out the image of the flower being stripped of its innocence.

The first beautiful thing she had seen in two months, and the crazy old fool had destroyed it—right in front of her.

She didn't feel so bad about taking his money now.

Xander cleared the table and returned her tray to Cedric. His foul, mud-colored dishwater smelled like decomposing vegetables.

Dish suds were supposed to be white, weren't they? But then, she also remembered sweet tea and hand sanitizer. What did she know?

"Table five." Cedric pointed over her shoulder to the table in the corner. "Go."

She hurried to table five, cleared it, stacked the shot glasses, and started back toward the bar. She glanced at table seven without really meaning to. But it was empty. The old man was gone.

He'd pushed in his chair and abandoned the naked daisy stem on the tabletop, surrounded by the delicate petals he'd torn off.

She picked up the stem and held it between her fingers. Was it a good idea to take money from a crazy old man who liked to torture daisies?

"Xander! Move your ass!"

She clenched the stem until her palm ached from the pressure of her fingernails and let it fall to the filthy, discolored floorboards.

Credits were credits. The more of them she had, the better. The more of them she had, the sooner she could be free. And if a scary old daisy killer's money were the only way to accomplish that, she would do it. If one daisy had to suffer humiliation and death for her to escape a hellhole like Callisto, maybe it was worth it.

Daisies are perennials; they always grow back.

CHAPTER 2

Cuddles barely stirred on the filthy floorboards when the 11 o'clock tone rattled the Oasis walls. He had to be truly wasted. Nobody could lay with their face pressed against the nastiness on the floor for any amount of time and be sober.

Other Oasis regulars grunted at the frequency of the tone, set just right to buzz deep within their brains obnoxiously. A stern reminder: We close at midnight. Get out, or we'll kick you out.

Cuddles didn't budge. Someone even tripped over him. Still, he snored away.

"Don't just stare at him, stupid." Cedric dumped a tray of glasses glued together with filth into his equally filthy dishwater. "You know what to do."

Xander rolled her eyes.

Of the many aspects of this job she hated, this was one she didn't mind, truth be told.

She paused at the supply closet as she marched toward Cuddles's prone form. Xander snatched the mop and positioned herself next to Cuddles, carefully out of reach. The kicking and biting part was only funny if they couldn't reach you. She'd learned that the hard way.

The mop hissed as Xander primed it with the switch on the handle, harsh cleaning solution plumping up the sponge head like bread rising in an oven.

Xander swung the mop like a golf club, and the sponge

smacked against the side of Cuddles's upturned face. It was the sound of wet dough on a kneading board, at least until the acid in the cleaning solution started to burn.

Cuddles woke up pretty fast then.

First with a startled groan. Then the shrieking started. Cuddles flailed and thrashed on the floor and rolled away from the mop, cursing and spitting.

The cleaning solution didn't really hurt them. It just stung. And in an alcohol-induced coma, the drunks couldn't really tell it apart from real acid. Purportedly Oscar had used real acid on someone once, and once was all it took for a reputation.

The Oasis cleans their floors with acid. Stick around too long, and they'll clean your face with it too.

"First tone." Xander arched her eyebrows at him as though he could see her face through the haze of whiskey in his system. "Leave."

Cuddles moaned and slumped against the floorboards.

Xander tapped the mop close to his face, and he yelped in terror, backpedaling until he nearly knocked a table over.

Poor drunk idiot. At least he was one of the nice ones.

One of the nice ones who slobbered all over her on a regular basis.

Never mind. He was just a drunk.

Cuddles stumbled to a mostly upright position and weaved his way toward the door, dashing at the cleaning solution still dripping off his unshaven chin. Maybe it was cleaning solution. Maybe it was drool. Xander couldn't tell, and with Cuddles it could be either.

With the Oasis emptying rapidly, Xander started in on the floors, the mop whispering against the caked-on grime. After the first tone, the bar shut down. No more drinks. And for the regulars of the Cuddles variety, the ore miners and slag shifters, drinking was their only escape from the brutal reality of Callisto. So when the drinks ran out, it didn't take long for the downstairs to go from train station at rush hour to graveyard at midnight.

Upstairs was different.

Xander scrubbed the floor from the side stairwell to the far wall, until her arms ached with the effort. Mopping hardly made a dent in the deep-set layers of filth and grime, but the mud and spit on the top came up easily enough. When the sponge drooped like a dead animal from the end of the mop, Xander held it over the garbage pail and pressed the recycle button. The sponge let go and dropped into the bin, but the mop shuddered and wheezed.

Xander bit off a groan and whacked the mop stick against the side of the counter. Only then did the mop stick sprout a new sponge.

"Cedric, when are we going to buy a new mop?"

Cedric scoffed from the cupboard where he sorted the day's unopened decanters. "You want a new mop, you ask Oscar."

Yeah, like that was going to happen. The less she had to do with Oscar the better.

She returned the mop to the closet and tied off the garbage bag while Cedric started tallying tips in the safe. On the third yank, she dislodged the bag from the pail and carried it toward the door.

No dragging. The roughness of the floorboards could rip it open.

No slinging it over her shoulder. The bag might leak.

She held it as far away from her body as she could. When she first started working at the Oasis, she couldn't manage the dead weight of Cedric's stuffed-full trash bags for the length of time required to get them outside. It had taken months, but at least she knew how to get the trash outside to the dumpster without breaking the bags open—on the floor or on herself.

Xander forced the door open, carefully keeping the trash bag aloft, and walked down the steps to the dumpster on the side of the Oasis. The illuminator poles overhead cast enough light to direct her to the alley.

The Oasis was ramshackle and rundown, but compared to the rest of the buildings in Copernicus City, it was a high-class establishment.

The air outside made her gag. As disgusting as the Oasis was, it smelled far better inside than it did outside. The alley was worse. Festering with human filth and decay, rats scurried over her shoes as she walked toward the dumpster, and a child—probably six or seven—ate from a trashcan across the street.

Further down in the alley, the light was bright enough to reveal a half-clothed couple on the ground, wrapped around each other, jerking and gasping. She shut her eyes as she tossed the trash into the dumpster.

Bad enough she had to listen to it all day long, she didn't want to watch it on the street.

Shame had no meaning on Callisto. The rest of the solar system had to be different.

Callisto was the red light district of the Jupiter moons. A tired and dreary-looking world, Callisto had little to offer humanity except a place to get laid. No one ever slept because even when it should have been pitch black, Jupiter's planet light bathed the small, filthy moon in faint red glow.

Surely Callisto wasn't the standard for living in the solar system. Callisto was just dirty and dark and ugly; NUSaxony would be better, if she could only get there.

Xander kicked the rats out of her path on the way back to the Oasis. Some of the independent prostitutes who'd earned a reputation in the area stood on the muddied street across from the Oasis. They knew the business. The miners and line workers who couldn't afford a prostitute at the Oasis clustered in groups around them.

Xander ducked back inside before any of the men mistook her for one of those kinds of girls. That had happened once, and she'd never let it happen again. Getting caught outside alone on Callisto was never a good idea, no matter what time of day it was. She'd learned that the day the *Anastasia* had abandoned her.

She yanked the door shut with a grunt and turned back to Cedric, but she paused when she noticed a dark-haired woman in a dress like sparkling flame sitting at the bar. The woman glanced at her, almond-shaped eyes vivid, and smirked.

"Xander-girl, you look a mess." Sylphie always chewed her words, drawing them out lazily like a cat sunning on a summer day. "The missus running you too hard?"

Cedric slammed a glass of bourbon—Sylphie's choice—on the counter, glaring at her. "What does that mean? I run her too hard?" He scoffed. "I work harder than she does. She's as lazy as you."

Sylphie threw the glass of bourbon back in one swallow. "Just because I work on my back doesn't mean I'm lazy, Ced." Sylphie winked and slid the glass to him. "But you wouldn't know anything about that, would you?"

"Working on my back?" Cedric arched his thinning eyebrows. "You might be surprised."

"Anyway!" Xander stepped up to the bar and gathered the stack of credits Cedric had piled there. "We had a busy day."

NAMELESS

Sylphie hadn't stopped smirking. "You think so, Xander-girl?" She eyed the credits Xander stuffed in her pockets. "Decent take, it looks like."

"Very decent." Xander patted her pocket and moved the tray of glasses from the counter to a table so she could scrub the bar down.

"Probably have a nice sum in that little jar under your bed, yeah?"

Xander didn't commit to an answer. She didn't know what her jar of credits had to do with anything.

Sylphie kept smirking.

Xander picked at a hard knob of grime on the counter a little longer than she needed to, probably wearing a hole in her washcloth. Thinking under the weight of Sylphie's smirks never got easier. The woman lounged like a cat, lazy and self-satisfied, but she had claws. She didn't hesitate to use them when they suited her.

Xander glanced at the dark-haired beauty on the bar stool. Yep, still smirking.

"What?"

The smirk became a grin. "Xander-girl, you really need to get over yourself."

Xander rolled her eyes. "Like you, Sylphie?"

Sylphie laughed, a full sound like waves crashing on the beach. "I'm all over me, sweet pea." She spun on the stool and rested her elbows against the bar, watching Xander as she worked. "You're never gonna' make it to NUSaxony waiting tables, Xander."

Tension rippled through Xander's shoulders. "I'm doing fine, Sylphie."

She didn't want to have this conversation again.

"Xander-girl." Sylphie reached out and took her arm, pulling

17

her away from her constant scrubbing. "It'll take you fifty years to earn enough creds to buy a single visa. You know that."

"But if you whore like Sylphie, you'll earn it twice as fast." Cedric stripped off his apron and tossed it in the corner.

Xander dropped the washcloth on the bar and faced Sylphie with her chin up. "I won't whore, Sylphie."

"Nobody just waits tables in a bar, sweet pea." Sylphie patted her face.

Xander peeled Sylphie's hand off her face and held it. "Sylphie, you said I didn't have to. You said I could just wait tables. That's why I came with you."

The smirk returned. "No, you came with me because I was the only one on the street who didn't want to crawl up your legs."

Cedric popped over the edge of the counter. "Yeah, I don't get that."

Xander and Sylphie glanced at him.

"Even if she would tumble, would someone tumble her?"

Sylphie chuckled. "Some folks are desperate."

Cedric ducked down under the counter again, and Xander held tight to Sylphie's hand, the woman's long manicured fingernails as red as her dress. That day only months ago still felt fresh. Helpless, lost, alone, wandering the streets of Callisto at dusk with only two choices—whore or die, with rape an unavoidable expectation either way.

Sylphie saved her from the streets, probably thinking she'd whore for Oscar, but she'd thrown in on her side. Told her she could wait tables and made Oscar allow it.

The old man's 200 cred card felt obvious in her back pocket.

Xander squeezed her hand. "I don't need to whore, Sylphie. I'll make it just fine on my own."

Sylphie's expression hardened a bit, her eyes narrowing. "Xander, it's impossible."

Cedric set two jugs of whiskey on the counter as he stood up and brushed his hands off. "If she can dig up another old man, she might be set."

"Old man?" Sylphie straightened. "Xander-girl, you chattin' up the seniors? I bet he got a kick out of that. Not too many under-twenties will even look at somebody more mature."

"He was staring at her ass, Sylphie." Cedric winked. "I noticed."

"Sure it wasn't the hair? Not too many natural redheads out here."

"No, it was her ass."

"Well, she's got a nice ass."

"That's what I keep telling her, but you know she never listens to me."

"He overpaid." Xander held up her hands to stop them. "And he told me I could keep it."

Sylphie's eyebrows arrowed into her hairline. "Did he know he overpaid?"

Xander hesitated. "Not until I told him."

Sylphie dropped her hands and sagged against the counter. "Xander, what the hell?"

"See?" Cedric flapped his arms like a demented hummingbird. "See what you did to me? What I have to put up with since you dragged this brat in here?"

"Xander, are you out of your mind?" Sylphie seized her by the elbows. "Someone *gives* you free credits, and you try to give them back? What's wrong with you?"

"It wasn't right," Xander snapped. "I couldn't just take

money from a helpless old man, Sylphie."

Sylphie threw back her head and roared with laughter. "You're never going to get out of here, kid, if you keep giving back the money you make."

Xander clenched her teeth. "I'll make it, Sylphie. I will."

Sylphie rolled her eyes. "Ah, Xander-girl. What a piece of work you are."

Graceful as a dancer, Sylphie slid off the stool and patted Xander's face again. She smiled at her, a real smile instead of a smirk, but the light of it didn't really reach her eyes.

She turned and sauntered up the stairs, hips swaying with every step. The 30 minute tone resonated through the rickety halls as she hit the top step. Sylphie blew a kiss and ducked into her room as the exodus from the upper level began.

Metal workers, machiners, and drafters made up the bulk of the upstairs customers. They were the only ones who could afford Oasis rates. But they were just like the downstairs customers when they were drunk—loud, slobbering, clumsy, and rude.

Doors slammed. Feet pounded against the flooring. A stream of them marched down the steps, each with all the coordination of a dizzy, three-legged elephant.

Xander picked up the washcloth and started scrubbing tables as Cedric disappeared under the counter again.

She would make it. She would earn enough to buy a visa, and she'd do it without sleeping with people for money. She'd escape to NUSaxony like Dr. Zahn had told her, and she'd find a neurologist who could help her remember.

Then all of this—the filth and the fear and everything that was Callisto—would just be a memory, instead of reality.

CHAPTER 3

Xander finished wiping the table down and started to return the tray of glasses to the counter, but she jumped with a squeak as a man flopped into a chair right next to her in a flurry of leather and the scent of grease.

"Hey, little girl." The man smoothed his sand-colored hair with a gleaming smile. "Didn't mean to scare you."

Xander calmed her wild heart with two steady breaths.

"I'm sorry, sir. Bar's closed."

His eyes undressed her, an unwelcome caress across her shoulders, chest, hips, and thighs. Xander forced herself not to shudder in revulsion and swallowed the desperate urge to poke out his eyes with her fingers.

"What kinds of whiskey have you got, sweet thing?" His voice rumbled.

Well-dressed and bordering on handsome. But his ears apparently weren't working.

"We have three kinds. NUKeltian, Himalian and Theban. But the bar is closed."

"What do you recommend?"

"I don't like any of them."

The man shifted in his chair, and his long leather trench coat fell open to reveal hips crisscrossed with gun belts. The two blasters she could see looked heavy. Was he some kind of police officer?

"You like those?" The man noticed her gaze. "Or are you

looking at something else down there?"

She flushed. "The bar is closed, sir."

He shrugged. "That's no big. I wanted something sweeter anyway."

Xander started to point him to the door when he surged up from his chair and pinned her against the table with one hand between her thighs. He buried his face in her hair. "Yeah, you'll do nicely."

Heart throbbing, limbs shaking, Xander tried to shove him away, but the man was a solid wall of muscle.

"I just brought in a two thousand C head, and I've got some creds to spend." He breathed against her neck. "So how about you and me go find some place more comfortable?"

The hand between her thighs gripped hard. She couldn't twist out of his grasp, and the table blocked her escape. He was too tall and too strong.

"What are you, twenty? Less than twenty. Eighteen, I'd wager."

"Get off me!"

"The name's Lou, by the way, sweetheart." He blew in her ear. "Remember the name. I'll have you screaming it."

Xander flailed, smelling his musky, leathery scent everywhere. The studs on his belts dug into her skin through her thin uniform.

Where was Cedric? Why wasn't he helping?

She flung her arm out for the tray of glasses she'd set on the table earlier. She seized a stack and swung it against Lou's head as hard as she could. They shattered against the side of his face in a crash of tinkling glass and ruby-red blood.

Lou howled in surprise and jumped back, blood trickling

down his face and neck, staining his pressed shirt and leather coat.

"What the hell?" He touched the side of his bleeding face and stared in shock at his reddened hand. "What the hell?"

Xander gripped the table edge, trying to breathe.

Lou took another step toward her, and she grabbed another shot glass and brandished it. His face turned dark with fury.

"What kind of a whore doesn't whore?"

"I'm not a whore," Xander said. "I wait tables."

"I want a tumble!"

"Then come back tomorrow."

"Tomorrow's a head hunt on Osiris."

"Your problem. Not mine."

The darkness on his face softened with another smirk. Lou stepped forward again, but he was too fast for her to hurl the shot glass at him. He snatched her wrist and shoved himself against her again. The table edge stabbed into her lower back, jolting pain down her legs.

"You're saucy." The blood on his head dripped on her. "I like it."

Cedric cleared his throat beside them.

Cedric? Where had he come from?

Forget where he came from, where had he been?

"Well, now, what's all the fuss?" Cedric set his hands on his narrow hips, face cold with a thin smile.

"Back off, barkeep." Lou snarled. "I'm busy."

"You're a nice-looking boy." Cedric smirked. "And I know our little Xander is just asking for it. But we close in three."

"Trust me. That's plenty." Lou kept her pinned down and reached for his belt.

"I'm sure it is, sweet thing." Cedric patted him on the

23

shoulder and paused. "Oh, you've got some nice muscles on you."

Lou gripped Xander's wrist harder as he glared at Cedric with eyes full of disgust. "I don't swing that way," he growled. "Ever. So buzz off and let me and little Xander here get to it."

"So tense." Cedric let his hand rest on Lou's arm. "Trust me, handsome. Little Xander isn't worth the effort, but if you're looking for a good time—"

Lou dropped her and lashed out at Cedric with all the force of a bulldozer. Cedric ducked under it and shoved the disruptor he'd pulled from under his shirt into Lou's ribs.

Lou froze. Xander didn't dare breathe; she clutched the table edge.

Slowly, Lou raised his hands. "Didn't mean no harm, sir."

"You *are* nice looking." Cedric prodded Lou's ribcage with the disruptor. "And I hate threatening handsome men." He charged the disruptor with a whir. "But we're closed."

Lou, to his credit, didn't flinch. "If that's the case, then I'll be leaving."

Lou donned a bright grin that was absolutely fake. He stood still, coiled to spring the instant Cedric pulled the trigger.

"Yes," Cedric said. "You will."

The silence roared in Xander's ears. She wanted to run, to get as far away from Lou as she could, but she couldn't move. Not yet. If Cedric opened fire, she would need to dodge.

Lou dropped his hands and snapped the collar of his trench coat around his neck. He strode out of the bar, the door slamming behind him.

Cedric watched the door latch before he shoved the disruptor into the back of his pants.

Only then did Xander let herself breathe. Cedric turned his

gaze to her.

"You okay?" he asked.

She nodded. "Thanks."

"Tourists," he spat. "Bet you'll be glad for old Cuddles tomorrow, huh?"

Xander couldn't contain a shaky laugh, and Cedric smiled at her. But both of them fell silent as a long, low creaking reverberated across the back of the bar like a dying groan.

"Shit," Cedric muttered, glancing at the blood and broken glasses on the table and the floor.

Oscar would notice. He'd beat them both.

Cedric grabbed her arm and pulled her to the bar, where they stood for the evening inspection.

Oscar, owner of the Oasis, emerged from the room behind the bar counter, speaking in hushed tones with the well-dressed man beside him. Oscar, a broad-shouldered giant, always wore a white furry coat with a high collar. It was Earth mink, Sylphie had told her, an animal long extinct.

Xander startled as Cedric pressed a towel into her hands. She frowned at him, and he nodded at her right hand. She glanced down and tried not to gasp. The glasses she'd broken hadn't just bloodied Lou's head, they'd shredded her hand too.

Cedric winked at her and poked her hand through the towel.

Oscar and his guest shook hands, and the man left the bar, avoiding eye contact with anyone.

Then, Oscar turned a slow circle at the center of the Oasis before he pinned both of them with a glare that could have boiled paint off a wall.

"We leaving broken glass on the floor now?" His thundercloud face glowed in the dim illuminators.

"Tourist, Oscar," Cedric said. "Didn't know the rules. We tossed him out."

Oscar loomed over them, dark eyes piercing and cruel. "Tourist?"

"Bounty hunter."

Oscar's face twisted in an expression of disgust. "Bounty hunters. Think they can do whatever the hell they want."

The last tone echoed through the halls, and the mezzanine doors opened as Oscar's prostitutes took position against the railing so he could count. He turned away from the bar and focused his attention upstairs.

Xander spotted Sylphie at the end, makeup removed and hair brushed.

Oscar counted in silence until he was satisfied, and then he waved the women away. They all returned to their rooms, and he glanced over his shoulder at Cedric.

"Clean this shit up," he said.

Cedric nodded.

So did Xander, but Oscar ignored her. That was either a very good sign or a very bad sign.

His office door slammed, and she and Cedric traded a glance. They smiled together and hurriedly cleaned up the broken glass and blood. Xander wiped her bleeding hand down as best she could. She would have to wash it in the morning, since Oscar didn't allow time or power for showers at night.

When the bar was finally clean, or at least as clean as it could get, Cedric shut off the lights, and Xander followed him to their shared room at the back. Xander made a stop at the medicine cabinet to gather bandages for her hand.

They only had enough room for two cots and one dresser. A

single illuminator on the ceiling filled the room with squalid light.

"I need a shower." Cedric sniffed his armpit and stripped his shirt off. "So—how was your take today?"

"Not too bad." Xander averted her eyes and pulled her nightclothes from the dresser, a long-sleeved shirt and a pair of long pants. Nights on Callisto were cold, and Oscar didn't heat the back room.

"Especially with your old man's contribution too, huh?"

"He wasn't my old man, Cedric."

"If you say so. Wonder who he was."

"I keep thinking about him," Xander said. "I think he looked familiar."

Cedric stopped moving. "I didn't think anyone looked familiar to you."

"They don't."

"But your old man did?"

"He wasn't *my* old man, Cedric."

"But if he looked familiar, maybe he was."

"Was what?" She glanced over her shoulder and winced at the brief glimpse of exposed skin. Not for the first time, she wished Cedric cared who saw him naked.

"What if he was your father?"

"He was too old to be my father."

"Fine, your grandfather then."

"Then why wouldn't he have said something?" She shut her eyes and bunched her clothes in her fists. "I mean, I think I would have recognized him if he were related to me. If we were family, I would have known him. Even if I can't remember anything else."

"You never know, Xander. Your head is pretty screwed up."

She scoffed. "Yeah, it is."

Cedric stretched behind her, still naked. Waiting for him to put his clothes back on was a waste of time, so she moved behind her makeshift privacy screen in the corner. She unbuttoned her too-tight blouse and wriggled out of the ridiculous skirt and crawled into her nightclothes.

Cedric had little patience for her prudishness when he wanted to talk about something. Xander sensed he wanted to talk, so he could pop around the corner at any moment.

Cedric claimed he had no interest in women, but it still didn't mean she was okay with him seeing her unclothed. Cedric didn't understand; no one seemed to understand, at least not at the Oasis.

When she emerged from behind the screen, Cedric reclined against the wall beside his cot, wrapped in his ratty old quilt.

She sat on her cot to bandage her bleeding hand. "Cedric?"

"What?"

"Who was that man with Oscar today?" Xander tightened the bandage around her hand. "He was in his office. No one's allowed in Oscar's office."

"He's Oscar's partner. They set this place up together." Cedric laid his head back against the wall. "Oscar runs the bar; his partner runs Fantasy."

"Fantasy?"

"Oscar helps him run Fantasy, Xander," Cedric said. "His partner's a pusher, and Oscar's walking a tight line—since the Feds don't much care for the stuff."

"Oscar's running drug deals from inside the Oasis?" Xander's eyebrows arched.

"Yeah." Cedric gave a short laugh. "You didn't know that? The whole moon knows that. Where have you been, sweetie?"

Oscar was in business with a drug dealer. Somehow the

image fit, but that didn't bring her any comfort in working for him. How much longer could she keep working for Oscar? How many more close calls would she survive, like the one with Lou?

Xander glanced at her blouse and skirt in the pile at her feet. She gathered them up and scowled at the blood stains on her blouse. She set it out to be cleaned in the morning and folded her skirt.

Gathering her tips and the old man's cred card out of the back pocket, she deposited them in the small jar she kept under her cot.

"Why won't you whore for Oscar?"

Cedric's question surprised her. "I just—don't want to."

"Why not? Everyone does it."

"I'm not everyone."

"Xander, you don't actually think you're going to earn enough waiting tables to make it to NUSaxony, do you?" Cedric's voice sounded strangely gentle. "Entrance visas cost an arm and a leg. And since I'm pretty sure you aren't NUSaxon, you'd need an exit visa too—which costs another arm and a leg."

Xander rolled her eyes. "So you're saying I'll get to NUSaxony, but I'll be a quadriplegic?"

"I'm saying you're never going to do it waiting tables even *if* you keep getting lecherous old drunks who overpay for their drinks." Cedric laced his hands behind his head. "Two hundred creds a pop is equal to a foot on the arm-and-leg scale."

"Yeah." She looked down.

Cedric paused. "Did you really try to give it back to him?"

"Yes. He wouldn't take it."

Cedric made an incredulous sound. "That means he really was frickin' insane. And so are you. Stupid bitch."

Xander winced.

He was right. She'd been at the Oasis for two months. Her

daily tips barely paid her food and boarding expenses; anything extra she made went directly to her savings. With the crazy old man's contribution, those savings amounted to nearly three hundred credits. A ticket to NUSaxony was six hundred credits, but to even enter NUSaxon orbit, she needed an entrance visa—which cost twice that. And, as Cedric helpfully reminded her, she also needed an exit visa—which cost the same.

In two months, she had earned three hundred credits but she needed ten times that amount before she could even reach NUSaxony, let alone pay for the neuro-therapy services she needed. She wasn't going to meet another crazy old man, and Xander had the sneaking suspicion that Oscar didn't see the need for a waitress who didn't whore. Who knew when he'd get tired of giving her a place to sleep that didn't include ten to fifteen customers a day?

Xander reached under her cot and pulled out a plastic bag beside her precious jar of credits. She removed a gray jacket with a name emblazoned on the left breast pocket, *Xander*.

It was the only key to her past, the only piece of the puzzle she had, and even then it still made no sense. She'd spent hours staring at it in a futile search for memories she couldn't remember. It meant nothing and everything.

She folded the garment against her chest, embracing it as though proximity might help.

"Sylphie makes a killing every customer," Cedric said. "She charges five hundred for an hour, Xander. In a day, she can make more than you could in ten years."

"I think that's an exaggeration."

"Not saying you could compete with her. I mean, you've got the ass for it—and your legs aren't bad. And the hair is a plus. The only redheads around are Earthen, and they're too weird to tumble.

But the rest of you can't compare to her." He shrugged. "At least, that's what I hear most of the folks around here say."

"Right—because you've got no interest."

"None whatsoever." He smirked.

"I won't sleep with anyone for money, Cedric."

"Why not?"

"It's not right." Xander quietly tucked the jacket back into the bag and slipped it under her bed.

"It's not right? Where does anybody say getting paid for your services is wrong?"

She sighed. "I don't know. I just know it's wrong. That's something I *do* remember."

Cedric shook his head. "That just means you're going to be here for a long time, Xander."

Xander closed her eyes. "Then that's fine."

"Putting up with shit from customers? Being treated like a slave? Having to do all of Oscar's dirty work? That's fine with you?"

Xander rolled onto her back and gazed up at the dirty ceiling. "Well, of course, it's not *fine* with me, Ced. None of this is fine with me. But there isn't anything I can do about it." She smiled at him. "The only thing I can do is the best I can."

Cedric took a long, deep breath and let it out slowly. "It's your life, Xander. But I'm not staying here. This isn't where I belong. It's not my destiny."

Xander frowned. "Destiny." For some reason, the word resonated in her mind.

"That's right. I don't belong here. I belong somewhere else—someplace nice. With running water that don't smell like piss. Real, fresh air. Where I can be successful. Respected. Appreciated for my skills."

"That's your destiny?"

"Yeah. And I'll do anything to reach it." He turned his somber gaze on her. "Anything."

Xander smiled. "That's good, Ced. Everyone should do their best to reach their potential."

He searched her face. "You are so weird."

She laughed. "Yeah. I guess I don't belong here either."

"But you belong on NUSaxony?"

"No," Xander said. "But that's where I need to go."

Above, the illuminator flickered before it went dark. Lights out meant Oscar was going to bed, and everyone else should too. The only light in the room now was the dim glow from the outside hall illuminator that shone through the cracks around the door.

"Well," Cedric said softly, "I hope you make it."

"I will, Ced."

"You're a good kid, Xander." His voice sounded odd. "A good girl. I don't think I've ever met one of those before."

Xander smiled sleepily into her pillow. "I hope I'm not the last."

She closed her eyes and let the squeaking of the floorboards above her lull her to sleep. It was another familiar thing, the breathing of an old house at night, whispering in the ancient creaking language only other old houses could translate. It was comforting. She just wished she knew why.

CHAPTER 4

The blond man grabbed her jacket and dragged her away from the console. In too much shock to fight him, she stared at the frenetic fingers of electricity that arced around the control room. He shoved her into her room, and he locked the door. The gears in the wall whirred.

"You have to stay here."

The door was sliding shut. She could only see half his face.

"David!" she cried.

"You'll be all right."

The door shut and sealed, and the ship rocked—

Xander's eyes opened to darkness, heart thudding in her ears. She clutched at the tatty quilt and swallowed her scream.

What was that?

She had often dreamed of another life. Faceless people. Sounds and voices that made no sense. Images of a world she should have known but couldn't remember.

This had been vivid. Specific. But even as she lay rehashing the vision, its clarity began to fade until she couldn't remember it. She remembered a blond man—remembered his touch and the frantic timbre of his voice. She remembered the explosion. That was all.

She shook herself and rubbed the sleep from her eyes. The crooked digital clock on the wall told her it was time to get up.

She had to clean the blood off her blouse, and from the feel of her throbbing, cut-up hand, she probably needed to disinfect and rebandage it.

She reached for the backup illuminator in the corner. The murky light shone on Cedric's empty cot.

Empty? Cedric never got up this early. Where had he gone?

Xander strained her ears. She didn't hear him walking around upstairs. Maybe he had gone to the bathroom. If he had, it would take her twice as long to get ready. Cedric fussed more over his few thin hairs than she ever did over her mass of orange frizzy ones.

She needed a shower, but Callisto water did more damage than good. One more day wouldn't matter.

The bandages on her hand were a different story. Her palm stung as she open and shut her fist, the soiled dressings crumpling with the motion.

She threw her clothes on behind the screen, in case Cedric popped back in unannounced. He didn't.

The bathroom across the hall could have doubled as a storage closet if it weren't for the smell. Xander paused as she stepped out of the room. The bathroom door hung open. No Cedric.

Weird.

But consider the source.

Xander hurriedly unwrapped her cut hand, cleaned it, and bandaged it again. She sprayed her blouse with stain remover too, so the blood from yesterday wouldn't attract attention. Undoubtedly she'd be covered in blood again before the day was out.

Trying to be clean on Callisto just too too much effort in the end.

She tied the dressings off and taped them down, frowning at the rickety old sink as she did. Wrong. The sink looked wrong. But why? It was the same sink as always, dingy aluminum hammered into the shape of a basin, spigot rusted and dripping, mounted on the rotting wall beside the shelf for toiletries. Her hair brush and Cedric's comb.

No, just her hair brush.

Where was Cedric's comb? Had it fallen? No, not on the floor.

Cedric's toothbrush was missing too.

Xander straightened, stomach tightening. Why would Cedric have moved his comb and toothbrush? That didn't make sense.

She turned and walked back to their room, standing at the center, heart thrumming in her ears. Cedric's cot looked undisturbed, like he hadn't even slept there. But that was false because she knew he had.

The nail behind his cot cast a shadow on the rotting wood of the wall. Empty. His spare shirt was gone.

No comb. No toothbrush. No spare shirt. No Cedric.

What was going on? Had Oscar crept in last night and dragged him off in silence? She slept like a rock, but Cedric screamed like a banshee when he was scared.

She perched on the edge of his cot, puzzled, and the dim light above flared, just enough to shine off her jar of credits under her cot. But that was wrong too. She didn't keep it in sight like that. She pushed it back further. She had done it last night, hadn't she? So how had it gotten so far out from under her cot?

No.

No, no, no, no.

Xander pitched forward to the floor, knees thudding against the floorboards hollowly. She snatched the jar from under the cot and pulled it into the light.

35

Empty.

Her jar of credits had nothing in it.

It wasn't possible. How could it have happened? When could it have happened?

Panic rose in her brain like a tidal wave threatening to eradicate a city. Everything she owned, all her hope, her only chance of escape—stolen right from under her. Literally. Even the cred card the crazy old man had given her.

She rolled over to sit on her backside, room spinning, head aching.

No credits.

No Cedric.

She clutched the fabric over her heart. Cedric wouldn't have. He couldn't have. Why would he have?

No, there had to be another explanation. There had to be a reason. Cedric had his rough spots, but he wouldn't have just stolen from her, not when he knew what those credits had meant to her.

The light overhead flared again, Oscar's summons to start getting ready to open. On any other day, she would have followed Cedric upstairs, and they would have gotten the bar ready together. But Cedric was gone.

Xander set the empty jar under her cot and clambered to her feet as gracefully as she could. Cedric wouldn't get far with what he took from her. As he'd so helpfully pointed out so many times, with her meager savings, she couldn't even afford a visa, let alone a ticket anywhere off Callisto.

She hoped he spent it on a hotel and woke up with Amalthean cotton beetles.

Xander squeezed her eyes shut. No, she didn't. She didn't hope or wish for that. She wanted to walk upstairs and see Cedric behind the bar like always, flapping his arms and demanding instant obedience with a sparkle in his eye.

Squaring her shoulders, she marched for the front of the Oasis. Emptiness and darkness greeted her in the bar when she walked into it. Lights shone under the doors on the mezzanine.

Sylphie.

Maybe Sylphie knew where he had gone.

Xander glanced at Oscar's door. He hadn't shown up yet. She had time before they opened. Xander scaled the steps to Sylphie's room and knocked.

Probably a horrible idea. If Sylphie knew where he had gone, what was she going to do about it? See couldn't exactly go after him.

The door swung open, revealing Sylphie with her hair up and a cigarette hanging out of her mouth.

"Morning, Xander-girl!"

Xander started to speak but found that her voice had disappeared.

Definitely a terrible idea. What was she going to do, point fingers? What did she want from Sylphie, sympathy? Ridiculous. Sylphie didn't care. Nobody did.

Sylphie watched her with eyes narrowed. "What's wrong?"

Not the question Xander expected. Maybe Sylphie could read her moods after all.

"Cedric." It was all she could say.

What was wrong with her? Her voice felt glued to her throat. She wanted to rage. She wanted to scream. She wanted to tell Sylphie exactly what had happened and exactly what she thought about friends who stabbed friends in the back. But all that would come out was a muted snarl that ended in something like a whimper.

Pathetic.

"What about him?"

And, of course, Sylphie never made it easy. She never made anything easy.

"Cedric," Xander tried again.

"You said that already, dumb ass."

"Cedric stole my credits."

Sylphie scowled. "What?" She took a drag from her cigarette. "Your little jar of bits and bobs? What the hell would he want with that?"

"I don't know. But he took them, and he's gone."

Gone. Left her alone to run the bar by herself, wait tables by herself, manage Oscar by herself.

"Get in." Sylphie grabbed her arm and pulled her inside.

Xander sagged against the wall in Sylphie's room when the door shut.

"Why would he do it, Sylphie? Why?" Xander pressed her hands into her face. "He's my friend. We were friends."

Sylphie blew lungful of smoke toward the ceiling and regarded her with a smirk. "Oh, come on, kid. Did you come up here to whine?"

Xander let her hands fall to her sides. "I'm not whining, Sylphie."

"Cedric stole my credits!" Sylphie mimicked in a squeaky voice. "He hurt my feelings!"

"Shut up."

Sylphie smashed her cigarette into the ashtray on her vanity. "What do you want me to do about it? Chase him down?"

"No."

"Call the cops? That'd be rich."

"No."

Sylphie slid closer to her. "Or did you just need a kiss?"

Xander dodged out of reach when Sylphie moved to embrace her. "Stop it." She held up her hands. "I just wanted to tell someone."

"Whining."

Xander shrugged. "Yeah. I guess so."

Sylphie rolled her eyes and scoffed. And slapped her hard enough to send her reeling sideways.

Xander scrambled to stay upright, clinging to the edge of Sylphie's bedpost. "What—what was that for?"

"Are you done?" Sylphie snapped.

"You hit me!"

"You needed it."

Xander rubbed the side of her face, red hot to the touch. "Ow."

"You think you've got it so bad, kid." Sylphie lit another cigarette. "You're full of it. You don't know what bad is. You've got a place to sleep and a job to work and food to eat. That's one more place, job, and meal than half the girls on this damned moon have." She puffed smoke out her nose, her eyes sparkling like black diamonds. "So some boy lover ran off with your credits? Tough shit. Go make some more, and leave me the hell out of it."

Xander stared at her, couldn't tear her eyes away.

Sylphie never made anything easy. But she didn't lie either.

A loud knock on the door startled them both. Sylphie's expression hardened, and Xander dropped to the floor and rolled under Sylphie's bed. If Oscar found her in Sylphie's room, he'd be furious. Barkeeps were never allowed upstairs, especially in the off hours.

Xander stilled her breathing as Sylphie opened her door. The hinges groaned.

"Oscar?" Sylphie said, puffing out another breath of smoke—presumably in Oscar's face.

"Cedric is gone."

Xander bit her tongue. How would Oscar know that? He didn't make a habit of venturing into the back room where Xander and Cedric slept, so he wouldn't know that Cedric's things were missing.

"Gone?" Sylphie scowled. "What do you mean gone?"

"He's gone." Oscar's voice was little more than a growl. "Took off. You know where he went?"

Sylphie snorted. "No. Why would I? You hired him. I thought you two were—"

"Shut your trap, bitch." Oscar slapped his hand against the door so hard that Xander jumped under Sylphie's bed. "You're a moneymaker, but I won't hesitate to throw you out."

Sylphie kept her tone even. "I don't know where he is, Oscar. How do you know he's gone?"

"He's not here," Oscar repeated slowly, "and he ran off with some of my merchandise."

"What kind of merchandise?"

Xander held her breath and imagined the glowering expression on Oscar's face.

"Fine then, don't tell me." Sylphie's voice held a smirk. "Did you want something other than to bother me?"

"Your little bitch is gonna' have the floor alone today. Think she can take it?"

Xander squeezed her eyes shut. Could she handle it? Could she take orders, mix drinks, deliver orders, fight off the rapists, clean up the vomit, and all the other things that she and Cedric used to tackle together? Could she do it alone?

NAMELESS

Sylphie puffed out another mouthful of smoke. "Of course, she can. She's a tough mother."

Oscar made a disbelieving sound Xander wanted to mimic.

She set her palm against the hand-shaped hot spot on the side of her face. She had been whining. She had just wanted to complain. She had just wanted someone to know what had happened, so someone would feel sorry for her.

But what good did that do?

Sylphie did care. She just cared enough not to coddle her.

The door slammed shut, but Sylphie didn't call her out.

Slowly, Xander rolled out from under the bed and got to her feet. She brushed herself off and almost drew back when Sylphie slid into her personal space and touched her cheek.

"Damn," Sylphie said. "I left a mark."

Xander smiled. "I needed it. Thank you."

Sylphie dragged on the cigarette again, brow furrowed and eyes still narrowed. "You are such a weird kid. Why the hell did I save you anyway?"

"Because you care?"

"Naw, kid." Sylphie pulled away and sat on the chair in front of her vanity. "I don't care."

"No," Xander said. "I didn't think so."

Sylphie put out her cigarette. "And neither did Cedric."

Xander froze.

"Don't you forget that, Xander-girl," Sylphie said, her tone full of warning. "Nobody cares."

Xander met her eyes. "Even if they do?"

Sylphie didn't answer right away. She started dotting powder on her face, looking only in her mirror.

Xander watched her in silence. Learn from it and move on.

41

Learn to suspect everyone; trust no one. Not even your friends. That was life on Callisto, on the Oasis, but was it life everywhere? What if it were?

The lights in the room flashed twice.

Sylphie dropped her powder puff. "That's your cue, carrots," she said. "Get down to the bar, or Oscar will really give you something cry about."

Xander stopped with her hand on the door. "Thanks."

"Go, stupid."

Xander smiled. "It's just nice to know."

"What is?"

"That you don't care."

Sylphie tilted her head and snarled. "Get your dumb ass downstairs." But her eyes smiled.

Xander flung the door open and ran down the stairs. She donned Cedric's apron and tied it just as Oscar stepped out of his office and started to count his whores.

She set her hands on the counter and tried to calm her breathing. She would be running the bar alone, as well as cleaning, mixing drinks, and waiting tables. How was she to do it all? And with an injured hand?

Only an idiot would even try it. Only a crazy person would even think it could be done.

Sylphie smirked at her from the second floor mezzanine, and Xander held her gaze.

The burn of Sylphie's hand on the side of her face began to recede. She couldn't focus on it anyway. Too much to do.

She pinned her hair back with a drink stirrer and smirked back at Sylphie.

Maybe they were both crazy, idiot people, but that didn't

mean they couldn't attempt the impossible anyway.

Oscar opened the door, and customers from all over Copernicus City flooded through the entryway. Xander tightened the bandages on her hand, checked the stores of liquor under the bar cabinet, and made sure she had a datapad to take orders. She took a deep, steadying breath and wove her way through the crowd into the tables.

CHAPTER 5

A Ganymede Sunrise: Himalian whiskey, NUGerman wormwood, bourbon, Adrastean Cointreau, bitters, a thin layer of thick cherry liqueur, and synthetic orange zest. The reddish-orange cocktail was the most complicated mixed drink in the Oasis. It even gave Cedric fits. And Xander had made four in the last six hours.

Her cut hand throbbed and bled through her bandages, but she ignored it. She left blood stains on the highballs and collins glasses, but all the customers were too drunk to notice. The glassware was all so dirty anyway that adding another layer of filth to them didn't make much difference.

Xander delivered the fourth Ganymede Sunrise of the day, along with another round of straight Himalian whiskey and rye to table eight. On the way back to the bar, she took another order for seven beers, a Copernicus, a Bleeding Leda, and something called a Lunar Rainbow.

The moment she got back to the bar, she dug out Cedric's drink mixing manual. She'd never heard of a Lunar Rainbow.

As she skimmed the book for the recipe, she listened to the satisfied hum of conversation in the Oasis. The customers were happy. That meant Oscar would be happy, and that was her only goal.

She found the Lunar Rainbow recipe and cringed. It looked even more complicated than the Ganymede Sunrise. And Cedric had scribbled something in the upper right corner of the page: "Damn thing never turns out!"

That didn't inspire confidence.

She pulled out bottles of liquor she would need, but she stopped when a shadow crossed her. A man in a suit stood at the bar.

"Can I get you something?" she asked.

"Aren't you a little young to be bartending?"

Xander narrowed her eyes at him. He was tall and slender, and his hair was neatly combed. And he was *clean*. Not just rinsed but *washed*. She could smell soap on him—real soap. Like he had bathed that morning in clean water. Who was he?

"If you say so," she said. The alternative was telling him she didn't know how old she was.

He was well dressed and bordering on handsome, and he absolutely didn't belong on Callisto. With his loosened tie, he reminded her of a businessman after a long day at the office.

Motion at his side drew Xander's eyes away from his face.

Sylphie glided to his side and took his arm, smiling like a temptress. "Careful, Mr. Clayton. I might get jealous if you start chatting up the waitresses."

The man gave a brief, tight smile. "What's your price, little one?"

Xander bristled. "I wait tables. I'm not a whore."

The man frowned. "You work in a place like this—and you're not a whore?"

"That's right. I wait tables. I make drinks." She emphasized the point by setting a pitcher of beer on the counter. The motion hurt her hand, but she didn't let it show.

The man didn't look impressed. "I don't drink," he said, as though it excused him from his other obvious vices. "I'll be returning in a week or so." His eyes were dark when he smiled. "Let me know your price then."

"I haven't got one."

"No woman on Callisto doesn't have a price." Mr. Clayton adjusted his tie and pecked Sylphie on the cheek. "Wonderful to see you again, Sylphie."

Sylphie seemed to find something funny and started chuckling. She winked at him and leaned back on the counter. "Good day, Mr. Clayton."

He marched out of the bar, scowling at the men who lay drunk and unconscious around the bar. As he left, the dim light outside revealed the wrinkles in his suit jacket.

Sylphie took a seat at the bar, and Xander poured her a tumbler of bourbon.

"He a regular?"

"Not too regular." Sylphie threw the drink back in a single swallow. "He's from the Sanctum. It's pretty far out, so he's not around very much. Him and all the other Sanctum types either come here or they go to the Lady Luck, in the outer rim."

"The Sanctum."

"I don't get him." Sylphie leaned her head back. "Or any of his people."

"What do you mean?"

"They're all goody-goodies."

"Goody-goodies?"

Sylphie groaned. "They're like you, kid."

Xander straightened. "Like me? What does that mean?"

"Too good for everybody else. Too good to live among the lowlifes. Too good to be bad."

Xander gaped at her, mouth open and eyes wide. She knew she was different. She knew she didn't fit in with the rest of the

46

crowd that frequented the Oasis, but Sylphie didn't really believe that. Did she?

"You don't really think that, do you?" Xander asked. "That I'm stuck up like that?"

Sylphie stared at her for a moment, perfectly polished red nails tapping on the side of her glass.

"You might have been the first time I met you." She smirked. "But not now. Now you got some sense knocked into you. And that happens when you're down in the gutters with the rest of us. But those Sanctimonians—"

Sylphie slid the empty glass to Xander. "They screw around just like everybody else, and then they act like they're better. It don't make no sense to me, sweetheart. They all belong to some super secret club so they all get to be jackasses and act all superior. I can't stand them."

Xander filled two glasses with beer and set them aside. She started on the Lunar Rainbow and winced at the pain in her hand when she lifted a heavy decanter of cognac.

Sylphie noticed. "How you holding up?"

"I'm alive."

"I can see that. But how are you holding up?"

"I'll make it, Sylphie."

"Good. I was worried for a bit there."

Xander stopped. "You were worried? About me?"

Sylphie shrugged.

"But I thought we all had to look out for number one."

"That's the rule," Sylphie said. "But you've been a breath of fresh air around this place, kid. Cedric might have screwed you over, but he felt it too. Probably why he left."

Xander frowned. "I don't understand."

"You make people uncomfortable, Xander-girl."

"How?"

"Don't know. You just—do."

"I don't mean to."

Sylphie stretched her arms out again. "That's what's so damn annoying about it."

Xander picked up the beer glasses and stepped around the side of the bar counter to deliver them, and the Oasis doors crashed open. A tall man in a rumpled suit stumbled inside, his brown hair mussed and blood dribbling from his mouth. Six visible plasma burns smoldered on his clothing.

It was Oscar's partner—his drug dealer friend.

He only made one more step before he belted out a bloodcurdling scream that stopped all motion in the Oasis.

Sylphie jumped to her feet at Xander's side, and Oscar barged out of his office.

Oscar's partner made a strangled sound, took another step, and fell dead to the floor.

Sylphie grabbed her, trembling.

Oscar cleared his throat, his expression carefully guarded. "Xander."

Xander faced him. "Yes, sir?"

"Close up early."

She studied Oscar's face. They never closed early.

"Xander," Sylphie hissed. "Do it."

Xander set the beers down and moved to flash the lights, and a window shattered on the side of the building. Something round and metallic rolled across the floor and came to a halt at the center of the bar, a blinking red light on the cylinder's head.

"What is—"

"Grenade!" A customer screamed.

"It's the police!"

Chaos erupted, and so did the grenade. The force of the explosion blasted Xander and Sylphie into the bar wall, glass raining around them. It turned the tables to splinters and flung scattered pieces of Oasis customers to the far corners of the room.

Xander's ears burned. Was that what it felt like to have Himalian whiskey poured in them? Oh, she'd never do that to anyone again. Her ribs pinched and ached. She couldn't hear, and she couldn't see, and something in the air made her eyes burn and water. Sylphie jumped to her feet in the smoke and the ash, the light of the fires illuminating her torn gown. She said something, but Xander couldn't hear her. Her lips moved, but there was no sound.

Sylphie tugged at her arm. Wanted her to get up. So she got up.

Sylphie helped her, and they limped for the stairs together. Halfway, Xander glanced back.

One wall had come down. Customers lay dead all over the floor. The ones who were still alive pulled themselves toward the entrance. Above them, the whores and their clients rushed around trying to make sense of the pandemonium below them. Some were climbing out windows. Others raced down the stairs, not bothering to offer help to either Xander or Sylphie.

As Sylphie and Xander stood on the steps, Oscar's office door opened. He wore his white coat and carried a large case. He looked up at them silently before he turned to the front of the bar.

It was too late. A thick steel battering ram bashed the front door in, and the Oasis filled with men in dark uniforms armed with plasma weapons.

Oscar didn't stand a chance. The police didn't even give him an opportunity to speak before they opened fire. And they didn't care who they hit.

Plasma bursts streamed all around them. Xander smothered a scream as one exploded near her head. The rush of heat against her face made her dizzy.

Sylphie shoved her up the steps toward the room. They both stumbled, and Xander fell against the steps. The blow sent massive waves of nauseating pain surging through her chest. Had her ribs broken?

Sylphie dragged her up the last step, plasma shots bursting like firecrackers around them.

Did the police want to kill everyone inside?

Sylphie flung them into her room and locked the door before she sagged against it, gasping for breath.

"Sylphie!" Xander cried. "What is this? Why are they doing this?"

"They found out about the Fantasy." Sylphie sounded agonized. She pushed off the door and limped to her dresser. She ripped the top drawer open. "They won't leave till we're all dead."

"Why? We didn't do anything!"

"Doesn't matter," Sylphie said, her voice faint. "Doesn't matter. They'll kill us all. Less paperwork."

Sylphie jerked a leather bag out of her drawer. She lost her balance and fell to the floor. She lay there, gasping as more explosions shuddered through the building.

Xander crawled to her side. "Sylphie?"

Sylphie grabbed Xander's arm with one hand, and with the other she shoved the leather bag into Xander's arms. Something else exploded downstairs—the biggest yet. A loud rushing sound outside the door indicated the building was on fire. A woman screeched next door.

"Xander," Sylphie said, her tone calm. "You do what I tell you."

"Sylphie?"

"You take this." She nodded at the bag. "And you get the hell out of here."

"What?"

Sylphie looked over her shoulder at a panel on her wall. "Secret exit. I found it on accident some time back. Even Oscar didn't know it was there. Take—the credits and go."

"Credits?"

Xander opened the bag. Credits. Credits upon credits upon credits. More than she could count. How long had Sylphie been saving?

"Sylphie!" she whispered. "I—I can't—no. I won't take these."

"I'm not going to use them, kid."

Xander met Sylphie's eyes, and Sylphie pulled her hand away from her chest where she'd been shot. More than once. The blood and plasma burns all over her blended in with her torn red dress.

Sylphie was dying.

"No."

"Stop it, kid." Sylphie's harsh laugh grated at the back of her throat. "Do you think—denying it will stop it? Thought you were smarter than that."

Another explosion rocked the main level.

"Now—you take those credits. Get yourself to NUSaxony. Find whatever you're looking for." Blood seeped from the corner of her mouth. "Find yourself."

51

"I can't take these."

Sylphie tilted her head, her black hair tumbling over her shoulders. "You wouldn't even have stole them, would you?"

"Stealing is wrong."

"You—you're such a weird kid." Sylphie gurgled from the blood pooling at the back of her throat.

"Why would you help me?"

"Take them. I'm giving them to you." She patted Xander on the knee again and left a bloody hand print. "Now get out of here. Get to the docks and get the hell off Callisto." Her smile was weak. "You don't belong here, Xander-girl."

"Sylphie."

"Go. Before this place comes down around us." Sylphie groaned. "Go to the docks, kid. Run. Just get out of here! Go!"

Sylphie shoved her. Xander ran for the secret passage and threw it open. She ran down the concealed spiral staircase inside as fast as she could. She didn't look back.

The stairs emptied into a crawl space, and Xander kicked the wall in. It led to her room. But Sylphie had said the passage led outside!

Xander dove into the passage again and searched for another door, some other way to escape. It only took a few seconds to find the other door latch. She pushed it open, and peered into the alley behind the Oasis.

Xander tucked the bag of credits into her blouse. But she paused and jumped back into the room. She reached under her cot and grabbed the bag with her gray jacket in it. She flung it over her shoulder and ran for the alley just as the Oasis collapsed.

She didn't stop running.

She pushed herself fast and hard. Were the police chasing

her? Had anyone seen her? Would they detain her, suspect her of setting the bar on fire?

Xander shoved her fears to the back of her mind as she darted into the shifting crowds that lined the sidewalks of Copernicus City, running and elbowing, ducking and dodging. She didn't stop until she got to the docks where the shuttle had dropped her off two months earlier. She flung herself into the short line in front of the ticket booth.

The old woman at the desk glared at her. "Destination?"

"NUSaxony."

"What the hell you wanna' go there for?"

"That's where I want to go."

"Six hundred creds, sweetheart. You got that much?"

Xander dug around in the bag until she found cards of the right amount, and she handed them to the old lady, who eyed her suspiciously.

"You staying or visiting?"

"Why?"

"Visas."

Xander tried to keep her voice from shaking. "I'm just visiting."

"Then I need another twelve hundred credits for an entrance visa and twelve hundred for the exit visa." The woman held out her hand. "Twenty-four." She sounded pleased with herself, as though she looked forward to dashing Xander's hopes.

Xander dug in the bag and retrieved another bundle of cards, handing them to the woman.

The woman was incredulous. "Skinny little whore like you couldn't have earned that much." But she took the cards anyway and handed her a ticket. "Hold out your hand."

Xander did, and the woman pressed the flat side of the ring she was wearing to Xander's thumb. In a moment, the computer screen on the woman's desk flashed green letters, *CLEAR*.

"No warrants out for you, and you're not NUChungqwo," she said. "Hold still."

Xander didn't have time to ask why her heritage mattered before the woman lifted a small plastic machine with a lens on the front and snapped a picture. Moments later, the machine spit out two blue cards with her picture on it.

The woman handed her the cards.

It was a horrible picture. Her hair was matted and tangled. Her face was bruised and smudged with soot and Sylphie's blood. She looked terrified.

"Move your ass." The woman nodded at the passenger ships behind her.

Xander plunged past the ticket booth, and one of the conductors directed her to a large passenger ship, the *Acheron*, digital displays indicating that it was bound for NUSaxony.

She raced up the boarding platform and found an unoccupied corner of the cavernous cargo bay. The other passengers clustered in groups and kept to themselves. She settled down in the corner and folded herself around the leather bag of credits and her visas which would secure her entrance into NUSaxony.

After two long months of scrimping and saving, trust and betrayal, she had made it. She was on her way to NUSaxony.

But at what cost? Could knowing her name, her home, her past possibly be worth it anymore?

Xander rested her forehead against her knees.

She would be brave, if for no other reason than Sylphie had sacrificed herself to give her this chance. She would pursue this course until the path disappeared, for Sylphie's sake and for Dr. Zahn, the two women who had saved her and protected her and cared for her more than they needed to.

Two women who had broken every rule they held dear about the universe—Dr. Zahn who Xander had not spoken to since the *Anastasia* abandoned her on Callisto; Sylphie who Xander would never see again.

Xander wept against her knees and hoped whatever she found on NUSaxony would be worth the price she'd already paid.

CHAPTER 6

The *Acheron* shivered as its sublight engines kicked in. The motion jarred Xander awake from a dream about Sylphie, smoking a cigarette and entertaining a customer with a gaping hole in her chest.

Her stomach churned, either from the dream or from the jump into hyperspace.

Old illuminators flickered on the bulkheads so the passenger bay wasn't pitch black inside. A few family groups clustered in the expanse of the bay, some sleeping, some talking, all eying each other with suspicion. A man in a white coat huddled in the corner, wringing his hands and glancing all around as though he expected the shadows to bite him.

Maybe he'd spent time in the alleys of Callisto. Why else would he act that way? He also seemed to be traveling alone, much like herself. But the more he twitched, the stranger he seemed. And she had enough trouble as it was; there was no need to go chasing it.

She stood and stretched, feeling the pain of her bruises and the sickening sensation of the blood dried on her arms and face. Her ribs and her hand throbbed, sharp pains jolting through her with every breath.

Movement would help. At least she could focus on something else other than the pain.

Xander walked to one of the portholes and frowned. She didn't see stars, as she was expecting, but rippling waves of bluish-green energy, like a gossamer curtain over the stars in real space.

"Never seen hyperspace before?"

Xander whirled. A freckle-faced boy about her age stood behind her. His clothes were threadbare, and she couldn't tell if his hair were actually brown or if it were just dirty, but his smile was honest.

"No," Xander said.

"I'm going to be a space pilot someday." He looked past her out the window. "Maybe even a bounty hunter."

A bounty hunter. That man Lou from Callisto had talked about head hunting. He was a bounty hunter. The boy obviously didn't know what he was talking about.

"I don't think that's a good career move," Xander said.

The boy grinned. "I'm Franklin."

"I'm—well, people call me Xander."

"Xander," Franklin said. "Where are you from?"

"I really don't know."

"But you got on at Callisto. That's where we're from."

"And you're going to NUSaxony?" Xander asked.

"We're transferring at NUSaxony. From there we're going to Earth. We won't live on the colonies. Mom says they're not a good place to live."

Xander glanced beyond Franklin to where a frail woman observed their conversation. Xander felt exposed in nothing but her waitressing outfit and the gray jacket, which she pulled tighter around her shoulders.

"Why aren't the colonies a good place to live?" She recalled Sylphie saying once that colony life was far easier than life on a moon or a planet.

"All the colonies are like NUJenesis." Franklin stepped closer to her. "They're all trying to start a war with the world-dwellers. That's what mom says."

"NUJenesis?" Xander pressed her fingers into her brow. "NUJenesis."

"Yeah." He leaned closer. "Do you know something about NUJenesis?"

"No." Xander held up her hands. "It just—sounds familiar somehow."

"No one really knows anything about NUJenesis," Franklin said. "Just that it's dangerous. Like all the other colonies." He tilted his head. "Ma says you're a whore. Are you?"

Xander blushed. "I am not."

"But you're from Callisto."

He was close enough now Xander could smell the dirt on his clothes and in his hair, could see the flecks of green in his brown eyes.

"I'm not a whore," she said firmly.

"Oh."

"You sound disappointed." Xander scowled.

Franklin grinned. "Well, we still have a ways to go." He touched her face. "And I'm bored."

Xander closed her eyes and stepped backward. "No. Thank you."

"Hey, just because I'm young—" He advanced again.

"How old are you?"

He straightened. "Twenty."

Xander arched an eyebrow. "Twenty?"

He shrunk a bit. "Sixteen."

"You don't need to be talking about this." Her stomach turned somersaults.

"Why not?" Franklin shrugged and took her hand. "Won't be

my first time, and anybody I find on Earth'll probably give me something catching."

Xander pulled her hand away. "Not interested."

He stepped a bit closer. "I'll be gentle. I promise. Girls always tell me I'm real gentle."

"Look." Xander set her hand on his chest firmly. "I'm not interested. Go away."

Franklin hesitated for a moment before he shrugged. "Okay. But if you change your mind—"

"I won't."

He grinned again and stepped back. He waved as he returned to sit by the frail woman Xander assumed was his mother.

Xander slid back down to the floor and closed her eyes.

It was okay. If he'd grown up on Callisto, he had to assume that every woman he met was a prostitute. It didn't mean anything.

She rubbed her temples and eyed Franklin as he walked to the other end of the bay, where another family was sitting. A woman with three children gathered close, two boys and a girl. Franklin knelt to talk to the girl, and in moments she was giggling behind her hand.

Franklin said something in her ear, and she accepted his help up as he led her to the shadows in the corner of the bay.

The girl's mother said nothing. Franklin's mother didn't look bothered at all.

Pain pulsed behind Xander's eyes and she squeezed them shut. Franklin might have grown up on Callisto, but the girl he'd just lured into the shadows hadn't. She was too clean. She'd been on the *Acheron* when Xander had boarded.

What if Callisto *was* the standard after all? And if that was the case, why was she so certain it was wrong? Where had that idea come from?

Xander laid her forehead on her knees. Nothing made sense. She had to be out of her mind.

She wrapped her arms around her shins and held on to herself until the trembling stopped. She propped her chin on one of her knees and stared at the bulkhead across from her.

"NUJenesis," she mumbled. "Like the Book of Genesis."

She froze.

Like the Book of Genesis? What is that?

The phrase had simply appeared in her mind, but she couldn't link it to anything else. What was it? How had she remembered it? *Why* had she remembered it?

She breathed, long and deep, and forced her shoulders to relax as she leaned her head back against the wall. She blanked her mind, willed herself to stop trying to remember. She felt the hum of the engines through the floor. She heard babies crying on the other end of the bay. Ozone and coolant hung in the air, like perfume, thick and heady.

Genesis. She allowed herself to think only the word.

Nothing.

Genesis.

She waited. Still nothing.

She kept calm. Quiet. Still.

But she couldn't remember.

She fought against the disappointment that weighed her shoulders down. The word was important, but she couldn't remember what it meant.

Maybe it would come to her in time. She tucked the word away in her mind and hoped whatever it meant would become clear soon.

She sat in the dark in silence long enough for her legs to go to sleep. Long enough for Franklin and the girl to move out of the shadows.

Xander started as the *Acheron* shuddered and lurched under her feet. She got up and peered out the porthole. The stars were back. She craned her neck at a difficult angle and could see a massive round gateway some distance behind the back end of the ship.

"What's going on?" Franklin asked his mother. The woman didn't answer.

"We can't be there already," a man across the bay shouted. "It ain't been long enough."

The ship quaked and rolled on its side. All the passengers in the bay fell, tumbling over the bulkheads, scrambling, trying to right themselves. Xander grabbed a strap attached to one of the walls.

After a moment, the ship straightened, but the feel of the engines through the floor panels was different. If a ship could be afraid, the *Acheron* was terrified.

Shouting, loud and frightened, came from the other side of the main entryway.

The families in the bay gathered their children and huddled around them. The bay reverberated with sobbing and crying, exclamations of fear. Fears of pirates, of raids, of attacks by bandits from the outer rim. The entryway doors slid open. A man wearing an ill-fitting captain's jacket stepped inside and tried to look official, though he only managed to look scared.

Xander didn't blame him. Behind him, half-submerged in shadows, stood six men in dark uniforms. Black pants. Dark shirts. Leather boots. Military hats. Each carried a long blaster of some kind. They weren't scatterguns. Maybe some kind of energy weapon. She'd seen her share of them at the Oasis, but these weapons looked deadlier than the common blasters she had noted on customers in the bar.

The six men marched into the room in tight formation, their half-hidden faces somber. They parted down the middle to allow another man, their commander, to pass through them.

Xander wanted to cower behind the crate next to her.

More than six feet tall, the man's shiny black hair fell over his brow and down to his neck in stylish disarray. His volatile eyes smoldered black, luminous in spite of their darkness. His face was all hard angles and infuriating confidence, a mask of serenity enshrouding what had to be a turbulent soul.

His presence snuffed out all noise and replaced it with sheer, silent terror, as though his very existence doomed everyone aboard to death. Not even the infants made a sound.

He didn't speak. Only his eyes moved, passing over the huddled families and trembling couples. Absorbing every detail, he scanned the passenger bay until his eyes found Xander.

His gaze stopped on her and didn't move further.

Her heart leapt to her throat. She wanted to run, to escape the look in his eyes. They stripped away every fear she had tried to hide, every secret she couldn't remember. His eyes pierced her soul and revealed the frightened little girl inside, the one she had tried to ignore since she'd awakened on the *Anastasia*.

He stepped forward, his eyes not leaving hers. She couldn't look away. Was he a snake that his gaze had mesmerized her? Her body wouldn't obey. Her legs wouldn't move. Her face wouldn't even look down.

Something crashed at the other end of the passenger bay. Everyone clenched, expecting the black-eyed man or his troops to open fire. He didn't move. He only looked away from her and glared at the other end of the bay where the shifty man in the long white coat stood.

The black-eyed man smirked, a wicked expression. "Zen Mitchem." His voice chilled Xander's blood.

The man in the white coat had turned ashen. The black-eyed man jerked his head ever so slightly—hardly enough to cause his hair to ripple in the overhead lights—and the six-man squad charged.

Zen Mitchem didn't stand a chance. The squad reached him before he even had time to run. They had stripped him of his coat, bound him, and led him away in less time than Xander had to draw two breaths.

"Zen Mitchem?" one of the men near Xander whispered. "He's a Fantasy dealer."

The squad led Zen Mitchem toward the entryway. A blubbering wreck, Mitchem didn't fight them. He didn't even try to resist.

Slowly, the huddled couples and family groups relaxed, all breathing a collective sigh of relief.

Xander didn't. The man with the black eyes hadn't moved at all.

Almost like the people on the ship noticed at the same time she did, everyone fell silent again. The troops had left, their drug dealer secured. The black-eyed man stayed.

Slowly, so slowly, the man turned his head to stare at her again, and he resumed his course toward her.

Toward her.

What did he want?

A horrifying thought blossomed at the back of her mind. What if the man knew her? What if he recognized her? What if he knew who she was? No. She didn't even want to think about that.

63

Certainly there was no way a man like him could have anything to do with someone like her.

She still couldn't move. Rooted to the spot, her feet were heavy, her arms like lead, and she could only gape as he stopped before her.

Her lungs seized when he raised his hand and slid his fingers into her hair. He didn't touch her scalp. Just her hair. His fingers clutched it.

"What is your name?"

His voice was so sudden, Xander almost didn't realize he had spoken.

He was too close. His scent was overwhelming. Something strong and sharp and cold that burned the back of her nostrils.

His fingers tightened in her hair. "What is your name?"

She saw his lips move. His voice was different than before. Lower. Softer. Full of something she didn't want to identify. Just the sound of his voice sent blood rushing to her cheeks.

"Xander."

"Xander," he repeated, the same tone as before. "Odd name for a common whore."

Anger flared in her. "I am *not* a whore!" She stepped back from him before she thought about it.

The man gripped the hair in his fingers and yanked her back toward him. Tears sprang to her eyes, and then the force on her scalp was gone. Xander regained her balance and backed out of his reach, holding the sore spot on her scalp.

The black-eyed man hadn't moved. He stood before her, gazing at the thick lock of red hair he held in his hand.

Her hair.

The man had cut her hair!

Xander sputtered indignantly. Somewhere in the depths of her consciousness, she knew the man could probably kill her with his little finger, but it didn't seem to matter in the face of her outrage.

The man smirked at her with arrogant eyes. "You have some spark in you," he said. "I like that."

He tucked her hair in his pocket and started toward the entryway. The overhead lights revealed the knife he held. The sight of the glinting silver blade kept her from throwing something at the back of his head.

He'd cut the hair from her head without her even seeing the knife. And she'd been looking right at him.

She quivered in anger as the black-eyed man left and the captain followed him. Only when the *Acheron* started moving again did everyone truly allow themselves to breathe again.

Xander wanted to know who the black-eyed man was and what he wanted from her. But even if anyone else in the bay knew, she didn't think they would tell her. The rest of the passengers seemed unhappier with her now than when she first boarded.

So she sat in the corner and curled her knees to her aching ribs.

The light above her shifted as the *Acheron* jumped back into hyperspace.

What is going on? What's happening to me? Where am I? What am I doing here? She forced herself to breathe long and slow. *Who am I? Who was that man, and why did he—why did he do that?*

She combed her fingers through the shortened lock of hair by her face.

She wasn't getting any answers. What would happen if she couldn't find answers on NUSaxony either?

The man had asked for her name so maybe that meant he

didn't know her, but the familiar way that he'd looked at her told her something different. The man's expression told her that he'd been looking for her, waiting for her, maybe even expecting her. That would have been the worst possible explanation.

She didn't want anything to do with the black-eyed man. Even though her mind was broken, that was one thing she knew for sure.

CHAPTER 7

Xander spent the rest of the voyage pressed against the chilly bulkhead, trying to sleep. She didn't have much luck, but she stayed out of sight until the *Acheron* fell out of hyperspace and into the shipping lanes outside NUSaxony.

The ship landed with a grinding crunch, the motion jostling the passengers. Once the ship was down, Xander waited for everyone else to disembark before she followed down the ramp. Franklin waved at her in spite of the glare she gave him.

NUSaxony spread out before her, a sprawling metropolis encased in a superglass dome under more stars than she could count. Giant signs in many languages—*Welcome to Victoria Dome!* and *You've Reached New London!*—flashed in her peripheral vision as she descended the ramp. Giant skyscrapers stretched toward the stars outside the dome, and even before she exited the freighter she could taste the clean air streaming out of the city center.

People stared at her. Some even pointed, but most ignored her entirely, pretending she didn't exist. Was it because of her clothes? Everyone around her wore tailored skirts and sweaters or business suits; her tatty, blood-stained waitress outfit and jacket looked out of place.

She decided to ignore them back.

Xander flowed with the other people who exited other docking tubes and moved into a building identified by signage as the Interplanetary Arrival Section of the Victoria Dome Colony-National

Transportation Center. Men and women at small desks seemed to be sorting through single file lines of arrivals, examining their proffered paperwork and forms.

"Customs," Xander muttered under her breath, the familiar term returning to her mind without her even seeking it. Mimicking the man in front of her, she pulled the entrance visa out of her leather bag.

She moved up for her turn, and a man in an ugly suit trained an appraising glance on her. She handed him her visa. He snatched it from her with two fingers and an expression that said he didn't believe she knew how to write. He handed it back with a cocked eyebrow. "Oitums ta' deecleh?"

"Excuse me?"

"Oitums ta' deecleh?"

"I don't understand."

"'Ave'ee any oitums ta' deecleh?" The tips of his ears burned red with frustration.

Customs. This is customs. Items to declare. Xander realized. *Items to declare!* "N—no. Nothing."

"Aw'right. Well, go on then."

He opened the gate, and Xander entered the lobby. She could hardly breathe for the stifling sense of disapproval she felt from everyone she passed.

Xander slipped into the crowd.

She walked by a woman who glared at her like she didn't deserve to be breathing.

Xander steeled herself. It was because she had come from Callisto. Everyone probably knew what Callisto was, and NUSaxons likely preferred a higher class of people. That had to be it.

Xander passed a man who covered his nose with a

68

handkerchief when she came close to him. Other people pointed at her and laughed.

She swallowed hard and kept walking forward.

She hadn't expected the people of NUSaxony to trust her, but she had hoped to find a bit of compassion.

Dr. Zahn and Sylphie had believed nobody cared about anyone, but that was just the *Anastasia*. That was just Callisto. It couldn't be true everywhere.

A woman approaching her on the sidewalk stopped when she saw her and crossed the street in order to keep walking. Xander felt like shouting at her.

Hadn't there been a time when people helped each other? Some part of her expected the universe to be sympathetic, to be concerned when a young woman wandered alone into a transport center covered in blood. Wasn't there a world like that anywhere?

Maybe her memories of that world were like hand sanitizer— something she had imagined.

No one helped each other in this universe. Dr. Zahn and Sylphie had, but they got something out of it. Sylphie escaped the harassment of a male bartender, and Dr. Zahn used her as an excuse to forgo the sexual advances of the *Anastasia's* crewmen.

Had there ever been a time in the universe where people just helped each other for no other reason than kindness? The concept didn't seem to apply to anyone she had met thus far.

Maybe she needed to chalk it up to her broken mind, fabricating fanciful stories about a dream world that had never been. A dream world where people drank sweet tea.

Xander stopped in an alley and took a moment to just breathe the fresh air. Unfriendly and cold as NUSaxony was, they had beautiful, clean air. She hadn't realized how much she had missed breathing it.

Moving sidewalks carried pedestrians on her right and left. Static sidewalks shimmered with some sort of polymer coating. Some people walked; some ran; some carried arm loads of luggage; most had devices strapped to their luggage that caused them to float, gliding seamlessly above the metallic sidewalks.

Some people carried luggage for others. At first, Xander was glad to see it, hoping that she had misjudged the universe after all, but she stopped after she watched the interaction between them.

A man who carried three large suitcases for a woman moved awkwardly, one stiff leg in front of the other. And the woman shouted orders at him, commanding him as though he were a slave. The man simply did as he was told.

The man's ungainly motions didn't look natural. He wasn't disproportionate or disabled, but his legs were too stiff, his back too rigid, and his expression seemed almost artificial. Was he even human?

Human or not didn't matter. A person had every right to live free, not as a step stool for other people's ambitions. People were created equal and deserved to be treated equally. Slavery in such an immaculate world sent Xander's head spinning. Maybe it happened on the moons, but a colony seemed Utopian in comparison to a moon.

How could they have slaves?

Xander shook herself. So many things didn't make sense to her. Her broken brain always confused everything. How could she have forgotten so much about herself and about the universe?

Everything was spectacularly clean. The people. The buildings. The alleyways. No one looked destitute or homeless. Everyone moved with a purpose.

It was a different world, and Xander felt just as misplaced as she had on Callisto.

Flashing neon lights caught her attention. A small kiosk stood at one end of a sidewalk with a bright sign above displaying the word, *Information*.

Xander gathered her courage and walked toward the booth. On her approach, a woman materialized behind the counter, holographic smile brightening her holographic face. Her teeth were too white, and her eyes looked too happy.

"Welcome to New London, visitor," the hologram said in a light English accent. "How may I assist you?"

"I'm—looking for Dr. Evylin Berkley."

"Dr. Evylin Berkley," the hologram repeated. "Dr. Evylin Berkley is located at the New London Neurology Center on Card and Hambly."

"Where is that?"

The hologram gestured to a slot on the counter, and it spit out a map with glowing directions to the neurology center.

"Thank you," Xander said.

"You are welcome, visitor. Have a pleasant afternoon."

The holographic woman dissipated, and Xander followed the directions. She was halfway there before she realized that she didn't have a clue what Dr. Berkley even looked like. Dr. Zahn had only given her the name.

She shook away the worry and kept walking. She turned the corner and stared at the neurology center, a massive building with high towers that stretched toward the dome center. The windows caught the rays of the distant sun and the much-closer artificial light matrix, shining like liquid silver. Doctors and patients in starched, clean clothing buzzed around the entry doors.

Xander took a deep breath and entered the neurology center. With the help of a floor guide and index, she located the name on the list: *Dr. Evylin Berkley – Chief Neuro-Therapist.*

Xander found the lift and entered. The doors closed, but the lift didn't move. Xander looked for a panel of buttons to select the thirty-fifth floor, but there were no buttons. No dials. No knobs.

Brilliant. Spotless Utopia, advanced medical technology, and elevators that didn't elevate. What sense did that make?

"State your desired floor, please." A woman's voice above her made her look to see if someone was hanging from the ceiling tiles.

"Oh."

"'Oh,' is not a correct choice. Please state your desired floor."

"Thirty-five."

"Thank you."

The lift ascended. It carried her up, up, up until Xander was certain she was going to need an oxygen mask, and the doors opened.

"Have a pleasant day," the lift said.

Outside the lift was a nicely furnished lobby with a woman at the desk—not a hologram. Xander approached the desk.

"Good day, visitor." The woman tilted her head unnaturally. "Which doctor are you here to see?"

"Dr. Evylin Berkley."

"Do you have an appointment?"

"No."

"Dr. Berkley does not see patients without an appointment."

"Please." Xander leaned against the counter top and stared into the woman's unfeeling face. "I need to see her. I must see her. I've come a very long way. One of her friends referred me. Dr. Helga

NAMELESS

Zahn."

"One moment," the woman said.

She seemed to be thinking, staring into space. As she sat there, Xander looked at her more carefully. Her skin seemed too perfect, and her hair had a plastic-like quality to it. Her eyes shifted strangely, and her face seemed frozen in an expression that resembled a human but only slightly. She was just like the man Xander had seen carrying luggage. Human, but not human and obviously so. A zombie, maybe?

The woman turned her head. "Dr. Berkley will see you." She pointed. "Last office at the end of the hallway."

"Thank you," Xander said and started down the hallway.

The last office door was shut, and Xander knocked.

"Come in." The voice behind the door was lightly accented and very proper.

Xander pushed the door open.

The blond queen sitting at the desk inside wore spectacles and regarded Xander with calm expectation that rapidly faded to sheer dread. Her mouth turned down into a dark, unfriendly frown.

"Are you Dr. Berkley?"

"Would that I weren't." She went back to her work. "What do you want?"

"Dr. Zahn told me I needed to see you."

"What for?"

"I have amnesia."

"Sorry to hear." Dr. Berkley didn't look up from her digital readout screens. "I'm certain your memory will return in time, and you'll live a full and happy life. Good night."

Xander started. "Dr. Zahn said you would help me."

"I'm quite certain that Helga meant the very best when she

referred you to me, but I have no interest in helping you at all."

"Why not?"

Dr. Berkley dropped her datapad and looked Xander up and down. "What are you wearing?"

Xander glanced down at her skimpy skirt and bloodstained blouse under the wrinkled Xander jacket. What was she wearing? What kind of a dumb question was that?

"Clothes."

"That is a matter of opinion. My services are for paying clients, young lady."

Oh, yes. Dr. Berkley would help her.

Right. Dr. Berkley was a drama queen, and Xander was the orphan child off the street begging for scraps.

"I *can* pay you."

"I'm very expensive." Dr. Berkley flashed a condescending smile. "Far too expensive for you. Now please be on your way."

"You won't help me because of the way I'm dressed?"

Dr. Berkley shrugged, pushed her glasses up, and started looking at her datapad again. "I believe businesses on Old Earth had a saying—no shoes, no shirt, no service."

"I'm dressed, Dr. Berkley."

"I'm simply trying to point out that businesses in the past have declined services to clients who were in a state of undress. And, according to my standards, young lady, you are definitely in a state of undress." She stood up. "Now, get out of my office."

Xander's face flushed. "Someone—my clothes were stolen."

"Stolen? Who would steal your clothes?" Dr. Berkley scoffed.

"Dr. Zahn's ship left me on Callisto."

"Callisto?" Xander hadn't though Dr. Berkley's voice could

NAMELESS

raise another notch, but she managed it somehow. "Why would they leave you on Callisto?"

"The captain made the decision," Xander said. "They didn't have the rations to support me, and Callisto was on the way." She took a slow breath and let it out. "So they left me."

"And you're still alive?"

"For the most part."

"No one bit you, did they?"

"Uh—no."

"Were you active in their society?"

"Active?"

"Sexually?" she asked, as though she were speaking to a child.

"No!" Xander exclaimed. She probably should have expected the question by now. "But I got knocked around a lot. It's really a long story."

Dr. Berkley made an antagonized sound. "I'm sure it's very long, and I'm sure I'm not interested in the least."

"A prostitute found me. Got me a job. Waiting tables!" She amended quickly, lest Dr. Berkley think less of her. "All I had to wear was this—uniform. The jacket's mine, I think; I had it with me when the *Anastasia* found me. The bar was attacked, and I ran. This was all I had."

The blond NUSaxon doctor was thinking, her expression pensive. She peeled her glasses off and chewed on the left arm of the frames.

After a long time, she set her glasses down and leaned forward, her blue eyes intense. "What's your name?"

"Everyone calls me Xander."

Dr. Berkley pointed to her jacket. "Xander. Like that patch."

75

"The *Anastasia* found me wearing this." Xander fingered the patch absently. "But I don't think it's really my name."

"Have you remembered anything else?"

"Some names and words," Xander said. "But nothing else really."

"How old are you?"

"I can't remember."

"Your home?"

Xander shook her head.

"Family? Job? Pets? Likes? Dislikes? Allergies?"

Xander didn't have an answer for any of it.

Dr. Berkley leaned back in her chair again and crossed one leg over the other, fingers steepling over her chest. "What happened to you?"

"The *Anastasia* found me on a derelict ship." Xander shifted uncomfortably under Dr. Berkley's frank gaze. "The only survivor. Seven others dead. I couldn't remember anything."

"I see." Dr. Berkley laid her arms on her desk. "Why are you here?"

"I'm here because Dr. Zahn told me you would help me."

Dr. Berkley chose her words very carefully. "What do you want me to help you do?"

Xander shut her eyes and forced her tone to be even and calm, rather than loud and angry. "I want you to help me remember."

"Remember what?"

"Who I am. Where I come from. If I have family and friends. A home. I want you to help me remember who I am."

"You said you could pay."

Xander tossed the bag of credits Sylphie had given her on the desk. "The prostitute who helped me gave me those."

Dr. Berkley looked through the stash of credits. "You probably stole these."

"I did not."

Again, Dr. Berkley looked at her, staring and thinking. She scrutinized Xander's face, her body, her stance. "No, you didn't," she finally said.

Xander pulled her eyebrows together in a scowl.

"I don't think you could lie if you tried. Your face is far too open."

"Does that mean you'll help me?"

Dr. Berkley closed the bag. "It means that I will accept your payment." She looked at Xander. "But before we make any decisions, we are calling Dr. Zahn." She grunted. "At least, we're going to try. NUSovian communications are barbaric." She stood. "I want her to verify you really are the one she told me about."

Xander stared in shock. "You knew I was coming?"

"Helga only told me that you might come. I fully anticipated you would never make it." She shuddered. "And that was before I knew they left you on Callisto."

Dr. Berkley turned her screen around, showing it to Xander and dialing a number. The moment the line connected, Xander felt a rush of emotion nearly overwhelm her. It had been two months since she had seen Dr. Zahn.

There were a lot of things about Dr. Zahn that Xander didn't like, but she had missed her.

The screen flashed to life, and Dr. Zahn's severe features appeared. Seeing the stern-faced NUGerman medic destroyed whatever composure Xander had left. Tears rolled down her cheeks, and she made no effort to stop them.

For just a second, Dr. Zahn's face brightened. Then, it was

gone, replaced by her usual staid expression.

"Xander," she said. "I am glad to see you alive."

"More or less." Xander managed to keep her voice relatively even. "I'm—glad to see you too, Dr. Zahn."

Dr. Berkley leaned over her shoulder. "So this is the same one, is it, Helga?"

Dr. Zahn's eyes sparkled when she addressed Dr. Berkley. "*Ja, ja.* The same." Dr. Zahn's voice even sounded happier than it had before. "You must help her, my friend. I pay you whatever you need."

"That's very kind of you, Helga, but your friend has already provided me with enough money for a few months."

"A few months?" Dr. Zahn flashed a smug smile. "Xander, you must be very popular."

Xander blushed and didn't answer.

"All right, Helga," Dr. Berkley said. "I'll help her. For you, darling."

"My thanks to you, Evy," Dr. Zahn said, her face softening in a rare smile.

"But only on the promise that you'll visit soon. I've missed you."

"Yes. The same."

Xander rubbed at her eyes, trying not to listen to the conversation between the two women, which suddenly seemed intensely intimate. Xander felt the old blush creeping up her face. Weren't there any straight women in the universe who weren't prostitutes? If there were, she hadn't met one yet.

"We will be passing close to NUSaxony in three months," Dr. Zahn said. "I schedule shuttle to come for visit. I look forward to see you, Evy." She smiled. "And Xander."

NAMELESS

"It will be good to see you too, Dr. Zahn."

Dr. Zahn nodded, and the screen went dead.

"Very good." Dr. Berkley straightened. "Now, get out of my office."

Xander stood up. "Where do I go?"

"That's not my problem." Dr. Berkley shooed her to the office door and into the hallway. "Good night."

Xander stood in the corridor, shocked silent. Dr. Berkley had taken all the credits in the bag, leaving none for Xander to use. How was she supposed to find a place to stay? Or clothes to wear?

She stood there, almost panicking. Did she try to find a free place to stay? Would anyone accept work for board? Would anyone even hire her? From what she had experienced in NUSaxony so far, no one would even speak to her before she'd had a shower.

She stood in the hall, trying to figure out what she needed to do, losing track of time until Dr. Berkley's office door opened again.

Dr. Berkley stopped dead in her tracks, glaring. "Why are you still here?"

It took Xander a moment to answer. "I don't know where to go."

"You can't stay here."

Xander took a deep breath. "Then, you need to give me back the credits I gave you."

"I have no intention of doing that. You paid for my services. I'll help you tomorrow morning at eight o'clock. No sooner."

"So where am I supposed to stay?"

"There's a hostel down the way," Dr. Berkley said, stepping out of her office and letting the door close behind her. "It's fairly inexpensive."

She started down the hallway. Xander followed. "Inexpensive

is still too expensive for me. You have all my credits."

"Then go earn more the way you earned those."

Xander wanted to cry, but she held them back and used the emotion to fuel the anger that had been simmering at the back of her mind.

"Dr. Berkley, I did *not* earn those credits."

The neuro-therapist stopped and turned back to her.

"They were a gift. I wouldn't even know how to earn credits! I mean, I know how you all are saying to do it, but I refuse to sell my body for money. And if that's the only answer you're going to give me, then—" Xander thrust out her hand. "Then give them back, and I'll remember on my own."

Dr. Berkley didn't move, only stared at her.

There really wasn't any chance at all that the neuro-therapist was going to help her. Dr. Berkley probably saw her as a pest, a lower life form. It didn't matter with the rest of the people on NUSaxony, but Dr. Berkley had been her one hope. Now it was clear that they didn't belong in the same room, let alone as doctor and patient.

She'd have to remember on her own then. And that was fine by her.

"You didn't steal them," Dr. Berkley said, jarring Xander out of her thoughts.

"No."

"You didn't earn them."

"No."

"Someone on Callisto *gave* them to you."

"Yes."

Dr. Berkley scoffed. "That's the most ridiculous thing I've ever heard." Dr. Berkley's blue gaze was steely and penetrating.

NAMELESS

"How do you expect me to believe such a thing?"

"Because it's the truth."

Dr. Berkley exhaled at a measured pace and pinched the bridge of her nose with her perfectly manicured index finger and thumb. The woman said nothing for a long time.

Xander swallowed the lump in her throat. "Are there any parks around that I can sleep in?"

"New London has curfews. You couldn't sleep out of doors."

"Aren't there any homeless people here?"

"Homeless? No. No one in a colony is homeless."

"Except me."

Dr. Berkley walked a few steps away from her, obviously struggling with something. Xander didn't move, wishing her hand would stop stinging.

Finally, Dr. Berkley dropped her hand and turned back to Xander.

"This is highly inappropriate," she announced. "It is unprecedented and uncivilized." She sighed. "But I see no other choice at the moment." She tucked Xander's bag of credits into her purse. "And you are a friend of Helga's. So—for tonight, you may stay with me."

Xander couldn't believe her ears.

"But, mind you, I'm not happy about it," Dr. Berkley said. "We're going to stop by a public showering facility first, and you're going to clean up before you set foot in my home. And you're not going to touch anything. And you're going to sleep on the sofa because it's easier to clean. I suppose you have lice or some other sort of parasite that's going to ruin my upholstery."

Xander was too excited to listen to anything she was saying. She simply stood still and waited until Dr. Berkley finished

81

lecturing, and then she followed obediently as the attractive neuro-therapist led her out of the building and down the street.

"This is not a permanent arrangement." Dr. Berkley continued to rant. "After tonight, you'll go somewhere else. And I hope you appreciate how unsuitable this is." She shifted her bag on her shoulder. "Just don't get too comfortable. This is not a permanent arrangement. We are to remain strictly professional at all times."

Xander shook her head. "I don't want anything else, Dr. Berkley."

The neuro-therapist narrowed her eyes. "You and Helga are close?"

Xander's stomach rolled. Did Dr. Berkley suspect that she and Dr. Zahn had been lovers?

"Dr. Zahn rescued me," Xander said.

"Rescued you?"

"She saved my life. She's my friend. Nothing more."

"Very well." Dr. Berkley drew a deep breath. "Strictly professional. Platonic, you understand? I'm certain that under all that blood and grime you are an attractive young woman, but I'll have it understood that this arrangement is strictly for your benefit. Are we clear?"

"Yes, Dr. Berkley." Xander looked down. "Thank you, Dr. Berkley."

"Don't thank me yet. You may not remember anything."

"It doesn't matter."

Dr. Berkley looked over her shoulder, a blond eyebrow cocked in confusion.

"What I mean," Xander said, "is that—I just want you to know that I'm grateful for whatever help you can give me."

Dr. Berkley didn't smile. She didn't nod. She didn't speak.

She only looked forward again and kept walking. But Xander thought she might have seen the doctor's stride break just slightly.

CHAPTER 8

Kale Ravenwood tapped the frames of his gold-tinted scanners, and the lenses rotated clockwise, irises focused on the nondescript man in the corner booth. The left lens displayed a digital readout of the man's estimated height, weight, build and ethnicity. The skull mapping would take a little longer, especially since the dim lighting made the measurements more difficult.

Conamara, and other posh restaurants like it on Venus, seemed to operate under the assumption that the dimmer a dining room, the more their customers would spend. They said it had something to do with romantic ambiance or some bullshit like that; it was more likely the customers couldn't see well enough to read the menus.

"Gross."

Kale glanced at his partner, Devon Chase. The blond man on the other side of the table poked his slimy entree with his fork as though he expected it to come alive and bite him.

"This is just nasty."

Conamara was one of the only restaurants on Venus licensed to import seafood from the Jovian moons, though Kale wasn't sure why anyone would want to eat Jovian fish. Devon had thought the dish worth it, apparently, and, from the expression on his face, he had discovered exactly why Kale had sworn off eating anything that didn't come out of a box.

"It's your own fault for ordering it, Dev."

NAMELESS

"Yeah, well, whoever said Europan lobster was yummy should be shot." Devon threw down his fork and pouted at the multi-armed creature splayed out on his plate. "Jupiter moons produce the best seafood, my ass. It doesn't even *look* like lobster. Sure as hell don't taste like it."

Kale turned his attention back to the mark. "Talon didn't say it tasted good, Devon. He just said it was a delicacy."

"Yeah, whatever. Is that our guy or not?"

"Gimme a second."

"You've had a second, Kale." Devon whined. "More than a second. Like five whole seconds, dude. Is it Mr. Shivs or not?"

Kale tapped the frames again, and the left lens projected the image of the mark's skull, highlighting the consistencies with the head they were seeking.

"That's him all right," Kale said. "All the plastic surgery in the world can't change his skull."

"I'll change his skull." Devon checked for the blaster hidden in his coat. "I'll beat my two hundred creds out of it."

Kale pulled the scanners off to glare at his partner. "You spent two hundred creds on that?"

"Talon said it was good!"

"Talon said it was a delicacy, stupid." Kale leaned closer and hissed, "That's coming out of your cut."

"Fine." Devon stuck out his tongue. "Shouldn't matter, since Parker over there's worth twenty mil, as is. Even with Vix's trips to the races and you racking up legal fees, that'll more than cover my scrumptious lobster dinner."

They stopped talking as the waitress approached on wobbly high heels and refilled their water glasses. "Can I get you gentlemen anything else?"

85

She fluttered fake eyelashes at Kale, and he did his best to keep smiling.

Women. The system would be a much more pleasant place if they'd just keep their too-tight corsets out of his face.

"That man over there." Kale gestured to Parker with a plastered-on smile. "Would you get me his check? I want to pay for his meal."

The waitress pressed her hand to her heart and leaned over, giving him an unobstructed view down her corset. "Why, how generous of you, sir!" She bustled away, rounded hips swaying exaggeratedly.

Devon watched her go with his hands spread against the velvet tablecloth. "Now, she's a hottie."

"Shut up."

"Well, she *is*."

"I didn't notice."

"Yeah, right, you didn't notice. It was all over her. In neon holosigns. Hottie!"

Kale pinched the bridge of his nose.

"I refuse to believe that display of woman-ness didn't knock you flat over with desire, Kale." Devon chortled. "That's a real catch, that one."

"Can we just get this over with, Devon?"

"Damn, you're grouchier than usual today."

"I'm tired, all right? I was up all night listening to Claude snore through the vent shaft. So I got no sleep. I want to nab this squatter, get the reward, and go to bed."

"Aw, poor little Kaley-waley. Didn't get his beauty sleep."

The waitress returned with three tickets and another flirtatious smile. Devon whined about his seafood disaster but paid

NAMELESS

anyway. Kale paid for his own drink and for Parker's outrageous feast of more than four hundred credits and dismissed her with a wave.

Devon tried unsuccessfully to catch her attention. He pouted again.

They watched for a moment as a different waitress informed Parker that his bill had been paid. The waitress gestured to Kale and Devon, and Parker stood and approached them.

"All right, brother." Devon leaned back in his chair. "Here we go."

Kale slid the scanners in his coat and tapped the radio transceiver clipped to his shirt. "Mark's on the way. Back us up, ladies."

"Roger that," Jaz responded, all businesslike, as usual. She was stationed outside but wouldn't come barging in unless she was needed.

She wouldn't be. Parker was one guy. Kale could take him alone, but Devon needed something to do.

In a moment, Gil Parker approached at their table. His dark eyes glared from behind a curtain of thick graying eyebrows. His clothes were neat, and his pants were perfectly creased, though his brown hair was untidy.

"You paid for my meal?" His voice sounded like sandpaper on plastic.

"Yes, I did," Kale said.

"Why?"

"I felt like it."

"Why?"

"Can't a man do a good deed every once in a while?" Kale shrugged.

87

"Not for me," Parker set gargantuan fists on the table top. "What do you want?"

"Whatever happened to gratitude?" Devon effected a flawlessly pathetic expression. "We reach out a hand of caring to a stranger, and he takes offense. What's the system coming to these days? I *knew* I should have moved to Mars, taken my mother's advice. These Venus types are just too unpredictable."

"You." Parker pointed at Devon. "Shut your mouth. And you—" He pointed to Kale. "Tell me what you want."

"I just wanted you to have a nice dinner, Mr. Parker." Kale jeered. "It's the last one you'll have for a long time."

Parker's antagonistic face slackened. "Cops!"

"Nope." Devon pulled out his blaster and took aim. "Guess again."

The other restaurant customers screamed when they saw Devon's blaster, running away or diving under their tables.

Kale stood, head and shoulders taller than Parker, and drew his arondight disruptor. Parker didn't move, eyes darting from Kale to Devon and back to Kale again.

"Bounty hunters," he said. "You're bounty hunters."

Kale charged the disruptor with a whir. "Got it in two."

"You're coming with us, buddy," Devon said. "And I don't know about my partner over there, but I'm a pretty fair shot with this thing, so I wouldn't be trying anything if I was you."

"Slow, Parker." Kale gestured toward the door. "I see a shiv and you lose a limb."

Parker turned and raised his hands. Kale and Devon, side-by-side, walked him to the door.

"How did you find me?"

"Your record," Kale said. "Shows you hit a fancy restaurant

after every heist."

"Yeah, and what's up with that?" Devon said. "You trying to impress the ladies or something?"

"Since you nabbed that sixty C and Conamara is the most expensive place on this rock," Kale said, "there was only one thing to do."

"Yeah, and I ordered the Europan lobster." Devon shoved Parker's left shoulder. "Slimy plate of crap!"

They were almost at the door.

Parker's fists clenched.

Kale saw it first. Candle flame from one of the tables reflected on smooth metal protruding from Parker's left fist.

Parker swung around, shiv arcing through the air. Kale jumped back fast enough to avoid it, but the sharp blade slashed Devon's left arm. He cried out, and Kale fired. The laser burst creased Parker's right leg but he only stumbled briefly. He took a step, landed a punch square on Kale's face, and ran.

Kale shook himself and tapped his transceiver. "Mark is on the run. Move, ladies." He looked at Devon. "You all right?"

"Son of a bitch! Stupid, idiot. Stupid. Yes, Kale. Fine."

"You sure?"

"Just go!" Devon grabbed a napkin from a table and pressed the cloth into the wound. "I'm fine, Kale! Go get him!"

Kale raced out of the restaurant, dashing the blood from beneath his nose.

People lined the main street of the Aphrodite Spaceport, but he spotted Parker's blue coat easily through the crowd.

"Vix, Jaz," he said into the transceiver, "he's heading north on Bradbury."

Kale cornered and dashed down an alley, a shortcut to the

other end of the street. His long legs stretched as he ran. He turned another corner, and his face slammed into a sharp-knuckled fist. The impact snapped his head back so hard he nearly fell.

"Damn it, Kale!" He heard a distraught cry.

Vix Valentine, one of the hunters who was supposed to be backing him up, stood beside him, angry in a red halter top and a pair of tight leather shorts.

Women. They just needed to disappear. Especially Vix.

"Vix!" He cradled his nose in agony for the second time that half-hour. "Do I look anything like Parker?"

"No."

"So why are you punching me?"

"What are you doing, running around corners like a madman?"

"Chasing Parker!"

A crashing trashcan lid interrupted them. Parker stood at the head of the alley staring in wild-eyed shock. He started to back off, but Vix drew her disruptor. "Don't move!"

Kale dashed the blood from his face yet again. "Yeah, like we didn't try that."

Parker took another step.

A long leg snapped out of the shadows of the alley and smashed into Parker's face. The blow drove him backward into the cement. He laid there groaning, blood gushing from his broken nose.

A woman with blond hair tipped with hot pink highlights slid out of the darkness, her hazel eyes intense. She pulled a G-60 Bolt Caster from her belt and held it against Parker's forehead.

Jaz Carver, the other hunter from the *Prodigal*. At least she served more of a purpose than constantly pissing him off, which seemed to be Vix's entire mission in life.

"Jaz!" Vix wore a confident smirk. "About time you showed up."

Jaz glared at Kale. "Two bounty hunters in an enclosed restaurant can't bring in one slagging squatter?"

"He hit me." Kale pointed to his red nose and then to Vix. "And then this idiot—"

"Shut up!" Vix shoved him.

Parker drove the heels of his shoes into Jaz's knees. She tumbled backward, and Parker jumped up and ran.

"Damn it!" Kale chased him.

Parker darted in and out of the crowds that filled the spaceport sidewalks. Kale kept up, but just barely. Finally, Kale stopped and leaned against a light post, aiming his arondight. At the sight of his disruptor, the crowds screamed and took cover. He fired.

Parker came to an abrupt halt as the laser blast pierced his left knee. He stumbled, grabbing for the post near him. His fingers missed it, and he fell into the street—right in front of oncoming traffic.

Kale ran for him.

Parker managed to avoid a small electric sedan. He rolled and stood but couldn't evade the oncoming construction hover. And Kale couldn't get to him in time.

The hover smashed into Parker. He didn't stand a chance.

The hover wailed as its drive engines shut down. Hovers and other mobiles all around it squealed to sudden stops.

Not good. Really not good. The reward was only for a living, breathing Gil Parker—not a collection of Gil Parker pieces.

Talon was going to have a fit.

Vix and Jaz reached him a few moments later. Jaz narrowed her eyes at the bloody spot on the road.

A.C. WILLIAMS

Vix covered her mouth, her face distinctly green. "That him?"

Kale hung his head. "What's left of him."

"Great." Vix shoved her blaster into the waistband of her shorts. "Well, it's coming out of your part of the reward."

"What reward, Vix?" Jaz crossed her arms. "We only got paid if we brought Parker in alive. And maybe Kale could do it, but I somehow doubt that we can convince the authorities that that greasy spot is Gil Parker."

Kale sighed as a squadron of police arrived and began shooing bystanders away. "Talon's not going to like this."

⊕

Captain Talon McLeod sat in furious silence, drumming his fingers on the conference room tabletop. His dark blue eyes bored holes in Kale's face, and Kale glared right back.

"Twenty mil, Kale." Talon's thick NUKeltian brogue turned his voice into a growl. "A whole twenty mil, in the tank. What have you to say of it?"

"Whoops?"

If Talon didn't make a habit of overreacting about every little issue, these meetings wouldn't be so uncomfortable.

"Whoops?" Talon's fingers stopped. "We chase this bugger for three months, use resources we don't have, drain contacts dry, and you up and shoot him. He kicks, and all you've to say is *whoops*?"

"Yeah, whoops, Talon. He was supposed to fall the other way."

"Eh?" Talon quirked a flaming red eyebrow.

"He was supposed to fall the other way." Kale's eyes flared. "I shot him in the left leg. He was supposed to fall to the left. He fell to the right. How the hell was I supposed to know what was gonna' happen?" Kale pounded the table. "You're acting like I killed him on purpose. Think I didn't know what was riding on this, Talon? Screw you."

Talon snorted and leaned back in his chair, his gaze not softening. "That so, *Mr. Sullivan*?"

Mr. Sullivan. Damn, he hated that alias. Why had he agreed to it anyway? It wasn't actually useful. Maybe it had been a good idea years ago when the Syndicates were actively searching for him, but now it was just something else Talon could hold over his head.

"You gonna' threaten me, Talon?"

"You gonna' keep losin' heads, lad?"

"Do you think I wanted him dead?" Kale let some of his frustration make his voice dangerous. "If I'd wanted him dead, I'd have thought of a better way to do him than knocking him into a hover. You and I both know that."

"Since killing's what you're good at, right, mate? I remember." Talon scratched his full red beard. "But what I want from you is less killing and more detaining, and it seems you can never tell the difference 'tween the two."

Devon, Vix, and Jaz lined the far wall, listening quietly. Only the telltale twitch at the back of Devon's jaw indicated his concern at the direction of the conversation.

It wasn't worth it today. Talon was right to be pissy. They'd needed the reward Parker would have brought them, and it really had been his fault, if he was going to be honest with himself about it.

Kale exhaled out his nose.

He flopped back in his chair and rolled a half-credit across

A.C. WILLIAMS

his knuckles. "Why don't you pick on Chase for a change?"

Talon detected the change in his mood and relaxed somewhat, his tone more patronizing than angry. "Because Chase didn't screw up, lad."

"What about that time on Ganymede?"

Devon sagged against the wall. "Damn, Kale, you always got to bring that up?"

"There's the ticket, Talon. Get off my screw ups and focus on his." Kale leaned back in the squeaky conference room chair, leather creaking under his weight. "His was bigger."

"That was two years ago, you loser!"

"Uh-huh," Kale shook a fist at Devon, "and that was a *hundred* mil. Not a lousy twenty."

"Well at least when Devon brings someone in, we get to *keep* the payoff," Vix said, flipping her hair. "With you, Kale, we're paying over half of it on damages."

"At least I don't gamble my cut away."

Vix snarled. "You want to go there, Ravenwood?"

Talon ran his hands through his graying red hair and heaved a sigh like a man twice his age. "You'll all be the death of me."

The hiss of a sliding door drew their attention to the other end of the room. Ben Turner, the long-haired NUGaulian navigator, poked his head into the conference room. "Marty says we are ready to go."

"Thanks, Ben," Talon said. "Plot a course for Ursa-Five, Epsilon Sector. We should deliver the news of Mr. Parker's demise to our contact in person, I think." He scowled. "Actually, I think Kale should deliver the news to our contact in person."

"Thanks, Talon. Thanks a lot."

"It's your fault he's dead then, isn't it, lad?" Talon arched his eyebrows. "You should be the messenger on this one, I think."

"Hey, you were the messenger last time, weren't you?" Vix lit a cigarette and blew smoke at the back of his head. "You should be really good at that now."

Kale rolled his eyes.

"Ursa-Five is quite a jump, Captain," Ben said with his typical indifference. "We should arrive in a few days."

"Make it happen, Benny," Talon said.

Ben nodded and disappeared, and Kale stood.

Talon glared at him. "Don't think this conversation is over, Kale." Talon pointed at Vix. "And, Valentine, if you blow any more smoke in this room, I'll have your ass in a sling."

She made a face at him and pushed off the wall, stalking for the door, swaying her hips. "How about I pop a window, Talon? And let some air in?"

"Aye, do it in your own quarters, and kill two birds with one stone." Talon waved her off as she left in a huff, and he turned his attention back to Kale. "We're not done talking about this, Kale."

"What more is there to say, Talon?" Kale set his hands on his hips. "I screwed up. Fine. Let's move on and nab the next mark so we can get on with our lives."

The ship gave a long shudder before the telltale leap into hyperspace. Kale felt the familiar clenching from the jump deep in his stomach. He'd learned to ignore the urge to wretch over the years of living in space, but it never really went away.

Talon rolled his eyes and stood. "We'll speak of it later when you feel like concentrating." He strode purposefully out of the conference room.

Kale moved for the door, and Devon landed a staggering punch on his chin. Kale howled and jumped backward.

"His was bigger," Devon mimicked.

Kale threw a fake punch, which Devon avoided with little trouble. Jaz walked around them, mumbling about the immaturity of men.

"How's your arm?" Kale asked as soon as Jaz was out of earshot.

"Aw, it's all right." Devon patted the new bandage on his left arm. "Scraps fixed me up real good." He shook his head. "When are you going to learn not to piss McLeod off, man?"

"I can't help it." Kale shrugged. "It's old habit."

The two bounty hunters left the conference room and walked down the dimly lit corridor in comfortable silence.

The *Prodigal*, converted for space flight from an Old Earth yacht, was one of the many bounty hunter ships in the system. And while the *Prodigal* had never been called the best of them, it certainly hadn't been called the worst either. Talon McLeod, the decorated NUKeltian veteran of the Titan War, and his crew had earned quite a name for themselves, even though oftentimes they tended to do more damage than good in their pursuits.

A sharp bark from behind was Kale and Devon's only warning before a Pomeranian barreled around the turn at the end of the hallway. She dashed between their legs, a streak of white fur against the sterile metallic hull plating, and leapt excitedly to bite Devon's fingers.

Devon laughed and teased the dog.

"Hey there, Newt! How's my girl? How's my girl?" Devon lunged at the dog, who lunged back at him with as ferocious a growl as a Pomeranian could make.

"You shouldn't encourage her." Kale rolled his eyes.

Devon always had a soft spot for dogs. Personally, Kale

thought a spaceship was the worst place in the universe for a pet. But if they were going to have a dog on board, Newt wasn't too bad. If Kale had to choose, he'd jettison Vix long before the Pomeranian.

"Newt!" bellowed a giant voice.

"Down here, Claude," Kale called.

Claude, the loader, poked his huge head around the corner and grinned, his face red-cheeked and pale blue eyes jolly.

"Kale, Devon." Claude passed between them and scooped up the dog. Claude's monstrous arms dwarfed the tiny creature. "Newt, here, manage to find coolant leak in Marty's refrigerant system. She think she need a treat, *ja*."

"No one deserves it more." Devon scratched the dog's ears.

"I return to engine to help Marty," Claude said. "He is such a little man."

"Yeah, don't let him hear you say that." Devon grinned.

Claude's booming laughter resonated in the sparse metallic corridors. He smacked Devon on the back of his shoulder, and Devon nearly toppled over. Kale snickered.

"No!" Claude kept laughing. "Claude think saying so to Marty would be bad idea! Ha!" He lifted Newt higher against his chest and headed back toward engine room, where he helped Marty Fixx, the chief engineer, manage the ship's propellant system.

Devon straightened and whimpered. "Owie."

"Oh, suck it up."

"That man hits like a Sagittarian battle cruiser."

"You only think that because you hit like a girl."

Devon shoved him, and Kale laughed.

The ship shuddered again, shaking the ceiling tiles and causing the bulkheads to groan.

"It's a rougher ride than usual, huh?" Devon commented.

"Yeah," Kale said, wincing. "We really could have used the payday on Parker."

Devon shrugged. "Plenty of stars in the sky." He paused. "Or is it plenty of fish in the sea?"

"How about plenty of shit left to shovel?"

"That probably works better for the grease spot formerly known as Parker. Yeah."

They continued together until they reached the short stairs leading up to the bridge. Superglass windows protected the bridge of the *Prodigal* from space. Sensitive tracking computers and hacking equipment lined the back wall, and a single helmsman dais stood at the front, which Ben occupied. Four strategically placed gunner turrets indented the otherwise smooth walls.

Talon sat in his captain's chair, slouching and shaking his head, undoubtedly in mourning for the twenty million credits that had slipped through his fingers.

Devon stood beside Ben Turner, and they spoke briefly. Kale leaned against the back of Talon's chair.

"What, boy?" Talon snarled.

"You going to deep six me, McLeod?"

"No." Talon looked up at him. "You're too good to drop." He sighed. "And I won't be turning any names in either."

Kale gave a sharp nod. He hadn't really thought Talon was stupid enough to announce his true identity to the whole system, but whenever Talon brought up the alias they'd created for him, it worried him.

"You don't know the shit storm we'd be in if you started waving my name around where everyone could see it, Talon."

"Aye, lad. You just piss me off."

"Sorry."

"No, you're not."

Kale grinned.

Talon shook his head. "Just," he looked up, "watch yourself. You go losin' many more marks worth as much as Parker was, and we'll be out of a job." He waved his hand. "This isn't a hobby, lad."

A quiet alarm sounded overhead.

Talon sat up in his chair. "Benny?"

"It's a subspace distress beacon, sir." Ben pressed a flashing button on his navigation console. "It's coming from a few light years ahead."

Talon sat back in his chair, steepling his fingers, obviously thinking about stopping to investigate.

Talon's weak spot: he always insisted on helping other people no matter who they were or what else should have taken precedence.

"Talon." Kale leaned over the back of the chair again. "Ursa-Five, remember? Touching base with the boss for the hit? Me getting shot for turning Parker into a grease spot?"

"I know, I know." Talon held up his hand and shook it.

It was his normal gesture when he was trying to think and someone was bothering him.

"Maybe we should stop," Devon said from Ben's side. "Might be something we could help with."

"You're as bad as Talon," Kale said. "Stopping is a bad idea."

"You always think stopping is a bad idea," Devon said.

"And when has it done anything for us? Last time it was those three weird gypsy ladies who gave us the pandemic of cotton beetles in the bedding."

"Well, what about the time before that?"

"Oh." Kale set his hands on his hips. "The lawyer. It took six weeks to get the smell of his cologne out of the air filters, and his hair was so greasy, Scraps took a week to get the stains out of the pillow cases."

"Enough, Kale," Talon said.

"Don't stop," Kale said. "It's always nothing but trouble."

"Perhaps in this instance Monsieur Ravenwood is correct," Ben said. "From my calculations, we are very close to the Themis family belt asteroids."

"See?" Kale said. "Good reason not to stop. We try to help folks and get smashed to pieces. There's a good reason right there, Talon."

"You're just afraid it'll be miners," Devon said. "Who knows what *they'd* do to the linens?"

"Shut up, Dev."

Talon scratched his beard. "Benny, can you drop us out of hyperspace before we get there?"

"Of course, Captain." Ben looked over his shoulder. "I am the best pilot in the system. Is that not why you hired me?"

"Sure as hell wasn't for your humility, Ben," Kale said.

"Ignore him, Ben," Talon ordered. "And do it. We're stopping."

"Aw, Talon!"

"We're stopping, Kale." Talon held on to his arm rests. "Get over it."

The shivering bluish-green light of hyperspace faded, and the *Prodigal* lurched. The black void of space, dotted with stars, slowly reappeared, but asteroids weren't all that hovered in the vast emptiness before them. The uneven masses drifting through space were hull fragments, bulk heads, and great chunks of superglass.

"Whoa," Devon murmured.

"What the hell?" Kale moved down to where Devon stood.

"Looks like a freighter of some kind," Talon said behind them. "Something big."

"It would have had to be big to leave this kind of debris," Devon said. "Look at it all."

Kale could see where the asteroid field began. It was still some distance off. True to his word, Ben had dropped them into empty space just before the debris field, far enough away from any danger of impact.

The ship fragments spread out before them like the ice crystal sands on the beaches of Europa, irregular hunks of metals and glasses, some still spinning from the initial explosion that tore the ship apart.

"From the radiation levels on what's left of the core," Ben said, "I'd say it's NUSovian."

"A mineral harvester," Talon deduced. "That's the only reason it'd be this close to an asteroid field."

Devon whistled under his breath. "Talon, NUSovian mineral harvesters are fortresses. It's a big deal to take one out, let alone rip it apart."

"It was probably a reactor breach," Ben said.

"I doubt that," Kale said. "NUSovian birds don't have a history of reactor instability, and even if they did, they'd need six reactors to vaporize just one mineral harvester."

"They're designed to work in asteroid fields," Devon said. "They're practically indestructible."

"Obviously not, Monsieur Chase," Ben said.

"Ben, where are you getting that distress signal from?"

Ben entered more information into his console and searched for a few moments. "Straight out," he said. "From dimensional scans, I would say it's a life pod."

Talon glanced at Kale.

Kale crossed his arms. "No."

"Kale, I swear."

"No, Talon. I'm not going out there." He looked away. "This is a bad idea. This is the worst idea in a long history of bad ideas, and I don't want anything to do with it."

Talon uttered a growl.

"I'll go, Talon," Devon said. "Whoever it is needs help." Devon threw a significant look at his best friend. "I'm sure they'll make it worth our while."

Kale didn't answer, arms still crossed, fuming in silence.

"Fine," Talon said. "Devon, you go out and get it. Kale." Talon paused to collect himself. "You go down and get Scraps. I've a feeling we'll be needing his help."

Devon hurried off the bridge, not looking back at Kale as he left. Kale glared after him.

"Ravenwood?"

Kale glanced at Talon. "What?"

"Scraps? To the loading bay?" Talon snarled. "Now!"

Kale glared back. "This is a bad idea, Talon."

"Why? I know you don't generally go in for helping people, lad, but this is pushing it even for you."

"You want to know what could do that to a NUSovian mineral harvester?"

Talon didn't answer. He leaned back in his chair and grunted.

"A syndicate, Talon." Kale leaned in closer to Talon. "That's what could destroy a NUSovian mineral harvester. It could have been the Dragons or it could have been Knightshade. Either of them could have done it."

"I'm assuming you have a point, lad."

"We need to stay away from syndicates, Talon."

"No, lad. You need to stay away from syndicates."

Kale ground his teeth.

"Kale, listen." Talon turned to him. "If it was a syndicate, it's likely they got what they wanted, right?"

"Maybe."

"In either case, if somebody's out there still alive, I see it that it's our job to help them."

"Why is that?"

"Because we found them. That makes it our responsibility, and I'm not leaving anyone behind if I can help it."

"You're a dinosaur, Talon." Kale rolled his head on his shoulders. "That mindset'll get you killed someday."

"Maybe so," Talon said, "but it'll be a death worth dying. That's the way I see it." He smirked. "You should try it sometime."

"Try what, Talon?"

"Saving people instead of shooting them." Talon grinned. "You might like it."

Kale scoffed. Talon could think what he wanted, but risking your own life to save somebody else was a waste of time and effort.

"So go down and get Scraps," Talon said. "And tell him to go to the loading bay."

The intercom system hissed, and Claude's booming voice shook the bridge floors. "*Invader* away."

Moments later, Devon's blue short-range fighter shot into view, aimed directly for the life pod Ben had pointed out.

"And you'd better hurry, lad," Talon said. "Devon seems to be in a hurry."

"You and your save-the-world syndrome," Kale spat. "You've been a bad influence on him."

A.C. WILLIAMS

Talon glared. "Would you go already?"

Kale turned on his heel and strode down the back steps, heading for the galley. The closer he came, the stronger the smell of frying food became.

Scraps, the *Prodigal's* chef and medic, stood at the stove top tossing some random medley of proteins and vegetables in a skillet. His threadbare, oil-spattered apron screamed *Kiss the Cook!* and his thinning gray hair seemed a little crazier than normal.

He looked over his shoulder when Kale entered.

Scraps always knew when it was him, which usually made Kale extremely nervous since people weren't supposed to know when he came and went.

"Kale!" Scraps beamed at him. "Care for a cup of tea? I have a new box of *matcha*."

"Get your med kit, Scraps," Kale said. "Talon wants you in the loading bay."

Scraps frowned and set the skillet to the side. He pulled off his apron. "Someone hurt?"

"Not yet," Kale said. "But the day's still young."

He turned for the corridor and waited while Scraps scurried downstairs to the medical bay to grab his first aid kit. He stepped into the hallway moments later, still smelling vaguely of grease.

"You going to tell me what's happening, boy?"

"Talon stopped to help somebody out. Again."

"Ah, Kale, you make it sound like such a bad thing."

Kale didn't see the point of even trying to point out the obvious reasons why it was a horrible idea. Scraps was even harder to argue with than Talon.

"You should learn to like helping people, Kale." Scraps's NUSovian accent always got a little stronger when he lectured. "It

104

will be good for you."

"Sure, Scraps. Whatever."

Good for me. Right. Wait till the Dragons catch up with us someday because we were too slow dragging our asses helping somebody to run for it. Then we'll see how good helping people turns out for me.

By the time they reached the loading bay, the *Invader* was gliding in, the life pod attached to the undercarriage by its magnetic grapple. Claude, looking all the more like a giant in his patched up enviro-suit and magnetic boots, guided Devon into the bay and indicated when he needed to stop.

While anti-gravity was still offline in the bay, Devon released the life pod. Claude guided it easily to the side and left it while he carried the *Invader* to its harness on the rotating winch in the corner.

As soon as the *Invader* was in place and the force field on the bay door was active, Claude announced, "*Invader* secure!" over the ship's intercom system. He moved back to the pod and made sure it was pressed close against the floor before he reactivated the gravity in the loading bay.

The pod wobbled on the floor, and Claude raised the energy field at the door for Kale and Scraps to enter.

"Get it open, Claude," Scraps said.

Devon climbed down the winch as Claude knelt and entered the standard open code for the life pod. The seal on the pod cracked open, and Claude lifted the lid.

Kale peered inside.

A woman lay in the pod. Her hair was blond, so blond it was nearly white. Her features were severe but not unattractive. She wore typical NUSovian army fatigues, dark green and bulky, and heavy combat boots.

105

Even from where he stood, Kale could see the blood pooling inside the life pod. The woman had three severe puncture wounds in her chest, abdomen, and stomach. Scraps didn't even need to examine her for Kale to know the woman had a few minutes left to live—if she wasn't dead already.

The woman gasped, and her eyelids sprung open, revealing stern blue eyes full of pain. She uttered a groan and a whimper and clutched at the wounds on her body. Scraps grabbed her hands and held her steady.

"Easy," he said. "Easy." He began to speak in Sovianese as Talon arrived.

If Talon were here, that meant Jaz had taken over the bridge. Where Vix had slithered off to didn't matter—as long as it wasn't there.

He stood at Scraps's side and smiled down at the woman. She looked at him first and then to Scraps in confusion. She blinked and took another gasping breath.

"No," the woman said. Her voice trembled with agony. "Not—NUSovian. Was—on the ship. Crew exchange from NUGermania."

Claude straightened and pulled his helmet off, gazing down at the woman in the pod. He didn't smile. "You are NUGerman, *ja?*"

"*Ja, ja.*" The woman clutched at Scraps's hands with bloodied fingers. "Zahn. Dr. Helga Zahn." She grimaced. "Where is the ship?"

"Destroyed," Talon said. "We received your distress beacon."

"No." Zahn shook her head. "Not the *Anastasia*. Not it. The other one. The *Destiny.*"

"Which one was the harvester?" Talon asked.

"*Anastasia*," Zahn struggled to say. "The *Destiny*—was

NAMELESS

derelict. We found it. And they took it." Tears welled in her eyes. She shuddered and clung to Scraps's hands as she choked down a scream of pain. "Chung bastards!"

Kale and Devon glanced at each other.

That didn't make any sense. NUChungqwo was only interested in technology that benefited their rabid nationalistic empire. They wouldn't want an abandoned ship a NUSovian harvesting crew had found drifting in space.

"Dr. Zahn," Devon started, "why would anyone from NUChungqwo want a derelict ship?"

"Not—the colony." Zahn struggled to breathe. "Chungs. Seekers."

Kale closed his eyes. "Knightshade."

Zahn nodded. "*Ja.*"

Talon made an unhappy sound and crossed his arms.

Zahn tried to take a breath. "Boarded the ship. Killed everyone. I—barely made it out. They took—the *Destiny*."

"Same difference," Devon said softly. "Knightshade wouldn't want a derelict ship just like the Chungs wouldn't want it."

"The man," Zahn hissed. "The man with black eyes."

Kale snapped to attention and leaned into the pod. "What man?"

"He was—with them."

"A Chung?"

"No."

"NUUSA?"

"Don't know." Zahn was turning gray. "He had—black eyes. Black soul. Killed everyone. Killed me."

Kale felt Devon's hand on his back. He'd made the connection too, Kale realized. If Knightshade and the Seekers, their

107

personal Chung army, had been the ones to attack the *Anastasia*, they only had one black-eyed operative in their employ who wasn't of NUChungqwo heritage.

"Xander." Zahn's voice was faint. "Xander—her ship."

"Dr. Zahn." Talon took her hand.

"Don't help me." The NUGerman medic snarled, seizing Talon's shirt, the blood from her fingers soaking into the fabric. "Find Xander. They took her ship. They want her too."

"Xander?" Talon asked. "Is that a woman?"

Zahn's eyes unfocused. "Evy." Her breath rattled as she exhaled, and she grew still, her hand still fisted in Talon's shirt.

After a few moments, Talon slowly shut her eyes and stood, disentangling her fingers from his shirt. Scraps sighed beside him.

"I'm sorry, Talon," Scraps said.

"It doesn't look like there was anything you could have done," Talon said. "I know you would have tried."

Talon looked at Kale. "What do you know about this?"

"Why should I know anything, Talon?"

"You're the syndicate expert, lad."

"I know Dragons, Talon. Knightshade's a different animal." Kale glanced at the dead woman in the pod. "Braedon Knight is trouble, and anything connected with his syndicate is trouble. We should forget this happened."

"What about the ship she was talking about?" Devon asked. "What about that person she was talking about? What do we do about them?"

"Nothing," Kale said. "We do nothing. It's not our problem."

"Kale." Devon grabbed his arm. "You know damn well the man she mentioned was Darien Stone."

"Probably."

"Knightshade wouldn't have sent Darien to get that ship if it wasn't important," Devon said.

"I'm sure it is important, Devon." Kale pulled out of his hold. "It's just not important to us." Kale glared at Talon. "If you even think about going after that ship or that Xander person, Talon, I'm gone."

"Kale."

"It's suicide, Devon!" Kale snapped.

"But what if we can stop them?"

"We can't stop the syndicates," Kale said. "Nobody can." He held Talon with his eyes. "And you know that, Talon. You know it. So don't you dare try to tell me different."

Talon took a long, deep breath and regarded the dead NUGerman medic.

"Aye, Kale. You're right."

Devon huffed angrily.

"We should close her up, shut off that beacon, and put her back out to space," Kale said. "And nobody will know the difference. No other idiots will stop. And we stay out of Knightshade's way."

Talon hesitated.

"You know I'm right, Talon."

Talon nodded. "Aye. Likely you are, Kale." He turned from the pod. "It doesn't make me feel any better about it, though."

Devon started shedding his enviro-suit and stormed out of the bay. From the set of his shoulders, Kale knew he was upset. But Devon didn't know what he was talking about. Neither did Talon.

Knightshade was the last problem they needed. Braedon Knight might have started out as a small fish years ago, but he had been gaining popularity throughout the system due to his involvement with bioengineered prosthetics, making them available on the black markets to anyone who could afford them. And having Darien Stone in Knightshade's employ made them all the more dangerous.

The Dragons would only kill him.

Darien Stone would kill everybody else just to hurt him.

"Close her up, Claude," Kale said.

"*Ja*, Kale. *Ja*." Claude sniffled and shut the life pod lid.

Kale watched Dr. Zahn disappear beneath it and turned away. Right or not, it was what needed to happen. Whatever Knightshade wanted with the ship called *Destiny* was none of his business.

Whoever Xander was, she was on her own.

CHAPTER 9

Downtown New London buzzed with activity as Xander and Evy walked to the neurology center. Xander stopped on the sidewalk to watch one of the holographic billboards overhead advertise a cosmetic product.

"Xander."

Xander looked to where Evy waited, eyebrows arched impatiently.

"Sorry." Xander hurried to catch up with her.

"I don't know why you find them so alluring," Evy said. "They're just advertisements."

"But they're holograms."

"And that's impressive how? Holograms are everywhere, Xander."

"I know, Evy."

Evy waited for a car to hover past before they crossed the street. Evy's heels clicked on the polymer-coated street as they walked side-by-side. They reached the other side of the street and continued toward the neurology center.

Xander checked her reflection in the windows of a café. From the credits Sylphie had given her, Evy had helped her purchase new clothing, a few shirts and a pair of cargo pants. Evy didn't call them cargo pants, though. Evy had never heard that term before. But then, Evy hadn't heard of hand sanitizer either.

"What are we testing today?" Xander raked her hands

through her frizzy orange mess of hair.

"It's a simple neurological exam, but it should reveal some fundamental areas of your brain." Evy patted her shoulder. "I imagine you're growing weary of all these tests after these few months."

"It's all right. I don't mind."

Xander stretched her arms over her head and smiled at the clouded sky as they walked. Dr. Zahn had told her that NUSaxons despised nice weather and forced their engineers to make most of the days rainy, overcast, and depressing. But Xander had grown attached to the cloudy days that prevailed in NUSaxony.

"Xander, here, look at this." Evy slowed her pace and motioned Xander closer, holding out her datapad. "That delightful dessert you made last week. I found a reference to it."

Evy leaned into her personal space and indicated a photo on her datapad. Xander smiled, the scent of Evy's hand lotion tickling her nose. Two months ago, Evy wouldn't have been caught dead standing this close to her in public.

"Chocolate chip cookies." Evy pointed to the photo. "A food item from Old Earth."

"Old Earth?"

Xander had needed to do something productive and making cookies always calmed her down. She didn't know how she knew that, but she'd been so certain of it, she'd purchased all the ingredients for chocolate chip cookies and made use of Evy's stove. Evy had never baked before, never used her stove before, and had never heard of cookies before.

Actually, no one had. Another mystery from Xander's broken brain. Like hand sanitizer and cargo pants.

"Yes." Evy frowned at the datapad. "I thought perhaps to find a reference of it in NUUSA records, but from what I can tell, it's not a common dish among their people either. It was a recipe utilized on Old Earth, before the colonization of space began."

Xander gaped at her. "You're kidding. Cookies are everywhere."

Evy shut the datapad. "Apparently not. Fascinating." She patted Xander's shoulders. "Don't worry, dear. We'll sort it all out."

She smiled fondly and increased her pace again. Xander jogged to catch up.

"Do you think I might have read something about Old Earth on the *Anastasia*? And then just forgot about it?"

"Anything is possible," Evy said. "But I doubt a NUSovian mining ship like the *Anastasia* would keep a library of Old Earth recipes." Evy tightened her hold on the datapad. "If Helga would call again, we could ask."

Dr. Zahn had not been in contact with them again. She hadn't even attempted to call. It troubled her, but Dr. Zahn was a grown woman who could take care of herself. She was probably fine.

Xander glanced at Evy as they walked together.

So far, the only kind people she had encountered in the universe were prostitutes and lesbians. That bothered her. She had never kept company with those kinds of people before. At least, she couldn't remember ever doing so. And now they were the only ones who were willing to help her.

What had happened to the universe? And why was she so certain it hadn't always been this way?

The neurology center came into view. Evy entered through the main doors. Xander paused in the doorway. A dark form appeared in her peripheral vision, and she turned to look. A small man stood some distance down the street. He wore a black suit, a black coat, and he glared at her with dark almond-shaped eyes. Xander blinked, and he disappeared.

Had she imagined him?

She lost track of how long she stood there, but it must have been a significant amount of time because Evy touched her shoulder, looking worried.

"Xander? Are you all right?"

"Y—yes." *Don't say anything. She'll think you're nuts!* "I'm fine. Sorry. I was just—thinking."

"Well, think away, dear. Just think inside the center."

Evy led the way inside, chin high and spectacles perched on her nose. Xander scrambled along behind her, taking two steps for each one of Evy's. Being short sucked no matter where you were in the solar system.

That man, she thought. *He was Asian. He looked Chinese. Like Sylphie. He would be—what is it called?—from NUChungqwo. And no one from NUChungqwo is allowed into NUSaxony. You imagined him.*

Xander and Evy walked into the lift, and Evy directed it to the thirty-seventh floor where the majority of the neurological testing took place. By now, the thirty-seventh floor felt like home.

Once there, they went to the main testing room where Xander grabbed one of the patient uniforms, and Evy set up the testing equipment.

"Evy?"

"Yes?" Evy remained focused on the diagnostic screen.

"Why were NUChungqwos banned from NUSaxony?"

Evy stopped working for a moment to look over her shoulder at Xander. "Because they tried, on numerous occasions, to breech colony security and commit acts of terror."

114

"But why would they do that?"

"Their ancestors were against building the Earth-Gate."

"The Earth-Gate?"

"The hyperspace gate," Evy said.

"Oh."

"It's frequently called the Earth-Gate because—well—it was at Earth."

"Why isn't there a Mars-Gate? Or a—Jupiter-Gate?"

"After the Earth-Gate exploded, the Transport Council decided to build them far away from the planets themselves, to avoid another catastrophe."

"All right. So the Chinese—the NUChungqwo ancestors—didn't want the gate. What does that have to do with anything?"

"The Chinese didn't want it," Evy said, "but the rest of Earth, namely those of the United Kingdom, my ancestors, didn't listen and built it anyway. When it exploded, it eradicated the majority of mainland China."

"They blame NUSaxony for the gate explosion? For killing their ancestors?"

"Ancestry is extremely important to them," Evy said. "The only people of Asian descent who are alive any longer are from NUChungqwo, and the people of NUChungqwo are strongly nationalistic and heavily militarized."

"I see."

"Why?"

"No reason."

Evy faced her. "Xander, why are you asking me about NUChungqwo all of a sudden?"

Xander dropped her arms, letting the uniform drag on the carpeted floor. "I'm crazy, Evy. I know that. And I probably shouldn't trust anything I see. I mean, I have mental problems. Otherwise I wouldn't be here."

"What Xander?"

"I'm just sure I saw a NUChungqwo man outside."

"Impossible."

"I know," Xander said. "But—Evy, he looked Chinese."

"You imagined it, Xander," she said. "That is the only explanation. The people of NUChungqwo are not allowed entrance visas. At all. There's no way one could have made it into New London."

Xander nodded. She peeled off her shirt and started changing into the uniform behind a screen while Evy went back to setting the scanner.

A flash of light outside the door caught Xander's eye. She pulled the uniform shirt on and moved away from the screen toward the door. She peered outside the glass.

Across the hallway to the open thirty-seventh floor lobby, huge windows provided a spectacular view of New London.

The white hot flash sparkled again outside the windows.

"Evy?" Xander started.

"What, Xander?"

"What is that light?"

Evy made an impatient sound and moved behind her. "What light, Xander?"

She barely made it to Xander's shoulder when the light outside the lobby windows grew brighter and bigger and hotter, flooding the thirty-seventh floor with scorching heat.

"Evy?" Xander whispered.

Evy's face washed out under the intense white light, her blue eyes full of fear.

She didn't speak. She seized Xander by the back of her shirt and dragged her back into the room. She slammed the door behind them as the lobby windows erupted, sending a wave of hot glass shooting through walls, doors, windows, offices and people. The screams and shrieks of the office personnel in the other room filled the corridors.

Xander tried to breathe, but the air seared her lungs. The carpet chafed against her right cheek, and something heavy on her back made moving nearly impossible.

It was the Oasis all over again. Not again. Why her? Was she going to lose Evy the same way she lost Sylphie?

Before Xander could say anything, Evy hauled her to her feet with surprising strength.

The room spun. Xander couldn't hear, her ears ringing with the sound of the explosion. She couldn't tell if the building itself had blown up or if something had exploded outside.

Xander's skin could have cooked an egg. Her arms and legs and face, any skin in the open, might as well have been a live burner on a stove.

Evy searched her for injuries, face red and scratched. Her lips pressed together in a tight line, and then pulled Xander toward the emergency fire exit. A few other office workers had the same idea.

Panicked footsteps echoed in the stairwell, punctuated by cries of pain and outrage uttered by others fleeing the top floors. They ran down, down, down.

They had to be close, right? Her side ached like they had to be near the ground floor.

Nope. 25.

They reached the twentieth floor before Evy slowed, her adrenaline exhausted. Many of the other office workers had dropped off behind them. There were no other explosions. No other sounds from the surrounding floors.

"Evy?" Xander panted. "Evy, what happened back there?"

"I don't know." Evy still dragged her down the stairs. "I don't have any idea."

Soon more doctors, nurses, and aides joined them in the trek downstairs. Some were injured; others were not; all of them were terrified.

Xander's ribs throbbed. And her skin—had someone tried to flay her alive with a butter knife? That's what it felt like. Every inch stung like alcohol in a paper cut. Maybe the heat from the explosion had burned her.

The crowd of doctors, nurses, aides, and office workers ahead of them had been hurrying, flowing without pause or delay since they left the thirty-seventh floor.

Then, five nurses in front of them shrieked and whirled. Their panic ignited a new chorus of screams as the neat, orderly evacuation line became a jostling mob terrified to stupidity.

The entire crowd shifted and began to run back up the stairs. Panicked. Evy nearly lost her balance and could only grip the rail as the mob of people reversed course. The sound of plasma fire echoed in the stairwell.

Plasma fire?

Evy gripped Xander's arm, and they tried to go back up the stairs, but it was too late. The rush of people pressed them against the wall; neither of them could move.

Polymer shards on the walls crumbled and fell as plasma bullets from below pierced them. The crowd around them began to fall with bloody wounds on their backs; they fell until their bodies layered the stairs.

NAMELESS

The gunmen approached.

The moment the crowd thinned, Evy tried to get up, tried to get Xander up, but a pulse blast pierced Evy's left leg. She lost her balance with a cry and fell, still clinging to Xander's shirt. Both of them tumbled down the stairs, now littered with dead and dying bodies, steps stained with crimson blood.

When they stopped, Evy pulled herself up. Xander felt the motion, even though her head spun. She stared at Evy's back.

Evy's back?

Evy stood before her, arms stretched back around her, holding her between her shoulder blades. Shielding her. But from what?

Xander peered around Evy's slender waist and saw three men in black suits, black coats, and black sunglasses, all carrying disruptors. A sharp voice came from behind the men, and another man entered the stairwell. The man Xander had seen outside the neurological center.

Ha! I knew it. My brain isn't that broken.

"Dr. Evylin Berkley?" The man spoke in a flawless, unaccented voice.

"Y—yes?" Evy's hands trembled as she cradled Xander between her shoulders, but her voice didn't.

"Move aside."

Evy lifted her chin and straightened her spectacles. The man's perpetual frown deepened.

Xander knew how he felt. What was Evy doing?

"You are not the one we are after," the man clarified. "We want the girl. Move aside."

Me? They want me? Xander's mind whirled. *Why? What could they want with me?*

119

Evy's grip on Xander's arms tightened. "No."

No? Xander stared up at Evy's bloody, ruined hair. *She's protecting me?*

"Dr. Berkley." The man's expression slowly grew into something more frightening. "I highly suggest you cooperate."

"I have no intention of cooperating with you," Evy said, a bit of her old snobbishness returning to her voice.

The gunmen raised their weapons.

Xander grabbed Evy's left hand and pushed it aside, trying to duck under her arm.

The crazy neuro-therapist didn't realize what she was doing. She couldn't know. These men would kill her. They'd shoot her without any remorse, and Xander wouldn't let that happen. Not if she could do something about it.

But Evy didn't budge and shoved Xander back behind her again, trapping her between her hands.

"You've already shot me," Evy said. "If you shoot again, you might hit someone else." Her grip tightened again. "Someone more important."

The first man scowled, but he said something sharp to the three gunmen, who nodded and lowered their weapons. He pulled out a radio and spoke into it, the language harsh, fast—like a trilling angry bird. Moments later, the radio squealed a response.

"Very well, Dr. Berkley," the man said. "You will come with us."

The gunmen dropped their weapons and lunged. The first one punched Evy in the stomach, and she doubled over. The second man seized Xander's arm, yanked her out from behind Evy's body, and threw her at the third man, who grabbed her arms and bound them. The other two men secured Evy, who still struggled between them.

NAMELESS

"Good." The lead man clapped his hands once. "Go."

He strode away, and the others towed Evy and Xander behind him.

Xander took Evy's hand. "Evy? Evy, why?"

"Why what, Xander?"

"Why did you do that? Why did you say that?"

"Not now, Xander."

"They could have killed you. They still might."

"Yes, and they might kill you too," Evy said. "Let's not focus on the whys, Xander. Let's focus on the now. Understanding why they've done this or why I did what I did won't help us escape."

The soldiers dragged them out of the stairwell and into the choking smoke of a battlefield. Xander only knew the lobby by the one sign still standing. Chairs lay strewn and splintered. Glass shards sparkled like diamonds in the light, like rubies where they'd fallen in puddles of blood. Bodies littered the torn carpets.

The entire neurology center had been destroyed. The explosion had taken out half of its main structure, as well as half the block. Alarms wailed all around them. Military vessels sailed overhead but didn't get very far. Stationed high in the dome, a large warship blasted every sky vessel apart. It seemed to have stronger weapons than any of the NUSaxon ships.

Xander had been wrong, so wrong. The Oasis didn't compare to this. The Oasis was nothing.

These people wanted war.

"What is this?" Evy gasped. "What are you doing? Why are you doing this?"

"Evy?" Xander cried.

"Lockdown." Evy voice wavered. "NUSaxony is in lockdown. You invaded us?" She steadied her voice and glared at

121

their captors like a queen in chains. "This is an act of war!"

The first man struck her. "Silence, woman."

Evy gasped, blood dribbling from the corner of her lips. The man dragged them onward, pressing toward a shuttle that had landed in the middle of the road. He boarded. The three men dragged Evy and Xander onboard and shoved them in a corner.

Xander tried to breathe, tried to focus. The Spartan interior of the shuttle seemed at odds with the soft, lush carpet and the scent of harsh incense. A blood-red banner emblazoned with four-point golden star hung from the back wall. In spite of the warm, spicy incense, the air in the shuttle smelled cold.

The shuttle lifted off the ground and started for the sky. Outside the windows, Xander could see the warship allow them passage.

From above, the damage to New London looked worse than on the ground. They hadn't just attacked the neurology center; NUChungqwo had attacked the entire city.

What did they want? Why were they doing this? And what did they want with her?

Harsh light washed over the shuttle as they sped into space. From the corner, Xander could see a large ship out in front of them, the name *Shuriken* emblazoned on its hull in imposing letters.

"What is it?" Evy whispered in her ear.

"A ship," Xander breathed. "They're taking us to a ship."

"Hold on to me, Xander."

"Evy—Evy, why did you do that?"

Evy's arms wrapped around her again. "I don't know, Xander, but somehow you've become precious to me. I couldn't just let them take you without a fight."

Xander rested her head on Evy's shoulder.

The shuttle decelerated, and the light changed again as they flew into a shuttle bay. The gunmen surrounded them again and pulled them to their feet, shoving them into a corridor and forcing them to march.

There's nothing special about me. Xander clung to Evy's arm, not caring what the men thought. *I don't know who I am, but if I'm important, I wouldn't have been lost. And I was. So what can they possibly want with me?*

The expansive shuttle bay of the *Shuriken* contained more warships exactly like the one still laying siege to New London. The soldiers shoved Evy and Xander down the walkway and into a corridor, barely illuminated with gray light. They stopped at a door and opened it. The room beyond had no windows, no furniture, and no lights.

"You will stay here." The lead man gestured inside the room, and the soldiers pushed them inside.

Xander stumbled but didn't fall. Evy did the same but somehow managed to make it look much more graceful.

Evy regarded the man like a Neanderthal. "Where are you taking us?"

"NUJenesis."

"NUJenesis?" Evy gasped. "Why—?"

"Mr. Braedon Knight wants to speak to your little friend." The man glared at Xander. "Attempt to escape, and we will kill you."

Xander stepped from behind Evy and faced him. "If this man wants to speak to me, why would you kill us?"

"I didn't say we would kill both of you. I said we would kill *you*." The man leveled a cruel smirk at Evy. "Mr. Knight doesn't like doctors."

He shut the door.

CHAPTER 10

The gears in the wall turned and whirred.

"You have to stay here."

The door was sliding shut. She could only see half his face.

"David!" she cried.

"You'll be all right."

The door shut and sealed, and the ship rocked—

Xander lunged forward, arm outstretched. "David!"

Evy caught her and held her close. "Shh." Evy stroked her hair. "It's all right. You were only dreaming."

Xander looked around the shadowed room. They were on board the NUChungqwo ship, the *Shuriken*, headed toward NUJenesis.

NUJenesis. Like the Book of Genesis. David. Xander. Rats and silver stones and electricity like claws raking through the air. Time stood still. No, time never stood still. What was wrong with her? Muddled, jumbled images and thoughts crowded together on the projector screen at the back of her brain, like a silent movie with no captions. Like sand slipping through her fingers.

"Xander?"

Xander gripped Evy's hand. "What time is it?"

"I wish I knew," Evy said. "They've left us a meal."

She nodded to the trays by the door. "Not that I would

endorse consuming it. What were you dreaming about?"

"I'm not sure."

"Was it a dream, or was it a memory?"

"I'm not sure," Xander said. "But I've seen it before. On Callisto. I was on a ship, and someone was locking me inside a room." She scowled. "So many things. People. Faces."

"Who is David?"

David.

The name twisted in her stomach, throbbed like a splinter in her mind. Someone important, but who? And if he mattered so much, where was he?

"Someone I know."

That would have to be enough of an explanation for both of them. It was all Xander had.

Evy patted Xander on the shoulder and stretched her arms out. In the darkness, Xander could see that Evy had used her suit coat to bind her wounded leg.

"Are you in pain?" Xander asked.

"Yes. But I'll live."

"How far is NUJenesis from NUSaxony?"

"I'm not certain. I only know what's come over the wires, and from that I've always surmised it was very far." She rested the back of her head against the wall. "It's a militia center or so they say."

"What about this Mr. Knight guy? Do you know anything about him?"

Evy hesitated. "Again. All I know is from the wires. But they say Braedon Knight is the head of the Knightshade Syndicate."

"That makes sense."

"Knightshade, though, I do know something about," Evy

continued. "They control many of the trade routes, and they have their hands in most businesses on each planet and colony. There's nowhere to go to get away from them."

Evy grimaced and shifted positions on the floor.

"Evy, are you okay?"

"It hurts," she said. "But I'm—peachy."

Xander lifted her eyebrows. "Peachy?"

"Yes, isn't that what you say? I chose the correct fruit, yes?"

Xander chuckled. "Yes, you did. You just don't strike me as peachy."

"No?"

"No." Xander leaned against her. "You're a rock star."

Evy's eyes twinkled. "Well, that does sound significantly more substantial than a fuzzy fruit." Evy hugged her with one arm. "Are you all right?"

"Thanks to you." She looked down. "Why does Knightshade want me?"

"That is the question, Xander." She smiled. "But I'd rather not stay long enough to find out."

Xander pulled back with a laugh. "What? You're going to stage a jailbreak now?"

"You'd rather stay?"

"Of course not, but—how?"

"When they brought the food, I got a glimpse outside. They're not guarding us."

"They aren't?"

"Xander, you're a scrawny teenage amnesia victim, and I'm a blonde," Evy said.

"Hey, I'm not scrawny." Xander pouted.

Evy's dry expression didn't change.

"I'm just slim."

"The point."

"Is a good point." Xander rolled her eyes. "But unless you know how to pick a digital lock, that fact isn't going to do us much good."

Evy flashed a brilliant smile.

"You do?"

"The problem is, I don't want to get out and have to run around the ship waiting for them to find us."

"And something tells me we don't want to be running loose on NUJenesis either."

The door clicked.

"It's too early for another meal," Evy said, "though calling it a meal scarcely does it justice."

Xander stood as the door unlocked and slid open. The light from the hallway silhouetted a tall man in a trench coat. Like a black smudge, he blocked the light, but even though Xander couldn't see him, she could sense the smirk on his face. She felt the chill of his presence across the room.

"Hello, Xander," he said.

Evy took hold of Xander's hand.

The man stepped into the cell, and Xander gripped Evy's hand in panic.

The black-eyed man from the *Acheron*.

She felt a sudden, hysterical fear that he would cut the rest of her hair off.

"Xander," Evy said quietly from the floor, "do you know this man?"

The man gazed at her with his too-black eyes.

"He was on the *Acheron*."

A.C. WILLIAMS

"That's right," the man said. He stepped closer. "My name is Darien Stone."

Xander hated the way he looked at her. His eyes pierced through her, as though she was no more substantial than a wisp of smoke.

"You're a very difficult woman to keep up with," he said.

Evy's grip increased, but Xander hardly felt it.

"I am?" Xander's heart beat wildly.

Keep up with? Had he been chasing her? Was the attack on NUSaxony and their kidnapping his doing? What for?

Good grief, what if he did want her hair?

"It's taken me nearly two months to find you again." Darien Stone's face curled in a devious smile that turned his face into something predatory. "That's unheard of for someone in my profession."

"You mustn't be very good at what you do then," Evy said sharply, "for she hasn't left NUSaxony at all."

Xander gazed out into the empty hallway beyond him. Evy was right. They weren't being guarded.

"What do you want with her?" Evy asked.

His only answer was another smirk, and Xander blushed. The redness of her face only deepened when his eyes took her in from head to toe, slowly.

"Mr. Braedon Knight is the one who wants to speak to her," Stone said. "As for what I want? Well, I'll leave that to your imaginations."

If he'd been a customer at the Oasis, Xander would have beaten him with her serving tray.

"You're with Knightshade," Evy said.

"Excellent deduction, Dr. Berkley."

128

NAMELESS

"So what does Knightshade want with her?"

"No clue." Stone folded his arms across his chest. "That's not my job. My job is to deliver the girl, Xander, to the care of Mr. Braedon Knight, and that is what I will do." He frowned at Evy. "And if you hadn't been so willing to sacrifice yourself for her, Dr. Berkley, you might have survived this ordeal. But, as it turns out, you won't."

Xander clenched. Beating him with a serving tray wouldn't have done enough damage.

"As soon as we reach NUJenesis, Xander will come with me and you, Dr. Berkley, will be executed." He smiled as he turned. "You really should have minded your own business."

He stepped into the hallway, still smiling.

"Enjoy the next few hours together, ladies," he said. "You won't see each other again."

The door shut and locked, leaving Evy and Xander in darkness.

Evy released a heavy breath in a rush. "Dear heavens, what was that man?"

"Don't you mean who?" Xander shook.

"That wasn't a who, Xander."

Xander narrowed her eyes at her friend. What did that mean? Evy sounded genuinely frightened. Not that Xander blamed her. Darien Stone scared her silly, but Evy had no history with him. So did Evy know him or did she just know his type? Neither possibility made Xander feel better.

The ship shuddered as it slipped out of hyperspace.

Evy went rigid. "We're stopping?"

"We haven't been gone that long," Xander mumbled. "Stone said hours."

129

Evy glanced down at her. "Yes. Yes, you're right." She frowned. "Perhaps they need to recharge. This could be a charge station."

"A what?"

"Come on." Evy got up and limped to the door. Xander grabbed her waist and held her up.

Evy pried a small metal panel off of the wall to reveal an intricate lattice-work of colored wires and microchips. Evy unfastened her left earring and poked at certain microchips with the stud.

"When one of them shocks you," Evy said, "that's the one to pull."

"How do you know that?"

She pulled out one of the microchips, an oblong slice of clear plastic covered in a web of silicon wiring. Evy used the earring to slide one small switch in the upper right corner to the side. She slipped the microchip back into the panel. The door slid open.

A ship full of NUChungqwo bad guys and a demon barber from the pit of hell—and a blond neuro-therapist could outsmart them. Maybe they didn't have as much to be scared of as Xander had originally thought. Either that or Evy was just that legit.

"Wow," Xander whispered.

She stuck her head out into the hallway. There was no one in sight.

"Hurry." Evy took her hand after she refastened the earring.

"How did you learn how to do that?"

"My brother taught me."

"You have a brother?"

"Had, darling. I *had* a brother. He died in a freighter accident six years ago."

"Sorry."

"It's all right," Evy said, although her voice sounded sad. "It happens."

Evy leaned heavily on her as they past a row of windows and stopped.

"This isn't NUJenesis." Evy beamed, slapping the wall quietly. "It's Ursa-Five, a space port in the Epsilon Sector."

"So why are they docking?"

"I'm certain I'm right," Evy said. "The attack on New London must have drained them, and they'll have to recharge their power cells before continuing on. Maybe they're just stopping for tea. I don't know, but let's not pass on this opportunity, dear. This way."

So she was an expert on ships too? This Evy made less sense than the first one Xander had met. At least that Evy looked the part of a queen. This Evy, the bloodstained, jail breaking version, didn't look right in the spectacles.

"Evy, how do you know where you're going?" Xander jogged to keep up as Evy led them down a long hallway and turned right.

"Why, Xander, I'm guessing, of course."

"Great."

"We need to find a vent shaft or something that we can get into that leads to the outside." Evy looked around.

"What we need is a blueprint."

"Whenever ships dock for recharging, they have to show their registered transport visas," Evy said aloud. "And they have to drop their shields." She pressed her index fingers against her temples. "And dump their trash."

"Their trash?"

"Yes, yes, trash. All ships dump trash when they recharge. We just need to find the ship's garbage dump."

"You're kidding, right? Evy, how do you know all this?"

For a moment, Evy looked startled and then flustered. She started to answer and then stopped. Finally, she shook her head. "It's common knowledge, dear. Everyone knows that."

Everyone knew it? That might be possible. Xander had forgotten so many things everyone else seemed to know, but did everyone know how to break out of a prison cell? Did everyone know protocol for registered transport ships? Did everyone know those things?

Maybe. But maybe not.

Evy dragged Xander down the hall to a door marked with indistinguishable characters.

"Everything's in Chinese," Xander said. "Can you read it?"

"No, but I can smell." She sniffed the air. "And it smells like rubbish." She pushed the door, and it opened.

The scent of garbage got stronger as they poked their heads into the room beyond. It was stacked high with tall crates of trash and piled full of white and black garbage bags.

Evy and Xander limped together on the tips of their toes, sneaking into the bay. A set of NUChungqwo soldiers trilled back and forth to each other as they unloaded the garbage.

Xander peered around a tower of crates. A gigantic doorway led to a bright, clean exterior where the soldiers tossed crates of garbage. Evy motioned forward with her head, and they sneaked toward the light.

The *Shuriken's* intercom rattled. It must have been an announcement that the ship was ready to leave because the soldiers unloading the garbage began to work faster.

Evy and Xander slipped out of the door behind a large crate and hurried through the piles of garbage to the exit at the other end of the bay. As they reached the door, Xander looked back. The cargo bay of the *Shuriken* closed, and the ship moved away.

"We did it, Evy! We got away!" Xander hugged her. "You're amazing!"

The ship's docking thrusters fired, and the bay door began to lower again. Xander heard the alarms blazing inside the ship even from within the garbage bay.

"Oh, dear." Evy murmured.

"What are they doing? They're coming back?"

"Go, Xander. Hurry!"

Evy balanced on one leg while Xander pried the exit door open. She reached out to Evy, and they struggled through as a dozen soldiers jumped out of the cargo bay doors and began to rummage through the mountains of trash.

"They're on to us!" Xander gasped.

"Quickly!" Evy dragged her out of the bay area in spite of her bleeding leg.

They ran into the garbage management facility. The scent of the trash nearly overwhelmed Xander, but she choked down the urge to vomit and helped Evy run toward the exit.

Doorway after doorway, corridor after corridor passed before Evy and Xander emerged into a brightly lit colony dome full of people.

The cloudless artificial sky above shimmered blinding blue. The marketplace scent of apples and woodcarving filled the air, and the hum of the crowds harmonized in the breeze. Birds tweeted, people chattered, but none of it could drown out the bang of the door behind them. It blew open, and seven NUChungqwo soldiers burst out of it.

"Evy!"

Two of the men rushed at them.

If a serving tray could be a weapon, so could a garbage bag.

Xander grabbed one of the trash bags and flung it at them.
The bag hit and erupted. Trash spewed over both men and filled the
alleyway with the smell of rotten eggs and spoiled milk.

The two soldiers went down, but it didn't stop the other five.

"Xander, run!"

The two women raced down the sidewalk and plunged into
the crowds, the soldiers chasing them. People scattered and spread
apart, all clutching at their belongings like they were in danger of
being stolen.

The people all seemed to realize that something was wrong,
and they cleared a path for Xander and Evy.

How kind of them. Idiots.

Xander would have preferred to fight their way through
them. As it was, the soldiers could find them easily.

Evy stumbled and choked on a sob, but she wouldn't stop
running. She pushed Xander in front of her.

"Go, Xander. Run!"

Xander steered them around a corner, and burst out of the end
of the alleyway. The sidewalks stretched out in front of them. Evy
struggled to keep up, and Xander didn't want to outdistance her. But
the soldiers closed in.

Evy clutched Xander's hand as they raced down the
sidewalk, looking over their shoulders for any sign of their pursuers.

"Evy, where do we go?"

"Somewhere." Evy gasped with every step on her injured
knee. "Anywhere. I think—I think there's a battalion of colony

NAMELESS

police here on Ursa-Five. Maybe they'll know what to do."

Evy turned a quick corner, and Xander twisted to look back. The NUChungqwo soldiers shouted and pointed at them.

Great, they see us. Xander refocused on running. *I should have taken the stairs at the Oasis more often.*

Evy couldn't run anymore, but if they stopped, the men would kill Evy and drag Xander back to the ship. They couldn't stop. They had to fight. But how? With what? She was fresh out of serving trays and trash bags.

"What do we do if the police don't help us?"

"They will."

"What if they don't? Shouldn't they have been here by now with all this noise?"

Evy shoved Xander ahead of her again. "Run!"

A section of roof above them gave way and crashed into the sidewalk. Evy and Xander narrowly avoided it and looked up. Another division of soldiers scattered across the rooftops.

"Run, Xander!"

Evy barely spoke the words before laser fire scarred the pavement all around them. Xander covered her head as she ran. Evy stepped wrong. Her knee wrenched, and she struck the sidewalk, leaving skin behind.

They weren't going to make it. Stone's men would catch them. Evy would die.

But she wouldn't die alone. Xander stopped and ran back to her.

"No!" Evy pushed her away. "Don't stop!"

She wanted to be left behind. Evy wanted her to run away. Well, that was never going to happen.

"Go!" Evy scrambled up. "Go!" She limped and ran, shoving

135

Xander forward.

"Not alone. You're coming."

"Then, go, you fool." Evy surged up, unsteady but still running.

Xander bolted forward and crashed into something solid. She tumbled to the sidewalk in a tangle of arms and legs.

Perfect. She ran into someone? With her luck it would be a soldier—or a pervert. After her day so far, she'd gladly take the pervert.

She pushed herself up and stared into brilliant blue eyes that left her mouth dry. His dark red hair spilled like blood on the pavement.

And she straddled his waist.

Great. Running for your life was a perfect opportunity for an awkward moment with a handsome stranger. A stranger with blue, blue eyes.

For the briefest moment, those blue eyes stared at her openly in amazement, curiosity, surprise. Then, like a steel door slamming shut, they turned cold as a winter sky.

What? It wasn't her fault. He stepped in front of her.

Who was he?

And why was she still straddling him?

Perfect. No chance for misinterpreting that.

She hadn't even thought about climbing off him.

CHAPTER 11

Kale whistled a joyful tune as he walked out of the Ursa-Five police station with a data scanner.

The Parker hit was a bust; so what? They'd picked up a bounty on a counterfeiter just before entering the Epsilon Sector, which had turned into one of the easiest grabs in Kale's recent memory. The idiot hacker had practically turned himself in.

Devon grinned at him like a dog in a meat market. "Did you get it all, Mr. Sullivan?"

"All fifty grand, Mr. Chase."

Devon winced. "Chump change."

"It's better than nothing."

"Let's see." Devon scrunched up his face as they walked. "Talon gets the first ten grand for ship functions. So that leaves forty to split among all nine of us."

"Four thousand, four hundred forty-four creds each."

Devon's shoulders fell, and he groaned. "Damn. Not even half what I need for the blaster cannon I wanted for my SRF."

"Just going to have to save it, then."

Devon held up his hand. "Or we could talk some of the others out of their cuts."

"Who?" Kale rolled his eyes.

"Scraps."

"Uh, no."

"What does Scraps need with four thousand creds?" Devon

circled to Kale's other side. "What's he going to do? Buy new pots and pans for the galley?"

"Or revamp the med bay?" Kale said. "Which you commented needed it—drastically."

"Oh. Right." Devon thought a moment. "What about Marty?"

"Do you really want to hack him off?"

"Right. Never piss off the engineer." His face brightened. "What about Claude?"

"Claude would break your face. Newt needs vaccinations, and they don't come cheap." Kale pounded on his back. "Face it. You're slagged."

"There you are!"

Kale and Devon stopped as Vix stormed toward them, hair swaying at her waistline.

"What took you two so long? I've been waiting forever." She tapped her black boot as she extended a cred card toward Kale.

"Yes?" Kale sneered at her.

"Anytime, Ravenwood."

"What?"

"I want my cut. Now." She held the card out again.

"You couldn't wait till we got back to the *Prodigal*?" Devon curled his lip. "What's so important?"

"None of your business."

Kale took the card from her and punched numbers into the scanner. "You're probably going to the races."

"Like I said. None of your business."

Kale slid the card through the scanner and handed it back to Vix. She snatched it out of his grasp and walked away, her hips swaying under a too-short red leather skirt.

"She's crazy," Devon said. "She's going to blow her whole

cut on her stupid dogs."

"Not all of it." Kale slid his arm around Devon's shoulders.

"How do you know?"

"Well, I only gave her four thousand."

Devon gaped at him. "You skimped her more than four hundred creds?"

"She didn't notice, did she?"

"You sly son of a bitch." Devon laughed and pounded Kale's shoulder.

"Care for a drink? Vix's treat." Kale pointed around the corner. "And McElroy's is right here."

"Brother, you are so on."

The hub of bounty hunter activity on Ursa-Five, McElroy's was loud and dark, the beer was cold, and the women were eager to please. Generally, Kale didn't much care for prostitutes, but McElroy's girls didn't push too hard, and he was in a mood to celebrate.

Devon had one foot in the door when Kale heard the shots, the repetitious zings of laser pulses.

He grabbed Devon's shoulder. "Do you hear that?"

"How couldn't I?" Devon rolled his eyes, craning his neck to look inside the bar. "It's Beulah singing. She should stick to bartending."

"Not that." Kale smacked the back of his friend's head and walked away from the bar. He stopped at the corner, straining his ears. "Pulse fire."

"Pulse fire?" Devon stood beside his friend, listening. His face sobered. "Yeah. Sounds like new model Luparas—military grade. I hear it. Wonder what's up."

They stood quietly, still listening.

"It's coming closer."

"Yeah." Devon checked his holster.

Above them, across the street—motion. Instincts kicked in, and Kale shoved Devon over as a rogue blast erupted from one of the roofs and crashed into the sidewalk, right where Devon had stood. Kale dodged another blast and aimed his arondight at the shooters on the roof.

He didn't get the chance to shoot.

A blurry orange streak punched into his chest. The back of his head struck the sidewalk, and he saw stars. And then—red hair.

A woman with terrified gray eyes under a shroud of flaming carrot-colored hair. She straddled his waist, staring at him.

A real redhead. How long had it been since he'd seen a real redhead? Let alone have one across his—Kale shook himself.

"What the hell?" he snarled at her.

For a moment, it seemed she hadn't even thought about getting off him. Kale tried to ignore how appealing that sounded.

"Sorry." She gasped and scrambled off him.

The instant she got off, Kale's eyes darted to the roof, where five soldiers aimed at her. He grabbed the back of her neck, yanked her against his chest and rolled, blasting off eight shots that knocked all five of the soldiers down.

"Kale!" Devon fired over his head at another roof. The soldiers convulsed as Devon's shots pierced their hearts, and they collapsed like empty flour sacks.

Kale grabbed the redhead's arm and dragged her to her feet. "They're after you?"

The girl—she was just a girl—whirled to see the other side of the street. A woman with a bleeding leg wound limped into view, followed by an entire battalion of soldiers.

NAMELESS

"Kale."

"I see them."

"They're Chungs!"

"Yeah, Dev, I kind of picked up on that." Kale shot a soldier through the eye. "You get the blonde!" Kale gripped the girl's hand and dragged her down the street behind him.

Devon flung the injured woman over his shoulder, and raced after Kale, the blasts from the soldiers' high-powered disruptors pinging off the pavement at their heels.

"What do they want?" Kale demanded as he pulled the girl after him.

"I don't know," she said.

"Fine, well stick with us. I'm Kale." He pointed at Devon behind them. "That's my partner, Devon."

"Kale?"

"Yeah."

"Why are you helping us?"

Kale started to answer and stopped.

Why was he helping them? He hated helping people. It was always more trouble than it was worth. But there was something about the girl—the hair maybe? Or maybe it was her eyes. She was just a kid, running for her life. What sort of an ass would he be to leave two defenseless women to the Chungs?

"Just be grateful," he said to the girl. He turned a corner and shot two more soldiers. Kale holstered his blaster and pulled out a radio. "Talon!"

A crackling voice responded. "You sound rushed, lad. Who'd you piss off this time?"

"Call everybody back."

"What?"

141

"Just do it, McLeod. And tell Marty to warm up the engines."

"You have my payday?"

"Yes!"

"All right, then."

Kale clipped the radio back on his belt. "Devon?"

"Here!" Devon still carried the injured blonde over his shoulder a couple of yards behind them.

"We're going back to the ship," Kale said. "Follow me."

"Follow you?" Devon whined. "You mean I have to stare at your ass the whole way there?"

$\oplus$

Xander stared in awe at the man with the wild auburn hair. How could he sound so calm while the world fell apart around them? He ran with long, graceful strides, dragging her behind him, so fast she had to scurry to keep up.

A cheetah. That's what he reminded her of. Long-limbed. Elegant. Fast as lightning.

Who was he? What did he want? And why had he saved her? He didn't know her, and nobody else had been willing to interfere? So who was he?

Was he expecting payment of a different sort after their rescue? Or was he simply helping them because he could? But that was impossible. People didn't help each other just because they could. Not in this world.

Kale nearly pulled her arm out of socket as he dragged her around a corner.

Could she and Evy trust them? At the moment, Xander didn't feel they had much choice.

The blasts from the rooftops diminished as they ran out of the commercial district and into the military district, where the spaceport stretched out before them.

"Almost there."

Kale dragged her toward a rusty spaceship on the spaceport tarmac, with *Prodigal* barely visible on its grimy hull. The patched-together spaceship looked like a yacht with an engine strapped to its backside. Could it actually fly? Its clawed feet gripped the landing pad, and a set of maneuvering thrusters sprouted from its sides. Above a large bay door hatch, an ovular superglass canopy shimmered on a flat deck, surrounded by four gunner turrets. Heat waves rippled around the engines, sizzling in the processed air.

The *Prodigal*. The name of a ship or the name of a man?

The mismatched ship blurred in her eyes as her mind twisted. Her feet stopped running. Was a prodigal a ship or a man? A son or a story? Or both?

Splinters in her mind.

"Come on!" Kale's grip bruised her elbow.

His rough jerk startled her out of her daze, and she scrambled to keep up with him as he ran.

A loading ramp on the ship's side lowered, and a woman with long blond hair ran down the ramp with an energy cannon longer than her arm. She aimed and fired, each shot cutting down multiple soldiers.

How did she shoot that thing? It looked too heavy to lift let alone shoot with any accuracy, but apparently no one had told her that.

Kale's boots thumped on the ramp as they ran up it. He shoved Xander to the bulkhead floor and grabbed Evy, sputtering indignantly, from Devon's shoulder. Devon turned and opened fire as

Kale dropped Evy next to Xander.

The blond woman kept firing. The cannon should have knocked her over with every blast, but she barely budged. What was she? Superhuman? A super human blond with pink highlights.

She killed three more soldiers and glared at the back of Kale's head. "Can't you two go anywhere without getting in trouble?"

Kale didn't answer, and Devon made a pouty face. If the superwoman saw it, she ignored it.

"Why are we still here?" Kale adjusted his position and shot a soldier in the head.

"Vix," superwoman said between cannon blasts.

Kale sagged. "Of course. Let's leave without her."

Superwoman smirked. "I'll tell her you said so."

"Like I give a shit." Kale snapped the charge unit out of the base of his disruptor and replaced it with a new one.

Devon pointed to the north. "There! North. It's Vix, coming in."

"Cover the east," superwoman ordered. "I have north."

Kale and Devon changed direction on cue and fired. Superwoman did the same. In moments, another woman vaulted into the ship, black hair flying and an impossible amount of leg showing.

"What is wrong with you idiots?" She collapsed against the wall. "We just got here, and you have the whole freaking Chung army coming after you!" She froze when she spotted Evy and Xander.

"Not us." Devon panted. "Them."

"We need to go." Kale grabbed Xander and dragged her out of the cargo bay and into a hallway. Devon followed, swinging Evy into his arms as he ran.

NAMELESS

Xander tripped, trying to keep up with Kale, her shoes slapping on the metal-plated floors of the rickety ship. Kale didn't brake for the stairwell either and hauled her up the steps behind him. The ship rocked with every outside gun blast, sparks glittering outside the command deck windows.

Kale shoved her into a seat on the back wall. "Sit."

"You'll be the death of me, boy!" A man with a bright red beard pointed at Kale, his face nearly the same color as his hair. "The Chungs are blowing holes in my ship!"

He sounded Scottish. Were there Scottish people in space?

Devon set Evy in the seat next to Xander. Evy cringed away from him, but Devin didn't seem to notice.

"Evy?" Xander took her hand. "Are you okay?"

"I've been shot, kidnapped, chased through a space port, and manhandled like a feed sack."

"Yeah. But are you okay?"

Evy dropped her head and nodded. "I'll live, Xander."

Xander strained to see more of the command deck. Kale stood beside the man with the red beard. A man with a long brown ponytail sat at a console near the superglass windows.

"Is there a reason we're still sitting on the tarmac?" Kale snapped.

"Chung boat in orbit, Kale," the red-bearded man said. "We're not going anywhere."

Evy lifted her head. "The *Shuriken*," she said.

Redbeard glared at her. "I'm sorry, lass?"

"The name of the ship is the *Shuriken*." Evy wrinkled her nose at him and then adjusted her spectacles. "They are after us. Your men were kind enough to help."

Even as the ship rocked from the explosions outside, the man with the red beard faced them calmly, hands on his hips, face quirked in a half-smile. "They're after you? What in the seven hells could the Chungs want with you?"

Superwoman jogged up the steps. "Bay doors secure, Captain."

The whole ship lurched. Kale and Devon flailed to grab the railing around the bridge before they fell, and Redbeard--Captain Redbeard--seized the big chair at the center of the command deck.

"What the hell was that?" the leggy woman shrieked from the bottom of the stairwell.

The ship's intercom system squeaked. "Them dung beetles out there just shot us with a bazooka, Cap!"

The captain paused for a moment before he sighed explosively. "Get us off the ground, Fixx."

"With the Chungs up there?"

"Chungs up there, Chungs down here. I'd rather take our chances with Benny on the helm then stay down here and get pounded." The captain gestured to ponytail-man at the helm.

"Got it." The intercom squeaked again.

The ship rattled like every bolt holding it together was loose. Was that because they were under fire or because the ship belonged in a scrap yard? Neither option gave her any confidence. Xander gripped the seat, and her heart leapt into her throat.

"Easy, Benny-boy." The captain sat in his chair at the middle of the bridge. He looked at Evy and Xander. "You ladies better strap in. This could be rough."

Evy grappled with her belt and got it fastened. Xander fumbled with the restraints, and Devon knelt and wrapped the complicated belt around her.

"Kale, Devon, Vix, Jaz—gunner turrets. Now."

Devon smiled, made sure Evy and Xander were secured, and raced across the bridge to a glassed-in chamber on the side. Kale and the two women slid into the other two gunner turrets.

The ship jerked as it passed through the colony scanning systems. Xander craned her neck to see out the superglass screen at the front of the bridge. Ponytail maneuvered the large ship through a narrow shipping lane.

"There she is," Captain McLeod said.

The *Shuriken* hovered close to the main exit lane. Its rear thrusters flared the moment the *Prodigal* came into view.

"Go, Ben."

The *Prodigal* groaned as the pilot wheeled it into a shipping lane.

"Talon!" Devon spun in his gunner chair. "*Shuriken* just launched chasers!"

"What's a chaser?" Xander leaned against Evy.

"I'm not certain I know." Evy gripped her bleeding leg, face gray.

She looked awful. How much blood had she lost?

"McLeod, they're firing." Devon turned his chair around again.

The captain tapped the intercom. "All hands, brace for impact."

The first laser blast merely shook the ship, but the second knocked it sideways, sending bits and pieces of bridge systems scattering across the floors.

"Ben, break out of this."

"I can't get around the shippers, sir." The man spoke with a NUGaulian accent.

"Find a way, lad. They'll shoot us to bits."

"Captain?"

"Aye, lad."

"I have an idea. There's a choke point coming up, a maintenance duct."

"Can you squeeze this bird's ass through that?" Kale didn't turn from his gunner screen.

Ponytail ignored Kale. "The duct leads to the lanes outside the colony traffic."

The captain sagged in his chair with a round of muttered profanity. "Do it."

The *Prodigal* shuddered as another blast hit. Xander peered out the glass again and spied the narrow maintenance duct. Much narrower. Kale's worry made sense. Ponytail turned the ship and blasted toward the duct, the two chaser vessels close enough to hear the whine of their engines through the hull.

"Sir, sensors show them switching to torpedoes!"

"Talon, they just fired."

"Incoming!"

The first torpedo skimmed off the ship's side in a ball of fire. Another blew a hole through the front deck. Xander clung to her seat.

Xander squeezed her eyes shut.

The ship lurched. She'd been here before. She'd lived this moment already. Clinging to her seat for her life, the ship falling apart around her. No one would survive. No one except her.

The ship rocked on its side. Xander forced her eyes open in time to see Ponytail thread the maintenance duct with a foot of clearance on either wing. The chasers behind them couldn't make the maneuver and crashed into the walls, the force of their explosion tilting the *Prodigal's* back side upward.

The *Prodigal* burst from the other end of the maintenance duct, meeting a fleet of small fighters, all sparkling with laser cannons primed to fire.

"Gunners, ready."

The fighters swooped in, and the four gunners opened fire. Kale nailed the first fighter directly in its fusion core, and it erupted in a fiery blaze. The deafening jackhammer sound of the gunner turrets discharging rattled Xander's lungs like the bass beat at a rock concert.

"Woo!" Devon blew two fighters away. "What you got, bitch?"

The ship rocked, and Xander gripped the harness with white-knuckled hands.

Deep breath. Breathe. Just breathe. Xander clenched her jaw shut to keep her teeth from rattling. *They know what they're doing. They've done this before. Right?*

She trained her gaze on Kale's gunning station. She caught her breath at the look of intense concentration on his face. His eyes shone stunning blue, a blue that pierced and warmed and chilled at the same time. His deep red hair shivered every time the ship took a hit. Xander couldn't take her eyes off him, the strangest combination of grace and power she could ever remember encountering.

Another torpedo crashed into the side of the *Prodigal*, and the bolts holding her seat to the wall strained. The ship groaned under the assault and reeled to the side. The force of the blow threw Xander against her restraints and drove the air out of her lungs.

"Ben, go to notch seven on my mark." The captain clutched his arm rests.

The ship shuddered again.

"Mark!"

Ponytail hit the engines, and the powerful turbines fired. The ship thrust forward out of firing range.

CHAPTER 12

Xander pried her shaking fingers off her seat and tried to remember how to breathe normally. The ship clunked and moaned as it lumbered through the blue-green light of hyperspace. Was it supposed to make that sound? Had the chasers damaged them?

The captain slumped in his chair, thick fingers scratching his red beard.

He tapped the intercom. "Marty?"

"Yeah, Cap?"

"Damage report."

"Yeah." The man paused in his response. "I'll get back to you on that."

"Great." The captain let his head hang.

The nice blond man—Devon, was it?—spun in his gunner chair to look at her and Evy. Not a mean look. No, a worried one, wanting to see if they were all right. Kale, her handsome rescuer, the one she steamrolled, hadn't looked at her like that. Actually, he hadn't looked at her again.

"What the hell was that?" The leggy woman with the long black hair burst out of her gunner turret and stormed toward Devon.

Devon rolled his eyes at her temper and unhooked his belts. "They were Chungs, Vix."

The black-haired tantrum with legs—Vix, apparently—slugged his arm hard enough to knock him sideways in his chair.

"I know that, you idiot," Vix said. "Do you think I'm stupid?

Of course, they were Chungs. Why were they attacking us?"

"We got into the middle of something." Devon winced and rubbed his arm as he threw a glance at Kale. "Didn't we, Kale?"

Kale didn't answer. He glared instead. Oh boy, did he glare.

He checked his disruptor's charge as he sat in his gunner's chair. A threat? Warning Devon to shut up or else? Devon didn't seem concerned. More amused.

The captain didn't seem concerned or amused. He just looked pissed, like a shaggy red dog with its teeth barred at a trespasser. "Kale?"

"Yeah, what, Talon?" Kale slipped out of his gunner's chair and set his hands on his hips.

"Didn't we just talk *recently*, lad, about sticking our noses in other people's business?"

Captain Redbeard, Talon McLeod, leaned forward in his chair with his eyebrows raised. Could he talk to Kale like a child and not get shot?

"Yeah. We did. So?"

Xander gaped. Could Kale smart off to his captain and not get shot? What kind of crew was this?

"And wasn't it *you* who said we should stay out of it?"

"Yeah, it was. That was different."

"How so?"

Kale's shoulders stiffened, dangerous light in his eyes.

"What were we supposed to do?" Devon clambered to his feet from his gunner's chair. "Leave the ladies behind?"

"Damn it." Vix growled as she joined Kale beside Captain McLeod. "Does this matter? They're gone, and they have no reason to come after us again."

"Except that we have their prisoners," superwoman said from

152

her gunner chair, one leg crossed, back stiff, face set like an ivory carving. Her hazel eyes glowed like embers.

The bridge crew turned piercing gazes on Evy and Xander, and Xander sat straighter. Evy didn't budge, her face carefully blank. Captain McLeod winced and rubbed his forehead.

Kale folded his arms, his face darkening. "Probably should have left them."

Xander blinked in surprise. Why would he say that? Not that it mattered now. But still—not reassuring.

"No, lad." Captain McLeod said, sounding very much like an exasperated parent speaking to a naughty child. "You shouldn'a. But the question is what to do with them now."

Xander stiffened and tried not to show it. They didn't need to know her heart hammered against her ribs or that the back of her neck dripped with sweat.

What would they do with them? McLeod could do whatever he wanted.

"I'm needing to know something," Captain McLeod said. "I need to know what two lovely ladies like yourselves were doing with the Chungs."

"You're bounty hunters." Evy fisted her hands in the fabric of her bloodied trousers.

Bounty hunters? Evy had to be wrong. Kale was a bounty hunter? And Devon too?

What if they're just like that creep Lou? From Callisto? Are all bounty hunters the same? What have you gotten yourself into? And worse, you dragged Evy into it too. You can't even run away this time.

"Aye." Captain McLeod focused on her. "You be havin' a problem with that, lass?"

Evy's grip on Xander's arm strengthened. "I don't make a habit of dealing with scum."

Xander fought the urge to stare at her. What was she doing?

"Lady," Kale said, his tone stunned, "unless you've already forgotten, we just saved your asses back there."

"At significant risk to our own asses, I might add," Devon put in. "Which is a sacrifice. Because I like my ass."

"And what payment are you expecting to receive from that service? Because I don't intend to pay at all. We didn't ask for your help." Evy glanced from Captain McLeod to Kale and back to Captain McLeod again. "You may drop us at the nearest base."

"Why?" Devon snorted. "So the Chungs can catch up with you again?"

"What did they want with a pair of self-righteous NUSaxons anyway?" Vix sneered.

"We are not certain," Evy said.

"You don't look like much." Vix crossed her arms and lifted her nose. "Are you important or something?"

"Not particularly." Evy winced as she put weight on her injured leg. "I'm a doctor. This is my patient. And that's all I'd like to tell you."

"What, we don't even get names?" Devon pouted.

Evy glared at him.

Captain McLeod frowned and approached. Evy's fingers tightened in a bruising grip on Xander's arm. Captain McLeod knelt before them and inspected Evy's bleeding leg. She didn't react, but her jaw tightened at his proximity.

"You're wounded there, lass."

"Your powers of observation are astonishing, Captain."

Captain McLeod took a deep breath. "Chase. Take them

down to Scraps. Have him patch them up. Then bring them back up here, and we'll have a chat."

Devon nodded and held out his hand to Evy. She did not accept it. Captain McLeod stood and walked toward Kale.

"You come with me, lad. We need to talk." He punched Kale's shoulder as he walked.

"About what?" Kale snorted.

"Cotton beetles."

Xander doubted that was the case. Kale followed Captain McLeod to the other end of the bridge. He didn't glance their way.

Devon offered his hand to Evy again. "Are you coming or not?"

Evy grudgingly took his hand, and he lifted her easily into his arms. Xander followed.

Devon led the way into a long metal corridor, through a few bulkheads, and down some short stairwells, to an open area with a large window on one side. A makeshift kitchen took up one end of the room, and a large round table occupied the rest of the space. Cabinets, painted cheery yellow, lined the walls, and the counter tops held jars of utensils and shelves of preserves. The kitchen was designed to look like something out of a home, comfortable and pleasant. Maybe after being in a spaceship for months, it would start to look like a home, but painted yellow cabinets really didn't make a difference.

Devon veered left as they entered the galley and descended a winding stairwell. The dim room below the eating area contained two medical beds against the far wall. Halogen lights illuminated the room, and a balding man stood at a table with a microscope. He looked up as they entered, his blue eyes sparkling.

Wild white hair grew around his ears and on the back of his

head, tied in a pony tail that reached below his neck. He wore a turtleneck with a bright blue apron with lettering that read, "Kiss the Cook."

Good Lord. Who were these people?

"Hey, Scraps." Devon grinned as he laid Evy on one of the medical beds. "Got some patients for you."

"Hopefully they'll be better patients than you, boy," the old man said pleasantly as he approached. He had a light NUSovian accent.

"I refuse to be treated by anyone named *Scraps*." Evy glared at him.

Scraps and Devon hazarded a glance.

"Well, if it helps," the old man smiled, "my name is Elek Ivanov. They just call me 'Scraps' here."

"Why?" Xander asked.

If it had to do with the apron, Xander would run away.

He smiled at her. "Because I cook exquisite meals with whatever Talon can buy me, and," Scraps turned a gentle gaze to Evy, "I also happen to be a very accomplished physician."

"Which a nice lady like yourself, Dr. Snooty Pants, should appreciate," Devon said.

"That's Dr. Berkley, to you."

"A fellow doctor?" Scraps brightened. "Fantastic!"

Evy looked away from him. "I'm a neuro-therapist."

Devon stuck out his jaw and furrowed his brow. "A neuro-what's-it?"

"A doctor who studies the mind." Scraps got out his first aid kit, pawing through it.

"A brain doc?" Devon yelped and glared at Xander. "And she's your patient? What is she? A psycho?"

NAMELESS

Xander stepped back from him. What a rude thing to say! And she'd called him the nice one.

"No," Evy said, "she's an amnesiac."

"Oh!" Devon arched his eyebrows. "An amnesiac! Hey, Scraps, what's an amnesiac?"

"She has no memory, Devon." Scraps examined the laser wound on Evy's leg. He glanced at Xander from the corner of his eye. "Fascinating."

"Got it." Devon snapped his fingers. "That's what Kale is."

"He is?" Xander's ears perked up.

"No, my dear." Scraps pulled out a roll of bandages and chuckled. "Kale suffers from something else entirely. I prefer to call it *selective hearing*."

"Is that why he forgets stuff all the time?"

"Devon, out."

"Yes, sir."

Devon tipped a pretend hat at Xander and scurried up the stairs.

"Now, hold still, little doctor." Scraps smiled as he pulled out an anesthetic hypospray. He pressed it against Evy's arm. It hissed, and the lines of pain on Evy's brow faded.

"So," Scraps said as he began to work on Evy's wound, "how did two nice young ladies end up out here?"

"That's not your business."

Scraps smiled. "Ah, so I see. Self-righteous colony dwellers who want nothing to do with the likes of us bounty hunters. Right?"

Evy said nothing, but Xander couldn't look away from the old man.

The only other person she'd met old enough to be a grandfather had been the crazy old daisy killer at the Oasis. And

157

even though that old coot had remembered sweet tea, Xander didn't want anything to do with him. If her grandfather was still alive, she hoped that he would be like Scraps.

"Well, I like to talk while I work," Scraps said, "so if you'll forgive me, I'll just chatter on as though you care what I'm saying."

Evy remained silent, looking away from him.

"People like you have such poor opinions of us," Scraps said as he worked on her leg. "Not that our peers give us a very good name, but we on the *Prodigal* make an honest living. And I really didn't have much other choice, honestly, when faced with choosing what life I would lead."

He smiled again.

"I had just buried my wife and daughter on Ganymede when I met Talon McLeod. Uh, he's the captain, by the way. He asked me if I wanted to come onboard his ship, search for greater—oh, how did he put it—financial opportunities." Scraps wrapped the bandages around her leg. "Thought it was kind of strange, a NUKeltian approaching a widower NUSovian like me. Our types don't usually get along.

"Well, I saw through him. I called him a bounty hunter. He didn't deny it. Then he told me he already had his hunters. He just needed a cook and a medic. Wanted to know if I could do one of those. I told him both. And he asked me again." Scraps patted Evy's leg. "I told him I'd give him a week. If I didn't like it, I was out. And he agreed."

"And he forced you to stay," Evy said.

"No!" Scraps laughed out loud. "Talon never forced anyone to do anything, except maybe Kale. I didn't leave because—this is home now, with people I love."

That didn't seem right. He loved the people here? He loved

the grouchy captain and the icy superwoman? He loved the black-haired harpy? Devon seemed lovable, sure, but what about Kale? Yeah, he'd saved them, but then he changed his mind about it moments later. Could anyone love people like that?

Could he love a ship that rattled as it flew? A kitchen that looked like a tin shed with painted cabinets? A life constantly on the run, constantly under fire, constantly afraid?

That could never be a home. That could never be a life. So how could it make Scraps happy?

But it did. So maybe there was more to it than what she'd seen so far.

Evy stared at him.

"So I didn't leave. And I won't. Going on three years I been here. Just turned sixty yesterday."

"Happy birthday," Xander said.

"Thank you." He bowed his head at her and pinned Evy with a powerful look. "Bounty hunters aren't all bad."

"But they're not all good either."

"Who is?" He stepped back for a moment. "That done to your liking, doctor lady?"

Evy glanced at her bandaged leg. "It doesn't pain me as much."

Scraps lifted his eyebrows.

"Admittedly," Evy began, not meeting his eyes, "I haven't much experience in—field dressing."

"As a neuro-therapist, I wouldn't expect it," Scraps said. "Now, little girl, let me have a look at you."

Evy fell silent as Scraps started examining Xander.

"Well," the cook/medic said after a few moments, "you seem to be fine, young lady. Few scratches but nothing that won't heal up." He frowned. "Both you got some burning on your faces. Seen some fire?"

"Nothing we want to talk about," Evy snapped.

"As you like it, little doctor." The intercom beeped, and Scraps touched it. "Yeah?"

"Scraps, ye got them fixed up yet?" Captain McLeod's impatient brogue filtered over the speaker.

"*Da*," Scraps said. "They'll be up in a flash."

"I'm sending Jaz down for them."

"Ah, the inscrutable Miss Jezebel. Whatever you need, Captain."

The intercom clicked, and Scraps started putting the first aid kit up.

"Jezebel?" Xander asked.

"Nice lady once you get to know her. She's real quiet. Doesn't open up to too many folks."

"But she does to you?" Evy fingered the bandage on her leg.

"Everybody does." Scraps put away his medical supplies. "Well, almost everybody."

"Everybody except Kale?" Xander said, lifting her brows.

Scraps looked down at her surprised.

"He seems to be the exception to a lot of things," Xander said.

Scraps eyed her suspiciously before he continued. "Yeah. He's a special one, that Kale is. He's the best shot we've got on this boat, though Devon would argue that."

"They seem to know each other very well." Evy slid off the bed and stood on her own.

"NUUSA, both of them," Scraps said. "Don't know if I should be saying, though."

NAMELESS

"Why not?" Xander asked.

"We're not supposed to talk about Kale often," Scraps shrugged. "Not with strangers anyhow."

Evy straightened her singed, stained blouse and lifted her chin. "Every bounty hunter I've ever heard of has been a scoundrel. A troublemaker. A lower class of person that people of civilized society should avoid."

Scraps nodded, his expression respectful, yet amused. "And if you don't mind me asking, Miss, how many bounty hunters have you actually met?"

Evy pursed her lips. "You all are the first."

"That so?"

"Yes."

"Hm."

Evy folded her arms and held her chin aloft. "I suppose you're going to say that I'm jumping to conclusions. Or that I'm basing all my assumptions on information that may or may not be correct."

"I don't believe I was going to say anything, Miss Doctor." Scraps grinned with a twinkle in his eyes. "Is that what you're thinking?"

Xander swallowed a giggle rising in the back of her throat. Now wasn't the time to be laughing, but not many could so easily turn Evy's own words against her. Scraps was obviously much more intelligent than he let on.

The sound of rapid footfalls on the stairwell quieted Evy and Xander, and superwoman appeared.

Jaz. So that was superwoman's name.

"Talon wants you." She jerked her head toward the stairs. "Follow me."

161

A.C. WILLIAMS

Evy took Xander's hand and started after the female bounty hunter.

"Thanks, Mr. Scraps." Xander waved at him.

"Don't mention it."

Evy and Xander had just reached the steps when Scraps called out, "And Miss Doctor?"

Evy turned back to him, face impassive.

"Don't you be fearing Talon McLeod. He don't mean you harm."

Evy's expression remained guarded. Why was Evy afraid? The kind old man had taken care of their wounds. Why was Evy determined to dislike him?

Xander squeezed her hand, trying to communicate her sincere desire to trust the bounty hunters. If Scraps were any indication, the rest of the crew meant well—even if they didn't know how to have a civilized conversation.

To Xander's immense surprise, Evy squeezed her hand in return.

"Mr. Scraps," Evy said.

"Just Scraps, dear."

"Scraps, then. Thank you for your care."

"You're welcome, Miss Doctor."

"My name is Evy, Scraps."

Scraps grinned, showing his bright white teeth. "Evy. Nice to meet you, Dr. Evy. Welcome aboard the *Prodigal*."

162

CHAPTER 13

Jaz's pace back to the command deck strained Xander's breathing. She didn't want to think about what it did to Evy's injury, though Evy didn't complain.

Captain McLeod stood as they entered, and Jaz took the place at his side. Kale and Devon leaned on the far wall and Vix hovered near them. Ponytail piloted without looking at anyone.

"All right, ladies." Captain McLeod offered a half-smile and gestured to a bench. "Have a seat."

Xander and Evy obeyed.

"While Scraps was patching you two up, Kale and I had a little chat about what went down on Ursa-Five." Captain McLeod grabbed a stool from under one of the science consoles. "Would one or both of you be willing to tell me why an army of NUChungqwo soldiers would be after a doctor and her patient?"

"We don't know," Evy said. "They just abducted us."

"From where?"

"NUSaxony."

Captain McLeod scratched his red beard. "Well, that would explain it."

Evy stiffened. "Explain what?"

Captain McLeod took a deep breath and leaned back on the stool, careful not to lose his balance. "Let's talk a little more about these circumstances first."

"What I'd like best of all, Captain McLeod, is for you to

return us to NUSaxony."

"NUSaxony isn't a good place to be right now, doll face." Vix light a cigarette and blew smoke out her nostrils.

"Why not?" Evy pursed her lips.

"NUSaxony is a war zone," Vix spat, despite Captain McLeod's vicious glare which clearly told her to keep her mouth shut.

"What do you mean?" Evy's voice trembled. "NUChungqwo attacked us. The colony was fighting back even as we were being brought on board the *Shuriken*."

"War's still raging, Doc," Devon said. "NUChungqwo's opened a can of worms, that's for sure. But NUSaxony will probably be gone by the time it's done."

All the color drained from Evy's face.

"Enough of that," Captain McLeod snapped.

"What are you so uppity about, McLeod?" Vix blew out a lungful of smoke. "You hate NUSaxons. I'd think you'd say they had it coming."

"What does this mean?" Xander took Evy's hand and held it to stop its shaking.

"It was bound to happen someday." Kale shrugged. "Surprised it didn't happen sooner. But what nobody can figure out is what made the Chungs invade in the first place."

Kale trained his eyes on Xander and held her in his gaze.

Oh, look at that. He did remember she existed.

Stupid Kale. It should be illegal for a boy to have eyes that pretty.

"The Chungs invaded NUSaxony to kidnap a doctor and her patient," Talon said. "Seems unlikely to be the catalyst for the war that started, but I don't see another option." Talon shook his head. "A

NAMELESS

conflict the size of what's going down between NUChungqwo and NUSaxony hasn't blown up since the Duranium Wars on the outer rim when NUGaul and NUEspan clashed. Colony wars are messy, and military commanders hate fighting them. No matter what nationality they are."

"So the real question is, what do the Chungs want with you two?" Kale narrowed his eyes.

"I told you already," Evy said, poised and cold. "I don't know."

"Do you know where they were taking you?" Talon leaned closer.

"No."

"Ye be lying, Doc."

"I have no intention of telling you anything, you brute."

Evy's tone had taken on a hysterical edge. No surprise there. All her friends, her colleagues, had been caught in the crossfire. If they couldn't go back, letting McLeod help was the next best option, and Evy seemed dead set against trusting him or any of his crew.

Xander gripped Evy's hand and took a deep breath. "They said they were taking us to NUJenesis."

Silence fell over the bridge.

Captain McLeod sat back, his eyes shocked. "NUJenesis? What for?"

"Stop." Evy turned to her. "They don't need to—"

"They wanted to talk to me," Xander said. "They said someone named Braedon Knight wanted to talk to me."

Kale and Devon shoved off the wall. Vix stopped smoking. Jaz stared, and Captain McLeod's jaw dropped. Even Ponytail cursed under his breath.

Geez. All that from a name? Not a good sign. I guess that

165

means they've heard of him.

"Braedon Knight?" Kale spoke in little more than a soft hiss, his blue gaze colder than ice.

Captain McLeod cleared his throat. "Braedon Knight? *The* Braedon Knight? Of the Knightshade Syndicate?"

Xander started to say something clever, but the weight of their combined stares stole the words from her mouth. "That's all they said. They were taking me to see Braedon Knight."

"Why the hell would Braedon Knight want to talk to *her*?" Vix said. "She's just a little girl."

"Apparently, there's more to her than meets the eye." Kale's eyes traced Xander's frame. He approached Captain McLeod and leveled a dangerous look at Xander. "Who are you?"

"What?"

"It's a simple question." His blue eyes burned into her. "Who are you?"

"She doesn't know." Evy set a gentle hand on Xander's leg.

"Excuse me?" Captain McLeod sat down in his chair and gripped his knees.

Evy glanced at him and sighed. "My name is Dr. Evylin Berkley. I'm a neuro-therapist."

Captain McLeod's face took on a different expression Xander couldn't read. "Dr. Evylin Berkley," he repeated. "You go by Evylin, then?"

Evy kept glaring at him. "I go by Evy. But you may call me Dr. Berkley."

"Evy, you say." Captain McLeod glanced at Xander. "And you, little one? Your name?"

"I just told you. She doesn't know her name." Evy scowled.

"Then what do you go by?" Kale asked.

NAMELESS

"Xander," she said. "It's the only thing I can remember."

The silence on the bridge grew deeper. Xander feared to breathe as if it would shatter the recycled air.

"Xander," Kale said. "Your name is Xander."

"I go by Xander," she said. "I don't know my real name." Was that a difficult concept to understand? Hadn't he just asked her what name she went by?

"Holy hell," Devon muttered.

Kale grabbed another stool and sat down next to Captain McLeod. "Where did she come from?" He directed the question to Evy.

"We don't know."

"Well, how did you come to have her then?" Captain McLeod crossed his arms.

Evy hesitated for a moment. "If your medic hadn't made such a good impression on me, I wouldn't be telling you this at all."

"That's what we pay him for," Kale said. "Now, answer the question."

Evy glanced from Captain McLeod's face to Kale. "Xander came to me—indirectly—by way of a friend of mine. Her crew found Xander in an abandoned spaceship. Xander was the only survivor."

Captain McLeod's face tensed. "What ship was she on?"

"The *Anastasia*."

Gasps rippled like lightning across the bridge.

"She has to be the same, Talon," Devon said.

Captain McLeod held up a hand. "A few days ago, we saw the *Anastasia*," Captain McLeod said. "I'm sorry to say she was in pieces. We found a survivor in a hull fragment barely alive, but she passed on soon after we rescued her."

"She?" Evy whispered.

"Her name was Helga Zahn."

Helga Zahn. The name resonated like thunder in Xander's mind, and the overwhelming panic she used to feel in the bowels of the Oasis rushed back on her like a tidal wave.

Dr. Zahn was dead.

"Dead?" Evy asked.

Evy's face went ashen, her hands shaking as they pressed against her stomach.

"Aye," Captain McLeod said. "She died just after we brought her on board."

"It must be a different Helga Zahn."

"How many NUGermans serve on NUSovian mineral harvesters?" Devon asked. "Face it, Doc, I think we're talking about the same person."

Dr. Zahn was dead.

Tears welled behind Xander's eyes, so many of them she couldn't prevent them from spilling over. Dr. Zahn's severe face and her cold blue eyes sparkled in her memory. The stern doctor who'd saved her, who'd protected her, who'd showed her friendship when she hadn't had to—she was dead.

Breath hitching, tears streaming down her face, Xander clutched the sides of her pants, wrinkling them. Panic and despair did no good now. Sobbing wouldn't help. She had to be strong. Dr. Zahn wouldn't have wanted anyone to cry over her; she would have thought the emotional display distasteful.

Evy sat silent beside her, head bowed, shoulders trembling. Not crying.

"Dr. Zahn mentioned that the *Anastasia* had gone to get an old ship from deep space," Captain McLeod said. "A ship called the

Destiny."

Xander met his eyes and kept her voice steady. "The *Destiny* was the ship they found me on."

"What do you know about it?" Captain McLeod asked.

"I don't remember." Xander dashed the tears off her cheeks.

"Have you tried, lass?"

"Yes."

"Really hard?" Kale asked.

Xander glared. "Yes. Really hard. You don't need to talk to me like I'm an infant."

He smirked. "Touchy, aren't you?"

"You said the brat was the only survivor." Vix pointed a slender finger at Evy as she slid around Kale's side. "Were there other people on board the ship?"

Xander glanced at Evy; she still didn't move or speak. Was she even breathing?

"Seven." Xander turned back to the crew. "At least, that's what Dr. Zahn told me."

Kale still glared at her. "And you have no idea who they were?"

Xander scowled. "If I knew, I would have told someone before now."

"Okay." Vix blew a ring of smoke above her head, drawing a pointed glare from Captain McLeod. "So the dead NUGerman said the ship and this brat are important. And they're obviously important enough for Knightshade to want them."

"What are you getting at, Valentine?" Captain McLeod snarled.

"This is deep shit, McLeod," Vix said. "Sounds to me like it wasn't the Chungs invaded NUSaxony; it was Seekers. But since nobody can tell them apart, NUSaxony thought it was the Chungs which explains their counterattack on NUChungqwo yesterday."

"Vix," Captain McLeod warned.

"Knightshade wants this brat bad enough to start a war between NUSaxony and NUChungqwo, just to get at her?" Vix set her hands on her hips, smoke curling from the end of her cigarette. "Messy business, McLeod. I want to know why Knightshade wants them."

"I think everybody wants to know that, Vix," Devon said.

"I don't think anyone but Braedon Knight knows," Xander said. "I tried to find out too—from the goon who was on the ship we were held on."

"From the what?" Vix scowled. "What the hell is a *goon*?"

"Yeah." Devon wrinkled his nose. "Is that some kind of new kid lingo? A *goon*?"

"A goon is—a creep," Xander said. "A jerk. A butt head. A goon."

They all stared at her until Xander felt her face turning scarlet.

"Never mind," Xander finally said. "He was—creepy. And scary. And I'd run into him before, and he said he had been tracking me for Knightshade."

Again, silence fell over the bridge. Kale hung his head, shaking it slightly and mumbling under his breath.

"This goon," Devon started. "Did he have a name?"

"Darien Stone."

Kale leaned his head back and uttered a soft groan.

"Enough, Kale," Captain McLeod snapped.

"We're done, Talon," Kale said. "Throw them back. This is the worst thing that could have possibly happened."

170

NAMELESS

"Hey, you're the one who rescued them," Vix said.

"It was a mistake. It was a bad idea." Kale held up his hands. "You get to hear me say it, Vix. I was wrong."

Xander gaped at him. He wasn't serious, was he?

How could he say that and mean it? He'd been a jerk already, but now he seemed to know what danger they were facing and he still didn't care? Why had he even saved her in the first place?

"We're not taking them back anywhere," Devon said. "We need to go find that ship."

Jaz shifted, as if surprised to hear Devon suggest such a rash course of action.

"Well, that's what Dr. Zahn thought we should do," Captain McLeod said. "Isn't it?"

"Maybe the answer is with that ship," Devon said. "If Knightshade is willing to go to those lengths for it, it has to be important. Maybe we can stop—"

"Stop what, Devon?" Kale faced him. "You can't stop a syndicate. You can't stop Knight."

"But you didn't hesitate to jump right into a Chung-fest to save two people you've never met?" Devon shoved a finger in his face. "Explain that to me."

Xander crossed her arms and waited for Kale to explain. Devon had a point. Xander didn't really know the back story, but Devon definitely had a point. And she suspected no one else could talk to Kale that way and live.

"That was different." Kale leaned into Devon's face. "They're saved now. They can go their own way, and we can go ours."

"Boys. Enough." Captain McLeod took a steadying breath. "I've been thinking a great deal about what Dr. Zahn had to say.

171

Personally, I think it's suicide to go after that ship."

Again, Jaz shifted her weight, the motion so slight Xander thought she'd imagined it. The woman's hazel eyes darted back and forth between Devon and Captain McLeod.

"Why not go after it?" Devon turned to Captain McLeod with his palms up.

"Don't you remember what the dead doctor said?" Vix mimed a noose around her neck. "Knightshade has it."

"If Knightshade is interested in the ship," Kale said, "they're interested in whoever is after the ship."

Jaz lifted her chin and spoke at last. "Seems to me that all Knight is interested in is Xander. And since you decided to play hero for once, we've already become a target."

"You're not pinning this one on me, Jaz," Kale said. "You would have done the same thing if you'd been in my place."

"It doesn't matter if we throw them to the wolves or not. Since we stepped in between them, they'll seek us out no matter what we do." Jaz sat down and crossed one leg over the other, keeping her gaze trained on Kale. "I think we should go after the ship. I, for one, am tired of allowing Knightshade to do as they please without anyone standing up to them."

Devon smirked. His eyes sparkled with victory. Had Jaz's agreement put that expression in his eyes?

Xander glanced from Jaz to Devon. They didn't act like a couple, at least not like any couples Xander had seen. But they seemed to be on each other's side.

Captain McLeod drummed his fingers against the outside of his thigh.

"Jaz, you're not making sense," Kale whirled on her. "You realize what we would be up against? Going after the *Tempest*? It's

Knightshade's flagship, Talon."

"Aye," Captain McLeod said. "That's true."

"Everybody but Jaz seems to be missing the point here," Devon said. "We have the girl." He gestured at Xander. "That's what he wants anyway, and Knightshade has the resources to find us no matter where we go. Even if we dump them, Knightshade will still track us down to find out where we left them. So whether or not we go after the ship isn't important. I say we go after it, and maybe we'll find out what he's up to."

Captain McLeod leaned forward on the stool and ran his hands through his wild, red hair. The action disturbed a thick layer of silver underneath. He grumbled into his palms.

"This is all against my better judgment," he said. "We're out here to stay away from the syndicates, and now we're going to go and piss them all off." He sat up and looked at Evy again. She sat, pale, shaking, trying desperately to contain her emotions. "But what can I say?"

"You can say no," Kale said.

"Aye, Kale, but the pretty NUSaxon doctor wants answers just like her patient does," Captain McLeod said. "And I'll admit I'm curious myself. Maybe it's got some tech on it Knightshade's wanting."

Kale shook his head. "I should have left them."

Xander didn't believe him. How could he say something like that? Surely he didn't mean it.

Kale hadn't looked at her again since his declaration that saving her had been a mistake. He avoided her, like he'd built a wall around her and papered it with signs that said, "Don't look!"

What about her scared him? He didn't seem scared of Braedon Knight or of NUChungqwo. He didn't seem scared of anything except her.

"Well, you didn't," Captain McLeod said. "And I see only one path now, Kale." A light on the armrest of his chair flickered on, and he pressed it. "Marty? I was just getting ready to call you."

Over the intercom, Marty made a whining noise that reminded her of a wounded animal. "Hate to break it to you, Cap, but I don't think we're going to make it half a clic further on our power cells."

"Why not?"

"We left before they charged up."

Vix moaned. "Are you serious?"

"Fine," Captain McLeod said, pinning a dark glare at her. "Kepler-Three is close, and they've got a charging facility we've used before. Set us down there, Ben. Marty, once we're charged up, we're gone. Understood?"

"Yeah."

"And keep your ears open for Seeker pings. They'll likely be hot on our trail if they're tracking us, so pay attention. Got it?"

"Yeah, McLeod. I got it already. Geez."

Captain McLeod sat in his chair and cast a glance at Evy and Xander. His eyebrows cocked.

"While the ship's charging," he said, "I recommend you ladies go out and get some clothes that don't smell like garbage."

Evy didn't respond. She still hadn't moved, tears trickling down her face now.

Xander's heart twisted.

Evy and Dr. Zahn had been close, very close. But Evy was the strong one, the confident one, the one who always knew what to do and never hesitated. Evy was falling apart in front of her, and she couldn't do anything to help.

174

NAMELESS

"Kale," Captain McLeod continued, "you'll go with them."

Kale's face went slack. He balled up his fists. Was he going to punch the captain?

"Me? Why do I have to go with them?"

"Seems to me you're the one signing up for babysitting duty." Captain McLeod folded his arms and crossed one leg over the other. "You brought 'em here, so you have the watch of 'em."

Kale murmured something profane, and Xander scooted closer to Evy.

At least, Captain McLeod seemed ready to help them stop whatever Braedon Knight was planning, but she would have felt better about it if Kale had expressed the same sentiment.

She sent Kale a furtive glance. A chill crept down her spine. Why had he gone to all the trouble to save her and Evy if he wanted nothing to do with them?

I guess I should take help where I can find it, she thought. *But is taking help from these people wise?*

The harsh set of Kale's square, rigid shoulders indicated their foray onto the planet wouldn't be cheerful.

"Jaz," Captain McLeod said, "you take 'em down to one of the passenger berths and get 'em settled in. Kale'll come for them when we reach Kepler."

Jaz nodded and glanced at Xander and Evy. Xander stood and offered her arm to Evy. Evy accepted the help without a word, and they followed Jaz off the bridge and down into the interior of the ship.

Jaz glided through the corridors, far too graceful to simply walk. Her hair swayed with the motion, waving around her hips in strands of gold and pink. The knives on her belt clinked, a threatening reminder that she wasn't just a pretty face.

175

She led Xander and Evy into a dark room.

"Lights," she said.

The room brightened, revealing two small, hard bunk beds with a little table in between them.

"It's not much, since we don't often take on passengers." Jaz turned to them. "But it should be enough for you two."

Evy didn't thank her and limped to the nearest bunk. Evy sat, the pain lines on her forehead standing out in sharp relief on her pale face.

"Thank you," Xander said.

Jaz's eyes hadn't left Evy. "What changed your mind?"

Evy looked up at her, tear streaks on her face. "What do you mean?" Her voice shook.

"When you first came on the ship, you didn't want anything to do with us," Jaz said, hazel eyes cold.

"I still don't want anything to do with you."

"But you spoke to us," Jaz said. "Before—you would say nothing. You only growled like a puppy—which was amusing to say the least."

"Amusing?"

"You're helpless. So I found your posturing amusing." Jaz tilted her head. "But after you spoke to Scraps, your posturing was gone. For the most part. And though you may not have liked speaking to us, you talked nonetheless."

"Your cook is an insightful person."

Jaz smiled for the first time since Xander had met her, even though it didn't brighten her eyes much. "Elek is a good man."

"You don't call him Scraps?" Xander sat on the side of her cot.

"I don't go for nicknames."

"But everyone calls you Jaz. That's a nickname isn't it?"

"It's not my decision what they call me. My name is Jezebel Carver. If they choose to call me something else, that is their prerogative."

Xander stood. "How long have you been here?"

"I have known Talon for ten years, and for seven of them, I have worked with him."

"Worked with him?" Evy asked. "Is that all?"

Jaz drew back in surprise. She gave a short laugh. "Yes. He is my superior, and, outside of Kale, I am his best hunter."

"Just a hunter. And nothing more?"

"You're suggesting I am a prostitute."

Evy scowled. "No. It just strikes me as odd that this Captain McLeod fellow would keep two beautiful women in his employ and not take advantage of their finer qualities. That's all."

Jaz's expression suddenly seemed annoyed. "You swing that way, do you?"

"What does that mean?"

"Nothing, Dr. Berkley. I'm simply trying to make you out." Jaz shook her head. "Vix and I are bounty hunters. Nothing more, although I classify as first mate aboard ship." She gave a thin smile. "I don't have much fondness for prostitutes; neither does Talon."

"Is that so?"

"He won't even allow them on the ship."

"How fortunate for you, although I imagine the male quotient of your crew finds such a ruling highly distasteful."

Jaz's eyes were unreadable. "I couldn't speak for them, Dr. Berkley, although in my experience, I know the majority of the crew shares Talon's sentiments."

"Seems unlikely, you must admit."

A.C. WILLIAMS

"Well," Jaz said with the strange little smile again, "very little is ever as it seems, Dr. Berkley."

"Miss Carver?" Xander asked before she realized she'd opened her mouth.

Jaz turned her eyes to face her. "You needn't bother with formalities."

"Should I call you—do I call you Jaz or Jezebel, though?"

"Whatever you prefer."

She's not very helpful about this, is she? Xander sighed. "What made you want to be a bounty hunter?"

Jaz frowned. "That is irrelevant."

"I'm just wondering, is all," Xander said. "None of this really makes any sense. I guess—maybe I'm trying to figure out why you all are helping us."

"We want to stop Knightshade," Jaz said. "That's all you really need to know."

"I see."

"Get some rest. We'll reach Kepler at nineteen hundred, and then you're Kale's problem."

"Nineteen?" Xander asked.

"Seven o'clock." Jaz backed out of the room, and the door shut behind her.

178

CHAPTER 14

Kale reminded her of an ill-humored stork, his hands shoved in his pockets and shoulders bunched up around his neck, head bent forward and his long legs strangely graceful in their awkwardness. Occasionally, the slight breeze blew the sound of his grumbling back to her. It was mostly profane.

Xander glanced at her reflection in a window. She looked like she'd been rolling around in a garbage dump. Between the messy hair and bruises, no wonder people stared. Evy didn't look much better, but her limp didn't garner much sympathy.

What? They didn't dumpster dive on this moon?

Dumpster dive. Xander suspected no one would know that term. She needed to start keeping an index of words no one knew.

"Any of these will do." Kale stopped. He jerked his head toward a line of vendor booths that sold clothing. "Just don't take forever."

Evy passed him. Xander followed, and Kale leaned on the side of a nearby building, dropping his gaze and folding his arms across his chest.

He had no interest in being there. Captain McLeod had probably sent him as punishment.

"Xander."

Evy frowned at her from a few paces ahead. With a reddening face, Xander tore her eyes off Kale and hurried after Evy. They stopped at the first booth and sorted through the clothing on display.

Xander decided quickly on a pair of pants and a t-shirt. Evy chose a pair of slacks and a blouse. Evy gathered the clothing and handed it to the vendor who gestured for her to place her thumb on a scanner.

As Evy stretched out her hand, Xander noted a woven bracelet around her right wrist. Xander didn't remember seeing it before. It didn't look familiar, but maybe she'd missed it. She didn't make a point of staring at peoples' wrists.

Evy didn't often accessorize. She wore nice clothing, matching suits and shoes. Sometimes earrings. On occasion, Evy had been known to wear a necklace. She never wore watches, since she always had her datapad nearby equipped with a clock app. The strange woven bracelet looked homemade, braided of coarse colorful threads. On someone like Evy, its homespun quality seemed incongruous.

The cashier completed the transaction and handed Evy a receipt, which she folded neatly and tucked in her back pocket. She noticed Xander's stare.

"Xander, what's wrong?"

Before Xander could reply, Kale called out, "Are you finished?"

Evy's face darkened. "Quite."

Kale whirled on his heel and started back toward the landing zone. Evy fell into step behind him and held Xander close to her side.

"Obstinate, bull-headed pig," Evy grumbled.

Relieved to hear some of the neuro-therapist's spunk had returned, Xander couldn't stop a giggle. "What do you really think, Evy?"

NAMELESS

Evy scoffed. "Just telling the truth, Xander."

Xander stepped double fast to keep up with both Evy and Kale's longer legs. Kale outdistanced them with ease and had to stop before they reached the landing zone and wait for them to catch up. He didn't seem very happy about it either, but Xander didn't really care.

"Can you two be any slower?"

"Evy's still hurt." Xander shifted her bag of clothes to her left hand when she felt the urge to hit him coming on. "And if you had any brains, you'd noticed that you're a lot taller than I am. So I have to walk twice as fast to keep up with you."

"Missed the part where that's my problem."

"Not your problem," Xander said. "It's mine. But you aren't helping any."

"So I should drag my feet? Is that it?"

"Do you always misinterpret everything people say?"

"Do you always answer a question with another question?"

Xander stopped walking. "Do I?"

Kale paused too and looked back at her. "I—don't know."

Not the response she expected. He was actually thinking about it? Had he been paying enough attention that he could think about it?

"You don't have to answer that." Xander grimaced and clutched both handles of her clothing sack.

Slowly, like a blade of grass trying to poke through a layer of snow, a smile started to curve Kale's lips. A smile? He was handsome enough glaring like a startled grizzly bear, so what would a smile look like? A grin? A laugh?

Her stomach tightened in anticipation. Before his smile fully formed, it faded with a sharp glance to a distant point behind her.

181

She turned to look, but he seized her shoulder and shoved her in front of him. "Go back to the ship."

"What are you—"

"Well, good afternoon, Mr. Sullivan!"

Xander and Evy froze as a barrel-chested police officer sporting a nightstick and a bottle of whiskey (Himalian, by the looks of it) swaggered toward them with a red face and a crooked hat.

Kale took a slow breath and turned to the man with a grin that showed too many teeth to be genuine. "Baker."

"Still bringing heads in?"

Kale pushed Xander toward the ship, and she nearly fell. Kale covered her stumble by blocking her from the officer's view.

"We sure are. That's where we're headed now."

The officer, Baker, narrowed his eyes and stared at Evy. "This don't look like one of your ladies. You picking up passengers now?"

"You could say that."

"I could say that?" Baker drawled and let out a sharp, raspy laugh. "Matt, I didn't think McLeod liked whores much."

Xander leaned around Kale's back, her face hot with anger. "We're not prostitutes."

Baker took a step back when his bleary eyes made contact with hers.

Xander heard Kale's jaw snap shut. "Aren't you on patrol, Baker?"

"Why—yes, I am."

"You supposed to be wasted when you're on patrol?"

Baker shuffled his feet and nearly fell over. "No."

"Well then—you go sober up, and we'll be on our way."

Baker smirked. "Trying to get rid of me, huh, Matt?"

"You could say that."

"I could, huh? Huh." The man shrugged. "Just drop by more often. We don't get a lot of business anymore, and our numbers are down. More heads you folks drop off here, better we get in with the main branch."

"I'll pass that on to McLeod."

Baker chuckled. "You're a swell guy, Sullivan. A swell guy." He waved at Evy. "Nice to meet you, ladies."

He sauntered down the street, but Kale didn't move until he was certain the man was gone. Kale seized them both by the arms and hauled them toward the *Prodigal*.

"What on earth was that about?" Evy spat. "Mr. Sullivan? Who is that?"

"Just shut up."

Xander planted her foot and jerked out of Kale's hold. He halted in surprise and glared back at her. "So are you Kale? Or are you Matt?"

His face was fierce. "Both. Get back to the ship."

"But—"

"No buts." He grabbed both of them again and shoved them. "Get on board now."

Evy made an irritated noise. She stomped up the loading ramp and headed for their room. Xander stood in the cargo bay and watched Kale.

Why does he have two names? Why do the people on the ship call him Kale when that man knew him as Matt? Xander frowned. *Is one an alias? And if he has an alias, does that mean he's undercover?*

Two names. What did that mean? What was he hiding? Whatever it was, the whole crew had to be in on it.

His long, slender fingers danced across the controls to raise the ramp.

He couldn't be both people. She wanted to trust him. He'd saved her. He'd saved Evy. Even if he'd been a jerk to them afterward, he'd still chosen to rescue them. But secrets had a price. Were Kale's secrets worth Evy's safety?

"So you have two names?" Xander slid closer to him.

"Why are you still going on about that? It's none of your business."

"Maybe I'm curious."

"Forget it."

He had to be the most frustrating man in the universe.

"I just want to know."

"I said forget it."

"But that man called you—"

"I know what he called me."

"But you—"

Kale leaned down and glared into her eyes. "What part of this not concerning you are you having trouble with?"

"I just want—"

"No."

"Won't—"

"No."

"But—"

"No!"

Xander flinched at the edge in his voice. His eyes sparkled angrily. She'd seen him shoot people, but would he hit someone? Would he hit her if she pushed too far?

Had she ever known anyone with eyes like that? Deep, stunning blue. Like blue-eyed grass.

Blue-eyed grass? Yes. A wildflower with slender petals the same dazzling color as Kale's eyes. Why did she remember blue-eyed grass? Where had she seen a flower like that before?

Blue-eyed grass belonged in that fantasy world with hand sanitizer and sweet tea, the world she only glimpsed in cherished fragments from her broken memory.

"What are you looking at?" His furious tone dragged her out of her reverie.

She blinked. Had she been staring at him?

She flushed. She had.

Would he understand? Was there any possibility that he might know what it was like to live in one world and remember bits and pieces from a different one that nobody else had heard of?

His fists clenched, and his mouth twisted downward in a scowl.

Maybe it wasn't worth finding out.

Yet.

Xander forced her shoulders to relax and lifted her chin. "Fine."

She brushed past him and followed after Evy, her heart thumping in her chest. She tried to ignore it and walk normally, even though his eyes stared daggers at her back.

Kale Ravenwood—or Matt Sullivan—or whoever he was—was an obstinate, bull-headed pig, in spite of the fact that he did have very pretty eyes.

Xander escaped the burn of Kale's eyes and walked right into the glare of Vix's. Vix leaned on one of the exposed bulkheads, smoking a cigarette, eyes narrowed and scarlet lips scowling. The cigarette flared red at its end as she dragged on it and blew smoke out her nostrils.

"Shopping's a bitch, huh?" Vix snarled. "Feel better now?"

Xander opened her mouth and closed it with a snap. She could tear that horrible woman up one side and down the other, but she wasn't worth it. Vix had no cause to be angry at her, so there was no point in giving her one.

Xander hadn't asked to be rescued, hadn't forced Captain McLeod to help them, hadn't wanted them to stop for new clothing.

Vix was just a miserable person; that was the best explanation.

CHAPTER 15

Xander half-jogged down the corridor to the passenger berth designated for her and Evy. Xander reached the door and paused as it slid open.

"Evy?"

"Come in, dear."

Xander stepped inside and spotted Evy sitting on the side of her cot. Her stack of clothing lay beside her, still folded.

"Are you all right?" Xander hovered in the doorway, unsure whether she should enter or not.

"Fine, dear."

She was lying.

Xander moved to her own cot, across from Evy's, and set her clothing down as she sat beside it. "What are you thinking about?"

"Nothing of consequence, dear."

Xander searched Evy's face. "Evy, why don't you like bounty hunters?"

"Do you like bounty hunters, Xander?"

Lou from Callisto was a bounty hunter. He would have raped her on the table in the middle of the Oasis. He was the only other bounty hunter she'd ever met.

"I've only known one," she admitted.

"Did you like him?"

"No." Xander shivered. "But—maybe he was an exception."

"Meaning?"

"Maybe all bounty hunters aren't like him."

Evy leaned back against the wall and folded her hands in her lap. "My father was a pilot. A shipper. He ran a route between NUSaxony and NUGaul, and he ran into bounty hunters often." She laced her fingers together. "He didn't have a high opinion of them. So perhaps his opinion wore off on me."

With her arms stretched out, Xander could see the bracelet around Evy's wrist again.

"Evy?"

The blond neuro-therapist looked up.

"Have you always had that bracelet on?"

Evy glanced down at her wrist. "Yes, I have. Just now noticed it, have you?"

"Yeah. It's pretty. I like it."

"Helga made it for me."

Xander winced. "Oh." She looked down. "Evy—I'm sorry."

Evy didn't say anything. Xander wished she would. Evy stared blankly at the floor, fingering the homespun bracelet on her wrist.

On the *Anastasia*, Dr. Zahn had been frank about her choice in sexual partners. It wasn't unusual, but it made Xander uncomfortable.

"Helga and I met at University," Evy said. "We were together for many years."

Xander swallowed. "Were?"

"We separated. After medical school. We decided we would do better apart." Evy turned the woven bracelet around her wrist. "We kept in touch, of course, but it was never quite the same."

"Why did you separate?"

Evy leaned back against the wall. "I don't think that's

something that you need to know, dear."

Xander flushed. "I'm sorry. I was just—I just—I don't know. I've known you for all these months, Evy, and I feel like I don't know you at all. Not really."

Evy didn't meet her eyes. "No matter how you look at it, darling, you're my patient. That's the way it's supposed to be." She sat up. "Captain McLeod said there's a shower down the hall. It's stocked with soap. You should go first. You'll feel far better afterward, I'm certain."

"You need a shower too, don't you?"

"I'll need to bandage my leg," Evy said, "or have Scraps do it. Either way, it will take me longer. You should go first."

Xander knew a dismissal when she heard it. If it were anyone else on any other day, she might have been offended. But not with Evy. Not after what they'd been through.

Xander gathered her clothes and hoped she hadn't dug too deeply.

She found the shower without much difficulty. At least, she thought it was a shower. She hauled the heavy metal door open and switched on the single illuminator, which provided enough dim light to make her wish she didn't need a shower. But one sniff of her hair and she leapt into the cramped antechamper and threw herself against the door to close it.

It had probably been a storage closet in another life. As it stood, Xander doubted it even produced water. Maybe engine oil from the state of the floor.

She'd probably smell worse afterward, but at least she wouldn't smell like garbage.

Xander dumped her new clothes on the stool in the corner and pulled back the dark vinyl curtain that separated the

189

antechamber from the shower itself.

She could stand up, but did Kale shower in a room this cramped? Someone that tall wouldn't fit.

Not that she needed to be thinking about Kale in the shower. The image her mind conjured came unbidden and wouldn't leave.

"Stupid Kale. Stupid me." She pressed the heels of her hands into her eyes and stripped off her clothes, leaving them in a pile on the oily floor.

The dimness in the antechamber couldn't hide the lines of bruising that encircled her arms and legs and ribs and waist. At first, she'd thought it dirt, but rubbing at them hurt. Her skin still glowed red and burned in places too.

She pulled the curtain back and stepped into the shower. The bulkhead sapped the warmth from her bare feet. The controls were standard—a button to begin the flow of water, one to stop. No temperature gauges since the system regulated the flow automatically. She shut the curtain and pressed the first button.

Streams of water knifed into her like a million icicles, and she squealed like a girl. She couldn't help it. The sound just escaped her throat while she tried to dodge the icy bullets flying at her garbage-scented head.

Stupid bounty hunters. Stupid bounty hunter ships.

Did she need to be clean? Maybe if she stunk of rotten eggs people would leave her alone. She flattened herself against the frigid bulkhead.

"Stop it. Stop being a wuss. You can do this." She whimpered. "It'll be worth it. You'll smell like stale ship water instead of bad chicken."

Grimacing, she launched into the stream with a choked gurgle.

Skip burning buildings down with fire. Drown them in water this temperature and they would collapse out of self-preservation. The water didn't even sooth her burns. It was just too cold.

She stayed in long enough to get her hair thoroughly wet and stepped out to obtain the soap from the dispenser on the shower wall. The soap foamed in the frizzyness of her hair, smelling like an awkward combination of flowers and cooking oil. Still better than bad chicken.

"Okay. Okay. Chin up." She bounced from bare foot to bare foot on the bulkhead. "Wash. Get the soap out. That's easy. And fast." She moaned. "Oh, God, let it be fast."

The antechamber door banged.

Xander stopped moving. She didn't breathe. Had she imagined it? The shower door locked, but the antechamber didn't. Did someone else want the shower?

"Hello?" Her shivering voice echoed like she spoke in a tin can.

No one answered.

Was someone waiting for her on the opposite side of the curtain? What if the worst had happened? What if the *Prodigal* had been attacked by the Seekers? What if a NUChungqwo operative lurked on the other side of that curtain? What if Captain McLeod had second thoughts about letting non-crew members use the shower facilities? He was a bounty hunter; who knew what he would do? Drag her out by her hair?

Had she locked the door?

Xander shut her eyes. Her imagination didn't need to be calling the shots, not while she still didn't know her own name.

Stop worrying. Finish your shower.

And if someone interrupted her, she'd splash them with frigid water. After that they'd freeze on the spot and drop dead and would never bother anyone again.

Maybe that was a slight exaggeration. But having a defense plan helped, even if it were lame.

She took a deep breath and leaned into the water, barely stifling the whine of discomfort from the freezing water. She rinsed all the soap out of her hair and stepped out of the stream, shutting the shower off.

She wrung her hair out as best she could, straining her ears for any movement on the other side of the shower door. Whatever she'd heard didn't return. She only heard the vague rumble of the ship's engines.

The shower drained itself, and she pressed the towel dispenser, which unrolled a full body length of soft disposable fabric. She wrapped it around her hair and opened the shower door to peek outside.

At least no one was standing on her side of the curtain.

She shut the shower door and reached for her underwear. She froze in mid-reach. The clothes she left on the stool were gone.

Don't panic. Don't freak. She took a breath. *You probably just didn't put them where you thought you did.*

She moved to pull the curtain back and paused. She unwrapped her hair and folded the towel around her body instead, leaving her frizzy mass of orange hair to fall wildly to her shoulders.

Xander pulled the curtain back.

No one. No one there. The door shut, her clothes gone, even the dirty ones.

Don't panic.

She stepped back and looked on either side of the wall seat. Not on the seat. Not on the floor. Not in the shower. Not anywhere.

The inevitable panic caught up with her.

Okay. My room isn't far from the shower. Horror gripped her. *I'll just get to my room. Evy will be there, and she'll help.*

Xander secured the towel. It gapped at her waist and revealed far too much of her legs for comfort, but what alternative did she have? Stay in the shower? Wander the corridors naked? No, the towel would do, until she found out who'd taken her clothes. Then she'd need a serving tray.

She pushed the antechamber door open and peered into the corridor beyond, looking both ways multiple times until satisfied no one crouched in the shadows. She started toward the room, but she hesitated. Something lay in a dark pile on the floor at the end of the corridor.

Xander checked the shadows again and approached the darkened object. She reached it, and her stomach flip-flopped. Her pants.

She knelt and gripped the waistband in her fingers. They were her pants all right, but how had they gotten in the hallway?

The hallway forked in two directions, one to the right and the other to the left. Halfway down the left branching hallway, she spied something green on the floor panels. She walked toward the object on the floor.

Was that her shirt? It couldn't be.

Yes, it was.

Her shirt. First the pants Evy had purchased for her on NUSaxony, then the shirt from Kepler.

Someone took my clothes. But why? And who?

She let her shoulders slump as she stood in the hall wearing only the towel. A nightmare. Couldn't she wake up? It wasn't enough to lose her memory and be chased across the solar system by a psychotic assassin. She had to end up on the pirate ship that time forgot with a clothes snatcher too?

She growled under her breath.

Giving up was easy. But then she'd have to explain why her clothes were scattered all over the ship. And she didn't want them to think she was a prostitute.

Yeah. Great job on that score.

Reluctantly, Xander peered through the darkness of the corridor and spotted another pile of clothes at the end of the hall. Clutching the clothes to her chest, she half-ran toward it. Her new pants, the ones Evy had just purchased for her on Kepler.

Just move. Go. Fast. Get the rest of it before anyone sees you.

She followed the hallway until she found the garbage-stained blouse Evy had bought her on NUSaxony. Her faced burned and not from the fires of the attack on NUSaxony. She ran down a connecting corridor and snatched her bra off the floor panels. She wrapped it in her shirt and looked down the hall for the last item of clothing, the one piece she hadn't found yet.

Whoever did this had a sick sense of humor.

Surely Vix and Jaz didn't wear the same kind of underwear. They'd know it wasn't theirs.

Xander took a deep breath and hurried to grab her panties from the floor, but just as she drew within arm's reach, a white puffball darted between her legs, yapping and barking.

A Pomeranian? On a spaceship?

Xander tried to ignore the dog and reached for her panties. No good. The dog wanted to play and snatched them up with a growl.

Could it get any worse? Could her face turn redder?

"Here, doggy!" She held out her hand. "Give it back, now.

Good doggy. What are you doing on a spaceship anyway, huh?"

She reached out to take them back, and the dog uttered a sharp bark and turned three quick circles, yapping.

"Shh, someone's going to hear you."

Xander lunged for the panties, and the dog jumped out of the way. Crouching, Xander tried again and managed to seize the waistband of the underwear. Her towel had ripped itself, but she was committed now. She wasn't going to let go until the dog did.

Playing tug-of-war with the only pair of underwear she owned probably wasn't a good idea, but what choice did she have?

The panties began to rip, and she shrieked in dismay. The dog lost interest and released the panties, yipping pleasantly before trotting away.

Xander sat on the floor for a moment and mourned her ripped underwear. What had she done to deserve this? She examined the undergarment; the rip wasn't too bad. If she could get a needle and thread, she could probably fix it herself. But now they were covered in dog drool.

Did bounty hunters have washing machines?

She clambered to her feet and struggled to keep the towel wrapped around her body. It had mostly come undone in the scuffle with the dog. She tucked it back around herself before picking up her bundle of clothing. As she stood, she came face to face with Kale, standing in the doorway of his room.

The crew berth. Kale had seen her little encounter with the bounty hunter Pomeranian.

Crap. Oh, crap.

She stared at him. He stared back, face unreadable.

What did she say? Could she even begin to explain? She couldn't very well claim it wasn't what it looked like because it had probably looked like a tug-of-war with a Pomeranian with a pair of panties. No use denying it.

She couldn't even think of a convincing lie.

No good jokes. Not even a bad joke.

"What the hell are you doing?" Kale leaned out of the doorway with his hands braced on the frame, looming over her like a thunderhead.

What was she doing? Mortified, humiliated, naked staring. That's what she was doing.

Definitely attractive.

At least she didn't smell like rotten chicken.

"Are you mute now?"

"No."

"Then answer the friggin' question."

"I was in the shower." *Stupid! Stupid! Just stop talking and run!*

"Obviously."

"Someone took my clothes." Why did she need to explain this to him? It was none of his business.

"What?" His face slackened, mouth open.

"My clothes—they disappeared. I got out and saw them and went to pick them up, and the dog—and I tried to get them back—and—"

Kale folded his arms across his chest and gazed down at her. It was the stance of a parent about to lecture an errant child, and it set every rebellious instinct flaring.

"I'm going to say this once, kid, so you'll know." He spoke carefully. Condescendingly. "I don't like pushy women."

She had anticipated mocking. Cruel jokes. Maybe even crude innuendos. But— "What?"

"It's not an attractive quality, not even in a whore."

She clamped her jaw shut. "I'm *not* a whore."

"Well, you're doing a fine job convincing me—standing on my doorstep in a towel and waving your panties around for the world to see."

Her face flamed so hot it stung. She couldn't even find the words to snap back at him.

Does he think I did this on purpose?

His expression told her he did. How could he think something like that? But then, what did he know about her? Only that she said she had no memory; that didn't make it true. He had no more reason to trust her than she had to trust him.

He turned. "Get the hell away from me. And stop making so much damn noise."

The door slid shut. Xander trembled in shame.

Somehow, she managed to stem the mortified tears building up inside. She walked down the hallway. She walked all the way to her room. She prepared herself to explain the entire story to Evy and sagged in relief at the empty room.

An empty room was better.

She changed into the clean clothes. She would ask Evy what to do about her underwear later. Right now, she just wanted to sleep. She wanted to shut her eyes and pretend she didn't exist, because if she didn't exist she wouldn't have to talk to Kale again. And nothing would have made her happier.

CHAPTER 16

The ship lurched. Her body bounced off the cabin wall and crashed onto the floor. She grabbed the side of the cot and pulled herself up, desperate for anything to keep herself steady. The universe reeled out of control—or maybe it was only the ship. She couldn't tell.

It stopped. She stumbled to her feet and ran for the door.

It slid open.

The command deck was aflame. Her father was bent over the computer at the center of the bridge, his brown eyes filled with some emotion between joy and terror.

"David," he cried. "Get her back in her room."

David appeared beside her, blond hair dark in the shadows. He grabbed her arm and forced her back into the room.

"David, stop!"

She lunged to get out, but he shoved her back in.

"Don't argue."

The gears in the wall turned and whirred.

"You have to stay here."

The door was sliding shut. She could only see half his face.

"David!" she cried.

"You'll be all right."

The door shut and sealed, and the ship rocked—

Xander's eyes opened, and she bolted upright in her bunk. Gasping, trembling, sweating. Why? Her head throbbed.

Evy slept across from her.

They were on the *Prodigal*. With the bounty hunters.

The same dream again. What did it mean? Who was David? And had that man really been her father? That's what her mind had told her, but did her mind really know what was real and what wasn't? Or was it just making things up?

Her head spun, her eyes pulsing in her skull.

Genesis.

The term flashed in her mind unbidden.

NUJenesis like the Book of Genesis. Her heart pounded. *What does it mean? Why is it important?*

She leaned back against the bed frame and watched Evy sleep. The woman's face was pale in the dimmed illuminators, streaks of obvious tears on her face.

Lamentations.

Xander froze. Lamentations. They were songs, weren't they? Sad songs about Israel turning away from God?

Her head gave a painful throb.

Israel? God? What?

She swung her legs out and set her feet on the cold floor tiles.

Genesis and Lamentations. They're books. She gripped the firm mattress. *Books in the Bible.* She held her breath, feeling pieces of her mind snapping into place without her even trying to force them there.

"Genesis," Xander whispered. "Exodus, Leviticus, Numbers, Deuteronomy—the Pentateuch."

Like a flood gate had been opened, the words appeared in her mind as though they had never left. Her head spun. The books of the

Bible, their familiar names rang true off her tongue like she had never forgotten them in the first place. She didn't stop until she had whispered all sixty-six to the silence, Genesis through the Revelation.

Verses she had memorized as a child rushed back to her. She clutched her head with rigid fingers, trembling in the darkness.

A Christian.

She was a Christian.

How could I have forgotten?

The passenger berth swam in front of her eyes. She was a Christian, but she hadn't lived like one. She'd had worked in a bar, befriended a gay man and a prostitute—and two lesbians now—and stayed silent.

But I didn't know! I couldn't remember. Her fingernails dug into the skin of her palms. *I didn't know it was wrong because I didn't know who I was.*

And no one else did either. How did that make sense? No one knew what a Christian was? She'd forgotten, but she had a reason. What about everyone else? Had the universe forgotten too? Could Christianity be dismissed as easily as hand sanitizer?

She managed a shallow breath. Then, another. She stemmed the panic rushing over her in waves and clenched her eyes shut.

"I didn't know who I was. So, who am I?"

She waited, straining her mind, desperately trying to remember something else. Nothing came. She remembered the Bible. She remembered her religion.

But who was she?

She leaned her head back one more time and closed her eyes, trying to find the place of discovery from which she had surfaced. She could hear all the same things, smell all the same scents, feel all the same sensations as before, but she couldn't remember.

Nothing would come, as though the door was shut and locked again and refused to open merely to spite her.

Her shoulders drooped. "I'm never going to remember my name."

A light groan sounded across from her, and Evy rolled over, her eyes flickering. Xander froze in her blue gaze.

"Xander?"

Xander didn't answer.

"Are you all right?"

"Yeah."

Evy sat up on her elbows. "Darling, did you remember something?"

Xander stared at her, uncertain. Evy was a lesbian. So she certainly wouldn't want anything to do with the Bible. For that matter, no one would want anything to do with it.

"Sort of," Xander said. "I remembered—Evy, have you ever heard of the Bible?"

There. She'd asked.

Evy frowned. "The Bible?" She thought for a moment. "No. No, darling, I haven't. Is that something you heard about on the *Anastasia*? Or on Callisto?"

Impossible. Evy loved literature, and even secular scholars recognized the Bible as ancient literature. How could she not know about the Bible?

Xander swallowed hard. "No. It's—uh—it's just something I remember reading."

"It's a book? What is it about?"

Xander shrugged, face burning. "Just—stuff. God. And faith."

Evy's face took on an expression Xander didn't like. "God?" she repeated. "And faith?"

"Yeah."

"Xander, that sounds like something out of the Sanctum."

Horror shook her. The Sanctum? Wasn't that where that horrible Mr. Clayton from the Oasis was from? Wasn't that the place Sylphie had told her about?

No, Evy had to be wrong. How could the Sanctum have anything to do with the Bible?

"I don't know," Xander said. She looked away, breathing hard. "I'm—I have to go."

"Where?"

"Just for a walk. I'm fine."

Evy called out to her as she hurried through the automated sliding door and into the corridor beyond, but she didn't turn back.

If the Sanctum talks about the Bible, and if the only people who know about the Bible are from the Sanctum, doesn't that make it the only place I could be from?

She didn't want to be from the Sanctum.

She didn't want anything to do with anyone like Mr. Clayton. How could someone with knowledge of the Bible go to a place like Callisto of their own free will? Do business—if one could call it that—with someone like Sylphie?

None of it made sense.

Remembering was supposed to help, not make it more confusing.

She leaned against the wall in the corridor, eyes closed, trying to calm down.

God, help me.

She had always talked to God like He stood beside her.

Someone had taught her that, told her that's what God did. She couldn't remember who.

Help me be calm. I remember You now, so I'll start doing this right. So I'm going to trust that You'll work everything out now that I remember You.

She stared at the floor.

Nothing was different. Her heart raced. Her brain whirled.

Maybe she hadn't remembered everything yet. Not that she remembered God ever speaking directly to her, but she had a vague memory of feeling at peace after talking to Him.

Peace was the one thing she didn't feel.

She'd accepted employment from a drug dealer. She'd served alcohol to addicts. She'd stood by and done nothing while children ate from garbage cans and women sold themselves for money.

How could that be Christian? So what if she couldn't remember how she was supposed to live? Sure, she'd been different—different enough to draw attention but not enough to make a difference.

Cedric betrayed her. Sylphie died alone, just like Dr. Zahn. And she hadn't even offered Evy comfort. She'd had the chance just now. But what had she done? Run away.

Some shining light.

Sleep would be impossible. Wandering seemed to be the best option. Maybe the activity would remind her frazzled brain that she did need to sleep. But she vowed to steer away from the crew berth. She didn't want to run into Kale again.

Leaning against the wall, she felt the loud, steady drone of the engines, singing softly in the dark, warming the cold shadows. Xander moved toward the sound, not thinking, needing to not think anymore.

Remembering wasn't supposed to be like this. It should have been happy. Instead, she wanted to cry.

She followed the engine song through the galley, past two doors emblazoned with red paint. Escape pods. In theory, they were a good idea, but if the pods functioned like the rest of the ship, it might be safer to stay on board.

Xander continued until her ear drums resonated with the thrumming sound. Eventually, the hallway emptied into a cavernous chamber with an enormous rotating pillar of pulsing radiation, contained by a superglass chamber at its heart. The luminous pillar connected to a huge machine on both sides and droned loud enough to rattle her lungs.

A sharp bark jolted her out of her reverie, and she looked down.

The dog!

The white Pomeranian grinned up at her with its tiny tongue hanging from its tiny mouth. The dog barked at her, almost vibrating in place, pouncing and bouncing and turning in circles as though it were happy to see her.

She certainly wasn't happy to see it. Good thing she left her underwear in the passenger berth. Of course, she wouldn't admit the fact that she wasn't wearing it to anyone but herself.

"I don't think I'm the kind of person who kicks cute little dogs," she said, "but for you I might make an exception."

"Newt!" bellowed a deep voice from inside the engine chamber. "Where did you go, you silly puppy?"

The dog barked a few times, and a giant appeared from behind the luminous pillar. His jolly blue eyes sparkled, deep set in a red face topped with white-blond hair.

"What is here, *ja*? A little girl!" He stopped beside her, and

Xander nearly toppled backward trying to see his face. "You must be the Xander-girl, *ja?*" The man set gargantuan hands on hips spanning a distance more than twice her shoulder width, and he grinned down so happily Xander couldn't help but smile in return.

"Uh, yeah." Looking into the huge man's happy face made her happy too.

He held out a massive hand, and Xander took it. His colossal fingers dwarfed her hand. "Claude is the name of me. Happy meeting you. Welcome to *Prodigal* engine room." He laughed.

Xander laughed with him. "Thanks."

How did he do that? She didn't want to laugh. She wanted to cry. Didn't she?

The dog jumped up and down and barked. Claude bent over and snatched the dog up, handing her toward Xander. "Ach! Dog, you getting very fat! Scraps feed you too much."

The Pomeranian licked its nose and barked at her.

"Little girl, she like you." Claude held the Pomeranian out to Xander.

Xander scowled. "Yeah, I figured that out."

"Little girl not like doggies?"

"No. I like dogs just fine. But that one has issues."

"Aw!" Claude bounced the dog on his arm. "All doggies have issues. All peoples have issues." He held out the dog and dropped her in Xander's arms. "That's why we make friends."

Xander held the dog away as it licked her face.

"Ah, she like you."

"How can you tell?"

"Has she chewed your shoes?"

Xander twitched. "No. She didn't chew on my shoes."

Dumb dog got a mouthful of something else.

"Then she like you." Claude laughed again. "She chew Vix's shoes all the time. Doesn't like her. Not at all."

Good grief, so what does chewing on my underwear mean? BFF?

Xander made a mental note to keep her shoes and any other clothing item of importance out of the dog's reach. "What's her name?"

"Newt." Claude puffed up like a parent at graduation.

"Newt?" What a ridiculous name for a dog! "Why Newt?"

Claude pressed a huge finger against the deep cleft of his chin. "Don't know."

"Claude, where the hell's my wrench?" The harsh voice echoed from deeper inside the engine chamber.

"Ach, I forgot. Marty need wrench," Claude said. "Marty, come meet the little girl."

"Little girl?"

A hatch opened on the far side of the engine room, and a man thrust out his head. A pair of smudged orange goggles hid his eyes, and his coveralls dripped with engine oil and grease.

"Don't care about no girl." He lifted himself out of the small maintenance tunnel and started toward Claude and Xander. "I want my wrench."

"Ah, be friendly, Marty." Claude hammered a sledge-sized fist against the engineer's back and nearly knocked the small man over. "She nice little girl."

Marty looked Xander up and down and glared at Claude. "Uh-huh." He held out his hand. "Wrench."

Claude reached for a shelf beside the doorway and pulled off a huge wrench covered in grease and oil. He handed it to Marty, who grunted as he took it.

Marty lugged the wrench back to his maintenance tunnel and disappeared inside.

"I go help him." Claude's white teeth shone in the light from the hyperdrive engine. "He thinks he do so much. But he is just a little man."

She held the dog out to Claude, who shook his head. "You keep Newt. She like you!"

The dog yapped, and Xander scowled. "Right. Thanks."

Claude waved and jogged toward the maintenance tunnel, shoving his head inside. "Marty."

"Ow! Don't bother me, you stupid—ow! Dropped that stupid wrench on my—oh, that smarts!"

Xander regarded Newt with an arched eyebrow. The dog showed all its teeth with its tongue lolling out. A happy expression maybe? Xander didn't trust it.

"You like me, huh?"

The dog licked her face again.

"Bleck. Okay." Xander held the dog out, looking into her face. "You stay away from my underwear, and we'll call a truce. Deal?"

The dog barked.

"Deal." Xander tucked the dog into her arm and heading for the corridor. "I think I just made a deal with a dog. I really must be out of my mind."

Xander wandered out of the engine room and through the corridors of the *Prodigal*. The hallways boasted bare bulkheads with only sheets of metal as the floor panels. Small portholes lined the narrow corridors, and the illuminators didn't do much to illuminate anything.

It seemed a small ship for a crew so large.

Large in more way than one. How a giant like Claude managed to even walk around inside a ship as dinky as the *Prodigal* astonished her. And Kale had to bang his head on every other bulkhead.

Did Captain McLeod seriously have a crew of nine on board this tiny ship? No wonder they seemed grouchy all the time. Nobody had enough space.

Xander stopped in the corridor as Newt uttered something between a whine and a growl.

"What?" Xander asked. "See another pair of panties to munch on?"

Xander noticed a line of doors on both sides of the corridor. The hallway suddenly looked disturbingly familiar.

The crew berth. How had she ended up back in the crew berth?

Newt growled in her arms. Xander tried to run, but the door beside her slid open before she could escape. And Vix stepped into the corridor.

Vix. Black-haired harpy woman. But not as bad as Kale. Kale would have been worse.

The woman stood and glared at Xander and Newt. Xander noted a lit cigarette in her right hand and an old beer can in her left. She bent over, took a drag on the cigarette, and blew smoke in the dog's face. Newt growled only louder.

"What are you doing?" Vix asked.

Xander coughed. "Just looking around."

"You've been to the engine room, I see," Vix gestured to the dog. She took Xander's arm and fingered a grease stain on the cuff of her sleeve.

"Yes." Xander pulled her arm away. "I'm—I guess—" What

NAMELESS

was she doing? Aimlessly wandering the ship? That wasn't suspicious at all. Telling her about the Bible was the last thing Xander intended to do, and Vix wouldn't understand the terrifying recurring nightmare.

Someone like Vix probably didn't even have scary dreams, and even if she did, she probably wasn't afraid of them.

Make something up. Xander held Newt close. *Who are you looking for? Who on this ship would you want to find if you were actually interested in talking to someone?* "Scraps."

"You're looking for Scraps?"

Xander hesitated. "Yeah. Yeah, I want to find Scraps."

"You hungry or something?"

"No."

Vix scoffed. "Didn't think you were a midnight snacker. You're too damned skinny." She drew on the cigarette again. "Did you try the galley?"

"It—it was dark."

"You afraid of the dark, kid?"

"No. It just—seemed too dark to go in there."

"Then turn on a light. Idiot."

Xander flushed and looked down. Maybe she *was* hungry. If she could eat, maybe she could sleep. Sleep always helped.

"Yeah," she mumbled. "Idiot. That's me."

Vix sneered and tucked the cigarette between her lips. She brushed past Xander and started down the corridor. Xander watched her. Vix stopped after a few steps.

"Well, come on, kid. Don't stand there looking stupid."

"Where are you going?"

"To the galley?" Vix blew out more smoke. "Damn. You really must have memory problems."

209

Xander lifted her chin and followed. Vix kept walking, and Xander stayed on her heels.

"Why are you really wandering around, kid?"

Xander broke stride. "What do you mean?"

"You're a shitty liar."

Xander scratched Newt's head. "Why do you care?"

"I don't. But if you're planning on planting a bomb and blowing the damn ship to hell, I want to know about it so I can get to the escape pods first."

Xander grimaced. She could lie, but what point would it serve?

Just tell the truth, even if it kills you. "I had a bad dream."

Vix stopped and looked over her shoulder at her. "Are you serious?"

Xander couldn't meet her eyes.

"You had a bad dream? What are you? Six?"

"I don't know how old I am."

"You're old enough to not piss yourself when you're scared of the dark."

Xander said nothing.

"Damn, kid. You got issues."

Vix shook her head and continued on. Xander followed in silence.

As they walked together, Xander watched in fascination as Vix tapped the ashes of her cigarette into the beer can.

"Why are you doing that?" Xander asked.

"Talon doesn't want ashes on his boat."

"Talon doesn't mind the smoke?"

"Slagging engine smokes enough for all of us."

They walked in silence for a few minutes.

NAMELESS

"Miss Vix?"

"Just Vix, kid."

"Okay. Vix. How long have you been here?"

Vix drew on her cigarette again. "About three years. Why?"

"Just wondering. Bounty hunting's dangerous, isn't it?"

"Life's dangerous, kid." She puffed a cloud of smoke out of her nostrils. "I used to work at a casino in the outer rim. Jaz happened to be there when a fight broke out. I bashed some freeloader's face in, and she thought I might make a good partner. So she signed me up." Vix curled her lip. "I think she was tired of Kale."

"Kale?"

"Yeah." Vix's tone turned cold. "Talon's poster child bounty hunter. Brings in his fair share of heads and more than his fair share of bills."

"You don't like him?"

"What's to like, kid?"

Xander held Newt tighter and stepped twice as fast to keep up with Vix's long-legged strides. "Are you friends with Jaz?"

"What?"

"Since you're partners, I just kind of assumed you were friends."

Vix faced her and dragged deeply on the cigarette. "Bounty hunters don't have friends." She blew the smoke out her nose in a long stream. "We're not exactly the most popular breed in the system, if you didn't know."

"Yeah." Xander held Newt tighter. "I've heard that."

Vix traced her teeth with her tongue and tapped the cigarette on the beer can. "Jaz's always got my back. I always got hers. If you want to call that being friends, knock yourself out."

211

"What about Kale and Devon? They're friends, aren't they?"

Vix dropped what remained of the cigarette into the beer can. "It's a right-brain, left-brain deal, sweetheart." She pulled another cigarette out and jabbed it between her red lips. She lit it and blew smoke toward the ceiling.

"I see."

Vix started walking again. "I doubt it. You've never been on a ship like this before, have you?"

Xander scowled at the woman's back. "I don't know."

"Right, right. You don't know. Memory problems." Vix blew out another puff of smoke. "Well, you sure don't look like you have. You got any idea where you're from?"

"Why do you care?"

"I don't."

"So why are you asking?"

Vix glanced back at her and with a curled lip snarled, "Just wondering."

Vix was not a nice person.

"After all," Vix snorted, "it's not every day you run into somebody who's got no friggin' clue who they are. Figure I'd better ask you all the friggin' questions I can think of so you can jump start your damned brain and get the hell off my ship."

Xander squared her shoulders. "Why does Kale have two names?"

Again, the woman stopped with no warning, and Xander nearly collided with her. Vix turned on her.

"What the hell kind of question is that?"

"On Kepler, someone—called him Matt Sullivan. And I— was just—why he has got two names?"

"None of your friggin' business."

NAMELESS

"That's what he said."

"Then you should take his word, kid. Don't mess with Kale. Trust me."

"Trust you?"

"Yeah. He's not worth it."

"Look—"

"No, you look, you little bitch." Vix turned on her so sharply, Xander backed up against the bulkhead. Vix leaned into her. "Stay away from Kale. You got that?"

Newt growled, and Vix snapped her fingers in the dog's face.

"You got it, kid?" Vix held her burning cigarette in Xander's face.

"I have no intention of talking to him again, okay?"

Vix leaned back slightly. "Glad to hear it, sweetheart."

"But I want to know why he has two names."

"Then you're just going to have to live with the disappointment, little girl, because that's something nobody's going to tell you."

"Why won't any of you talk about this?" Xander shifted Newt to the other arm.

"Because it's none of your friggin' business!" Vix leaned down in Xander's face and blew a puff of smoke into her eyes. "What part of that aren't you getting? You're not staying with us, you little shit. We're going to get your damned ship for you, and then we're never going to see you again. So there's no friggin' reason why you need to know all this."

Maybe it was all the months of standing up to belligerent drunks on Callisto. Maybe it was the lack of sleep or the overload of stress. Xander didn't feel like backing down.

She clenched her teeth. "It was just a question."

213

"Fine. It was just a question." Vix blew smoke in Xander's face again. "That don't mean I got to answer it. You're just going to cause more trouble around here, and that's something we don't need." She straightened. "So—I've answered your little questions. And there." She pointed to a nearby doorway. "That's the galley. Go find Scraps. Get yourself a snack or whatever the hell you're looking for, and go back to your friggin' berth."

Vix pushed past her, and Xander nearly made it to the galley door when Vix stopped and shouted back at her. "And don't come looking for a babysitter when you wet yourself again."

Xander turned to say something rude, but Vix had vanished. Anger simmered in her chest. Newt growled in her arms.

Xander patted the dog on the head. "So that's why you don't like her."

Newt yapped.

"I don't blame you."

She faced the galley door, and it slid open. Xander saw the dingy yellow cabinets again and eyed one of the chairs at the table in the center of the room. In spite of how much she disliked the feel of the room, sitting down sounded like a good idea. She could sit in the darkness for a little while until she felt tired enough to sleep without dreaming.

She sat in the chair and let Newt down on the floor.

"Well, this is a surprise."

Xander looked up at the voice. Scraps smiled at her from the top step of the stairway.

"I wasn't expecting company. Good evening." He approached her. "Or, should I say good morning?"

"I don't know what time it is."

"It is very late. Or very early. Depending on how you think

about it." Scraps chuckled as he walked past her. "Trouble sleeping?"

Would he make fun of her like Vix had? "Bad dreams."

"I don't doubt it, little one."

Xander had known there was a reason she liked him.

"Are you hungry?"

She hadn't eaten dinner, but she hadn't really been interested at the time. Just the thought of food at the moment turned her stomach.

"No," she said. "I'm not."

"Did you eat dinner?"

"No."

"Well, I won't have that," he said. "Not in my kitchen."

"If I eat, I might throw up."

"If you don't eat, you will be sick. That is against the rules of my kitchen." He smiled at her again. "I have just the thing."

He ducked behind the counter and rustled around for a moment before he stood up, holding a container of some kind. He retrieved a bowl from the cabinets and poured the contents of the container into it. He placed the bowl in a heater for a few seconds until it steamed, and then he brought it to the table and set it down in front of her.

"Potato soup?"

"Comfort food. Eat." He thrust a spoon at her.

From his expression, she knew she couldn't turn him down. She accepted the spoon and slowly took a bite of the soup. It was warm and salty, rich and buttery. The nausea faded, replaced by a gnawing hunger that rumbled in her stomach loud enough to rattle her lungs.

She devoured the soup while Scraps laughed at her.

"Feel better?" he asked as soon as she had finished.

"Much." She leaned back in the chair, surprised at how hungry she had been. "Scraps?"

"Yes?"

"Do you know—where exactly are we going? I mean, I understand that we're looking for this *Tempest* ship, but where are we now?"

"I couldn't tell you, Xander," Scraps said. "I stick with the cooking. Talon is better off with the decision making, but I'm sure wherever we are going, we'll find information."

He took the bowl and spoon and washed them. She stayed in the chair and enjoyed the comforting sounds of a kitchen. Comforting? Hadn't the room felt dreadfully eerie less than an hour before?

"If you don't mind me asking," he said, "what kind of dreams are you having?"

Do I tell him? What will he think?

His kind eyes smiled.

"I think it's a memory," she said.

"What of?"

"I don't really know. It's me and—a man—David, I think is his name. I don't remember how I know him. But we're on a ship and there's lightning everywhere. He shoves me in a room and locks it and tells me that everything is going to be okay. And then, the ship—just—rocks. Goes crazy. Shakes. Like it explodes."

"And then?"

"I wake up."

Scraps came to sit in front of her, folding his arms on the table. "What makes you think it is a memory?"

"Because—I keep having it. Seeing it. The same thing—just

NAMELESS

more details every time. Over and over and over. What else could it be?"

Scraps didn't answer. He stayed quiet for a long time before he finally stood up. Xander followed him with her eyes.

"Where are you going?" she asked.

"This way," he said. "You come with me." He took her arm and pulled her gently out of the chair. "Over here."

He led her to the opposite corner of the galley where a couple of round chairs lined a small den area. The chairs looked remarkably soft.

"Sit." Scraps indicated one of the chairs.

Xander obeyed and gasped as the soft upholstery swallowed her.

"Now," Scraps said, taking a chair across from her, "what do you think of that chair?"

"What?"

"What do you think of it?"

"It's nice," she said. "Really comfortable."

"Good." Scraps clapped his hands. "I keep telling them this is the kind of chair we need more of. But McLeod he says that chairs should be functional—and those are too soft for functional people. Jaz won't give me an opinion, and I don't trust Vix. Kale and Devon don't care, Marty's always covered in grease and I won't let him near anything with upholstery, and nothing I buy is big enough for Claude. So I wanted someone else's perspective."

Scraps's voice grew fuzzier and fuzzier.

Xander tried to focus on it, but the chair was soft and warm. It felt like being wrapped in someone's arms. Safe and secure.

Scraps's talking droned in her ears, buzzing until his words all melded together in a smooth flow that sounded like—music? No.

217

She must have been imagining it, even though it certainly did sound like someone was humming.

The room darkened. Sleep rushed over her senses. The dream might come back, but Scraps hadn't made fun of her for being frightened. So maybe it was okay to talk about it with him.

Scraps said something she couldn't make out, and she was certain his hand rested on the crown of her head. But Scraps didn't know her that well, and no one in this universe cared about people they didn't know. They barely cared about the people they did know.

So it had to be her imagination. Even so, it was the nicest thing she'd imagined in a long time.

CHAPTER 17

The scent and sound of frying onions woke her. Blankets tucked around her body bound her to the chair, far too deep and comfortable to consider leaving. She opened her eyes and spied the old man behind the cook stove tossing vegetables in a skillet.

"There you are." His grin lit up his wrinkled face. "Good morning. Welcome back to the land of the living."

"Did I—sleep?" Her voice sounded thick.

Scraps laughed.

"What time is it?"

"Time for breakfast."

Xander unfolded herself. Someone had draped a blanket over her while she'd slept. Had Scraps stayed up with her all night? Was it even possible he could have done such a thing? What made him care so much? Why would Scraps waste kindness on her when she had nothing to offer him?

But what about the Bible?

She stood up and folded the blanket.

The Bible says to treat others the way you want to be treated. To think better of others than you think of yourself. To love everyone, no matter what they do to you. Is that why I think the universe should be different? Because the Bible says it should be?

She scoffed to herself.

Just because the Bible says that's the way it should be doesn't mean it ever was that way.

"What's with the frowning?" Scraps asked. "Smile, little one. I have eggs for you."

Xander smiled for him, even though she didn't feel like it. If all he asked was a smile, she'd give it to him if it killed her. The man had already done far too much for her.

He set a plate of scrambled eggs and vegetables in front of her and handed her a fork.

"How do you feel?" he asked. "Better?"

"Yeah. I think so."

"Good to hear. You looked exhausted last night."

Xander ate her eggs. Funny how Scraps could make eggs taste excellent. Scraps handed her a glass of water, which she accepted gratefully.

"You didn't drug the potato soup, did you?"

He chortled. "What makes you say that?"

"I got really sleepy really fast."

"That's because I started talking. I can put anyone to sleep."

The smile she gave him this time was real.

"You slept for many hours," Scraps said. "It's well into the morning now."

Xander stretched her arms over her head and stood up. "I had probably better go back to my room," she said. "Evy may be worried."

Scraps patted her arm and went back to work, and Xander walked toward her and Evy's shared quarters. Xander reached their room and entered. Darkness greeted her.

Where could Evy have gone? Off by herself? With someone else on the crew?

Xander shut her eyes and sat on her bunk. Evy needed hope,

but at the moment Xander didn't have any to spare.

She needed to think, needed to sort out the things that had happened to her, the things she had begun to remember that conflicted so intimately with the life she knew here.

Xander sat in the solitude of the passenger berth, silence her only companion.

What was so important about her that a syndicate was willing to go to war, to slaughter innocent people to get her?

Evy and Dr. Zahn had been together. That's what Evy had told her. Xander didn't agree with it, didn't think it was right. The Bible said it was wrong. But either way, they had obviously cared about each other. Either way, losing someone you loved hurt.

Guilt twisted inside her. Why hadn't she told Dr. Zahn how much she'd appreciated her? Had she been so afraid? Had she been so uncomfortable? How was that right?

Maybe what Dr. Zahn believed was wrong and maybe how she'd lived her life had been wrong, but wasn't it just as wrong to dislike her for no other reason than her choices? How could she think poorly of Dr. Zahn when Dr. Zahn had been the first person to help her?

"No one is right. We're all wrong." Xander pressed her face into her palms. "Especially me."

She wanted the time back. She wanted to go back and tell Dr. Zahn she had been wrong. She wanted to go back and tell Sylphie she was sorry. And then she wanted to go home.

"Wherever that is."

The vision in her head hadn't gotten any clearer despite replaying it a thousand times, and though she could remember what the two men—David and her father—looked like, she didn't know anything else.

The entry bell rang.

"Come in."

The door slid open. Devon.

"Hey, kid." He grinned.

"Hi, Devon." She forced her face to smile at him.

He didn't buy it. "You all right?"

"Sure."

He sat on Evy's bunk and rested his elbows on his thighs. "I don't believe you."

Xander stared at the floor. "I'm not very good at lying."

"You remember that?"

"No. Just something I figured out along the way."

He chuckled. "Do you want to talk about it?"

Xander waited and took a long, deep breath. "I don't know. I don't know if it would help."

"Try."

A tear slipped down her face. "Dr. Zahn was like my protector. She took care of me on the ship when—the rest of the crew wanted something else."

Devon sat up. "NUSovian birds don't make port very often. I'm sure having you on board was thrilling."

"If you call waking up at night with three strange men in your bed and their hands all over you thrilling, then, yes."

Devon smiled.

"Dr. Zahn protected me. She told me about Evy. She helped me as much as she could. They still left me, but—Dr. Zahn didn't want to."

"Left you? Left you where?"

"Callisto."

Devon's eyes bulged. "Callisto? They left you on Callisto?

Alone?"

Xander nodded.

"And you're still alive?"

"Not infected or anything." Xander threaded her fingers together. "God was watching out for me, I guess."

Devon tilted his head. "God?"

Xander hazarded a glance at him. "Yeah. God."

He'd pulled back from her, eyes narrowed, mouth set in a straight line. Not angry. But not sure either.

"You've never heard of God?"

"Well, yes. Somewhat. I've heard of gods, plural. In myths."

"It's not a myth," Xander said. "I don't remember much, but I *do* remember that. I believe in God—One all-powerful God."

"Suppose that would make sense."

Xander lifted her head. "It would?"

Devon shrugged. "Well, sometimes I wonder. I've been from one end of this system to the other, Xander. And I've seen a lot of crap, yeah, but most of the time I see more beauty than anything else, and I guess I always thought that somebody had to make it all."

"Yeah," Xander said. "Someone did."

"So you believe in this One God."

"And in His Son."

"Son?" Devon chuckled. "One all-powerful God had a Son? That'd be something to talk about."

"Yeah."

"And you remember all this?"

"It's really the only thing I *have* remembered."

"Why didn't you say anything?"

Xander winced. "Because—I asked Evy and she said it was the same thing people believe at the Sanctum."

Devon's face darkened. "That so?"

"I guess, these people from the Sanctum, know about God and Jesus and the Bible, and they talk about it all the time, but no one likes them."

"Because they're assholes."

Xander looked down.

"Sanctimonians preach love and goodness and forgiveness and purity and then turn around and screw everyone else over. No one trusts anything they say."

"But they believe in God. Like me."

"They're not like you."

Xander raised her eyebrows. "They're not?"

"You can't actually think you're from the Sanctum."

"What if I am? No one else seems to know anything about God."

"There's got to be another explanation. You can't be from the Sanctum."

"Why?"

He shrugged again. "You're—different."

Devon's admission made her feel better. She straightened and leaned toward him. "Can I ask a question?"

"Sure."

"Why doesn't Kale want to do this? Why doesn't he want to try to stop Knightshade?"

Devon scratched the back of his neck. "Kale's got a certain perspective on the syndicates. He thinks it'd be better if we just left well enough alone."

"But if there's something we can do to stop what they're planning, shouldn't we do it?"

"That's what I think. But Kale—Kale has a good reason to

NAMELESS

feel the way he does."

"What?"

"You'll have to ask him." Devon sighed heavily and then grinned. "Okay. Enough of that. I need you to come with me." He thumped her knee with his fist. "Come on."

He stood, grabbed her hand, and pulled her to her feet.

"Where are we going?"

"To the conference room. I came down to get you." He still grinned. "I've got a great idea for how we're going to find your ship."

"Can't you just tell me?" Xander asked as he towed her out of the room and down the hall.

"You'll have to wait and see, Xander." He set his hand on her back to nudge her forward. "Trust me. It's a good idea."

They walked together to the conference room, where everyone else had already assembled.

Evy sat alone on the other side of the table. She glanced at Xander when she entered but said nothing and didn't smile.

Vix hung in the corner, smoking and tapping the ashes in her beer can. Captain McLeod sat at the end of the table, face neutral. Jaz sat beside him; anything she was thinking was carefully hidden. But Xander didn't miss the spark in her eyes when she saw Devon come into the room.

Kale hunkered in a chair, elbows on the armrests, hands dangling in his lap. He scowled, face drawn and eyes snapping in ill-concealed anger. Xander moved to run away from him, but Devon dragged her to the chair beside Kale and pushed her into it.

"Hey, guys," he announced.

Xander would have preferred to stand next to Vix.

"Took you long enough, Chase," Vix snarled from the corner.

225

"I couldn't just tell you guys and not tell Xander." Devon pouted and walked to the other end of the table. He leaned over the table with his knuckles against the polymer tabletop. "I figured out the best way to find Xander's ship."

Captain McLeod held out his hands. "We're waiting, lad."

Devon began to pace. "The *Tempest* has Xander's ship, right?"

"That's what the stiff said," Vix said, puffing smoke.

Evy shuddered, and Captain McLeod glared at Vix.

"Right." Devon didn't seem to notice. "Our problem is that the *Tempest* is the biggest, baddest ass mother of a ship in the whole quadrant. She's got the best weapons, the best tracking systems, the best radar jamming systems—the best of everything."

"She's the freakin' Knightshade military flagship," Kale growled under his breath.

"Old Stoney outfitted her himself," Devon said. "And he spared no expense."

"So even if we could find her, which we can't," Captain McLeod said, "she'd vaporize us before we got within a parsec."

"Maybe," Devon said. "Maybe not. The vaporizing thing—I haven't figured out yet. I'll get there. It's the finding her thing I got nailed."

Captain McLeod looked impatient. "Get on with it, Chase."

"We track the *Tempest*—which is untrackable—by tracking old Stoney." Devon grinned. "What do you think?"

Captain McLeod raised his eyebrows. Evy didn't really have much a reaction, but Vix choked on her smoke and erupted in violent fit of coughing.

"Tracking Stone?" Jaz repeated.

"That sounds kind of risky," Xander said.

"It's a terrible idea," Kale spat. "The worst idea he's ever had."

Devon leaned over the table again. "But?"

Kale rolled his eyes.

"But what, Kale? Come on, old buddy, tell 'em but what."

"Go to hell, Dev."

Devon grinned at him, and Kale sighed.

"Kale did it anyway," Devon said, standing up. "You just have to know how to ask."

Kale muttered something profane.

"Kale," Captain McLeod started slowly, "this is something you could do?"

Kale glared at Devon and then turned his glare to Captain McLeod. "Yes, Talon. Anybody can track anybody as long as you know enough about them."

"And we know everything about Stone," Devon said. "We grew up with him, so we know how he thinks."

Xander raised her eyebrows. Devon and Kale had grown up with Stone? As children? She shook herself. She could easily see Devon as a child, carefree and laughing, but Kale as a child? Difficult to picture. He'd probably been the kid that ran around pulling pigtails and skipping school. Darien Stone probably tortured animals.

"And Kale knows even better how he thinks." Devon cleared his throat and glanced at Kale as though he feared to tell a secret. "Because—well—you know."

Weird. What did that mean?

Captain McLeod leaned forward in his chair. "Kale, explain please."

Kale ground his teeth. "One of Stone's priorities in

Knightshade is Fantasy dealing," he said. "He's the head of the big dealers."

"Ghosts," Jaz said.

"Right, the ones who hide in the shadows and recruit the minor dealers to do the dirty work," Kale said. "The dealers get the creds and give them to the Ghosts. The Ghosts pass it on to Stone, and Stone gives it back to Knightshade."

"In theory," Devon said. "But old Stoney has a Ghost who likes to skim a little something-something off the top." Devon smirked. "His name's Zen Mitchem."

Xander gasped. "Zen Mitchem?"

Everybody looked at her, and her face burned.

"Sorry."

"What?" Kale glared. "You know him or something?"

"I saw him on the *Acheron*," Xander said. "That was the first time I saw Stone."

"Really?" Devon laughed. "I guess the galaxy is a small place after all. That would be two months ago or so when Stone went to collect him in person after Mitchem got caught with his pants down. I guess he weaseled his way back into a contract, and Stoney let him have one more shot."

"Which he screwed over," Kale said.

"And this time, Stone will probably kill him." Devon took the chair opposite Jaz, still beaming.

"Wouldn't it be better to just send somebody else to kill him?" Vix asked.

"Stone doesn't work like that," Kale said. "He likes it too much."

"So," Devon said, "Kale and I tracked down Zen Mitchem. He's got a bounty on his head on Ring-Seven. No small amount

NAMELESS

either. My plan is to hunt him and get the info on the *Tempest* out of him before we turn him in."

"And this Mitchem character will know the location of the *Tempest*?" Captain McLeod asked.

"Ghosts stay up on Stone's location." Kale said. "He'll know where it is. Or at least, where it's scheduled to be."

"And you've found him, you say?" Captain McLeod eyed Devon.

"Elara," Devon said. "Just a few clics off."

"Talon," Vix growled, "you're not seriously considering this. This is ridiculous."

Captain McLeod glanced at Evy, who hadn't said anything. Then, he glanced at Xander.

"Kale, what are the odds this will work?" Captain McLeod asked.

"That what will work? Catching Mitchem? That'll be easy." Kale folded his arms. "Convincing him to squeal? Easier. Attacking the *Tempest* and surviving?" He scoffed and rolled his eyes.

"Well, we'll come to that part later," Captain McLeod said.

"I think we should talk about it now," Kale said, "since that's the eventual outcome we're heading toward."

"Not now, Kale."

"It's asinine, Talon, and you know it. We don't stand a chance against the *Tempest* or Knightshade, and we're all going to end up dead."

Captain McLeod pounded the armrest with his fist. "Don't you be lecturing me, boy."

"You're an idiot, Talon."

"Shut up, Kale."

"If you'd get your head out of your ass, you'd see how stupid

229

this is."

"Ravenwood," Captain McLeod bellowed, standing to his feet and facing Kale with fire in his eyes. "When I tell you to shut it, you do it. My ship, my rules. You don't like it, get off."

Evy straightened where she sat, eyes widening at the display, and she stared at Captain McLeod with shock on her face. Xander wanted to crawl under the table and hide.

But no one else seemed concerned. Actually, Devon looked like he was enjoying the show.

"Weren't you getting off anyway?" Captain McLeod asked. "I seem to recall you saying something of that nature."

Kale didn't answer and looked away, apparently tired of the discussion.

Captain McLeod quieted. "Fine. We'll go to Elara."

He turned on his heel and stormed to the door. Vix uttered a heavy groan and followed him, whining. Kale waited until Vix disappeared and darted off in the other direction, not looking at anyone.

Devon grinned. "What do you think?"

"Devon," Xander said, "are you sure it will work?"

"Sure, I'm sure."

"It will work," Jaz said confidently. "I think it is a good idea."

The cockeyed grin Devon flashed at her lit his face up like a sun.

Evy stood and moved for the door, and Xander followed her. On the bridge, Captain McLeod perched in his chair. Scraps stood beside him.

"I understand we're heading to Elara," Scraps said. "Tityas is a good place for potatoes—which we're dreadfully low on, Talon."

NAMELESS

Captain McLeod looked up at him. "Potatoes, Scraps?"

"*Da.*"

Captain McLeod narrowed his eyes. "And I suppose you're going to want the ladies to go with you then?"

"*Da.* It would be good to give them a change of scenery, don't you agree?"

"You mean a distraction, Scraps?" Evy took Xander's arm.

Captain McLeod and Scraps glanced back at her. She folded her arms, her face stoic. Scraps smiled at her, and Evy looked down.

"I don't care," Captain McLeod said. "Do as you like. Just keep them out of trouble."

"*Da.*"

Captain McLeod moved toward the conference room. "Ben, you've got your coordinates. Take care of the rest."

Captain McLeod stood and left the bridge.

Scraps and Evy walked away together, leaving Xander alone with only the navigator.

Ben. Mr. Ponytail.

He paid no attention to her and continued guiding the ship through space. The artificial lights overhead made his long brown ponytail shine. His extraordinary posture and neat, trim style made her expect him to criticize her piecemeal Kepler outfit.

Had she introduced herself? He hadn't really spoken much, except in small phrases, and he'd said nothing to her at all.

She meandered to the helm console and stood beside it, watching the stars out the superglass view screen.

"There are so many of them," she said softly.

He said nothing.

"So," Xander said, her voice quiet. "How long have you been here?"

231

At first, he didn't answer. Presumably he was concentrating on flying the ship, thin fingers pressed against the console.

"Long enough," he said at long last.

Xander opened and closed her hands as she stood beside him, feeling uncomfortable with his silence.

"I'm sorry," Xander said after she couldn't take it any longer. "I just realized that—I hadn't really spoken to you. And I've spoken to everyone else. I really—just wanted to—say hello, I guess."

Ben answered only with a noncommittal grunt.

Maybe he didn't speak English. That could be. His thick NUGaulian accent already made him hard to understand, but maybe his vocabulary needed work. That could explain why he acted like a jerk.

Unless he was a jerk.

She kept her voice pleasant. "Where is Elara?"

He made a scoffing sound. "It is a moon of Jupiter."

His accent was very strong. Xander wondered if that was why he took so long to answer between questions. Maybe his English wasn't very good. At least, she was hoping that was the reason for his difficulty.

"Do you ever—go out to hunt?"

Ben uttered an exasperated sigh. "No. I stay here and fly the ship." He turned to glare at her. "That is my duty on board the *Prodigal*. I fly. I navigate. I maneuver. That is my job." His brown eyes darkened. "Unlike you, who have no job and are reduced to distracting me from mine. So I will kindly ask you to leave me alone."

Xander flushed. "I'm—very sorry."

Ben said nothing and turned back to the console.

Okay. Answers that question. He's a jerk.

She stepped back from the helm and hurried toward the lift. Scraps had said he would need help on the moon. If her presence was distracting for Ben, then she'd avoid him. He didn't seem like a person she'd want as a friend anyway.

She stopped short as Vix stepped out of the shadows and stood in her path.

"Excuse me." Xander tried to move around the bounty huntress. But Vix blocked her way. "What are you doing?"

"I'm going to tell you this once, kid. Cover your hair when you're on the moon."

"What?"

"Elarans don't like redheads. So cover your damn hair."

"With what?"

"A hat. A scarf. It doesn't matter. Just cover it up."

Xander narrowed her eyes. "Why are you telling me this? You don't care about me."

"Maybe I care about Scraps. If you're with him, and the Elarans decide to beat the shit out of you—kind of like you deserve—he'll step in to help you. And he'll get hurt. Maybe I want to avoid that."

Xander nodded. "Okay."

Vix brushed past her but stopped before she moved out of sight.

"Do yourself a favor, though," she said. "Don't tell the old man that's why you're doing it? He's enough of a man that he'll be offended."

Vix winked and stepped around the corner.

Xander stared after her, unconvinced she told the truth. Where was she supposed to find a hat anyway? If what Vix said was true, why hadn't Captain McLeod said anything about it? Or Devon?

Or Jaz? Any of them she wouldn't have doubted.

But, Vix seemed like she had been around the universe once or twice. So maybe she knew things the others didn't.

In any case, if it would keep Scraps safe, Xander would do it. She didn't want anyone else to get hurt because of her. She would find a hat and wear it, even if it made her look ridiculous.

CHAPTER 18

Xander stopped in the passenger berth and searched for something to cover her head. The only thing that could conceivably work was her pillow case, and while she wanted to do as Vix had said, she didn't want to look like an idiot.

I wonder if Scraps has a hat I can borrow.

She found Scraps going over a list of needed supplies with Evy looking over his shoulder. Focusing on something else other than Dr. Zahn had brought some color to her face.

"Tityas is the largest marketplace on Elara," Scraps said. "They'll have everything we need—and a lot of what we don't. So we'll do fine." He shoved the datapad into the woven bag slung around his shoulder. "And it's also the likeliest spot to find information on whatever head they're hunting."

"Do we need to bring anything, Scraps?" Evy rolled up the sleeves of her blouse.

"No," Scraps said. "You lovely ladies just stick with me. I'll take care of you."

"Scraps?" Xander flattened her hands on the table where Scraps worked.

"Yeah, Xander?"

"Do you have—a hat?"

Scraps straightened. "A hat? What for?"

"My hair," she said. "It's awfully greasy. I'd just feel better with it covered up."

Xander tried to cover her wince. She couldn't lie for beans. And the tilt of Evy's eyebrows indicated that she hadn't bought it.

"Well, of course I have a hat," he said with a laugh. "Have to hide my bald spot after all, don't I?" He reached into a cupboard at the far end of the row of cabinets and pulled out a large, floppy bucket hat. "Will this work?" He threw it to her.

Xander caught it. She wrapped her hair around her hand and thrust it into the hat as she secured it on her head. The hat was a little big for her, but it would do the job.

"It's perfect, Scraps. Thank you."

Scraps nodded and knelt behind the cabinet.

Evy stared at her but said nothing.

The ship shivered and rumbled. Xander's hand flew to the wall to brace herself.

"Reentry," Scraps said from the floor. "It'll be done with soon." He laughed. "Or we will crash, but it will still happen soon." He pulled out his datapad and made a note.

Not encouraging. At all.

"Quite exciting, isn't it?" Evy commented. "Never knowing if you're going to fall out of the sky."

Scraps grinned. "Always keeps life interesting."

True to his word, the *Prodigal* stopped quivering.

"Ben will set us down in a few minutes," Scraps said. "Let's go."

He started out the door, Evy on his heels and Xander right behind her. But Xander tripped and nearly fell, the instep of her right foot throbbing. A lever protruded from the galley floor where a hatch blended almost perfectly into the flooring.

Well, what was that? A hidden door? A secret route to the engine room? McLeod probably used it to smuggle black market

NAMELESS

goods. Or people. Did she care enough to open it?

"Xander, come on," Evy called.

No. The door didn't matter. The less she knew, the better.

Xander caught up to them as they reached the cargo bay. The *Prodigal* wobbled and groaned until it gave a relieved shudder. The whole ship seemed to droop with a contented sigh.

Scraps touched the intercom on the wall.

"Ben, we down?"

"Aye," Ben said.

"Good." Scraps opened the cargo bay door, and dry wind flooded inside.

Xander held her hat with one hand and clutched Evy with the other. Scraps led them out.

"Tityas is a pleasant enough place," Scraps said as he walked. "Just don't mess with the locals."

The dry, sandy ground reminded her of a beach, but the planet had no ocean and the air held a chill.

Scraps must have visited before, since he knew exactly where he was going. Xander didn't let go of Evy's hand. They weaved through groups of traders and vendors on the streets. Scraps didn't slow until they arrived at an open-air marketplace at the heart of the city.

Booths lined the street in both directions, brimming with sellers and buyers, each booth full of food and plants and clothes and everything else imaginable. It made the little marketplace they'd stopped at on Kepler look like a garage sale.

Scraps headed toward a booth loaded with all kinds of different produce. Apples and oranges and melons and peppers and potatoes and onions, everything a ship's cook could need in the never-ending search to prepare crew meals that didn't result in food

237

poisoning or scurvy.

Men, women, and children roamed the streets. The men wore mainly coveralls and steel-toed boots caked with mud. The women wore long dresses with full skirts. The children wore jumpers and denim and collared shirts, and most of them were barefoot. All of them seemed pleasant. None of them looked particularly threatening. And none of them wore hats.

Of course, none of them had red hair either.

Xander pulled the hat tighter over her hair.

Scraps stopped at the produce booth and picked out potatoes. She watched him turn them over, looking for bad spots or moldy areas. He handed a sack to Evy and set the approved potatoes inside.

Xander glanced at the vendor. His sour expression seemed directed at her.

Weird. She hadn't done anything to him. Maybe his face was stuck that way.

Maybe he didn't want to sell his potatoes. But that would be silly. If he didn't want to sell them, why would he offer them for sale?

Could he be angry at me? That's dumb. He's got no reason to be angry at me. Fruitcake.

Vix's warning just made her paranoid.

After filling the bag with potatoes, Scraps paid the vendor.

"I think I see some apples." Scraps shouldered the bag of potatoes. "We never get apples. So I think that would be a nice treat. Yes?"

Evy nodded.

"Apples sound great, Scraps," Xander said.

Scraps started back through the crowd, and Evy and Xander struggled to keep up.

238

More people stared at her, most with intense dislike.

Was she just being paranoid? Or were they really glaring at her?

She checked her hair. All suitably concealed. Maybe they didn't like pale skin either. Her fair complexion usually identified her as a redhead even if no one could see her hair. Maybe a hat hadn't been a good enough disguise.

Scraps stopped at a fruit booth, and he and Evy started picking through apples. Xander only listened with one ear as Scraps explained the particulars of finding good apples.

"Color is a good clue but it's not the only one," Scraps said. "You have to use all your senses. Smell it. Feel it. Listen to it."

She tuned him out. Didn't he notice how many people glared at her? Didn't either of them notice how angry the people around them looked?

Maybe they didn't like people who wore hats either.

Scraps chose a number of juicy, red apples and put them in a sack he retrieved from the vendor. He paid the vendor and handed the sack to Evy.

They started walking again.

"We should pick up some rosemary," Scraps said. "It didn't take in my garden, so I have to buy it."

"You have an herb garden on your ship?" Evy stared at him.

Scraps responded, but Xander didn't hear, too busy trying to avoid the Elarans.

They all seemed angry with her. But why?

They probably know I'm a redhead. Xander pulled the hat harder over her ears. *No one else here is wearing a hat. So that probably means that anyone they see in a hat is a redhead, which is how they know. That's why they don't like me. The best thing to do is just to hurry through the marketplace and get back to the ship as soon as possible.*

A cruel hand clamped down on her arm. She couldn't even yelp in surprise before her attacker dragged her into the shadows of an alley, shoved her against the wall, and covered her mouth with his hand.

He snarled something in her ear in a florid language she didn't know. Latin-based? She couldn't identify any of the words, and he spoke rapidly, breathing down her neck, pressing himself against her.

"Excuse me?" she squeaked.

What was this bozo doing? Who did he think he was?

He said something and laughed and ran his hands into her hair, tilting her head back.

He was going to kiss her!

Horror and rage surged through her, and she shoved him with all the strength in her arms. The man stopped and laughed and tried again, and she stomped hard on his foot.

He barked in pain and backed away, and she kicked him in the shin hard enough to send shudders of agony up her own leg.

The man shouted and fell backward, holding his lower leg in obvious pain. He spat at her, screaming in whatever language he knew as he rolled on the ground in agony. He looked enraged.

What did he have to be upset about? She was the one who had been assaulted. She tucked her hair into the hat again and stepped back onto the street.

Oh, no.

No Evy and Scraps anywhere. She hurried down the street, looking for any sign of them, but neither of them appeared. She stopped and glanced both ways down an intersection.

Herbs. Scraps wanted herbs. So who sells herbs?

A hand formed around her arm. Instinct took over, and she tried to jerk away.

"Calm down."

She looked up into the NUChungqwo man's face. She didn't recognize him, but that meant exactly nothing. She didn't recognize herself. At least this guy smiled.

But weren't Stone's goons from NUChungqwo? Did that mean everyone from NUChungqwo should be mistrusted? Sylphie was from NUChungqwo, and Sylphie had saved her. Judging his heart by his face was wrong.

So who was he? Did he know her?

"I won't hurt you." He pulled her to the side of the busy street.

"What do you want?"

"You must not be from around here."

Xander frowned. What did that mean?

"Are you lost?"

Xander hesitated. "No. Not really. I just—lost my group."

The man's cheerful black eyes sparkled. "I saw you with a blonde and an old man. Is that your group?" He released her arm.

"Yes."

"The old man. He's Elek Ivanov."

Xander straightened. "You—know him?"

"Of course. He comes here often. He's on Talon McLeod's bird, right?"

"Yes."

The man smiled again. "My name is Dai."

"Dai?"

"Dai Yukihara. Who are you? Are you a new hunter? That

seems unlikely."

"No. I'm a—a passenger. My name is Xander."

"I'm pleased to meet you, Xander," Dai said. "I saw Elek and his lady friend go this way." The man pointed and began to walk down the street.

There was no reason not to follow him. If the man was just a simple NUChungqwo citizen, he wouldn't have had anything to do with the Seekers, who only worked for Knightshade.

"The *Prodigal* comes through here on occasion," he said. "Elek and I go way back. You're very fortunate I found you."

"Yeah, I don't know what's going on. Everyone is looking at me like they hate me."

"That's because you've got that hat on."

She touched the hat and frowned. What did that have have to do with it?

"How is Captain McLeod these days?"

"Fine, I guess. I don't really know him. We've only been with them a few days."

"Traveling?"

"You could say that." *We're still looking for the* Destiny *but after we find the* Tempest *and get the* Destiny *back, what then? Where will we go? NUSaxony is in the middle of a war, and I'm sure Captain McLeod won't want us to stay on his ship.*

"Xander?"

She glanced up at him. Apparently, he'd asked her a question, and she hadn't heard him. "I'm sorry. What?"

"I asked if you liked the *Prodigal*."

"Oh. Sure. It's a nice ship."

"Really?"

Xander grimaced. "Well—it's awfully small. I suppose it

must be well known, if you've heard of it."

"Oh, I've heard of it all right," Dai said. "Lots of people have. Talon McLeod isn't exactly famous, but he *did* make quite a name for himself in the Titan War. And his hunters usually bring in more than their fair share of bounty heads. Especially that woman—what's her name? Jezebel Carver? She's his best hunter."

Xander shook her head. "I think Kale would argue with that."

Dai furrowed his brow. "Kale? Who is Kale?"

Xander's heart thudded. *Wait. Outside the ship, doesn't everyone know him as Matt Sullivan?*

"Oh," she said. "Well. Kale is—one of Captain McLeod's hunters."

"Kale," Dai frowned. "I know about Devon, and I've heard of Matt. But I don't know a Kale."

Xander swallowed and smiled, but the expression felt plastic on her face. She hoped Dai wouldn't notice.

"Yes. I've heard of a Mr. Sullivan on the crew. He also goes by Kale, you say?"

"Yeah. That's—how he introduced himself to me."

But Kale used a different name for a reason. What if he was hiding? What if she had just blown his cover?

Surely not. Telling one man on a moon like Elara didn't amount to blowing someone's cover. And if Kale wanted to hide, he should have done a better job of not using his real name. No way could he pin this on her if it went south.

"Interesting." Dai stopped and pointed. "There. You see? There are your friends. Still buried in their rosemary and thyme."

Xander smiled. "Thank you so much."

"Don't mention it." He turned. "But I really would take the hat off, if I were you." Dai winked at her and vanished into the crowd.

Xander touched the hat and thought better of it. Dai Yukihara had been very kind, but she still wasn't sure if she should trust him. She would ask Scraps about it later.

She pushed through the crowd and ran to where Scraps and Evy stood, deeply involved in a conversation on the different medicinal uses of herbs. Evy looked back as she approached.

"There you are," Evy said. "I thought we'd lost you."

"I'm fine. Just got turned around." Explaining that she'd been attacked felt like whining.

Scraps checked his datapad for the time. "Are the two of you hungry? It's getting close to lunch time."

"I could eat, I suppose. You, Xander?"

"Sure."

Scraps handed the bag of potatoes to Xander. She grunted at the weight but shouldered it anyway. Scraps headed for a stand selling boxed lunches. He purchased three.

"I don't usually splurge like this," he said, "but how often does an old man like me get to have lunch with two lovely ladies?"

To Xander's immense surprise, Evy smiled.

Xander ignored the looks the people in the area shot her and stayed between Evy and Scraps until they reached a park near the outskirts of the city, close to where the *Prodigal* had landed. Scraps indicated for them to set the bags down and eat.

The box lunches surprised her, rectangular dishes with five sections of varying sizes, each filled with a different sort of food. One had two rice balls, one had some kind of pickled vegetable, one had a cup of soup, and the other two sections had two different kinds of meat. Scraps handed her a fork.

"Scraps?"

"Yes, Xander?"

"Do you know someone named Dai Yukihara?"

Scraps frowned. "No. I don't think so. Why?"

"Oh, I was just wondering."

"Xander," Evy began, "did you talk to someone?"

"Yeah. He said—he knew you. That you went way back."

Scraps shrugged. "Oh, it's likely. I've met a lot of people. Was he friendly?"

"Yes, very."

"Then I wouldn't worry about it."

Xander drank the soup from the cup. If Scraps wasn't worried, she wouldn't worry either.

After they finished eating, they gathered their purchases and started back for the ship.

Yes, the *Prodigal* looked strange, like a patchwork quilt pieced together with mismatched fabrics, but it didn't seem so ugly anymore. She stopped walking and just gazed at the ship. Evy and Scraps stopped ahead of her.

"It's okay," Xander said. "I just want to enjoy the outside a little longer."

Evy nodded, and she and Scraps went inside. Xander looked out on Tityas. With Jupiter huge in the sky overhead, it could have reminded her of Callisto, except Elara was much cleaner.

What was happening to her? A few months ago, if a complete stranger had grabbed her and tried to assault her, she wouldn't have been able to function. Now? Well, she had gone on about her business. It hadn't even put a damper on her day.

Was this how life was supposed to be? Expecting to be assaulted or raped every moment she set foot outside the relative safety of her ship?

"What the hell?"

She turned at the sound of Kale's voice. He walked straight at her from the *Prodigal*, feet stomping, eyes on fire.

She didn't want to talk to him. She tried to dodge him, but he seized her arm, whirled her around, and snatched the hat off her head.

"What the *hell* are you doing?"

"Going back to the ship." Xander started to reach for the hat but stopped herself. Snatching it back from him would look childish.

"Back to the ship?" He pointed toward the market. "You came from Tityas already? What the hell is wrong with you?"

"Wrong with me? What's wrong with you?" Throwing her whole weight against his grip didn't budge him, but she tried anyway. "You shouldn't just go around grabbing people and screaming at them for no reason."

"No reason?"

"You have no reason to be angry at me. What did I do now?"

He gaped at her. "You're an idiot."

Enough. Enough of him yelling at her without provocation, enough of his attitude and condescension, enough of him in general.

"Why did you save me if you think I'm an idiot?" She punched his bicep in frustration, ignoring the painful throb in her knuckles on impact.

"Well, I didn't realize you were an idiot at the time."

"It takes one to know one. Let go!"

"Have you made it your life's mission to keep pissing me off?"

Xander gave a vicious yank and wrested her arm from his hold. "I'm trying to stay away from you. You're the one who keeps talking to me."

He leaned into her face. "You are the worst whore I've ever met."

She slapped him.

Kale didn't move. Didn't react. He stood in shock, a red mark the shape of her hand forming on the side of his face. Xander didn't even feel guilty about it.

"I am *not* a whore." Her voice trembled with rage.

He turned his face back to her, his eyes blazing as he held up the hat. "So why the hell do you keep acting like one?"

"Wearing a hat makes me a prostitute?"

"On Elara it does."

Her face went slack. Her heart stopped. She stared at him. "It—what?"

He straightened, towering over her head. "You want to get nailed, that's your business." He threw the hat at her feet. "Just don't say I didn't warn you."

Over his shoulder, she could see Vix and Jaz on the loading ramp of the *Prodigal*. Vix stopped at the end of the ramp and lit a cigarette. She puffed on it before she looked up.

She had seen everything, and Xander could see a cruel smirk on her face. She laughed and followed Jaz toward Tityas.

Xander couldn't move; she couldn't breathe. Vix had lied to her, had set her up, had planned it from the beginning.

Why? What could Xander have done to her to make her hate her so much?

Kale brushed past her and left her standing alone.

If Vix did that, Xander thought, *could she have—what if she's the one who took my clothes too? Is she trying to convince Kale that I'm a prostitute? But why? Why would she do that?*

Xander stared at the hat with tears in her eyes.

She steadied herself and picked it up. She brushed the dust off of it and walked toward the *Prodigal*. She should return it to Scraps.

Newt yapped at her as she entered the ship. She stopped and picked her up, scratching the dog's ears, and the dog promptly settled into her arm and went to sleep.

"So it wasn't your fault after all, huh?" Xander pressed her nose into the dog's warm fur. "I guess I owe you an apology."

She walked toward the galley, straining her memory to recall anything she had done to Vix to make her angry. They really hadn't spoken. They had only talked a few times, including the previous evening after the nightmare.

Vix must not want to help her. But why set Kale against her? Why endanger her like that?

Xander made it to the galley and found Scraps and Evy talking quietly at the table. Scraps smiled at her. Xander handed him his hat.

"Thank you for the hat," she said. "It—helped."

"Good." Scraps accepted the hat. "You should take another shower if you feel greasy."

"I might." *No way. Not as long as Vix is on this ship.*

"What's bothering you, Xander?" Evy asked.

Xander bit her lip. "I think—I don't think Vix likes me."

Scraps chuckled. "Vix doesn't like anyone."

"But I think she hates me. And I don't know why."

Scraps patted Xander's arm. "It wouldn't surprise me at all if she did."

"Why? What did I do to her?"

"Nothing." Scraps leaned back in his chair. "If anything, she would hate you because Kale doesn't."

NAMELESS

Xander frowned. What sense did that make?

"Don't worry about it," Scraps said. "Now—what shall we make for dinner?"

Evy glanced at her, and Xander hid all her concerns behind a cheerful smile.

She should just stay away from Kale. It would simplify everything, and Kale would probably appreciate it. But what would he think? He'd saved her from the Seekers. Then he'd tried to help on Elara—not well, but his intentions were true. And she'd done nothing but act like a child. It shouldn't matter what he thought about her, but it did.

Xander set Newt down and washed her hands. She would help Scraps cut up the apples they had bought and stop worrying about everything. She paused as she dried her hands. Dai knew she wasn't a prostitute. How had he figured that out? He didn't know her. Or did he?

Forget Dai. He didn't matter. She grabbed a knife and started slicing apples, but the dark knot of guilt in the pit of her stomach kept tightening.

She'd spent the afternoon walking around dressed like a prostitute. So far, her plan to convince Kale she wasn't a prostitute could have been going better.

Kale. Stupid Kale. He deserved to be slapped for screaming at her, for grabbing her, for calling her a whore.

He did.

Liar. No, he didn't. If anyone needed a good slap it was her.

249

CHAPTER 19

After all the hunters departed from the *Prodigal*, Captain McLeod ordered the ship back into space. Apparently, he didn't like having the ship on the planet surface while all the short-range fighters were out.

So the *Prodigal* waited in orbit above Elara while the four bounty hunters searched the moon for any sign of Mitchem. They'd left hours ago.

Xander stood in the galley with Scraps and Evy and a bowl of apples she had just finished slicing. She remembered apple salad. Apples. Raisins. Walnuts. Cheese. Celery. Chopped and mixed with mayonnaise. Evy and Scraps watched her work, surprised she remembered what she was doing.

Xander didn't dare tell them how her hands shook. She made it up as she worked, the next steps just coming to her one at a time until she finished. Then the only trick was making Scraps and Evy believe she'd done it all intentionally.

Maybe the key to finding her memory was not to look for it. If she could make apple salad without trying to remember how, maybe she could find her name the same way.

The blue loading lights rotated brightly above their heads.

Scraps grunted. "They're back."

The intercom system buzzed.

"Scraps." Captain McLeod's voice was impassive. "They need you in the loading bay. Jaz took one."

NAMELESS

"*Da.*" Scraps rinsed his hands and trotted downstairs to get his medical kit.

"Took one?" Xander looked at Evy. "What does that mean?"

Evy shrugged and sat down. Scraps ran up the stairs and jogged down the corridor.

"Evy?"

"I'm fine dear," Evy said. "Go with him, if you like."

Xander nodded and followed him.

"Scraps?" she asked as she ran behind him. "What did Captain McLeod mean? Is Jaz all right?"

"Since he weren't screaming at me to get there, she's likely fine," Scraps said. "But McLeod don't like blood on his floors."

That didn't help her anxiety level.

She followed him to the bay where Claude locked the *Invader* into position on the loading winch. Claude wore a dark blue enviro-suit and looked even more like a giant than normal. Inside the cockpit, Xander could see Devon waiting patiently until Claude finished securing the fighter and indicated he could get out.

Devon popped the cockpit and lowered himself down to the floor, but the impact of his boots made no noise. Xander frowned

She stepped toward the door, and Scraps stopped her with a hand on her shoulder. He smiled and held her still. Confused, Xander glanced up at him before she noticed the glittering lights along the edge of the door frame.

"Scraps?"

"It's a force field, Xander. Don't touch it."

"What would happen?"

"You'd get burned." He grinned at her. "And my supply of burn cream isn't what it used to be." He turned back to the bay. "When Claude is finished loading the ships, he'll shut the bay doors

251

and lower the field. Then we can go in."

Xander nodded and waited beside Scraps.

Devon scooted toward the back wall as Claude punched a button on his suit. The massive loading winch shivered and began to turn, revolving until Kale's sleek fighter appeared. At the same time, Jaz's fighter hovered into position outside the bay doors.

Xander could see Kale tapping his fingers inside his cockpit as the winch revolved until it stopped with an open harness. Claude stepped back, and Xander watched Jaz guide the *Gypsy* into the bay. She lined herself up with the winch and cut her power just as Claude initiated the grappling hooks around the *Gypsy's* chassis and secured it in the open harness. He made sure that all the mechanisms were tight.

"*Gypsy* loaded." Claude's voice echoed over the intercom system radio.

"Copy," Jaz said from her radio and popped her cockpit open.

Claude helped her climb out, and Xander spotted the bleeding wound on her shoulder, sealed with some kind of epoxy. Jaz moved to the back wall beside Devon who offered an arm to rest on. She shook her head.

Claude followed the same procedure with Vix's *Blackbird*. Once Vix was out and all four fighters were secure, Claude pressed the intercom.

"All loaded, Captain," he said.

"Aye." Talon's voice echoed in the empty chamber.

The bay doors shut, and the force field on the doorway dropped. Scraps made a beeline for Jaz. Vix helped her out of the top portion of the enviro-suit as Jaz shed her helmet.

Xander hung back to watch. Scraps pulled a device out of his bag and scanned the bloody wound on her shoulder.

NAMELESS

"Explosive round," she said through clenched teeth. "Mitchem. Son of a bitch."

The loading winch groaned as it spun. The intercom system squealed, and Kale's voice boomed over the speakers. "Claude, what the hell is taking so long?"

"One moment, Kale."

"You've had a moment. Get me out."

Claude ignored him and stopped the winch when it reached Devon's fighter. "Devon?" Claude called. "Where you put it?"

"Oh, it's in the back," Devon said.

"The bounty?" Scraps asked.

"No." Jaz growled in pain. "Something else."

Devon popped the hatch on the back end of the *Invader* and yanked the release open. As he did, a scrawny child tumbled out of the short-range fighter and hit the floor with a loud crash.

"Devon Chase!" Scraps snapped to his feet, angrier than Xander had ever heard him. "What are you doing?"

"Take it easy, Scraps." Devon held up his hands. "It's not what you think."

"It's not a child." Jaz snarled from the floor. "It's not even human."

Devon stepped aside, and the child sat up, blinking abnormally large green eyes in a slender face crowned with hair that constantly shifted colors.

"Woooo!" The child—a girl?—rolled her head around. "That was fun!" She spread her arms out wide and fell back to the floor panels, giggling maniacally.

"What?" Scraps stared. "Devon, what is that?"

The girl sat up again and let out a squeal. She jumped to her feet and clapped her hands and spun in circles, laughing and

253

giggling, her hair shifting from pink to blue to yellow to orange and bright purple in rapid, crazy sequence only to repeat all over again. She looked like a spinning top with a neon rainbow on her head.

Slender and lithe, the barefoot girl wore a shirt four sizes too big for her, and her pants seemed to be part of a military uniform.

"It's an android, Scraps," Jaz said. "It's a damned android."

"Wee! Woo-hoo! Wee-hee!" The girl screamed as she spun and spun until Xander felt dizzy.

"Would you stop?" Vix pulled her helmet off.

The girl instantly stopped spinning, so fast she couldn't regain her balance and fell flat on her face.

"Is that all it took?" Devon chuckled. "If I'd have known that, I wouldn't have had to listen to 'Ninety-nine Bottles of Beer on the Wall' all the way here."

"Forty-seven!" The little android bellowed into the floor tiles. "Al was at forty-seven!"

"Claude," Kale barked over the speakers. "Now."

Claude muttered and went to release Kale from his SRF. Scraps returned to Jaz, and Devon dragged the android's body away from the zone where Kale would fall. The *Scimitar* appeared on the winch, and Kale opened the cockpit. He tumbled out and barely landed straight.

"Damn. Keep me cooped up in there any longer, and I'd sprain something."

"To sprain something, you have to exert yourself, Kale." Scraps spoke from where he dressed Jaz's wound. "Not sitting still."

"Shut it, Scraps." Kale popped his neck and rotated his shoulders. "Where is it? We should jettison it now before it starts singing again."

"For once," Jaz said as Scraps stood, "I agree with Kale. We do not need an android on this ship."

"Wait." Xander finally found her voice and walked to where the android girl sat on the floor, rocking back and forth, singing to herself. "This is really an android?"

"You ever met a human with hair like that, kid?" Kale sneered.

"I saw androids on NUSaxony," Xander said. "This one doesn't act anything like they did. They were stiff. This one is— well—she's different. She's almost—human acting."

The little android stuck out its tongue, flopped face down on the floor tiles, and rolled over onto her back, kicking her bare feet into the air making glub-glubbing sounds.

"You were saying?" Kale cocked an eyebrow.

"It's a frickin' lunatic," Vix said. "We should put it out of its misery."

Jaz hadn't moved from the floor, her sharp gaze not missing one of the android's erratic movements.

"Al is malfunctioning." The android rolled over again, sounding very cheerful.

Vix jerked. "How?"

"Al was designed to mimic human behavior." The android jumped up and bowed. "Al's primary programming is faulty. That is why Al is the way she is." The little android collapsed in a heap on the floor. "That is what the prune-man says."

Devon knelt beside the android. "Hey," he said. "Can you sit up?"

The android popped upright like bread springing out of a toaster. "Al can sit up! Al can lay down! Al can do many things!"

"Yeah, I see that," Devon said. "Your name is Al?"

"Al's name is Alfonso Beneducci!" the girl said. "But you

can call Al, Al."

Jaz's face grew darker, and Vix lit a cigarette.

"Okay, Al," Devon said. "Where did you come from?"

"Al came from a ship-ship. Her beings all went to black, so she left." Her hair flashed from blue to orange to pink. "Al is happy to see beings again! Al does get very lonely."

"Okay, I've had enough of the bot," Kale said. "Scraps, would you get it out of here, please? I don't care if you blow the damn thing up. I don't want to see it anymore."

Scraps scowled at him and knelt in front of the android girl. "Here, little one," he said. "How about you come with me?"

"Al is not supposed to talk to strangers." The little android looked very solemn.

"Not supposed to talk to strangers but she jumps into the middle of our head hunt?" Vix threw her hands in the air. "Just shoot the damn thing."

"Well, my name is Scraps." Scraps didn't even bother to glare at Vix.

Al giggled. "Funny name-name!"

"Well, I think Al is a funny name."

Al flung herself at Scraps, giggling. "Al says we can be friends."

Scraps laughed. "I'm glad to hear it. Come with me. I want to introduce you to a friend of mine. His name is Marty, and he will love to meet you."

Scraps left the bay with Al in tow, but Xander hung back.

Kale walked to the back of his fighter, the *Scimitar*, and opened the rear hatch. He pulled out a man in a dirty white coat. Zen Mitchem. Exactly the same as Xander remembered.

The intercom system blared, and Captain McLeod spoke.

"Where are we, people?"

Kale pounded the talk button. "Head on to Ring-Seven," he said. "We're set down here."

Mitchem stirred. He looked up and spotted Xander, staring openly at her. He snapped back to reality when Devon knelt and grabbed the back of his dirty coat.

"Hey," he hissed, his bruised and bloody face frantic with fear. "Hey, look. You can't—you can't turn me in. They'll find me."

"You should have thought of that before you started running Fantasy." Devon seized Mitchem by his cuffs and dragged him to his feet. "Up."

Xander stepped back as Devon headed her way, struggling with Mitchem.

"Wait!" he cried, terror in his eyes. "You! You were on the ship. You saw Stone. You know what he's like. He'll kill me."

"Playing with fire." Devon hauled him toward the corridor.

"I'll give you information." Mitchem wailed. "Whatever you want."

"We'll talk, Mr. Mitchem," Devon said. "But not here." Devon dragged him out of the bay toward the brig.

Xander stared after them until she felt Kale's eyes on her. She turned to him and found him staring at her, his left cheek red with her hand print.

He held out his hand to Jaz. "Come on. Scraps will want a closer look at that after he drops the bot off with Marty. I'll walk you to the medbay."

"You don't need to do that, Kale."

"Yeah, Jaz. I do."

Kale and Jaz left together, Jaz leaning on Kale just enough to take a step without wincing. She must have lost a good deal of blood to be so lightheaded.

The smell of cigarette smoke drifted toward her. Vix leaned against the loading console, tapping her cigarette into a beer can. Xander narrowed her eyes at her. She didn't want to talk to Vix, but she needed to understand why. With the rest of the crew gone, this would be the best time to try it.

Talking to Vix was a bad idea, but if she had done something to make Vix angry, she needed to know how to make it right.

"Vix?"

"What?"

"Why did you tell me to wear a hat on Elara?"

"Figured that out, did you?"

That didn't deserve a response. "Why did you lie to me?"

Vix smirked. "Because I don't like you."

"Why?"

"I gotta' have a reason not to like you? Maybe I don't like you because you're you."

"I don't know me," Xander said. "How can you?"

"Sometimes a gal just knows." Vix picked up her enviro-suit helmet. "And I can tell. You're trouble."

Xander scowled.

"You can't deny it, kid. If Knightshade wants you, we should just let them have you, but Talon's got it in his head to be some kind of hero." Vix sneered. "You should just accept it. You're gonna' get us all killed."

"I didn't ask for your help."

"You didn't?"

"No."

Vix shoved another cigarette between her lips. "Actions speak louder than words, kid. I heard that somewhere and thought it was junk. But maybe it's true."

"Is that why you stole my clothes?"

Vix arched her eyebrows in mock denial.

"That was you, wasn't it? You did that too."

Vix smirked again.

"You did all that because you want me to leave?"

"Read whatever you want into it, kid. I just don't like you."

Xander took a calming breath. She wanted to get angry. She wanted to shout and fight. Didn't Vix know what could have happened? But fighting wouldn't change anything, and they still had a long way to go. They had to work this out.

"Vix, what did I do to you?"

Vix blew smoke in her face. "Not a damned thing."

She brushed past her and disappeared into the shadows of the corridor.

CHAPTER 20

Alfonso Beneducci sat in the chair, swaying back and forth and humming a strange little tune as Marty completed his examinations. As Scraps had predicted, Marty had taken charge of it immediately, fascinated by its odd behavior. Marty had called everyone down to see it when he was certain it wasn't a threat.

Ben had remained on the bridge, and only Jaz kept her distance, glaring at the android like she thought it would suddenly attack everyone.

Xander tilted her head as she looked at the android. "She really looks human. I mean, except for her hair."

Al's fiber-optic cable hair shimmered yellow in the engine lights before it slowly changed to blue.

"I've never seen an android like this before." Marty marveled as he scrutinized the movement of her arms and legs. "Sit up." The android obeyed, and Marty opened a panel hidden on the back of her neck. "This circuitry is way beyond me. I've never seen a design like this. This is nuts."

"I remember something about human-like androids being all the rage some number of years ago," Captain McLeod said. "But I never saw one." McLeod glanced at Kale. "Something out of NUJenesis, you think?"

"How would I know?"

"You seem to know an awful lot about NUJenesis and Braedon Knight," Vix said. "Maybe you'd know something about this too."

"Well, I don't."

Marty closed the panel in Al's neck and shook his head. "There's no danger." He brushed his hands off and put his gloves back on. "Looks like some of her circuits have been fused over."

"Which ones?" Captain McLeod asked.

"Some of her personality programming," Marty said, "which is probably why she's so weird. But—I don't know. I've never seen a matrix like it before. So maybe she's just goofy by design."

"Goofy by design!" Al laughed out loud.

Newt barked and ran up to the chair, sniffing at Al's bare feet. Al bent over and looked at the Pomeranian.

"A puppy!" The android lifted the dog into her arms. "Hello, little puppy." Newt licked her face.

"Ach, look." Claude bellowed a jolly laugh. "Newt likes her, *ja.*"

"It's not a *her*, Claude," Vix snipped. "It's an android."

"But she was designed to be a girl," Xander said. "So that's what we should call her."

Xander ignored the face Vix made at her.

"Al," Captain McLeod said, "who is your maker?"

"Al doesn't know."

"How did you come to be on Elara, and why did you get in my people's way?"

Al blinked for a moment, her verdant eyes sparkling. "Al was there—" Her face went blank. "Al doesn't know."

"You don't know?"

"Al was on a ship-ship."

"Yes?"

"And the ship-ship went to black so Al put the people-persons in the pod-pods. And then she was on the world-world and then she heard the boom-boom and ran-ran to see-see and wee-wee-wee!"

"Pods?" Evy arched her eyebrows.

"Stasis pods?" Captain McLeod's jaw muscles twitched with impatience. "You said you put them in stasis?"

"Al put the people-persons in stasis." The android nodded with every word.

"What happened?"

"They went to black."

"Went to black," Captain McLeod repeated. "What does that mean?"

"Ceased to exist. Ceased to be."

"They died?"

Al thought for a moment. "They went to black."

"How?"

The android's face fell. "Al does not know. But Al was very sad."

"Are they still in stasis?" Kale asked. "Where are they?"

"Yes, on the ship-ship in the deep-deep," Al said, "but Al thinks it is not wise for other beings to see them."

"Why not?" Devon asked.

"Al's crew of beings became very ill."

"Is that why they died?" Captain McLeod narrowed his eyes. "They died of a sickness?" He shot a look at Marty, who quickly began running viral scans.

"The possibility is possible," Al stated in a sing-song tone. "Al was very sad."

"How can an android be sad?" Evy asked. "I didn't think they could have emotions."

NAMELESS

"They can't." Captain McLeod stood. "But they can mimic them. This one seems to have the ability to mimic everything that *is* human, from grief to loneliness to joy. So well it's hard to tell she's *not* human."

Xander looked at Devon. "And that's not normal?"

"No." Devon shook his head. "That's not normal."

"Well, instead of us sitting around here staring at her," Scraps said, "how about we get to know her better?"

Jaz scoffed from the doorway, drawing all eyes to her. Her eyes shone with contempt. "It's a friggin' android, Elek. You don't get to know it."

Xander raised her eyebrows. What did Jaz have against androids?

"Is she clean, Marty?" Captain McLeod asked.

Marty closed his hand-held scanner. "All clean," Marty said. "No germs on this kid."

"Good," Captain McLeod said. "Scraps, you have responsibility for her. Make sure she doesn't get into something she shouldn't."

"Got it."

"The rest of you, go back to work. Marty, make sure the engines are running efficient like."

"But it said its crew died." Kale leaned on Marty's worktable and folded his arms. "Doesn't that bother you?"

"Oh, hush yourself." Captain McLeod glared at him. "We'll take care of it later. We can leave the damned thing at the next stop for all I care. If we're wanting to pursue this ship of Xander's, we need to go now. End of discussion."

Jaz scoffed again and stormed away. Vix followed her.

That didn't seem like normal behavior for Jaz. Maybe

263

Xander didn't know how Jaz should act, but the android's appearance seemed to have put her in a terrible mood.

Al stood on spindly legs and circled the chair. Captain McLeod sighed.

"Scraps," he said, "you sure you can handle her?"

"Not a problem," Scraps said. "But a question. Do androids eat?"

Al stopped and beamed. "Al is programmed to mimic all forms of human behavior. The consuming of num-nums is among them."

"So you eat." Captain McLeod raised his eyebrows.

"Al has not eaten since yesterday."

"Well, that won't do." Scraps took Al's hand. "Come with me, and we'll fix you something good to eat."

"Oo! Num-nums? Num-nums!"

Scraps led Al down the corridor.

"I'll go too," Xander said.

Evy nodded at her, and Xander started after them. She paused at the doorway when Captain McLeod began doling out orders.

"Kale, Devon," Captain McLeod turned to them, "one of you mates stay on the bridge and monitor our progress. And one of you go talk to Mr. Mitchem about our travel plans."

Both men nodded and headed together for the bridge.

"And, you, Dr. Berkley." Captain McLeod turned to look at her.

Evy stiffened and raised her chin. "Yes, Captain McLeod?"

"Would you care for a cup of tea?"

Xander expected Evy to snap at him. But Evy's expression shocked her. The blond neuro-therapist smiled—a real smile.

"Only if you have Earl Grey."

264

Captain McLeod laughed. "What self-respecting spaceship captain doesn't?"

Xander expected Evy to stomp off and tell him exactly where to put his tea kettle, but she didn't.

"That's very thoughtful of you, Captain McLeod."

Captain McLeod stopped by her side. "Call me Talon, please, lass. And it's not thoughtful at all. Purely selfish motivation."

"How is that?"

"Are you familiar with the legends of King Arthur?"

Evy looked skeptical. "Yes? Are you?"

Captain McLeod gave a hearty laugh. "I certainly am. One of my favorite topics of study." He grinned. "And I would honestly love to hear your take on the Excalibur legend."

Xander gaped as Evy gave a gentle laugh. She couldn't stop staring as Evy and Captain McLeod left the room together.

Motion out of the corner of her eye caused her shoulders to square. Kale stood in the opposite doorway. He stared in the direction Captain McLeod and Evy had gone, eyebrows angled in disbelief.

He picked up a beam light from Marty's worktable. As he grasped the handle, she noticed his long, slender fingers. How could a man with such delicate fingers end up in such a rough trade as bounty hunting?

And then he turned his eyes on her and stared, burning through her.

Her face went red. She didn't understand his eyes, didn't know what he was trying to communicate.

What did he want? He'd already expressed what he thought about her.

When he stared at her like that, her throat closed. Her tongue went numb, and her mind blanked, like she had forgotten how to speak. Face burning, she forced a smile and hoped it came off pleasantly as she walked toward the galley. He didn't follow, but she could feel his penetrating gaze on her back long after she'd left his sight.

Staying away from him would help them both. She only upset him, and his eyes only confused her. Keeping the peace mattered more than satisfying her curiosity.

Xander hurried to the galley. She arrived just as Scraps finished heating up a bowl of stew. He had seasoned it with the spice packets that came in bulk dehydrated roasts. Scraps had explained the packets weren't as good as fresh herbs but would do in a pinch.

"Hello, Xander." Scraps handed the bowl to the android.

Xander took a seat at the table and watched Al down the whole bowl in a few minutes. She also ate three fried slices of ham Scraps set in front of her and a bowl of instant ramen noodles. In between, she must have drunk a gallon of water, tea, and milk.

Scraps laughed. "Good to have someone who appreciates my cooking."

"Al is full now," Al drawled.

She leaned back in her chair and promptly went to sleep, snoring loudly.

Xander smiled. "She *does* mimic humans well, doesn't she?"

"Very well."

Xander pursed her lips as she watched the sleeping android.

Scraps noticed. "What is it, dear?"

"I'm just thinking. That's all."

"Thinking about what?"

Xander hesitated. "Al and I aren't all that different."

"How so?"

266

"She doesn't know who she is."

"She's an android, Xander. Androids don't struggle with self-identity because they have none."

"She doesn't know why she's here, what purpose she serves. She doesn't know if she has a family."

"Again, Xander, she's an—"

"Android. I got that, Scraps. But, still."

"I suppose, in a certain light, you *are* alike, but there's one main difference." Scraps took her hands. "An android can't forget. Al will only remember what she is programmed to remember. But you, Xander, *can* remember who you are and where you come from." He patted her hands. "It's just going to take some time."

Xander gripped his hands. What would he think if she hugged him? How long had it been since she'd had a real hug? Scraps might be okay with it, but it wasn't worth risking.

"Thanks, Scraps," she said instead.

They cleaned up the kitchen together while Al dozed, often breaking into song and making both Xander and Scraps laugh.

Xander stacked dishes in the cabinets above the stove burners.

You have remembered something, her mind said. *You've remembered your faith, and you haven't told anyone about it.*

That's what Christians were supposed to do, tell people what they believe. But she got the distinct feeling that no one would care. Maybe Talon and Evy would but from a literary perspective. Devon would because he was Devon, just like Scraps. But it wasn't Scraps or Devon or Talon or Evy she wanted to talk to. She wanted to talk to Kale, even though she always ended up making him angry. "So, Xander."

Xander glanced at him. "Yeah?"

"Where did you learn to make salad from apples?" Scraps propped his elbows on the counter.

Xander smiled at his flyaway hair and sparkling blue eyes. "I don't remember."

"Ah, a shame." Scraps arranged bowls and pans under the counter. "Perhaps you have some other recipes tucked away in your funny little brain. When you remember them, you must share. The salad of apples is quite wonderful."

"I'm glad you approve."

"Scraps-approved." He gave her a thumbs up.

What would she do without Scraps? Wonderful, brilliant, kind Scraps.

He set his hand on her shoulder. "What has you so quiet, Xander?"

She blinked at him. "I'm fine, Scraps. Just thinking."

"About?"

"It's complicated."

Scraps rolled his eyes. "Then it has to do with Kale, yes?"

She couldn't keep her jaw shut. It slanted open without her permission.

"Yes." Scraps patted her shoulder and started wiping down the counter. "You should go talk to him."

"Scraps, I—"

"No. Go talk to him."

"I'm trying to stay away from him, Scraps." Xander crossed her arms. "It's better for both of us."

"Ah, this is what you've told yourself, yes? Yes." Scraps laughed and hung the washcloth over the handle on the stove door.

"Yes. Because it's complicated."

"Kale is always complicated." Scraps sighed and set his

hands on his hips. "You should talk to him." He flashed her a grin. "You would be a good friend to him."

A friend? Friends with Kale? Xander almost laughed. What a ridiculous notion! Scraps couldn't be serious.

He beamed at her.

Okay, maybe he could be.

"Scraps," Xander leaned on the counter, "Kale doesn't want to be friends with me."

"Have you asked him?"

"Well-no."

Scraps waved his hand at her. "Go. Talk to him."

"We always misunderstand each other." Xander threaded her fingers together. "He never listens to what I'm saying. He puts words in my mouth. He hears things that I don't actually say."

"He is a man. You are a woman. You speak different languages." Scraps took off his apron and hung it on the hook in the corner. "Go. Talk to Kale. You will be happy. He will be happy. Then, I will be happy."

"I don't know, Scraps."

Scraps took her shoulders and smiled into her face. "Go."

The man was infuriating.

But what if he was right? What if just talking to Kale openly was the key?

Maybe if she tried to talk to him without aggression, without any expectations, without trying to make a point, he would talk to her. That's all she really wanted. A conversation. She'd spoken to everyone else. Even Vix. Even Ben. She'd had a longer conversation with the Pomeranian than she'd had with Kale.

Surely he didn't always want to be the exception.

She would apologize for Elara. She would thank him. She

wouldn't let him fluster her, as he seemed so talented at doing. And maybe—just maybe—they could be friends.

CHAPTER 21

Xander peeked into the darkened brig where Vix guarded Zen Mitchem in his cell. A row of green glowing energy bars penned him inside, but the flickering emerald light shone enough that Xander could make out his form against the cell wall. Sleeping maybe? Or unconscious.

She refused to talk to Vix. Vix had made her dislike perfectly clear to her. So if Kale wasn't guarding Mitchem, where was he?

Xander walked down the hall, trying to think of where Kale might go on the *Prodigal* when he had time to kill.

What would she say to him? How did she begin to apologize?

Just keep it simple. Just tell the truth. That's all.

A muted thump stopped her outside one of the open doors in the corridor. The sound echoed down the passageway, coming from beyond the darkened doorway at the far end.

She peered around the door jamb into a long, narrow room, walls lined with practice swords, staffs, and a vast array of firearms. The far end of the room featured a firing range. To the side of the room, a practice mat for sparring took up a whole corner. The rest of the space seemed dedicated to weights and boxing.

Only Kale was in the room, and he seemed to have a grudge against a punching bag in the corner.

Xander caught her breath as he turned an intricate kick that made the bag belch dust as though it could actually feel pain.

Beautiful.

Men were supposed to be rugged. Handsome. Rough and tough. Weren't they? Where had she gotten that idea?

He attacked, swinging, kicking, flowing with deceptively graceful blows. Xander strained her memory, seeking any thought or image of another person who had captured her attention; she couldn't find anything. Or maybe being so close to Kale made it hard for her to think clearly. That was a definite possibility.

She closed her eyes long enough to pull in a steadying breath.

Kale thought he knew everything, though. He acted like he did. He talked to her like he did.

Well, he didn't.

Maybe he knew criminals and crime. Maybe he knew about bounty hunting. Maybe he knew what made a good prostitute versus a bad one, but he didn't know anything about her. He couldn't, because she didn't.

And if he thought she would cower and run away from him, he was wrong. If he thought he could intimidate her with his beautiful eyes and his graceful limbs and his amazing, incredible hair—well he had another thing coming.

And if he told her off, fine. But she would have her say. And he could choose to reject her friendship based on what she was instead of who he thought she was.

She steeled herself and stepped forward. He dealt a resounding punch on the bag.

"You want something, kid?"

Xander pressed her lips together.

Kid. One strike against her already. He thought her a child. She wasn't. She'd fought off rapists and deadbeats. She'd looked a Knightshade assassin in the eye. Maybe she didn't know how old she was, but she wasn't a kid.

"I want to apologize."

He glared over his shoulder at her. "What?"

"For slapping you. You didn't deserve it. You were just trying to protect me. And I'm sorry."

He narrowed his eyes before he scoffed and set his hands on his hips, turning to face her fully. "You want to be friends."

Xander gawked. He couldn't have known that, not unless he could read her mind. And that possibility brought up a whole slew of other problems.

She blinked. "Yes."

"No."

"No?"

"You deaf?"

"You haven't even let me—"

Kale whirled on her. "You are trouble. I said it from the start, kid."

"I'm not a kid."

"You're more trouble than you're worth. We'll get your damned ship, and then you'll go your own way and leave me the hell alone."

Xander squared her shoulders. Arrogant, stupid Kale. Why was she apologizing to him again? Her hand print still flared red on the side of his face. Right. For slapping him. So they could be friends.

She was too much trouble?

"I'm still going to apologize," she said through clenched teeth.

"Fine. Apologize." He turned back to the punching bag and steadied it. "Then go away. I'm busy."

"I've talked to everyone else on this ship."

"You never stop talking, kid."

"I'm not a kid. And I just—"

"What?" He rolled his shoulders and glared back at her. "You feel bad because you hit me? You think you owe me something?" His eyes hardened. "You don't. You need to stay away from me."

Xander bristled, her cheeks burning. "Would you just give me—"

"Go away." He landed a brutal punch on the bag. "Go read a book or something if you're bored."

"I'm not bored. I just want to have a real conversation with you."

Kale whirled and leaned into her personal space in a single, fluid step, the motion bathing her in his scent like cedar and spice. Her head spun with the smell of him.

"You annoy the hell out of me." His voice rumbled, low and rough.

Jerk. Stupid, arrogant, beautiful jerk.

"You act like you know everything." He scoffed. "And that's bullshit. Because you don't even know your own name."

She craned her neck to look him in the eye. "Some things are more important than a name."

Kale folded his arm, still hanging too close to her for proper breath. "Such as?"

How could he expect her to think when he smelled like cedar and wouldn't get out of her face?

"Come on, smart ass. You've got it all figured out. What's more important than a name?"

She swallowed.

"What's more important than your name?" He poked her in

the shoulder. "Because you don't seem to hesitate about risking our lives to find it."

Anger colored her cheeks again. If he didn't shut up, she was going to slap him again.

"The way I see it," Kale wrinkled his lip, "enough people have already died for your name."

"They didn't die for my name," she whispered, voice harsh and trembling. "They died for me. And I never asked them to. Just like I didn't ask you either."

He leaned closer. Too close. Why was he so close?

"Why are you in here?"

"I came to apologize."

"Bull shit. Nobody does that."

"I do. Because I want to be your friend."

"Why?"

"You saved me. Why not?"

He stepped back, face cold, eyes distant. "You don't want to be my friend, kid. I don't have friends.

"What about Devon?"

Kale paused. For the briefest moment, she thought she saw light in his eyes, but it vanished, leaving his face colder than before. Kale turned away from her. "Devon is worth it. You aren't."

He left, and Xander watched him go, stunned silent, no longer finding the shift of his hair so attractive.

I guess that's my answer.

Kale wouldn't be her friend. He wouldn't have anything to do with her. He wouldn't forgive her.

The *Prodigal* shuddered.

She peered out the nearest porthole to see the ship docking alongside a small space station, nestled between the misty rings of

Jupiter. A blinking holosign flashed *Ring-Seven* some distance out.

Ring-Seven, where Zen Mitchem would earn the crew a bounty.

Kale didn't want her around, but that didn't mean she couldn't watch them lead Mitchem away.

She reached the docking bay just as the connection corridor opened.

Mitchem, a tremulous, frightened wreck, cowered between Kale and Devon. Ben stood behind them with his arms crossed, and he shifted his weight from one foot to the other as she approached, nervously as though he feared she would talk to him again.

He had nothing to be afraid of.

Kale noticed her too. He glanced over his shoulder, pressed his lips together in a thin line, and narrowed his eyes.

"All right, people," Kale said, his eyes on his partners. "Devon, you take Mr. Mitchem and get the payday. Ben, what is Talon sending you out for?"

"Captain has requested a few necessities," Ben said. "Marty needs a basic power coupling, Scraps needs syringes, and I'm out of wine."

"Well, don't take all day. Talon wants us gone ASAP."

"I won't be long." Ben stepped out of the bay and disappeared around the side of the ship.

Mitchem twisted in Devon's arms to look back at Xander. "Little girl!" He flailed. "Don't let them take me. Stone will find me. You saw what he's like."

Devon shoved him ahead.

"You know what he'll do to me," Mitchem screamed as Devon dragged him off the ship. "You were on Callisto, weren't you? Just let your imagination run wild. He'll do worse to me—and

NAMELESS

worse to you if he finds you."

Devon hauled Mitchem away. He didn't stop screaming.

Xander watched Devon and Mitchem until they disappeared from the ramp.

Kale stood in place, staring at her again. When she felt the weight of his gaze, she crossed her arms and glared at him. She didn't expect his arrogant smirk. What was that look for?

"Callisto?"

Oh, of course. Great. Xander's face warmed. "Yes."

"You were on Callisto?"

"What about it?"

He chuckled.

"What?"

"Don't be defensive, kid. Just saying."

"Look—I'm not—I waited tables."

"Uh-huh."

"I'm not a whore."

"Sure, kid."

He still hadn't moved. Why? What did he want? Hadn't he just told her he didn't want to be around her? Why was he hanging around?

Xander crossed her arms and gazed out over the bustling port. She froze when Kale's fingers brushed through her hair, isolating the short strands Stone had cut.

"Why is your hair shorter here?"

She ignored how good he smelled. "Stone. He cut my hair on the *Acheron*."

His fingers were in her hair. Why? He didn't want to be her friend. He didn't want to be her anything.

"What did he do with it?"

277

"He kept it."

"Huh." Kale withdrew his hand. "Interesting."

He started walking.

"Kale. Stone—he—"

He stopped. He didn't look back at her, his back straight. "Yes?"

"Stone frightened me."

Slowly, Kale looked over his shoulder at her, his eyes so deep there seemed no end to them.

"Then, you should be terrified of me."

He marched down the ramp with solid steps, shoulders square, wind in his hair.

CHAPTER 22

Ring-Seven was one of the seediest stations in the system. Kale didn't like it. There were too many dark alleys, too many places for an ambush. Great for tracking bounty heads, not so great when you were the target. And walking around in Ring-Seven always made him feel like a target.

Too many bars, too many ships, too much noise. Not that he disliked any of those, but having them all crammed together in one small area overloaded his senses. Knowing Stone was on the prowl didn't help his nerves either.

He leaned against the cold sheet metal lining the exterior of the Ring-Seven precinct, waiting for Devon to cash in their payday on Mitchem.

A woman with red hair pranced past him on heels like stakes. No, not red hair. Not really. It was the tawny apple shade of a low-quality dye. Not like Xander's hair.

Xander had real red hair, the color of Jupiter's atmospheric storms, the color of the sunlight in the Martian sky. A frizzy ridiculous mess softer than satin.

Why the hell had he touched her damned hair? It had been instinct, curiosity. He'd wanted to feel it, and now he couldn't stop feeling it.

She had to stay away from him.

A flash of blond hair alerted him to Devon's presence, but he didn't react and let his partner pound him on the shoulder. Then, he smiled and let Devon think he hadn't seen it coming.

"Full creds, partner." Devon grinned.

"Good. Let's get back to the ship." Kale turned and started back the way he'd come.

"Damn, Kale." Devon jogged to keep up with him. "Nose down. What's got your panties in a twist?"

"I don't like it here."

Devon doubled his pace to walk evenly with his best friend. "So."

"So, what?"

"What was that back on the ship?"

"What do you mean?"

"You staying behind. You never stay behind." Devon poked him in the ribs. "Isn't that right, Mr. Sullivan? Isn't that why we came up with that dumb alias in the first place? So you could turn in bounty heads without freaking the System Police out?"

"Let it go, Devon."

"Bull shit."

"Lay off. No reason." Kale growled under his breath. Devon knew exactly how to get under his skin.

"Xander was on Callisto."

Devon blinked. "Really."

Kale narrowed his eyes at his friend. "You knew, didn't you?"

"Knew what?"

"That she was on Callisto."

"Yeah, she told me," Devon said. "It's pretty amazing, if you think about it."

"Think about what?"

"Someone like her surviving a hellhole like Callisto?"

"It's not strange," Kale said. "She's probably just really good between the sheets."

Damn. Why had he said that?

Xander in bed. Xander with her hair like velvet firelight and her eyes like stars. Clear skin, ribs he could trace with his fingertips.

Stop it. You're not thinking about that.

Damn, Xander. Damn, Devon. Damn both of them.

Devon frowned. "No, Kale, I don't think that's it."

Kale forced a laugh. "Dev, there's no way that anyone—girl, boy, man, woman—can spend any time on Callisto and make it out alive without putting out. Even just a little."

That was a fact, and Kale ignored how his heart rate sped up at the thought of someone else with his hands in Xander's hair.

Stupid. Stupid kid.

"Kale, she said no one touched her."

"She's lying."

"She believes God protected her."

Kale stopped walking. "What?"

"That's what she said."

"God? What the hell does that mean?"

"Not really sure."

"God. Isn't that a Sanctum thing?"

"Yeah, I think so. But Xander's not from the Sanctum."

"She has her moments."

Devon leveled a glare at him, and Kale rolled his eyes.

"Okay, fine." He sank his hands into his pockets. "She's not from the Sanctum. You're right, but I don't get her, Dev. She makes no sense at all."

"Uh-huh."

"I mean, before we made port, she was trying to apologize to me."

"Apologize?"

"She's batshit insane."

"Crazy. Actually—"

"Like she could possibly understand anything about me. Like she could comprehend it. Acting like she can just tell me what do to and when to do it. She's the one who needed my help, damn it."

"That's—"

"She wore a hat on Elara, Devon. You say she's not a whore? Right. Wearing a hat on Elara means you're just asking to get jumped. Everybody knows that. Everybody except her."

"Great, Kale. But—"

"She annoys the hell out of me."

"Kale."

"Doesn't she bother you?" Kale uttered a frustrated growl. "The way she looks at you with those big damn gray eyes of hers."

"I thought they were green."

"No, they're gray."

"You sure?"

"Positive. Big gray eyes. And all those damn freckles."

Devon made a sound somewhere between a choke and a laugh. "Haven't noticed them."

"You have to look real hard."

"You been looking real hard, Kale?"

Kale froze.

What was Devon implying?

Kale glared at his best friend. What was his problem? The expression on Devon's face was positively giddy.

"Don't worry." Devon was laughing now. "I won't tell her."

"Tell her what?" Kale erupted. "There's nothing to tell! I'm just naturally observant."

"So naturally observant that you haven't noticed I've been trying to say something for the last five minutes?"

Kale blinked. "Of course, I noticed." He shifted his collar. "I was just—ignoring you."

"Right."

"Well, tell me, then."

Devon still chuckled as he and Kale started walking again.

Asshole. What did he know?

"I had a little heart to heart with Mr. Mitchem on the way to the precinct," Devon said, "and he decided he wanted the last laugh even if Stone and his men come to kill him. So he told me where the *Tempest* is meeting up with Knightshade to exchange the *Destiny*."

"You're kidding."

"Nope."

"I figured you would have asked him on the ship."

Devon shrugged. "I did, but he was tight-lipped. So I figured he'd crack just before we turned him in. Turns out I was right."

"You didn't have to torture him?"

"No, he just cracked. Right there. Said if he was gonna' die he wanted it to count for something."

"He must have been sneaking some of his own product."

"Likely."

Kale grimaced. "Was he sure?"

"Sounded sure. I was going to tell Talon when we get back."

Kale fell silent.

Part of him had hoped Mitchem wouldn't have known anything about the *Tempest*. Now that he'd spilled its location, they would have to pursue it. They would have to go after Xander's damned ship. Talon would insist.

It was the worst idea in a whole series of bad ideas, starting with letting the freckle-faced, gray-eyed redhead onboard to begin with.

Why had he saved her anyway? Had he just been thinking with his balls? That didn't make any sense. He hadn't thought with that part of his anatomy for years.

Even now, all he could figure was that he'd wanted to keep her safe. It had been a gut level reaction. He'd seen the terror in her eyes—those damned beautiful gray eyes—and the desperate need to protect her had been instinct.

He hadn't thought at all.

That was the problem.

"Kale, you *are* up for this, aren't you? I mean, you're not going back out all of a sudden and run off?"

Kale started and looked down at Devon.

"No. I'll stay in it. If for no other reason than to keep you dumb asses alive. But I don't like it, Dev. It's a bad idea."

Devon shoved his hands in his pockets. "Why are you so against it, Kale? Don't you want to stop them? Whatever they're doing, it can't be good."

"Say we find the *Tempest*, somehow get her damn ship back, do you honestly think Knight doesn't have a backup plan? Are you naïve enough to think people like us can stop something like Knightshade?"

Devon scowled but said nothing.

"You can't stop the syndicates, Devon. You of all people should remember that."

"And that means," Devon said, "we do nothing. We don't even try."

"Why try? We'll fail. Best case scenario, we'll die."

NAMELESS

Devon shook his head.

"And I don't know about you, Dev, but I'm not ready to go yet."

Kale stopped, and Devon stopped beside him.

The *Prodigal* still rested on the landing pad, but Xander sat on a bench outside the ship. Hair loose, shifting in the breeze, not paying attention to anything.

Anyone could have walked up to her. Anybody could have grabbed her and dragged her off. And she wouldn't have seen it coming.

A redheaded woman with legs like a colt sitting outside alone in a seedy port like Ring-Seven? She was just asking for trouble.

Devon poked his head around Kale's shoulder. "What's she doing outside the ship?"

"You see?" Kale snapped. "That's what I'm talking about. Annoying as hell."

Devon laughed.

"What?"

"Nothing."

"You laughed. Why did you laugh?"

"Because you just wasted a bunch of talk telling me you don't care about her, and it's obvious you do."

"I don't."

Devon was a jackass.

"Yeah, you do."

"I don't."

He needed to back off. He didn't know what he was talking about.

"Kale. You can't fool me, man." Devon grabbed his shoulder. "I'm your best friend. Stop denying you care about the kid. You

285

saved her ass, and you'll let her smart off to you—which you barely let me do."

Kale didn't look at him. Devon really knew how to get under his skin.

"And you get pissy when she does stupid stuff." Devon grabbed his elbow. "Which tells me that for some reason you don't want her to get hurt."

"Dev."

"And, the most interesting fact of all is that she annoys you."

Kale leveled a dark scowl at him.

"And you only let people you care about annoy you."

Kale said nothing, folding his arms and letting out a heavy sigh.

It had been a mistake joining the *Prodigal* crew. It had been a mistake trying to have a normal life. It had been a mistake letting Devon back into his head again. Devon had always known him too well. He'd always understood him, most of the time before he understood himself.

Devon was a jackass. But he was usually right.

"So why do you care about her?" Devon glanced back at her.

"Why do *you* care about her?" *Good. Redirection is the key.*

"She's sweet."

"Sweet?"

"Yeah."

"Dev, she's a pain in the ass."

"But a sweet pain in the ass."

"Damn it, Dev."

Devon laughed. "So what if she's wrong? So what if she's naïve?"

"She's ridiculous."

"So what?"

"She's going to get us killed."

"You don't know that. Kale, for all you know, maybe there's more we can do to stop the syndicates than you think. You can't exactly say you have a non-biased opinion of them, after all."

"Neither can you."

"No, neither can I. But I'm tired of running from it, Kale."

Kale stared into his best friend's face and remained quiet.

"And I think that's why I like her," Devon said. "She wants to know who she is. She'll do anything—even climb on a ship with people like us—to remember. She'll attack a syndicate to remember. She wants to know her past. She's not running from it. And I think that's why I like her." Devon glanced up at him. "I think that's why she annoys you."

Kale shut his eyes. "People have reasons for running, Dev."

"Sometimes they're good reasons. But you can't run forever."

Devon started toward Xander.

Kale held still, arms still crossed. Xander lifted her head as Devon approached. How could Devon not see the freckles? They were clear as day.

Devon was right. So was the kid right too?

Her face and eyes smiled as Devon spoke to her. She obviously had a lot of respect for him, which was deserved. Devon was a good person to respect.

Kale suppressed a chill as Xander's eyes found him.

Those huge damned gray eyes.

It was a quick look, barely more than a glance, but her expression revealed her thoughts. Confused. Hurt. Frustrated. And maybe a bit angry. Damn, she was beautiful angry.

She was even more beautiful flustered. When she'd appeared outside his quarters in the towel, holding all her clothes and squabbling with Newt, he'd thought he'd never seen anyone more beautiful.

For being so short, she had the longest legs he'd ever seen, and in that moment all he'd wanted to do was rip that towel off her and find out what it covered.

But she was just a kid. And he had no business getting close to anyone again. And she had no right to show up at his door waving her panties in his face, damn it! And he'd intended to tell her just that, but before he'd said anything, he'd seen her face.

Humiliation.

He'd expected her to crawl into a corner and never speak again; it was unthinkable for something so trivial to upset any woman he'd ever known.

He'd known then she couldn't have been a prostitute. But then the hat on Elara? Maybe she did it just to piss him off. But more likely, she was just a weird, stupid kid.

Why did he care about keeping her safe? Why the hell did it matter so much?

Maybe the naiveté, which she possessed in great quantities. Of course, she could never actually be as innocent as she looked. That was impossible for someone her age, whether she had spent time on Callisto or not. But she certainly did seem to need protection.

You're looking for redemption, his mind said softly. *And you think keeping her safe makes you a hero.*

He watched Devon pull her to her feet, and they both walked back toward him. She didn't look at him. She stared at the ground.

That's stupid. He clenched his jaw and blanked his face. *Even if it was my job to protect her, it wouldn't change anything.*

He wasn't a hero. He never had been.

And no girl could change that, not even an innocent one with freckles.

CHAPTER 23

Ring-Seven was noisy and crowded. Xander didn't like it at all, but she preferred watching people over lying on her bunk alone.

She had tried to sleep, but it hadn't come. And Captain McLeod had seen no issue with her sitting outside the ship waiting for Kale and Devon to return.

People choked the metal streets, all talking and selling and buying and shouting and haggling; the cacophony made her head spin.

She spotted a flash of dark red in the crowd. Easy to see, Kale stood so much taller than everyone else. He and Devon had stopped on the sidewalk, turned toward each other. In the set of their shoulders, Xander could tell how much they trusted each other.

Some distance behind them, another flash of red caught her eye. A scarf—a red scarf worn by an old man hobbling through the crowd. The scarf stood out, since no one else wore one. The old man had wrapped it around his neck and tied it.

Actually, she hadn't seen many people wearing scarves in the ports where they'd stopped. When was the last time she'd seen someone wearing a scarf? Had it been on Callisto? That sounded right. But who had it been?

Devon came toward her. Kale didn't approach. He hung back, deep in thought. Either that or he was trying collect himself. Her mere presence seemed enough to irritate him beyond reason.

She really needed to apologize, but that hadn't gone so well the last time she'd tried. Maybe Devon could help.

What had Devon done to earn Kale's friendship? Probably something ridiculous and masculine—like drinking too much and throwing knives at a fencepost. Or at each other.

Men.

"Hey, kid." Devon greeted her with a friendly smile.

"Hey, Devon."

Why did it bother her when Kale called her *kid* and not when Devon did?

"Why are you outside the ship?"

"I needed to get outside," she said.

She glanced past his shoulder to Kale. Xander would have given anything to know his thoughts. He just stood there with his arms crossed and his face like marble, the artificial light in his flyaway hair.

"Mitchem cracked, by the way."

"He what?"

"He told me where the *Tempest* is."

"So that means we can go after the *Destiny*?" Xander furrowed her brow.

"Yeah. That's what you want, isn't it?"

"Right." She glanced at Kale. "Devon?"

"Yeah?"

"Does Kale hate me?"

Devon cocked his eyebrows. "Hate you? No."

"Are you sure?"

"Yep."

"How do you know?"

"Because he hasn't killed you."

"I'm being serious, Devon."

291

"So am I."

She gave him a skeptical look.

"You do annoy the hell out of him."

"So he's said." Xander sighed. "I don't mean to. I guess I just can't help it."

"I think you're a sweet kid, Xander." Devon held out his hand. "And so does he. And I think that's part of it."

Xander took his hand. "I annoy him because I'm sweet?"

Devon helped her stand. "You annoy him because you're you."

"That's not very comforting, Devon."

He laughed again, and they started toward Kale together. As they got closer, her stomach fluttered. She couldn't look at him.

Okay, she thought, *we're going to talk, and he's going to start off antagonistic, but you can't snap back. Just take it and be nice. Don't say what you're actually thinking.*

She stopped walking and looked up. He was right there, his blue eyes drilling through her.

"Why are you outside the ship?"

See? Antagonistic. Right there. "I just needed some space." She forced cheerfulness. *Good job. No snapping back. Now he's calm and Devon is here, so try apologizing again.* "Kale, I really owe you a—"

A shadow crossed his face so abruptly her voice trailed off.

"Drink." He finished her sentence where she had faded.

"What?"

"You owe me a drink." He seized her under her arm and whirled her so quickly she nearly fell. He supported her entire weight, dragging her down the sidewalk.

His face was blank, his eyes alert.

NAMELESS

"Kale—what—"

"Tail?" Devon said, directly behind them.

"Yep."

"High road?"

"Go."

Devon made a big show of patting Kale on the back, and he disappeared into the crowd.

"I thought you were going back to the ship," Xander said.

"No."

"Where is Devon going?"

He didn't answer.

"A tail," she mumbled. "Someone's following us?"

"Yes."

"What are we doing? Where are we going?"

"This way."

"What do you want me to do?"

Kale glared down at her. "Stop talking."

She frowned. "What?"

"Do you ever stop?" He shook her arm. "Talking? Stop. No more. Just shut up."

Xander's jaw dropped. *Fine. No more talking. If that's what he wants. Jerk.*

Kale dragged her down the sidewalk, and he stopped, eyes sweeping the teeming marketplace. He hauled her into an alley off the side of the main road. It blocked most of the artificial sunlight.

She didn't like it. Not at all. It reminded her too much of the alleys on Callisto, rat-infested, smelling of garbage and human waste.

Kale didn't hesitate, didn't even slow down until they were midway down the alley.

293

Then, he shoved her against the wall, one hand under her arm holding her steady and the other hand against her waist, pushing her back.

Her heart leaped into her throat as he bent and pressed his face against her neck.

"Don't move," he muttered against her skin.

Move? She could hardly breathe. Whenever she could draw a full breath, all she could smell was him. He didn't smell like what she'd expected. Warm, cedar and spice. And far too much of it far too close.

Her face flooded with heat.

What is he doing? Am I letting him do this?

Just like every other man she'd met. Touching her, groping her, asking something of her she had absolutely no intention of giving.

After this, he didn't deserve an apology.

She shifted away.

"Stop," he hissed against her neck.

Stop what? He's the one who's—

"Calm down." The hand under her arm moved up, grabbed her neck, and bent her head back as he pinned her against the wall with his hips. "Hold still," he breathed in the shell of her ear. The hand on her waist slid across her back, cradling her in the crook of his elbow.

Calm down? Is he serious?

His enormous hands spanned her whole rib cage with long slender fingers.

Could he feel the rapid pounding of her heart? Her head whirled.

Like being held by a brick wall, his arms and chest were

NAMELESS

made of warm marble. Taut, strong muscles crushed her close, encircling her, enveloping her in a solid wall of stone with a beating heart and hot breath that tickled the back of her neck.

She felt dizzy, disoriented, either from not breathing or from breathing too much of him. He needed to let go. She needed him to let go of her right away, but she had no strength in her arms. Why was he doing this? Wasn't there someone following them?

His lips burned the side of her neck, turned the protesting muscles in her arms to jelly. She couldn't stop shivering. His lips found her jaw line, her ear lobe, the crease of her eyelids.

She would explode. He had to stop. What was he doing to her? And why didn't she want him to stop? What was wrong with her?

He found her lips, his breath ghosting across them.

She wanted him to kiss her.

In that instant, she needed to feel his lips against hers. She didn't understand, but she didn't care. She wanted it. She wanted it more than she wanted to remember her name.

His biceps tensed. She felt corded muscle, powerful and wiry, pressed against the soft curve of her ribcage. He angled her body against his in a way that forced every thought from her mind.

And then—something moved behind him.

A chill washed over her at motion in the shadows over Kale's shoulder. Something moved, something dark. But before she could breathe a single word of warning, Kale dropped her.

He dropped her!

And thrust his right elbow back with brutal force smashing the sharp bone into the sternum of a man directly behind him. In a single, smooth motion, Kale grasped the man by the hair and smashed his face into the brick wall.

295

Xander gawked in horror. Kale jammed his left elbow into the man's lower back, and bones snapped.

The man collapsed to the alley floor at Xander's feet. He wore a black jumpsuit and canvas belts loaded with ammunition for the two blasters in holsters under his arms.

Dead.

The man was dead. How hard had Kale hit him?

Light flashed through the darkness in the alley, and the bricks by Xander's head erupted in a spray of mortar. Dust showered her, and the air tingled with the smell of ozone.

Laser fire. Someone was shooting at her?

One moment, Kale stood gazing at the dead man at their feet. The next he threw the dead man's body on top of her and spun in place, the shadows sparkling with crimson bursts of laser pulses. She didn't even have time to be disgusted at the feel of the dead man's body against her.

Three laser blasts fizzled against the dead man's back.

Cringing, she ducked her head.

Was it Knightshade? It had to be. And Kale—he'd hidden her? Is that why he threw the dead man on top of her?

The numbness faded, but she couldn't stop trembling. Breath came in short, shallow gasps. Who were these people? Why were they attacking? What did they want? Where did they come from?

Xander wanted to get up, move, run away, but escaping the dead man's body meant probably getting shot. And throwing away the protection Kale had given her would probably make him angry, though at the moment, she wavered between gratitude and being furious at him.

Kale spun in the shadows like a dancer. Why? Attacking maybe? All the shooters fired from outside his reach.

296

Wrong. Kale's left arm caught an invisible opponent in the neck with a sickening crunch. Dressed in black, the men slipped through the darkness like ghosts. How could Kale see them?

Two men in the black jumpsuits ran at him through the shadows. Kale clotheslined one of them, spun a perfect kick, and snapped the second man's neck in a single blow.

The first man staggered to his knees, and Kale whirled, seized the man's head, and broke his neck. Kale bent and drew both blasters from the dead man's holsters, opening fire at the top of the alley.

Xander gaped as three men fell from the tops of the buildings and hit the alley floor.

He didn't stop; he kept shooting. Xander watched him move, anger melting away, replaced by utter terror at knowing someone capable of such immense destruction.

He snapped a man's neck like a twig with the same hands that had cradled her head. He crushed a man's windpipe with the same fingers that had spanned her ribs only moments early.

And she'd thought him a stranger before.

She didn't know this Kale at all.

The men in black jumpsuits just kept coming, streaming out of the shadows with guns, knives, and swords.

None of them got close enough to touch Kale. Not once. The blasters he'd stolen ran out of charge, and he resumed fighting hand-to-hand, using the hilts of the blasters.

It had to be Knightshade. Wasn't it possible for a syndicate as powerful as Knightshade to have tracked her? What if the men attacking Kale so viciously were really after her? What if this—all of this—was her fault?

Again.

How many of these stupid people did it take to capture her? This was ridiculous!

Kale dropped both blasters, twisted and bent from bludgeoning countless men to death, and faced the last attacker. The man didn't have a chance.

Kale drove his hand into the man's face, and he collapsed backward, unmoving.

Dead.

Some scientific part of Xander's mind knew Kale had driven the man's septum bone up into his brain. How could Kale could have possibly done something like that in a single blow?

After the last man fell, Kale stood like a statue, motionless and cold. Xander watched, not breathing, as his squared shoulders sloped a fraction. She sought out his eyes.

She wished she hadn't.

The clarity in his face stunned her, clarity on a level she hadn't expected to see in his expression. Blank. His face, his eyes were completely empty. Not guarded or hiding any emotion. His eyes simply lacked emotion. He had killed dozens of men in the span of ten minutes and felt nothing. No remorse. No regret. Nothing at all.

Kale Ravenwood was a killer.

She lay in stunned silence, staring at him.

Devon burst out of the shadows at the mouth of the alley. Whatever his high road plan had been, it seemed to have failed. His hair stuck out at every angle, and his mouth and nose gushed blood. But he didn't slow his approach. If anything, he ran faster.

Was he going to attack Kale? What was he doing? What was he thinking?

Sudden concern for Kale—and for Devon's sanity—surged

through Xander, and she shoved the body off, but her voice caught in her throat as Devon threw a brutal left-handed punch at Kale.

Bad idea. Such a bad idea. Kale would defend himself. Didn't Devon know that?

Kale leaned backward, Devon's knuckles barely grazing his chest, and Devon clobbered the man hidden in the shadows behind Kale.

Xander hadn't even seen him.

Kale turned and caught the man before he fell, snapping his neck.

"Kale."

"I know."

"They're Dragons."

"I know."

"How many more?"

"Too many."

In a blink, the alley swarmed with men in black jumpsuits, all firing blasters. The alley smelled like a closet full of burnt wires.

Kale and Devon didn't hesitate, drawing weapons and opening fire, and Xander cowered in her refuge behind the dead body. She could still see Kale and Devon. And she understood why Captain McLeod had made them partners. Kale and Devon moved completely in tune with each other.

Kale led, Devon followed, in perfect sequence, time after time after time. No holes, no breaks, no hesitations; they moved like one person. Kale kicked; Devon punched. Kale shot right; Devon shot left. Xander felt she could have danced to the rhythm they set.

Vix had said Devon and Kale were two halves of one brain, and Xander saw the truth of it now. Where Devon was weak, Kale was strong; where Kale needed support, Devon stood strong.

They were more than partners, more than brothers; they were very nearly the same person.

The generated cloud cover must have shifted, for the artificial solar matrix above brightened the dim murkiness of the alley, glinting on a dark metallic insignia emblazoned on her dead shield's jumpsuit, just over his heart.

The image of a dragon coiled around itself, barring its fangs, brandishing sharp claws.

A dragon? Her thoughts drifted to the terse conversation she had overhead between Devon and Kale. Devon had called the men *dragons.* Was that what the insignia meant?

She watched Kale and Devon shoot the same man through the chest at the same time. The dead man fell, and she could see the muted flash of the insignia on the man's jumpsuit as he hit the ground. Kale dropped the blaster, picked up another one, and killed the next attacker who moved.

Kale has a certain perspective on the syndicates, Devon had told her.

Xander blinked, the cold fist of icy panic tightening in her stomach.

Syndicates.

Her heart pounded in her chest. *Devon said syndicates. Plural. Are there—Is there more than one?* She looked again at the dead man on top of her. *Are the Dragons another syndicate?*

Her lungs clamped shut. Laser fire roared in her ears. Xander shook as she watched man after man throw himself at Kale, desperate to hurt him, to shoot him, to kill him. Not once—not once had any of them attempted to come after her.

Kale had never intended to hide her. His actions had been meant to protect her.

These people are after Kale.

In a flash, Kale and Devon separated. Xander heard Kale bellow, "Get the kid!"

The kid? She scowled to herself. *Oh. Me.*

She scurried out from under the dead body and crouched behind a trash dumpster. The alley still crawled with men in black jumpsuits. How many of them were there?

Kale hadn't stopped killing them. He had his arondight out, blasting away at each attacker. He didn't miss a shot. Everyone died.

Devon ran toward her, taking shelter behind another dumpster. He started shooting at the building roofs, where more laser blasts rained down on them.

"Xander, come on."

Too many lasers. Too many people. Xander didn't feel safe enough to simply run to Devon.

"Xander, now!"

He had to be joking. She didn't trust him that much.

Kale rammed the butt of his arondight into the underside of an attacker's jaw, jerked the man's blaster from his holster, kicked him in the stomach, and aimed the blaster—at Xander.

Her heart leapt into her throat.

Kale fired.

Xander couldn't move.

The pulse smashed into the dumpster a foot from her head.

"Move!" He thundered from across the alley.

Xander didn't wait to see what he would do if she hesitated again. She bolted to Devon. He snatched her arm and dragged her behind him as he kept firing.

Kale hadn't let up. He'd killed another dozen men in the time it took Xander to run to Devon. Whoever these men were, they had no qualms about throwing themselves at death. At the moment, Kale was death.

Devon started running, Xander on his heels. Somehow, Kale knew. He launched ahead of them, still shooting, still killing.

Would he ever stop? When they got back to the *Prodigal* could he switch it off and not kill his own crew? Or did killers work like that? Was the impulse to kill something they could turn on and off?

He shot at me. The thought kept running through her head. *He shot at me. Me.*

Yeah, she'd needed to move. But he didn't need to shoot at her.

Devon slid to a halt and knocked out an attacking soldier with an elbow to the throat. He snatched the man's blasters and started shooting again. They followed Kale through the alley to an open area with a large drainage grate. Dead men littered the ground.

What had he done to merit sending an army after him?

But someone had.

And Kale had killed them all.

He shot three more times; three more men fell dead.

A frightened yelp came from the shadows behind them. Without hesitation, Kale whirled, aimed, and fired. Someone gasped in pain.

Kale strode into the darkness and emerged, dragging a man with him. The man wore the same black jumpsuit with the black insignia of the dragon. Kale released him and let him fall to his knees. A wound gaped in his stomach.

Kale dropped the blaster and checked the charge in his arondight.

"Kale," Devon said.

Kale didn't respond.

Xander stared at the man kneeling before Kale.

Man? Hardly. He was young—maybe not even twenty. What was Kale going to do?

Kale lowered his weapon to the man's forehead, and the man's eyes widened.

"Don't!" Xander cried.

Kale pressed the muzzle of the arondight between the man's eyebrows.

"That was all of them, the whole platoon. I'm all that's left!" The man choked on a sob. "I'm just a medic!"

"You're a Dragon."

Kale shot him. The blast ripped through the man's head, and his body collapsed.

Xander's jaw hung open, but she couldn't help it. She couldn't stem the tears coursing down her cheeks.

If the man had been given the chance, he would have killed all of them without pause; but it didn't seem right that Kale hadn't hesitated to kill a wounded and defenseless man.

Kale searched the dead man's body, showing little respect for his remains.

Kale had killed the majority of the others; this was different.

"You killed him," Xander whispered.

The man had been helpless, and Kale killed him anyway.

"Kale," Devon said softly, his tone strained.

Kale didn't answer, still searching the dead man's body.

"We need to go, Kale."

Still no answer.

"Kale?"

Kale knelt, turned the dead man's body over, and started

snooping around in the pockets on the backs of his limp legs.

"Kale, we need to go."

"How many did you see before you got here?"

Devon blinked. "Three. Three or four."

"How many was it? Three or four?"

"Fine. Four."

"Did you kill them?"

"Eventually, yes. Kale—"

Kale glared up at him. "Are you sure?"

"About how many—"

"Are they dead?"

Devon sighed. "Yes, Kale. They're all dead. Now can we get the hell out of here?"

Kale turned his attention back to the dead man. "There's no rush." He pulled a package out of one of the dead man's pockets. "He was a medic. They stay back until the end."

"Why?"

"If the mission fails—to kill off everybody that's still alive in the platoon." Kale tossed the package to Devon. "Cyanide hyposprays. He's the last one here. We got them all."

"Are you sure?"

"They're on mission, Dev," Kale said. "They only carry those on mission." He turned to face them. "They know I'm here."

"Then, shouldn't we be in a hurry to leave?"

"No," Kale said. "The danger's gone." Kale's gaze narrowed on Xander. "I want answers."

Xander trembled under his gaze.

"How did they know I was here?" Kale's expression was dark and growing darker.

"Kale," Devon started, a warning in his voice Xander didn't

understand.

"Come here."

Xander stared at him.

"Come here *now*."

"Kale, calm down." Devon put his blaster up and reached out to his friend.

Kale smacked his hand away, seized Xander's arm, and hauled her toward him. "Do you know any of them?"

Her mouth dropped open. "Do I—what?"

"Do you know them?"

"What?"

Kale shook her. "These men. That one." He pointed. "Or that one." He pointed again. "Or any of them. Do you know them?"

"Kale, are you serious?" Devon grabbed his arm.

Kale shrugged him off and took her by both shoulders. "Talk."

"Kale, you're out of your mind." Devon grabbed Kale's shoulder. "Let her go."

"Answer the question, kid."

"No." Xander forced herself to speak. "I've never seen—any of them—before."

"Then, did you talk to anyone?"

"About what?"

"About me."

Xander stared up into his angry face. On Elara. The man, Dai Yukihara, the friend of Scraps. Is that what he was talking about?

"You did," Kale hissed. "You did, didn't you? Who was it?"

"I—"

"Who was it?"

"Kale—"

"Who was it?" He shook her.

"Kale, stop." Devon seized his shoulders again. "You're scaring her."

"She should be scared. Who did you talk to?"

"I didn't—He said he was a friend of Scraps."

"A friend of Scraps? What was his name?"

"Dai." Her shoulders throbbed from the pressure of his hands, and he only squeezed harder.

"Dai?" His voice was little more than a snarl. "Dai Yukihara?"

His fingers dug into her skin. He was crushing her, didn't he know? She couldn't restrain a whimper.

"Did you use my name?"

"Yes."

Would he kill her? Would he kill her without remorse like he killed the platoon of soldiers who'd attacked them?

He didn't hate her. Devon had said so. But he trembled with rage, his eyes blue fire, his face pale and drawn. Would he kill her if he were angry enough? Didn't she mean more to him than that? Even if he didn't like her, even if she were too much trouble, he wouldn't hurt her. Would he?

"Kale."

Xander peered through her eyelashes. Devon wrapped one arm around Kale's chest, facing away from him. The fury in Kale's eyes took her breath away.

"Kale," Devon said, "let her go. She didn't know. She didn't know any better."

Dai Yukihara used me. Kale is hiding. That's why he has two names.

"Kale, you can't think she did it on purpose."

Kale's grip loosened.

"If it's anyone's fault it's ours," Devon kept talking, "because we didn't warn her—her or the doctor. And it's not like they haven't been looking for you. If anyone was careless, it was us."

She stared into his furious face, tears rising in her eyes.

How long has he hidden? And you've ruined it. You led them right to him. Warm tears trailed down her cheeks.

"Kale," she whispered. "I—I'm sorry."

His expression darkened again. Kale released her one finger at a time. Her legs gave out, and she sank to the ground, not caring to brush away the tears. Kale tilted his head back and cracked his neck. Devon let go of him.

Kale took a deep, slow breath and muttered something to Devon before he turned and started down the alleyway again, this time toward the exit. Devon nodded and moved toward her, holding out his hand. "Come on, kid."

She frowned at him.

"We're late," he said. "We've got to go."

"What about—them?"

"Don't worry about them. Kale's right. They're not a threat anymore."

"Who are they?"

Devon helped her stand and sighed. "Don't ask questions, Xander. Not a good idea."

"Devon, I'm so sorry."

He stopped her. "It's okay. You didn't know. Come on."

They walked toward the docking area together. Neither of them spoke.

The marketplace buzzed around them like nothing had happened, like a platoon of syndicate hit men hadn't been slaughtered in a black alleyway.

Kale marched ahead of them, head high and hands fisted, not looking at anyone, not slowing down for anything. No more ill-tempered stork. He strode through the crowds like a lightning bolt slicing across a stormy sky.

Captain McLeod waited for them outside the docking port, tapping his boot with an impatient rhythm. His angry expression only intensified when he saw the state of Kale and Devon's clothing.

"What did you two do now?" he barked. "Can't you go anywhere without causing trouble?"

Kale didn't answer until he got closer, his voice low and muted. Xander couldn't hear his words. But she could guess. Captain McLeod glanced at her and sighed, his shoulders drooping.

"Is that so, eh?" he said. "Very well."

He turned, and Kale followed him back into the docking tube. Devon moved to go with them, and Xander stopped.

"Xander," Devon said, "come on."

She shook her head.

"Xander, it's okay."

"No, it's not."

It would be better for all of them to leave her. Kale was right. She made trouble for everyone.

"I led them to him," she said. "All of that was my fault, Devon. If he didn't hate me before, he should now."

Devon took her hand. "It's something we've been expecting, okay? It was going to happen sooner or later."

"But if I—"

"If you hadn't let it slip, Vix would've. Or I would've. It was just a matter of time." He cupped the side of her face in his hand. "Xander, he doesn't hate you. He hates himself. That's the problem."

Xander frowned at him, and he offered a soft smile.

How could he smile after what had just happened? After what they had just seen? Her heart thudded against her ribs.

Is this what it means to be Kale's friend?

Devon pulled her along the ramp. She followed, not sure where her feet were going but trusting Devon to catch her if she stepped wrong.

"It's okay, kid." He patted her back. "I promise."

"I messed up, Devon."

"Well, nobody's perfect."

The doors shut behind them, but Xander didn't release Devon's arm.

"Are you okay?" He tightened his arm around her shoulders. "You're not hurt, are you?"

"No. Just—he scared me."

"Yeah." Devon's eyes held sadness. "He does that."

They walked side by side, Devon's warm embrace around her shoulders chasing the fear from the alley away. As the terror wore off, the exhaustion settled in. Her legs turned to jelly. She needed to sit down, or she would pass out. And that would be a great way to prove to Devon that she wasn't hurt or weak.

Xander glanced at Devon's face as they walked across the bay.

Kale hated himself. What did that mean?

She held Devon's hand as it draped over her shoulder.

Xander wanted to know Kale. She wanted to be his friend, but she hadn't understood what that would mean. She still didn't. But Devon did.

Devon's eyes shone calm and clear, not worried, not afraid, not doubting. He'd seen Kale become death, and he hadn't flinched.

309

CHAPTER 24

Xander focused on the scribbles marked into the metal frame of her bunk. The crooked letters formed unintelligible words, like a toddler had tried to leave his life story in permanent ink. The *Prodigal* had taken on passengers before, so it was probably a child's tale of scary noises and frightening bumps, which seemed to be the *Prodigal's* forte.

Xander tried to focus on that child, on where he might be, on who he might have been. Anything was better than remember the fury in Kale's eyes. Even listening to Evy's light breathing didn't calm her.

Did Kale really hate himself? He shouldn't. Sure, he was arrogant and obnoxious and rude, but everyone had moments like that. He was also brave. And kind.

Yes, kindness. She'd seen it in his eyes more than once, even though he'd probably deny it. But she'd seen him.

If the Dragons found him, they'd kill him. So would Knightshade.

Xander rolled over and sat up. Her bunk creaked like it could feel pain, and she froze, hoping she hadn't woken Evy. The neuro-therapist didn't stir.

What would happen when they found the *Tempest?* Could they even stand up against a ship like that? The *Prodigal* might be small and fast, but even with Ben at the helm, a well-placed cannon round from a destroyer like the *Tempest* could obliterate them.

NAMELESS

"Is it even worth it?" she whispered to the shadows.

What would happen if they lost? Would they be taken prisoner? Would they be killed? Were her memories really so important? Was it worth risking the lives of the people who had vowed to help her?

Xander pressed her face into her hands. She wouldn't get to sleep any time soon.

They should have named the ship *Insomnia*.

Barefoot, she stood, wrapped her blanket around her shoulders and padded into the corridor. Maybe Scraps couldn't sleep either. Maybe he had some more potato soup. She crept down the metal passageway to the galley and waited for eyes adjust to the dimness inside.

No Scraps. But someone had been cooking.

Claude?

He sat at the table scraping the remains of a meal off a plate. His face brightened.

"Hello, little girl," he said, his booming voice strangely soft. "No sleeping for you, either, *ja*?"

Xander gathered the blanket around her shoulders more tightly and smiled at him. "No. I'm having some trouble."

Claude pushed a chair away from the table with one of his giant feet, and Xander sat beside him.

"Want some warm thing to drink?" Claude asked, standing.

Xander tried not to gawk at his size. She nodded.

Claude puffed out his chest and moved to the counter area in the galley and started shifting pans and cups around.

"I didn't know you could cook."

Considering his size, it seemed strange Claude could even use utensils too small for his huge hands.

311

"Claude cook, Claude cook," the NUGerman man said, waving a massive paw in the air and grinning so all his white teeth sparkled. "Claude cook meat. Claude cook potato. Claude cook meat and potato together. Claude cook." He nodded. "Claude live by his own self for many years before he meet Scraps, who cook more than meat and potato."

Xander watched him lumber around the small kitchen.

"Claude?"

"*Ja?*"

"How did you come to be here?" she asked. "How did you end up on the *Prodigal?*"

Claude chuckled. "Is simple story. Not funny. Not exciting either. Not like Kale or Devon or Jaz or Vix. Claude just come." He set a pan on the stove. "Claude hear bounty hunter ship need loader. Claude know he good at loading. So he join."

"You didn't know anyone here?"

"*Nein.*" Claude shook his head. "Claude born on NUGermania. Lived on some moons. Didn't meet no one really. Then he come to *Prodigal.*"

"You like it here?"

"*Ja.*" Claude poured something into the pan and lifted his head. "Why you not sleep? Not tired?"

"No, it's not that," Xander said. "I just—have a lot on my mind."

"Remember something?"

She scoffed. "No."

Claude's eyes softened. "Claude is sorry for little girl. Memory is important. He hopes she remember who she is."

Xander remained silent, and Claude stared at her for a long time.

NAMELESS

"What wrong?" he finally asked. "You no want to remember?"

"No, it's not that," Xander said. "But—it is."

Claude tilted his head. "Claude not understand."

Xander leaned back in her chair and pulled on her fingers. "What if I remember and I don't *like* what I remember?" She frowned. "What if the person I was—wasn't good?"

Claude chuckled. "How could the little girl not be good?"

"If I'm from the Sanctum," Xander said, "I might be bad."

Claude didn't look convinced. "The little girl is good."

"How do you know?"

"Because the little girl is good now." Claude shrugged and poured a rich, fragrant liquid into the pot on the stove.

"What if I'm not? What if I remember the truth, and I'm not a good person, Claude? Will it be worth it?"

"Worth what?"

Xander sank down in the chair. "All of you have done so much for me. Risked so much to help me. I'm afraid if I remember who I am and where I come from, in the end, it won't be worth it."

She sat up and looked into Claude's open face.

"I don't want to be from the Sanctum. I don't want to be like them. But that's the only option. That's the only choice I've got. For the things I know, I had to have come from there."

Claude stirred the pot before he leaned over the counter. "Then you come from there," he said gently. "It not mean you bad person."

"But everyone from the Sanctum is a hypocrite," Xander said. "And I don't want to be like that."

"Then don't." Claude's eyes twinkled. "If you remember you bad person, change. No one perfect, little girl. If us help you

313

remember that, then is worth it."

Xander watched him as he went back to stirring the concoction in the pot.

"No being afraid of truth," Claude said as he stirred. "Not any point in that. Truth is truth. It follow you no matter where you go, so it not smart to run from it. But people run from it anyway because people not smart."

"People are afraid of the truth," Xander murmured. "I am. I'm afraid of it to the point I almost don't want to know anymore. I almost want to stop looking."

Claude set his spoon down for a moment and looked at her. "Claude going to tell little girl a story. Does little girl like stories?"

Xander couldn't stop a smile. "Sure."

"Good," Claude said with a sharp nod. "Listen to Claude tell story."

Xander folded her legs on the seat of the chair and cuddled deeper into the blanket.

"Claude born on NUGermania. Big colony far away from here. Full of NUGermans. All big people who eat much bread."

Xander smiled.

"On NUGermania," Claude continued, "only three jobs. Best job is doctor. Make sick people well. Smart people. Claude try that. Claude not do so good. Claude not that smart."

Dr. Zahn's stern blue eyes flashed to the forefront of her memory, and Xander ignored them, swallowing the lump that formed in her throat.

"So, Claude try second best job. Miner."

"Miner?"

"*Ja.* Gas mining. Rock mining. Gem mining. Metal mining. Mining. With big machines. And big drills. Learn to mine on

NAMELESS

NUGermania, join mining team, and they take to a moon. And you mine. All day. Every day." Claude made a tired sound. "Hard work. Good work. But hard. Work very hard. And always very dirty."

Claude added something else to the pot and stirred it. A sweet, tantalizing smell filled the galley.

"It was—small Jovian moon. Praxidike. Small Jovian moon. Claude go there to work with friend Heinrich." Claude smiled. "Heinrich and Claude good friends. Go to mining school together. Best buddies."

"Like Kale and Devon?"

"Eh." Claude shrugged. "Maybe. Kale and Devon fight too much. They like brothers. Claude and Heinrich just friends." Claude was quiet for a moment. "Claude no have much credits. Claude have few shirts. Some pants. Underthings. Not much. Heinrich the same. One day, Claude see one of his shirts is missing. Claude look all over everywhere for his shirt—because it is warm shirt and Praxidike mine is cold. He no find it."

"What happened to it?"

"Heinrich take it." Claude stirred the pot again. "Claude was very angry. He get all red. He trusted Heinrich, and Heinrich took what did not belong. So Claude and Heinrich fight."

Xander waited.

"One week later," Claude said, "Heinrich die when mine fall in. He crushed under boulders. Claude could not save him."

"I'm sorry, Claude."

"Claude is sorry too," he said. "Claude was more sorry too. Because at Heinrich's funeral, a man stand up to speak. His name Johann. And he say he very poor. No credits. One shirt. That all. And it very thin. He say—he in mine freezing and his partner who mine with him is Heinrich."

315

Xander watched the emotions playing across the NUGerman's face.

"Heinrich give him clothes. His own clothes. But—not enough. He too skinny. Need more clothes. So Heinrich give him Claude's big, thick shirt. To keep him warm." Claude sighed. "Heinrich was going to tell Claude, but Claude got angry too fast."

Xander folded her arms. "He still should have asked you before he took them, though."

"*Nein*. Claude had three shirts. All warm. And Claude big boy. So he stay warm better than little skinny Johann." Claude looked down sadly. "Heinrich did right. Claude did wrong. That is truth."

Claude turned and pulled two mugs out of the cabinet behind him, one small and one enormous.

"When Claude know truth, he very sad. Because he find he not as good a person as he thought he was." He smiled. "Claude was afraid of truth, but it find him anyway. Claude and Johann became good friends."

"What happened to Johann?"

Claude didn't answer right away. He took hold of the pot and poured the liquid inside into the mugs. When he was finished, he looked up and found Xander's eyes. "Johann die. Explosion in mine."

"Claude. I'm—so sorry."

Claude shrugged. "Mining is dangerous. So Claude go back to NUGermania, and he decide to try third job."

"Which was?"

Claude came around the counter and handed the small mug to Xander. "Chocolatier."

"What?"

NAMELESS

Claude gestured to the mug. Hesitantly, Xander sipped the liquid and gasped in delight.

"Hot chocolate?"

"*Ja.*"

"Claude, this is amazing."

"*Ja.*" Claude looked pleased with himself. "Claude like chocolate."

Xander sipped the sweet, hot drink. She didn't know whether to laugh or cry for the big NUGerman who sat across from her with his red cheeks and sparkling eyes. His giant hand dwarfed his massive mug.

"So you work heavy equipment, blow things up, and know chocolate," Xander said.

"*Ja.*"

A laugh escaped her, and Claude joined in.

Xander jumped as something bumped her chair. She glanced down and spotted Newt on the floor. She bent over and pulled the little Pomeranian into her arms. The dog settled into her lap and went to sleep.

"Newt like you," Claude said. "You a good little girl."

Xander glanced up at him.

"No be afraid of truth," Claude said. "Being afraid not change it. If you not a good person or if you not who you think you supposed to be—change that. But no be afraid."

"Life teach you that?" Xander asked.

Claude's eyes shifted to the back of the room, and he smiled. "*Nein.*"

Xander looked over her shoulder and froze. Jaz, wearing a pair of loose slacks and a blouse, stood at the door.

"*Guten abend.*" Claude beamed. "Chocolate?"

317

Claude wanted her to join? But Jaz the ice woman didn't socialize.

Jaz smiled and moved to sit at the table with them.

"Thank you, Claude," she said.

Okay. Scratch that. Been wrong before.

Claude stood and went to fill another mug, while Jaz looked at Xander. "Are you joining our little chocolate-lovers, insomniac club?"

"I didn't know you had one."

Jaz leaned over the table, her long blond hair swaying with the motion. "We do. Claude doesn't sleep well, and neither do I. So we usually end up here, drinking chocolate and just talking."

"Does it help?"

Jaz smiled again. "Yes."

Xander held her mug closer. "Do you—why can't you sleep?"

Claude returned and handed Jaz a mug of the hot chocolate.

"Claude has loud dreams," Claude said. "Mine dreams." He sat and sipped his mug. "Jaz has dreams too." Claude straightened. "The little girl is worried she discover she not a good person, Jaz. Claude tells her she no should be afraid of it."

Jaz glanced at Xander. "You're afraid of remembering who you are?"

Xander looked down and nodded.

"I don't blame you. I should think it would be a frightening thing to lose everything you knew. It would frighten me."

Claude sipped his chocolate.

"I think I'm afraid the truth is going to change me," Xander said.

"Truth changes everything," Jaz said. "Truth makes people

uncomfortable. It makes us see things that we don't want to see, reveals things about ourselves and others that hurt, but it's better to accept it and move on."

"Why?"

"Because if you never accept the truth, you'll never be at peace with who you are and what your purpose is."

Xander turned her mug in her hands. "Sounds like you both have talked about this before."

"I guess you could say so. It's one of the things Claude and I talk about." She sipped her chocolate. "This is better than usual, Claude. Did you do something different?"

"Dark chocolate," Claude said. "With mint."

Jaz took another sip. "You shouldn't be afraid of the truth, Xander. It'll find you whether you run from it or not."

"You think so?"

"Xander, there are two certainties in life—death and truth." Jaz set her mug down. "They will both pursue you to your grave. There is no escaping them." She shrugged. "But we run from them anyway in hopes that somehow we can slip by unnoticed. In the end, one or both of them catch up. Running doesn't solve anything."

"Just delays the inevitable."

"That's right." Jaz picked up her mug again. "And the inevitable *is* inevitable."

"It's destiny."

Jaz looked at her for a long time, saying nothing.

Claude stretched his arms over his head with an enormous yawn. He stood and went to wash the pot.

Newt shifted in Xander's lap and jumped down to bother Claude's ankles as he worked.

"Claude dreams of the mines." Xander looked at Jaz. "What

do you dream about?"

Jaz shook her head. "Things I don't like to speak of."

Xander nodded. "Fair enough."

Something clanked behind them, and Xander and Jaz turned to the doorway. Al stood there, dazed and half-asleep.

"Ach, the little android girl." Claude lifted his hands and beamed. "She has the night dreams too?"

"Probably not, Claude," Jaz said, rolling her eyes.

Al turned a dopey, half-open stare at Xander and tilted her head, her hair turning deep blue as she wandered awkwardly to the table and sat down.

"She's pretty amazing, though, you have to admit," Xander said. "It's hard to believe she's a robot."

"Al-Units were always different," Jaz murmured.

Xander blinked at Jaz as her statement sank in. "You've seen androids like this before?"

Jaz's hazel eyes darkened. "Yeah."

"Why didn't you say anything earlier?"

Jaz sipped her chocolate. "It's not something I like talking about."

Xander set her empty mug down. "You don't like talking about much, do you?"

Jaz arched her eyebrows, a glint a laugh in her expression.

Humor? Jaz? Did she even know how to laugh?

"No," Jaz said finally. "I don't." She finished her chocolate and set her mug down, turning her gaze to Al.

The android stared straight ahead, not really seeing anything.

"Unlike you." Jaz glanced at her. "You seem to enjoy talking quite a bit."

Xander fidgeted with her fingers. "I guess so. I know it must really bother people."

"No, it's not that. It's—pleasant. It's just unusual to be around someone who enjoys talking with people instead of about them."

"I think it annoys Kale."

"Many things annoy Kale."

"Yeah." Xander shook her head. "I don't think he likes me very much."

"Does that bother you?" Jaz leaned back in her chair, her eyes serious.

"Yes," Xander said. "It does. I don't like it when people don't like me. I feel inadequate. Like I could have done something better or like I can fix it. I'm not naïve. I know there are just going to be people who don't like me, but it makes me sad."

"Why do you feel he dislikes you?"

"I don't know." She didn't need to go into detail.

Jaz's eyes were deep. "Kale is dangerous." Jaz stared into her mug. "He's the most dangerous man I've ever known." Her expression faltered with a smile. "Well, very nearly."

What did that mean? After her experience on Ring-Seven, Xander doubted anyone could be more dangerous than Kale.

"He's also a good man," Jaz said. "He just doesn't know it."

"Devon says he hates himself."

"If I'd lived his life, I would too." Jaz sipped her chocolate. "But he'll get over himself someday."

The AI-Unit made a gurgling sound and slumped in her chair. Xander laughed at her, and Jaz's face grew more sober than before.

"I don't see much point in them, I guess."

Xander frowned and then notices Jaz's eyes focused on AI. She'd changed subjects.

321

Not what she'd wanted. She wanted to keep talking about Kale.

"I always felt creating an android to do the work for a person is lazy. The easy way out." She sneered. "Like a character flaw or something." She pushed her mug between her hands. "They're trouble."

"So you don't like androids?" Xander asked.

"I suppose they have some uses."

"But you don't like them," Xander said. "In general? Or just Al-Units specifically?"

Jaz lifted her gaze and drew her eyes down the android's features slowly, taking in every detail.

"I knew someone who built them," Jaz said. "Someone who built Al-Units. It was a long time ago."

"Someone who built Al-Units?"

"Yes. It was his life. It was an obsession. It consumed him." Jaz looked down. "Until nothing and no one else mattered to him anymore. Not his friends. Not his family. No one. Only the perfect design mattered. He was so consumed with the idea of the perfect android that he missed the point of his life." She sighed. "That's truth, Xander. He was afraid of it too. Always running from it."

"The truth?"

"That life goes on," Jaz said. "That you can't change the past. That you can't fix everything. He thought he could, but he couldn't."

The expressions on Jaz's face changed from anger to sadness to something deep and penetrating.

"I guess I'm not so much angry at the Al-Units. They didn't do anything to me. Maybe it's just the idea of them." She shifted. "We should take care of it. It might be worth something someday."

Al's hair shifted to a bright orange color, and she lolled her head around, grinning, green eyes sparkling. "Eeny, meeny, miny! Catch a tiger by the toe!"

Jaz's face looked so haunted Xander felt chills down her spine.

"Tigers don't have toes," the blond-and-pink-haired bounty huntress whispered.

Al faced her. "They still have to pay."

Jaz and Al held each others' gazes for a long time, saying nothing. Finally, Jaz stood, taking both her mug and Xander's mug to Claude.

"I'm going to bed," she announced and walked out of the room without another word.

Xander watched her go and looked back at Al, who rocked in her chair, her hair alternating between blue and green, humming eerily to herself.

CHAPTER 25

The morning chimes rang throughout the ship. Time to get up and help Scraps make breakfast.

Xander enjoyed the time with him, learning about his kitchen and all his little tips for making stale, flavorless dehydrated food taste homemade. Xander remembered with pride telling him how she had once fixed Evy a whole meal with nothing rehydrated or precooked; he'd been suitably impressed and had trusted her in his kitchen.

Her apple salad had been a hit, and he'd even asked for her recipe. If she'd experienced a prouder moment in her life, she didn't remember it. That didn't mean much, of course, but every little bit helped.

Xander found him in the kitchen, whipping eggs and frying bacon already.

"Good morning, Xander." He greeted her with a smile.

"Morning, Scraps." She started to set the table.

"Did you sleep well?"

Xander didn't want to lie to him, but she didn't want to tell him the truth either. "Sure."

Scraps stopped whipping eggs for a moment and regarded her skeptically, his blue eyes searching her for the truth he knew she hid. He always knew. Xander only smiled at him and made sure to put a napkin with every plate.

Xander looked up as Devon stepped into the galley, yawning.

His wild blond hair looked like Newt had spent the night licking it.

"Morning." His voice sounded garbled and tired, like he spoke with a mouth full of marbles.

"Morning, Devon." Scraps gave him a cup of coffee.

Devon sat at the table, rubbing his eyes and drinking his coffee and yawning in between.

"Devon?" Xander perched on the edge of the chair across from him and pulled on her fingers.

He grunted.

"Can I ask you a question?"

"There's one."

Xander frowned at him.

"That was a joke, Xander."

"Oh." She bit her lip. "Yeah, I get it."

"Never mind." Devon set his coffee cup down. "What's your question, Xander?"

"Mitchem."

"Yeah?"

"He told you—where the *Tempest* is?"

"Or where it will be, yeah." Devon yawned again and took another drink of his coffee. "Io. In two days. Stoney's meeting Knightshade operatives there to exchange the *Destiny*." He leaned back in his chair. "And, actually, we're making a stop on Thebe this morning."

"We are?" Scraps asked.

"Talon figured we should charge up the power cells before we track the *Tempest* down," Devon said.

"Yes," Scraps said. "That's a good idea."

Jaz appeared in the door.

Xander stood to grab the coffee pot and poured a cup for her.

Jaz didn't exactly smile when she took it, but she didn't frown either.

Xander went back to the stove and stared at Al sprawled on the floor, snoring and whistling. Scraps noticed Xander's gaze and laughed.

"She was here when I woke up," he said. "I'd probably better keep an eye on her, or Talon'll throw her out the airlock. I need you to take Kale his tea."

Xander frowned. "Oh, Scraps, I don't think that's a good idea. Can't he come get it himself?"

Scraps shrugged. "Probably. But it's our little tradition. I take him green tea in the morning. He doesn't do breakfast."

He flash heated a mug of water and dropped a tea bag into it. He handed the cup to her. The teabag dissolved, leaving perfectly brewed green tea.

Xander glared at Devon and Jaz, who sat at the table watching her. Why? Was this a test? Oh, she really wasn't in the mood for a test.

Xander took the cup from him, the hot tea warming her hands. Devon and Jaz turned away from her and whispered to each other.

"Xander?" Scraps frowned. "Are you all right?"

"Fine, Scraps. Fine."

Scraps leaned over the counter to look at her, worried. "Xander, what? Did he hurt you?"

"No."

"Then, what?"

"I—I just cause him trouble, Scraps. I'm always making things more complicated for him."

Scraps wiped his hands on his apron and folded his arms. She knew that face. He didn't believe her, and he would stare at her until she cracked.

They were ganging up on her. It was a conspiracy.

"I'm trying to give him space."

Scraps glanced up at Devon and Jaz. They were still engaged in a conversation close to each other. Scraps gazed at her for a moment before he covered her hands with his. "Xander, what happened on Ring-Seven?"

Xander shut her eyes. Scraps wouldn't back down. She might as well save the time and just tell him.

"We were attacked—by people Devon called Dragons."

"Black Dragons?"

"Yeah. I guess."

Scraps rocked back on his heels. "I see. That makes a bit more sense." He leaned in again. "What happened? What did Kale do?"

She drew a steadying breath. "He—killed a lot of people."

"I'm sure. Did he do something to you?"

"Not really." Xander ignored the still aching bruises on her upper arms. "He—was angry. He yelled a lot."

"Did he frighten you?"

Xander nodded. Scraps patted her hands.

"Don't be afraid of Kale, Xander. He means you no harm."

She set the tea down. "I blew his cover, Scraps. All I want is to be his friend, but I keep making his life so difficult." She pointed to the tea. "If I take him that tea, he'll probably choke on it."

Scraps laughed. "Oh, Xander."

"Not funny."

"I'm sorry." Scraps squeezed her hand. "Xander, you don't need to worry."

"That's what Devon said." She looked back at Devon and

Jaz, still leaning close to each other, whispering.

"Take him the tea."

"I was even going to apologize to him."

She sighed and picked up the tea. "He won't let me. I tried. He got angry."

"Then, just talk to him."

"Tried that too." She rolled her eyes. "I'm telling you guys, if it's not hate then it's passionate dislike."

Scraps laughed again. "Most likely, Xander, he just doesn't know what to do with you." He leaned on the counter with his arms spread. "Why do you want to be his friend?"

"He saved me." Xander smiled. "I think he's amazing, even if he drives me insane." She shook her head. "But I think I just bother him. I just don't know why."

Scraps reached across the counter and tapped her chin. "Xander, do you know why he saved you?"

"No. I don't think he does either."

"He saved you because he is a good man. The Black Dragons chase him because he is a good man. Deep inside him, he is a good man." Scraps handed her the tea cup again. "Be afraid of him if you want, but he is a good man. Still a man, but a good man."

Xander frowned at Devon and Jaz again. They both understood Kale in a way she didn't.

"He hates himself," she mumbled.

Scraps smiled. "Yes. Good men forced to do horrible things often do. And it is up to their friends to help them see the good inside again."

Xander blinked at him.

Is that what Devon meant? And Jaz? Kale had been forced to do horrible things? After what she'd seen, she didn't doubt his

328

capability.

Xander gripped the mug. "Okay."

"Okay?"

"I'll take him the tea."

"Excellent."

"But if he shoots me, it's your fault."

Scraps laughed again and shooed her away.

She smiled at Devon and Jaz as she passed them. They smiled back at her, holding hands under the table. She wasn't sure what was stranger, the fact that they were holding hands or the fact that they were hiding it.

Xander walked confidently toward the loading bay, the scent of green tea tickling her nostrils.

Kale wanted her to stay away, but Kale's closest friends kept pushing her toward him. What did that mean?

Could she be friends with him? Was she strong enough? Scraps question rang in her ears.

Why do I want to be friends with him? I care about him. She scowled. *But why?*

Xander stood at the door of the loading bay and watched him. Kale had moved the *Scimitar* to the main floor, its hull covered in soap suds. He used a long-handled scrub brush to scour the ship's hull.

It couldn't be as simple as attraction. Maybe that's what drew her to him, but she wanted to be closer. She wanted to be someone he trusted, like Devon. She didn't know where the desire came from, but the strength of it choked her every time he came within arm's reach.

A dirty tank top and ratty jeans clung to his slender body. Graceful. Just looking at him you wouldn't know how strong he really was. He didn't look like a bounty hunter.

Lou, the vile bounty hunter from Callisto, had been thick and wide, barrel-chested and overly muscular. Lou looked like a bounty hunter.

Kale looked like a dancer.

But she'd been in both their arms, and she had no doubt Kale could wipe the floor with Lou.

What must it be like to hate yourself? It had to be a horrible way to live. She'd been afraid of hating the person she'd been, but Claude had helped her put those fears to rest. Had anyone done that for Kale? Would he allow anyone to do that?

Xander stepped toward him. She gripped the mug until her knuckles turned white. Kale paused and looked at her over his shoulder, his face blank.

She held out the mug. "Scraps made it for you."

He set the brush down and turned. "You going to make me walk all the way over there?"

Jerk. Did she really feel sorry for him?

He won the prize for the most frustrating, antagonistic man in the universe. Also the most dangerous. So as much as she wanted to throw it at him, she refrained and stepped close enough to set the mug in his hands. His hands and his long fingers could span the width of her back.

Just like that she felt the alley wall against her back, smelling his scent and feeling his fingers roaming across her skin and wanting him to kiss her so desperately she could hardly breathe.

She couldn't look at him. Even when their fingers brushed as he took the mug, she didn't lift her eyes. Was she blushing again? Was he thinking about the alley too? Was he remembering what she felt like in his arms?

He didn't say anything. Just sipped the tea.

Did she start? Did she need to say something?

Xander met his eyes.

No.

If he wanted to talk to her, he needed to start. She'd been chasing him since the day he rescued her. He knew what she wanted. He knew how she felt.

Gazing into his hollow blue eyes, Xander chose. She would be his friend whether he wanted it or not. He had no say. If he wanted to talk, she would talk, but he'd have to initiate. She'd listen when he was ready.

She smiled and turned to go.

"Why did you bring this?"

She faced him. His blue eyes still gave nothing away, but his lips turned down in a confused scowl.

"Scraps had to watch Al."

"Why didn't someone else bring it?"

Did she tell him the truth? Yes. Scraps said to. So she would. "I wanted to bring it."

"Why?"

"To see you."

"To see me? Why?"

She steeled herself. "To apologize."

"Again?"

His shoulders squared and he took a deep breath, but she held up her hand.

"And you're going to listen this time."

His breath came out in a rush, his beautiful eyes widening.

"You've done nothing but save me since Ursa-Five," she said. "And I've done nothing but make your life more complicated. I don't want anything from you, Kale. I don't expect anything from you. I just want to say thank you. And I'm sorry."

She dropped her hand and waited for his temper to flare.

Kale stared at her for much longer than was comfortable. And then, he laughed.

He laughed and laughed and set his tea down on the stool while he tried to get himself under control.

Xander ground her teeth.

Rude. Rude, beautiful man.

"Care to explain what's so funny?"

Kale surged forward and seized her elbow faster than she could dodge. He hauled her closer with one hand and snapped her sleeve up to reveal the bruises he'd left on her upper arm. Kale's blue eyes pierced her.

"I nearly broke both your arms, and you're apologizing to me?"

She lifted her chin, taking a deep breath, and he released her. She took a step back, yanking her arm out of his hold and pulling her sleeve down with a huff. He retrieved his tea cup.

"You were upset," she said.

"Bull shit."

"You're obviously hiding from those people. And if it hadn't been for me, they wouldn't have found you. And for that—I'm sorry."

"Devon was right. You couldn't have known."

"I should have."

"How?" He faced her. "How could you have known?"

"You have two names. It didn't even occur to me that it was an alias. I just—didn't think. And I'm sorry."

"So you said."

Xander ran her hands into her hair and bit off a frustrated groan. "Would you please just accept my apology?"

"No."

She drew back. "No?"

"No. I won't." He sipped the tea.

"Why not?"

"You didn't do anything wrong. So there's no need for you to apologize."

Xander shut her mouth with a snap. She'd said she didn't want anything from him. She didn't. But she really did want to be forgiven. Why wouldn't he?

"It really bugs you, doesn't it?" he said. "When I don't do what you want me to do."

"I want to be forgiven."

"There's nothing to forgive. And I won't forgive you of something you don't need to feel guilty for."

"But it's my fault."

"For what? Having a conversation with somebody? Being friendly? Which seems effortless for you, at least when it comes to everyone else but me."

Oh, he was impossible.

"Then what about me endangering your lives? I got people killed because I want to remember my name."

"All of that's out of your control."

"What?"

"I chose to save you. That was out of your hands."

"That doesn't—"

"And you never did ask for our help. Talon's just bound and determined to give it." He shrugged and sipped his tea. "He's dumb like that."

333

Xander tried to close her mouth so she didn't look like a suffocating trout, but her jaw wouldn't cooperate.

"So, no," he said. "I won't forgive you."

"You—"

"Kid, you don't need my forgiveness, all right? Hell, if anyone needs to be asking forgiveness, it's me. But I'm not going to do that—because you don't need to forgive me anyway. You'll live longer if you don't."

He set his tea down and grabbed the brush again. His hair shifted with the motion, deep red like the color of oak leaves in autumn.

That was it. If he forgave her, if they became friends, he would endanger her. Anyone close to Kale would share the danger following him. No wonder he pushed everyone away.

Devon's friendship was worth it. That's what Kale had said.

Devon could take care of himself, and that's why Kale could be friends with him. But Xander couldn't. Friendship with him would get her killed. His hostility acted as a shield around her, meant to protect her from himself.

She swallowed. "I do," she said, her voice resolute. "Forgive you."

He stopped scrubbing.

She took another step toward him. If she'd been closer, she would have taken his hand.

Would he turn and smile? Tell her everything would be all right? See that he couldn't scare her away with all his ridiculous, manly posturing? Would he hold her like on Ring-Seven? Would he kiss her?

He wouldn't. She knew it. But she wanted him to.

She wanted to understand him. She wanted to be free to look

into his eyes without having to be afraid.

But he gripped the brush handle and didn't turn around.

"Then, you're an idiot. And there's no help for you."

Her heart twisted.

She hadn't expected a hug, but she hadn't prepared for cruelty. The harsh words cut deep, slashing brutally at the quiet hope his earlier kindness had kindled. Any chance of friendship between them slipped through her fingers like blood seeping from a wound refusing to heal.

Xander straightened.

She'd tried. She'd asked, and he'd refused. She'd done her part. If he really didn't want anything to do with her, that was his choice.

But it hurt.

More than it probably should have.

He went back to scrubbing, so it should have been easy to turn away, but it felt like walking through mud, like her shoes had become weights. With every step she struggled to take, her heart screamed more loudly for her to go back, to plead with him, to force him to understand.

She didn't care what he had done. She didn't care who he used to be. She wanted him to know he could be himself and it was okay. He mattered to Devon, to Jaz, to everyone. They all thought he was worth risking their lives for.

But she couldn't convince him if he wouldn't listen, and trying to force him to hear would only push him further away. So she marched away from him one step at a time and didn't bother to wipe the tears from her face.

Someone needed to cry for him. It might as well be her.

CHAPTER 26

Kale didn't move until her footfalls no longer echoed in the corridor outside the bay. Then, he let the scrub brush fall to the stool. He leaned against the chassis of the *Scimitar* and closed his eyes.

He'd had seen her expression fall in the reflection of the *Scimitar's* polished hull. He watched the light drain out of her star-colored eyes.

Mission accomplished. Congratulations, you're a jackass.

He'd learned it a long time ago. Now finally the kid would figure it out too. Better for her if she did.

He stared at the tea cup on the stool, his hand still tingling with the softness of her fingers as she'd handed it to him.

She was ridiculous. And naïve. And foolish. And bossy and irritating and annoying and all he wanted was to get her in his arms again and smell her hair like he'd done on Ring-Seven.

What had he been thinking? There had been plenty of other ways to distract the Dragons. Why had he done that?

The feel of her, the scent of her invaded every private moment. He hadn't kissed her, but he should have. Then he could have known what she tasted like and he could stop dreaming about it.

The hair on the back of his neck stood up.

He recognized the feel of staring eyes. He turned and stifled a groan. Vix leaned against the far wall with her arms crossed and her blue eyes dark, an unlit cigarette behind her left ear.

NAMELESS

The snake. How long had she been there?

"Morning, Kale." She approached and ran her fingers over the fuselage of the *Scimitar*.

Kale ground his teeth, picked up the scrub brush, and started back to work. "Don't be greasing up my ship, fox-lady."

"It doesn't need grease from me, Kale. You're slippery enough."

"What's that supposed to mean?"

Vix leaned against the ship at a provocative angle. "You really don't know anything about girls do you?"

"Is that rhetorical, Vix?"

Vix slid between him and the chassis, crooking her neck to be able to see into his face. He drew back enough to communicate irritation at her invasion of his personal space. Even Vix knew not to push him too far.

"Xander likes you."

"No, Vix. She hates me."

"Kale, you don't honestly believe that, do you?"

He stepped around her silently and picked up the tea cup. Maybe he was dreaming, but it still smelled like Xander. Like lavender. A kind of flowery scent he wasn't sure he'd ever smelled on a woman before.

Vix smiled slyly. "Just watch yourself, Kale."

Kale rolled his eyes as she started for the door. "Vix?"

"What?"

"Do you think I'm stupid?"

"Do you really want me to answer that?"

"I know what you're doing to the kid."

Vix's face dimmed.

"And you need to stop."

337

She moved closer until she was almost pressed against him. "What am I doing, Kale?"

"You told her to wear a hat on Elara, didn't you?"

Vix's smirk increased. "What makes you think that?"

"She wouldn't have worn a hat unless someone told her to." Kale set the cup down and folded his arms. "And you're the only one shitty enough to do that to her."

"You think I want the kid to get hurt, Kale?"

"I'm not sure how you did it." He let anger seep into his voice. "But I'm almost certain you managed to get her outside my room in nothing but a towel the first day they were here."

"How could I have possibly arranged that?"

"It's not how, Vix, it's why."

Vix pretended to look as though she wasn't following, but Kale knew better. One of the benefits of having known her so long.

"You want me to think that she's loud, pushy, and rude. Just like you."

"And why would I want that, Kale?"

"Because you know I don't like loud, pushy, rude women. Because you don't want me to like her."

"I don't see why that would bother me at all, Kale."

"You don't, do you? That's interesting."

"Very."

"You're standing too close to me, Vix."

"Oh, I'm sorry. Didn't mean to invade your bubble." She slid her hands down her sides to rest on her hips. "So how'd you figure it out? Did our little amnesiac tell you?"

"No. She didn't say a word."

Vix blinked.

"She didn't. She's probably not even angry at you. She's kind

NAMELESS

of weird like that."

"So—what?" Vix tapped her foot. "Have you started preferring loud, pushy, rude women now?"

"No, Vix. Not at all. She's nothing like you."

"Good to know." She rolled her eyes. "Fine. I really hoped to save you the frustration. Relationships with kids really don't work well."

"I really don't care, Vix."

"My advice?"

"I don't want it."

"Just do her."

Kale narrowed his eyes.

"Come on, Kale. I know you want to. You've wanted to jump her since the first time you saw her, haven't you? Men, you're all alike." She spat. "I recommend it. Go get her. Take her like a man. Hm?"

Kale rolled his eyes and turned away from her, picking up the scrub brush. "Go away."

"It's the best way."

He glanced back at her. "How do you figure me tumbling her is going to help the situation any?"

"You'll get it out of your system." She stepped back and walked for the door. "And the brat'll learn that you're not worth it."

Vix stalked off into the corridor. Kale watched her go and set the brush back against the side of the ship before he sat down.

It was the most absurd conversation he'd ever had with Vix. She'd always been nothing but trouble. And there was no denying it now—she had been the one playing Xander for a fool. It was just like Vix to manipulate someone like the kid. And that was probably exactly what she was doing now, trying to manipulate him.

339

Well, it wasn't going to work this time. He'd learned his lesson where she was concerned.

But he couldn't deny the allure of the idea, even though he'd never had sex with anyone as young as Xander before. She had amazing skin—it had to be the freckles. Her hair was beautiful too. There just weren't enough redheads in the universe anymore.

On Ring-Seven when he'd had her against the wall, he hadn't expected her smell. He hadn't expected the softness of her skin. He'd felt her ribs, her narrow hips. Her curves weren't as pronounced as Vix's, but Xander had them. He'd felt them quite clearly in that alleyway, and some part of him was desperate to actually see them.

He'd been on fire since the moment she'd crashed into him on Ursa-Five, but being that close to her on Ring-Seven had done something to him. It had taken all his strength to drop her when the Dragon had come at him.

Was he actually thinking Vix could be right?

How would the kid react if he showed up in her bunk that night? Would she scream? Would she fight him? Or would she melt in his arms like she had on Ring-Seven?

He'd tangle his fingers in her hair, and she'd yield. She'd gasp in his mouth. She'd clutch his shoulders, his hair, his face. And she'd scream. Oh, he'd make her scream. She'd let him do whatever he wanted because she wanted it too.

He'd show her how it was supposed to be done, not a quick tumble in a Callisto whorehouse. He'd take his time, and he'd make sure she never forgot him. And he'd never forget her either. How could he? That hair? Those freckles? The taste of her skin and the way she trembled in his arms, like she'd never been kissed?

Her pale skin against the dark sheets of his bunk, hair like flame in his fingers, the length of her legs around him—

"Shit."

Kale drove the back of his head against the *Scimitar* chassis.

What the hell is wrong with me? He clutched his scalp with shaking fingers. Had it really been so long since he'd had sex that he'd jump at the chance to tumble the first girl who came along? Yeah, it'd been a long time, but not *that* long.

She was just a kid. And he was who he was. No one like him should touch someone like her.

A girl, he reminded himself. *She's just a girl.*

He chugged the rest of his tea, grabbed the scrub brush, and focused on scraping the last of the grime off the *Scimitar*.

And she'll be much better off if she stays away from me.

CHAPTER 27

The rumbling song of the engine echoed in the corridor and helped Xander get herself under control as she walked back to the galley. She imagined the engine's tuneless chugging composed an ode to the *Prodigal* crew, with the whiny bits dedicated to Vix, the loud thumps for Claude, the tinny whistles for Devon, and the strident clangs for Kale. Maybe the *Prodigal* was pissed off at him too.

Xander waited outside the galley door until her breathing evened out. If Devon or Scraps suspected that Kale had upset her, they'd either try to console her or they'd get angry at him. Neither would help. She'd cry harder, and Kale would only get angrier.

She waited until her face didn't burn.

"Had you seen this?" Jaz spoke solemnly from inside the galley. "It came across the wires yesterday."

"Gimme."

Xander peeked around the door frame. Devon and Jaz sat close to each other, shoulders touching, both holding a datapad that glowed brightly in the dim galley. The datapad displayed Xander's photograph, a candid shot from her days on Callisto.

What were they doing with a photograph of her from Callisto?

She started to ask.

"Are those decimals right?" Devon asked in awe.

Xander froze.

NAMELESS

"They are," Jaz said. "300 million."

Devon whistled low. "Shit."

Xander's heart jumped into her throat. What were they looking at? A wanted poster? Jaz had said it came across the wires the previous day. Why hadn't she said anything about it?

300 million credits? For what?

For me. Someone is offering a 300 million credit reward for turning me in.

The corridor began to spin. Xander gripped the door frame until her fingertips ached.

"That's a hell of a lot of creds." Devon sat back in his chair.

Xander slid farther away from the door frame. She didn't want him to see her. She didn't want them to know she'd heard them talking.

"What could we do with 300 million creds?" Devon chuckled.

"You could splurge on exotic seafood dishes."

Devon groaned. "I'm never going to live that down, am I?"

Xander tried to even her breathing out. If she didn't, she'd faint in the hallway. Panicking didn't help. She had to be calm. She had to breathe.

"Why would Knightshade offer that much for Xander?" Devon shifted in his chair. "Damn it, Jaz, why do they want her so bad?"

"Her ship?"

"They can't want her for her ship. They already have her ship."

"Maybe they need her to operate it?"

"Fat lot of good she'll do them as she is," Devon said. "She can't even remember her own name."

343

Xander peeked around the door frame again and tried not to stare. Jaz leaned against Devon with her head on his shoulder, her blond hair a waterfall down his back. Devon's hand rested on her knee.

"You realize this complicates things," Jaz said.

Devon pressed his lips together.

"If Knightshade is willing to put this much out for her, they want her. They want her worse than any of us suspected." Jaz threaded her fingers through Devon's. "They won't stop hunting her."

"And neither will anyone else," Devon said. "The minute this hits the net, anyone who's seen her with us is going to come after her, cannons blazing." He rested his cheek against her head. "We're going to have to fight them all off."

"And now the Dragons know Kale is with us too."

Devon grimaced. "Don't remind me."

Jaz shifted to wrap an arm around Devon's lower back. "Xander seemed very upset."

"It was bad." Devon's voice didn't tremble, but it was quiet. "He won't talk about it, but he hasn't had to fight like that for years." He sighed. "I'd expect him to be up with you and Claude some night. Just don't ask him why."

"He doesn't drink chocolate."

"Well, don't let him drink scotch. Then nobody's safe."

Xander fisted the front of her shirt in her hand and breathed as quietly as she could.

Devon kissed Jaz's cheek and sat up. "Don't worry, babe. We'll figure it out."

Jaz traced the line of his jaw with a slender finger as she pulled away from him. "I have no doubt, Devon. I believe we have done the right thing."

"But?"

Jaz leaned on the table and regarded the datapad with a frown. "Surviving Knightshade just got much less likely, whether we attack them or not."

Xander pulled away from the door and leaned against the corridor wall, her heart throbbing in her ears.

She couldn't think here, and she had to think. She pushed off the wall and half-ran for her room. She paused outside the door and composed herself before she peered inside.

Empty. Good.

Evy was probably with Captain McLeod. Since she'd learned of Dr. Zahn's death, Evy had truly become a different person. The Evy before Dr. Zahn's death wouldn't have been caught dead in the company of a man, let alone the captain of a bounty hunter ship.

Xander sat on her bunk and clutched her stomach.

Knightshade had issued a reward for her capture. They would stop at nothing to find her. They would kill everyone she loved, everyone she had associated with. Why didn't matter. That was the truth.

"Truth is a certainty of life," Xander whispered to the shadows. "You can't escape it, and running solves nothing." She doubled over and pressed her forehead against her knees.

With a bounty so extreme on her head, every hunter in the entire system would be coming after her. Not only would the *Prodigal* crew have to fight off Knightshade and now the Dragons, they'd have to fight off the rest of the bounty hunters too.

Her very presence endangered anyone close to her.

This must be how Kale feels all the time.

The *Prodigal* shuddered in flight, and her ears popped from the pressure as the ship began to descend. Were they landing?

Thebe. Devon had told her they were landing on Thebe to recharge the engines before they attacked the *Tempest.*

What would happen if I left?

The thought came sudden and strong.

I'm the one Knightshade wants. If I leave, Knightshade will leave them alone. Knightshade will come after me, just like the rest of the bounty hunters.

She'd be alone, yes, and she hadn't been alone since the *Anastasia* left her on Callisto. But if she could keep her friends safe, alone might be worth it.

Whatever Knightshade wanted with her couldn't be good. They had her ship, the *Destiny,* but they didn't have her. And it would be up to her to stay out of their hands.

But without the Destiny, *will I ever remember who I am?*

She looked at Evy's bed, neatly made and unwrinkled. Just like Evy, her friend who'd changed so much from the cold, distant woman she'd met on NUSaxony. Losing Evy would kill her.

Losing any of them would kill her. Ben she barely knew, and Vix she didn't like, but she didn't want their blood on her hands. Captain McLeod had been kind to her. Scraps had been her grandfather. Marty and Claude accepted her. Devon had been her brother, Jaz her sister, and Kale—Kale had been himself. And that's what she had wanted anyway.

"Some things are more important than a name."

She could live nameless as long as her friends were safe. Knowing her name paled in significance to knowing the people she loved were still flying, still chasing their dreams among the stars.

The ship shuddered around her as it touched down, the engines relaxing with a mechanical sigh of relief.

Decision made.

Time to go.

She stood and grabbed Evy's datapad from the shelf in the corner. Did she leave a note? No. If she left a note, they'd know she'd gone, and they'd come after her. None of them would be happy when they realized she had left, but it was for their own good.

You're acting just like Kale, her mind accused.

She shook herself and left the datapad on the shelf.

Xander checked the hallway and walked to the command deck. Even the bridge was abandoned. Ben wasn't at his customary place.

Perfect.

Xander didn't run into anyone in the corridors. She stepped into the loading bay, and stopped short as Newt jumped out at her. The little white Pomeranian yipped at her, and she knelt to scratch her ears.

Funny how she'd hated the dog when she'd first encountered it. She wouldn't see Newt again, wouldn't hear her bark or laugh at the silliness of their first meeting. That knowledge settled in her stomach like a painful knot.

Newt turned in a circle and plopped on the floor panels, rolling over for Xander to scratch her belly. Xander obliged, and then walked toward the loading ramp. The force field shimmered like a diamond curtain against the loading bay door.

Active. She couldn't get out that way. She turned and spotted the emergency hatch in the floor.

She opened it and slipped out, shutting it behind her, closing it against Newt's confused barks.

She jumped down to the sandy ground of the desolate Theban desert. Wide, rolling hills of sand stretched in every direction around the ship. Hot wind brushed her face, and the dry air sapped the moisture out of her hands.

The *Prodigal* rested on the tarmac of a ramshackle facility. *Martha Jean's Recharge and Meal Station*, the partially lit holosign flickered. It advertised fair prices.

Xander could hear conversation on the wind. She ducked under the *Prodigal's* belly and stood behind one of its landing claws. Marty and Captain McLeod spoke to a man in a greasy jumpsuit with a hat on backward, and he held a filthy rag in his hands. Xander could barely make out the writing embroidered on his jumpsuit. *Ed.*

Captain McLeod and Ed shook hands, and they parted while Ed unhooked the cable attached to the mount beneath the *Prodigal's* wing. Captain McLeod wiped his hands on his pants with a disgusted expression while Marty laughed at him.

They're finished. They're leaving.

As soon as she heard Captain McLeod and Marty slam the hatch door on their side of the *Prodigal*, Xander scrambled out from under the wing and knelt behind a large sand dune.

The engines flared to life, air distorted with the heat. Afterburners under the wings shot fire and lifted the *Prodigal* off the ground. The landing claws retracted, and the *Prodigal* shot into the stars.

Xander watched them go in silence, tears streaming down her face.

The rickety old ship flying away left a gaping hole in her heart. She hadn't even known it had taken up residence there. How would she sleep without the rumble of its engines singing?

What would Evy do now? She couldn't go back to NUSaxony. She would be alone too, but at least she would still be alive.

NAMELESS

Scraps would never get the hang of apple salad, and Kale would never know how much she cared.

She'd never see them again.

She waited, half expecting the *Prodigal* to turn around and come back, to see Scraps come storming out of the ship, enraged that she would leave without helping with the dishes first.

But they didn't.

When her skin began to burn, she walked toward Martha Jean's.

Martha Jean's reminded her of a truck stop. The term leapt into her mind when she stepped into the tumbledown duranium shed.

Ship repair supplies made up half the building. A restaurant took up the other half, complete with a bar and a holographic dancer in the process of stripping off what little holographic clothing she wore.

A few customers sat at the tables, most of whom were old and bent over their tables sleeping, drool running down their chins. Xander didn't see a waitress or a sign indicating where people should sit. So she seated herself—at the bar.

Martha Jean's made the Oasis look more like a shack than it already had. But then, the Oasis made a shack look like a four-star establishment. Hopefully it would take the crew a day to notice her missing. If she could wait at Martha' Jean's until another ship came through, she'd be able to barter passage or at least sneak aboard.

A woman with wild eyes set too far apart and crazy, flyaway hair stormed out of the kitchen, puffs of smoke belching out of the door as it opened. She smelled like burned eggs.

"What do you want?" The woman showed a mouth full of half-rotten teeth.

Xander ignored the stench. "I'd like a ride offworld."

The woman stopped. "You what?"

"I need a lift," Xander said. "And I'd like to wait here until someone comes along who'll take me. Can I?"

The woman stared at her like she'd sprouted another head. "We don't give rides." The woman passed her and marched out to the tables with a datapad to take orders.

Xander watched her. That wasn't what she'd asked.

She looked like the only waitress in the restaurant. And if the burning smell emanating from the kitchen were any indication, she was probably the only cook too.

Xander took another deep breath.

The woman came back, fuming and sputtering. "You still here? What do you want?"

"I told you," Xander said. "I'd like to wait here until I can charter a ride off world."

"I told you, little girl, we ain't a taxi service."

"I didn't think you were," Xander said. "I just need a place to stay out of the sun."

The woman scowled. "We ain't an inn."

"No, not stay overnight. Just until I can get a ride."

"We don't give rides."

"I know."

Maybe Martha Jean's looked nicer than the Oasis, but the intelligence of her staff seemed to be the equivalent of an orangutan.

"Are you going to order anything?"

"A glass of water?"

"Water?"

"Yes, ma'am."

"Have you got credits?"

"No, ma'am. I don't."

NAMELESS

"Then you can't have no water."

"Not even a small drink?"

"If you ain't got no credits, you can't have nothing we got." The woman tightened her apron. "And if you can't order nothing, you can't sit there."

Was she serious? Surely that was a joke.

The woman glared at her.

Okay. Not a joke.

Xander nodded and slid off the chair.

The heat from the desert air hit her like a solid wall when she stepped outside.

She'd forgotten what it was like in the universe. She'd gotten used to Evy. She'd gotten used to the crew.

The only person who had helped her no questions asked had been Kale. Saving her life on Ursa-Five had been a snap decision. There hadn't been time to negotiate who got what spoils. There had only been time to act—run away or help. And Kale had chosen to help.

Kale. Beautiful, blue-eyed bozo.

Why did he refuse to let people in? Why did he refuse to let her in? If he'd stop being so stubborn, maybe he'd understand that she didn't want anything from him. Just to be his friend.

Not that it mattered now.

Still, if she turned around and found him smiling at her, she'd say it all over again. Maybe he didn't think he was worth it, but she disagreed.

A footstep crunched behind her. Maybe it was the woman from inside, come to take pity on her.

Xander turned and came face to chest with Darien Stone.

CHAPTER 28

Darien Stone?

He didn't belong on Thebe. How could he possibly be on Thebe? Maybe someone who just looked like him.

But his expression, the shadows simmering in his eyes, told her everything. Somehow he'd had planned it all.

"Hello, Xander." He smirked.

She couldn't answer.

What was he doing there? How had he found her? What was he going to do with her?

Calm down. The crew is safe.

"You haven't remembered your name yet, have you?"

She took a step backward. He didn't move.

"I'm certain you're surprised to see me." He tilted his head. "You should be."

Xander took another step back. One step too many. Stone seized her arm in a grip like iron and jerked her to his chest. She pushed against his leather coat, but he held her steady.

"What do you want?" She tried to twist out of his hold.

He only smiled a black, evil smile that turned her blood to ice.

Not answering was bad. Smirking was worse.

The people in Martha Jean's wouldn't help her. The *Prodigal* crew was gone. She was on her own.

The sandy dirt mounded over her shoes as Stone dragged her

352

beside him. He could overpower her. He could fight. He could shoot her, but that didn't mean she had to let him push her around.

Or pull her around.

He would win a fight, but she'd make him fight for it all the way. She give him a fight he'd never forget.

Xander saw a rise in the sand. She drove the toe of her shoe into the base of it and ripped back, wrenching out of his grasp. But Stone anticipated it and spun, seizing her hair and jerking it hard enough to bring tears to her eyes.

"There's that lovely spark." He laughed. "Enough of a fuss to be fun. I like you."

"Everybody says that. Then they get to know me." She punched his chest.

He laughed again and clutched a handful of her hair, yanking her along at his side. Xander yelped at the strain on her scalp.

He'd concealed a small, sleek silver shuttle behind a tall dune. He opened the back hatch with a remote in his coat pocket. He hauled her inside and threw her on the floor, the door closing behind them. Xander rolled away from him and threw her shoulder against the door, hoping something might break loose inside it.

It didn't.

Trapped. Trapped in a shuttle with Darien Stone.

He stared at her.

His eyes consumed her, undressed her. If Stone had started poking and prodding her like a piece of fruit, she couldn't have felt more like a piece of merchandise.

Men at the Oasis had looked at her like that, but there she'd had a serving tray. There she'd had Cedric. For all he'd hurt her, he'd saved her more than once.

Here? Just her and Stone. No weapons. No friends. Nothing

to stop him except her fingernails and her teeth, and she intended to use them.

He slipped out of his long black trench coat and loosened his tie. Such a domestic action didn't suit him. It threatened her more than if he'd pulled a knife.

He sank into a rich leather chair across from where she leaned against the back hatch. "Water?"

She glared at him.

"I do love your spark, little girl."

She straightened against the wall and wiped her sweating palms on her pants. The shuttle smelled of incense and leather. Stone sat on one of the two chairs angled against the main wall. A wood-paneled chiller case against the back wall probably kept liquor cool, and a metal pole supported the leather-padded ceiling near the cockpit door.

"Good," he said.

She glared at him.

"You're thinking. You're noticing." His feral smile chilled her. "Notice away. Notice you have nothing in reach you can use to defend yourself with."

"You planned this, didn't you?" She lifted her chin and set her hands on her hips.

If she showed him her fear, he'd pounce. That's what happened at the Oasis. She had to hide it. Hide it and put on a brave face. Like Kale. That's what Kale did. He was alone and hurting, and he hid it all behind a smile and harsh words.

Well, if he could do it, so could she.

"Yes."

"All of it."

"Most of it." He smirked. "I'm certain Kale thought he was

playing me. After all, he and Devon know me better than anyone else. And Kale and I have a certain—similarity—in our backgrounds now. The only difference is that I'm still with my syndicate, and he washed out of his."

Xander frowned. What did that mean? The Dragons wanted Kale. That didn't mean he'd been a part of them. Or did it?

"Oh, he didn't tell you? Kale was the top hitter for the Black Dragon Syndicate for years." Stone flashed a predatory grin. "Yes, he was the best of the best until he lost his nerve and took up bounty hunting. He's really gone downhill, if you ask me."

"I didn't ask you."

"When I found out you were in his possession, you were easy to track. I could kick back and relax." He leaned back in his chair, his eyes caressing the length of her throat. "Once I figured out they intended to come after the *Destiny*, it was only a matter of time until Kale decided to trace my steps. Mitchem was the best option."

Stone stood and selected a bottle of water from the chiller.

"Mitchem is dead, by the way. He outlived his usefulness."

Xander watched him twist the top off the lid and take a long drink. His throat moved as he swallowed. If she lunged at him, could she get her hands around his neck? Was she strong enough to strangle him?

He set the bottle on the stand between the chairs. His eyes burned her. He hadn't once looked at her face.

"Why am I so important? What do you people want with me?"

Stone walked toward her.

"What Mr. Knight wants with you, little Xander, I honestly don't know." He fingered a strand of her hair. "I know what I want."

Fingernails. Teeth. Xander stiffened, holding his feral gaze.

Make him remember.

The instant his fingers clutched her hair, she slapped him, fingernails grazing his skin and leaving trails of blood across his face. But he didn't stumble sideways. He didn't let go of her hair.

He straightened, his face bleeding, his eyes black as space.

"Good." His grip on her hair tightened. "Show me that spark."

Xander threw a punch at his chin, but he grabbed her fist and threw her against the shuttle wall.

She gasped for air, clutching her ribs. *I'll show him spark.*

Stone grabbed her throat and yanked her up. Xander clawed at his face, and he let go, capturing both her wrists in one hand and pinning them to the wall.

So much for fingernails.

He sank his teeth into her neck and shoved his knee between her thighs, slipping his free hand up her shirt.

Too strong. So much stronger than she thought.

Teeth! Teeth!

But what could she bite? His coat? Right, that would hurt him.

He drew his tongue up the side of her neck to her ear, his hand sliding down the back of her pants to force her against him.

She couldn't kick with his knee between her thighs. Panic, like a fog in her brain, overpowered her anger. Teeth and fingernails would only get her so far.

Oh, God. His hand.

Why had she left the ship? Why had she thought she could survive on her own?

If Kale were here, he'd run to her rescue. He wouldn't know why. He just would because that's who he was.

Kale smelled like cedar and spice. Stone smelled like red wine, acidic and burning.

No Kale. He's not here. Xander beat against Stone's chest. "Get off me!"

The hand down her pants traced a cold line up to her ribs. He jerked her head back and shoved his lips against hers.

Stop him. Make him stop.

She pounded on his chest, but he didn't release her. She clawed at the skin of his neck. He only kissed her harder, forcing his tongue past her lips and into her mouth.

Teeth. Bite. Now.

Xander bit him.

He chuckled.

He thought it was funny? Their mouths were full of his blood, and he laughed?

His teeth clamped on her lower lip, and she yelped in shock and pain. He released her hair and trailed both hands across her stomach, across her lower back, cupping her breasts in his palms.

She arched her back, but she couldn't escape. She twisted in his arms, but astride his knee, she couldn't get any sort of balance.

He thrust his tongue into her mouth again, the copper taste of his kiss warning her not to bite him again.

That left fingernails, but she'd already scraped skin off his neck. He hadn't stopped.

He wouldn't stop.

Cold terror knotted in her chest. With every stroke of his tongue, squeeze of his fingers, cold lightning ripped through her body, tingling beneath her skin. What was he doing to her?

Xander landed one more desperate blow against the side of his face, and he pushed himself against her with a harsh laugh, breathing hot air into her mouth.

She didn't have the strength to make him stop.

The first choked sob tore itself out of her mouth, and his bruising grip doubled in strength. Stone's calloused hands scratched down her back and sides to her belt, fingers dipping beneath her waistline until they found her belt buckle and fumbled with it.

Terror she left on Callisto raged through her, Xander lunged sideways with a ragged cry. Maybe the fear made her stronger. Stone lost his balance, and they both fell to the floor.

Free. Free of his hands.

Not for long. Stone grabbed her hips and pulled her back to him. Xander clawed at the carpet, ripping her fingernails. He seized her belt loops and dragged her back, fighting with her belt. She kicked, thrashing away, and he laughed.

I'm just entertaining him. He wants me to fight.

He won over the belt buckle and whipped her belt out, bending to kiss her exposed belly and sliding down her zipper.

He lifted his head, and Xander shoved her palm into his nose. Cartilage crunched as his nose broke.

Music to her ears.

He roared in pain.

No, that was music.

Xander rolled over and scrambled away, getting to her knees.

"You little bitch!" Stone snatched her shirt and dragged her back. "You broke my nose, you little bitch."

"Did you want a medal?" Xander kicked his knee.

His fist struck her temple, and bright spots burst in her vision. Xander hit the floor. He kicked her in the stomach so hard she wretched.

Gasping for breath, Xander let the carpet absorb the tears

pouring down her face. Stone loomed over her, blood dripping off his broken nose.

She broke his nose. All by herself.

Kale would be proud.

"Sexy as hell." He dashed the blood off his face. "Don't stop fighting. Keep it up. Keep hoping, and I'll show you there's no hope. That's my favorite part—like snuffing out a candle flame."

She glared up, blood pooling in her ear.

"Come on, little girl. Don't give up now." He knelt, tracing the length of her legs with one hand. "Your friends are coming back for you."

His black eyes sparkled like cold jet.

"That's why you're fighting, isn't it? You're fighting because any moment that hatch is going to blow open, and your Kale is coming to the rescue." His face curled in a horrible smirk. "Because Kale already had you, didn't he? Son of a bitch always got first pick."

Xander glanced toward the hatch. What was he going on about?

His hand slid into her hair. She stilled under his eyes.

"We're not done yet. We haven't even started." His fingers tightened against her scalp. "You think Kale Ravenwood knew how to make you scream? You have no idea. But you need to crank up the volume so they can hear you, don't you think?" He leaned into her. "Scream your lungs out."

He wants me to fight. She swallowed, tasting her own blood. *The more I fight, the worse it will be.*

His fingers tightened against her scalp. "No?"

She glared at him.

"Spark's still there." Stone smirked. "But you're a smart one.

You'll just take it, won't you?" He rolled her over and nuzzled his face against her neck. "You won't fight anymore, will you?"

Xander didn't move, even as his hot breath flared down her collar.

"Shame. Would have been more fun if you'd held on longer." He kissed the hollow of her neck.

Stone pulled away and stood, straightening his coat. Xander lay on the floor, still glaring, not daring to move.

"Since you're done fighting, you might as well know," Stone said. "Your friends aren't coming. I had old Ed out there rig their engine to blow the second they hit hyperdrive."

She gaped at him in horror.

"So, chances are, they're already scattered in a million pieces."

No. No, that can't be. Xander turned her eyes away from him. *The ship can't be gone. Kale can't be gone. Not forever. They're still alive, and Stone's just trying to upset you.*

Liar.

He lied.

No, he didn't. He'd wanted her to fight. Now he knew she wouldn't anymore, so he'd told her what he'd done. He'd killed them. She'd run away to protect them, and he killed them anyway.

The shuttle spun. She couldn't breathe.

Why? Why, God? Why?

Xander sat up, fresh tears spilling down her face. "You didn't. You couldn't have."

"Why would I lie?" He knelt and touched her cheek. She pulled away, and he laughed. "That's right."

He pulled a pair of cuffs from his back pocket and fastened her right wrist to the shuttle's center support beam.

"You got them killed, little girl," Stone said. "Running away never would have made any difference. I would have killed them just because. Kale and I have history that goes way back." He squeezed the inside of her thigh. "I do wish he could have known I got to have you. He knows how I like it." His fingers trailed upward. "Nothing would piss him off faster than knowing I got to touch you after he did."

Xander's stomach turned over.

Stone stood again and smirked at her. "We'll make sure the exchange goes well at Io, and then you and I are going to NUJenesis." He brushed imaginary dust off his shirtsleeves, stained with her blood. "But don't worry. It's a long trip. I'll make sure you don't get bored."

Stone knocked on the cockpit door, and the shuttle's engines powered up.

Xander pressed her forehead against the pole and squeezed her eyes shut.

God, what have I done? How can this happen? I just wanted to do the right thing. How can this happen when I just wanted to do the right thing?

She let the tears come.

"There, there, little Xander." Stone sat back in his chair and resumed his leering. "Go ahead and cry. Just wait until I really give you something to cry about."

Stone would take her to NUJenesis. She didn't have to guess what he would take from her on the journey there.

CHAPTER 29

Even as Stone stared at her, Xander twisted in the cuffs. He thought crushing her hope would make her stop fighting? He didn't know anything about her. She'd lost everything more than once already. One more time wouldn't make a difference.

She'd give him the fight of his life. It would hurt. He would hurt her over and over again, and he wouldn't stop. But she'd never give in. He could never break her.

Something bang-bang-banged on the hull of Stone's shuttle, a dull, loud sound, and Stone scowled in his chair. He stood and pressed the comm button next to the cockpit door.

"Hold takeoff."

He walked to the side hatch.

Xander held her breath as he released the door latch.

The harsh light of the desert didn't shine into the shuttle, blocked by a figure in the doorway.

Stone yelped and leaped back as a massive wrench smashed into the floor where he'd been standing. A huge fist seized his shirt and ripped him out of the shuttle.

"*Guten Morgen,*" said a loud, angry voice outside. "*Du Hurensohn.*"

She knew that voice. She knew that wrench.

"Claude," she screamed. "Claude!"

Claude was alive. The *Prodigal* crew was alive.

Xander couldn't see, but she could hear. She couldn't tell

who was winning. She eyed the crater the wrench had left on the floor panels.

Claude was probably bludgeoning Stone to death, and she didn't feel a bit sorry for him.

A roar of pain sounded outside, and Xander flinched for Claude. She yanked on the chain binding her to the pole, but it didn't budge. And she didn't have a key.

No matter how big Claude was, Stone still had a blaster. She pulled and pried at the cuff, but it wouldn't release.

Scrambling to her feet, she leaned out as far as the chain would allow, reaching for the coat Stone had laid just beyond her fingertips. Maybe the key would be in it.

Another cry of pain from outside.

"God, let that be Stone this time."

If Claude were outside fighting, where was everyone else?

A shadow darkened the doorway, but she didn't turn. She wanted Stone to see her trying to escape, wanted him to know she hadn't given up and wouldn't give up. Not ever.

A firm hand grabbed her chained wrist, and Xander swung around, fist raised.

She stopped, her free hand restrained inches from Jaz's face.

"Jaz?" Xander gasped, eyes widening.

Jaz arched her eyebrows. "Were you expecting someone else?"

Jaz examined the cuff that bound her to the pole. Xander frowned.

"Jaz, why did you come back for me? You shouldn't have."

"Xander, now is not the time to discuss this."

"I left so you all would be safe," Xander said. "Now here you are charging back into trouble again."

"Oh, stop." Jaz pulled a card out of her pocket. She slid it between the locking mechanism of the cuff, and it sprang open. "Don't be ridiculous."

Someone howled in pain outside.

"But—Claude—"

"That wasn't Claude."

The shuttle rocked so hard it nearly toppled over.

Jaz grimaced. "That was Claude."

Devon appeared in the doorway—Devon, his face bloody. He leapt inside and ran to Xander, his eyes worried.

"Xander? You all right?"

"She's fine, Devon." Jaz touched his shoulder and replaced the lock-picking card in her jacket. She pulled her blaster out. "We need to go."

Devon turned her face from side to side, examining at the cuts and bruises Stone had left. He pressed his lips together.

"Okay, go." He turned and ran back outside, pulling his own blaster.

Jaz walked to the opposite side hatch and released it with a kick. Xander still stood at the center of the shuttle.

"Xander." Jaz held out her hand. "Are you coming or not?"

Xander met her eyes. "I'm going to get you all killed."

Jaz's expression turned fierce as she stormed back and seized her arm. "Oh, hell, Ravenwood is right." She yanked Xander to her feet. "You are a complete idiot." Jaz shoved her out the door. "Run!"

Thebe had become a war zone. Sand filled the air like smoke.

The *Prodigal* hovered overhead, its engines pulsing with energy, radiating extra heat on a desert already too hot. Jaz crouched behind the shuttle and held Xander at her side.

Why were they doing this? She'd given them the chance to

run, and they came back? Why? They shouldn't be here.

Five cables dangled from the underside of the *Prodigal*.

The shuttle rocked again, followed by another roar of pain.

"Go, Jaz, go!" Devon rolled in the sand and pointed at the cables.

Jaz bolted forward and dragged Xander with her. Xander tripped and stumbled, but Jaz didn't slow down.

Xander looked back.

Devon and Claude climbed to their feet, faces bleeding and clothing torn. And Stone—Stone was locked in combat with Kale.

Kale delivered two vicious spinning kicks and a knockdown punch that drove Stone to the sand. But he jumped up and punched Kale in the face.

Devon leapt in between them, and Stone threw him off without a glance.

Jaz jerked her away from the sight and ran to the cables. Vix popped out from behind a sand dune, blaster ready, radio hanging from her belt. She grabbed one of the cables as Jaz started wrapping a harness around Xander's hips.

"Wait," Xander said. "Jaz, please. Just wait. You can't do this. I'm dangerous."

Jaz grabbed her collar and shook her. "Xander, shut up."

Vix hooked the cable on the harness and spoke into the radio. "Got her. Pull her up."

Xander yelped as the cable jerked and dragged her upward toward the *Prodigal*. Now, dangling between the Theban desert and the bounty hunter ship above, she could see the fight at the shuttle.

Claude's face looked like he'd been beaten with a sledgehammer, but he kept throwing punches in between Kale and Devon's attacks. But the real fight seemed to be Kale and Devon against Stone.

Their grisly dance mesmerized her even from a distance. Kale danced around Stone's attacks like the wind, but Stone moved with deadly skill and malicious intent. Devon wasn't graceful, not like Kale, but he hit like a battering ram and held on like a bulldog with a bone.

A sand dune close to the shuttle exploded, another shuttle closing in. Sleek and silver like Stone's shuttle, it had to be Seeker reinforcements. It circled and laid down a line of fire close to the fight, while peppering the *Prodigal* with laser blasts.

Explosions rocked the ship above her. Sparks rained down from the loading bay, showering around her, and the winch stopped. The cable slid, and Xander shrieked as she fell ten feet. She grabbed at the cable as it jerked to a stop, the whiplash dotting her vision with white spots.

"Xander." Jaz clung to the cable on the ground as though she could steady it. "Unhook the harness and climb down."

Xander wrapped the cable around her arm and leg and unhooked the harness. Thebe's gravity pulled stronger than before.

She descended the cable, hands burning and arms trembling, praying it wouldn't let go. If it jerked again, she would fall. She could hardly hold on while it hung still.

Within five feet of the sand, the cable jerked.

She lost her grip and fell on top of Vix, who screeched with indignation.

"Get off me, bitch." Vix shoved her.

"Sorry." Xander scrambled away from her. "I'm sorry."

Another explosion came from above, and the *Prodigal* veered to starboard as one of the underwing engines choked in a plume of fire and black smoke. The turrets on the bridge lit up and started shooting at the shuttle flying circles around them.

Jaz grabbed Xander. "We need to take cover," she said. "Now."

Jaz turned, and Stone punched her in the face, knocking her to the ground.

Vix slipped in the sand but tackled him around the waist hard enough to drive him back a step. He threw her down with little trouble.

His face bleeding, his clothes torn, rage sparkled in the depths of his black eyes. He reached for Xander and yelped as Jaz kicked him in the back of his leg, his knee buckling.

Vix clawed his face and kneed him in the stomach, but he grabbed her hair and slammed her into the sand. Jaz regained her footing and lunged at him with a punch and a kick. But he connected a crushing blow to her stomach.

Neither got up.

"You're coming with me," he snarled.

Grabbing Xander's wrist, he gave it a vicious twist. He pinned her against his chest, blaster at her head. She froze, blood surging in her ears.

Vix and Jaz swapped dangerous expressions as they stumbled to their feet.

She knew it would happen. They'd come back for her out of some misplaced sense of duty, and Stone would kill them all.

Footsteps pounded the sand. Kale and Devon appeared around the dune. Both bleeding. Both stood red faced and panting, but Kale's eyes were ice. Claude came a moment later, breathing hard.

"Where the hell have you been?" Vix clutched her stomach as she bent over, black hair tumbling over her shoulders.

A.C. WILLIAMS

"Hashing out a clever strategy," Devon shouted.

"Hiding from lasers." Claude rested his giant wrench on his shoulder. "Lasers bad."

Devon punched his arm. "Shut up, Claude. That makes us sound like wimps."

Kale only glared at Stone.

"Looky what I found." Stone seized Xander's neck and displayed her like a trophy. "A hostage!"

"Let her go, Darien." Kale spread his hands.

"Oh, Kale, why would I do that?" Stone backed toward his shuttle. "Because you asked so nicely?"

"We'll track you down, Stone," Devon said. "No matter where you take her."

"Like you efficiently tracked me down this time, Devon?" Stone laughed. "I hardly think you're a threat. The only one of you who hit me hard enough to hurt was your dumbass NUGerman friend back there—and he had a wrench. What does that say about you, Kale? You've gotten soft."

Kale glowered, his blue eyes brilliant.

Vix and Jaz watched in silence with bleeding faces and worried eyes.

Stone circled them. With every step backward he used her as a shield between him and the bounty hunters. For every step he took, Kale and Devon followed.

"You going to come inside?" Stone backed up to his ship's ramp, fingers bruising Xander's neck. "That'd be fine with me. I'm certain the Dragons would pay a good price to have you back, Kale. And surely I could find some slaver den that needs a handsome, strapping boy like you, Devon."

Neither of them answered.

NAMELESS

Devon's eyes glittered green, his chin lowered.

"And Xander and I can provide the entertainment on the way." Stone pulled her tighter against his chest. "It'll be fun. I already had a taste. Just couldn't help myself."

Kale's face grew darker. A muscle twitched at the back of his jaw.

"Oh, you don't like that, do you, Kale?" Stone slid his hand to the front of her neck and down to her chest. "Well, too bad. You never had anything I couldn't have too."

He backed up to the open door.

"I'm taking little Xander with me," he said. "My associates up in the sky will shoot your ship down if it tries to interfere. And if you try to stop me, I'll hurt her."

"You're going to hurt her anyway, Darien." Kale's eyes simmered.

"Well, of course, I'm going to hurt her." Stone's voice resonated with malicious intent. "I'm going to lay her so hard she won't be able to walk for a month. I'll lay her so hard, Kale, she won't remember ever tumbling you." Stone chuckled. "But I don't have to skin her alive after."

Xander shut her eyes. She didn't want to think about what Stone planned to do to her.

She should think about something else. Scraps's hugs. Devon's smiles. The tingling in her stomach when Kale looked at her. Yeah, all around much more pleasant things to think about.

"Or pull out her fingernails. Or burn her." Stone pulled her tight against his hip. "Or break every bone she has? Do I, Kale?"

Kale didn't answer.

Xander clenched her eyes shut tighter.

Daisies. She liked daisies. Except the last daisy she'd seen

369

had died a brutal death—like it seemed she would.

"If you try to stop me, Kale, I'll do all of the above—and I'll video it—and send it to you for your birthday." Stone laughed. "I'll still get to have my fun either way. But it's up to you how much it hurts her."

Xander opened her eyes.

Kale's eyes were riveted on Stone. He had the most stunning eyes.

They could cut a deal. She would go with Stone, and Kale and the others could go their way. No one else had to get hurt. No one else had to die for her. The people she loved would be safe.

Yes. She loved them.

She forced herself to smile.

"It's okay," she said. "Just—let me go."

Kale and Devon stared at her. They didn't understand. Their eyes widened exactly the same way.

Tears clogged her throat. "Trust me. This is better."

It was a lie. Of course, it wasn't better this way. Going with Stone was insane.

But this way, she could say goodbye on her terms. She wouldn't have to carry the burden of their deaths.

"Xander." Devon reached for her.

"You see, boys?" Stone hugged her against his chest. "Little Xander knows what's best."

"Xander doesn't know shit." Kale dropped his blaster into its holster. "Get to know her better, and you'll figure that out, Darien." His eyes scathed her in their anger. "But she sure thinks she knows it all."

"She's a woman," Stone said. "They all do."

Kale stood with his hands on his hips. Cruel. Arrogant.

Smug. So confusing.

She wanted him to live. She wanted him to meet someone who would help him understand how beautiful life could be.

Devon and Kale stood, glaring together.

Why were they making this difficult? They had a way out. They didn't have to save her.

Then, their expressions changed. Disbelief?

Stone saw it too. But before he could react, Stone roared in shock and pain and dropped her. Xander hit the ground and glanced upward.

Al.

Somehow she'd thrown her skinny little artificial body at Stone and wrapped her spindly legs around his shoulders and neck. Growling like a wild animal, she chewed on his head. Her hair flashed red and orange and green and yellow and purple in rapid, dizzying sequence.

Frantic, Stone thrashed and flailed, but he couldn't reach her.

Devon lunged at Xander, grabbing her arm and dragging her away from Stone.

Stone peeled Al off and threw her away just in time for Kale to kick him in the chest. He fell back into the shuttle. Al slammed the door and locked it, giggling maniacally, and held out the thin cylindrical remote Stone had used earlier. She pressed it, and the ship started. The engines fired, and it launched into the sky.

Al clapped her hands and turned in a circle.

"Come on." Kale seized the little android.

Devon hauled Xander after him.

What? What had just happened? Had Al just defeated Stone? No way.

The *Prodigal* had stabilized and dropped the cables again.

Vix and Jaz were halfway up the cables by the time they got there, Claude already aboard. Al scrambled up the cable by herself.

"Hold on to me," Devon said.

"But—But—"

"Xander, for once in your damn life, don't argue." Kale wrapped her arms around Devon's neck.

Xander shut her eyes and clung to Devon, and he scaled the cable. Kale followed them, hand over hand. Above them, explosions still sounded. Xander peeked one eye open just in time to see the *Prodigal* launch a torpedo that took out the Seeker shuttle. It rained in fiery pieces down on the desert.

Devon reached the bay.

"Climb up, Xander," he said. "Do it now."

She didn't argue. She didn't have far to climb.

Claude grabbed her and pulled her into the bay, but he didn't set her down. He held her tight against his chest in a bear hug.

They made it impossible to leave. Did they know that? She couldn't stay. Knightshade would never stop chasing her, and as long as she stayed with them, their lives meant nothing.

Why did they have to be so wonderful?

Devon and Kale reached the bay, and Jaz closed the doors. Vix punched the intercom.

"Go, Talon," she said. "We're all here."

Claude set Xander on the floor, and Evy appeared out of nowhere and tackled her.

"Xander." She sobbed. "Oh, Xander, what were you thinking? Oh, you weren't thinking, were you? You silly, foolish girl."

Xander held her tears back.

This wasn't a time to cry. This was a time to reason.

Stupid Evy. Stupid everyone. Oh, there came the tears.

"Damn." Devon groaned as he got to his feet. "Where's Scraps? I need painkiller."

"Where the hell did that bastard Stone go?" Vix lit a cigarette. "Didn't seem the type to run away."

"He didn't run." Kale leveled a glare at Al who sat swaying on the floor panels, grinning eerily, her hair vivid purple. "What did you do to his shuttle, bot?"

Al giggled fiendishly. "Auto-auto pilot-pilot hacker-hacker Al is sneakish! Hee-hee!" She burst into giggles.

Kale knelt in front of her. "What did you do?"

"Al set the auto-pilot in the Stone-man's ship-ship." Al clapped her hands, and her hair turned yellow. "His ship-ship goes to Arche."

"Arky?" Devon scowled. "What?"

"Arche, Devon." Jaz touched his arm. "It's a moon."

"A small one," Kale said. "Nothing there but rocks."

"Moon-moon Arche!" Al sang. "Circle-circle says Al to the ship-ship until the vroom-vroom goes boom-boom!"

"What the hell is it talking about?" Vix blew smoke.

"She set the auto-pilot in Stone's shuttle to fly circles around Arche until its engines burn up." Kale grinned. "Not bad."

"And!" Al dug in the pocket of her pants and pulled out a disc, which she handed to Kale. "Plan-plans for the big-big ship-ship."

Kale took it from her and turned it over.

"Al," Jaz said, "you stole schematics for the *Tempest* out of Stone's memory banks?"

"Yep-yep." Al grinned. "Al is sneakish." She exaggerated a wink and flailed when her face nearly stuck with one eye closed.

"With any luck," Kale stood, "Stone will still be on board that shuttle when we hit the *Tempest*. They might still know we're coming, but he won't be able to command. That's a big advantage."

"Hit the *Tempest*?" Xander whispered. "We're still—going after the *Destiny*?"

The four hunters and Claude all gawked at her. Evy pulled back.

"Well, of course we are." Evy frowned. "Why wouldn't we?"

Xander looked from face to face, the people who had saved her when they didn't have to. Her friends.

"I left because I'm danger," she said. "As long as I'm with you, Knightshade will never leave any of you in peace." She steadied herself. "I want to remember who I am but not at the risk of losing you. Any of you."

"What about your name?" Jaz arched an eyebrow.

"Some things are more important than a name." Xander pinned Kale with a glare, which he pointedly returned in silence.

Devon took her arm. "Xander, we promised to do this. Running away won't change anything. Knightshade needs to be stopped."

"But you don't have to stop them."

"If we don't, nobody will," Jaz said. "And now we have the advantage."

Devon grinned. "We didn't agree to do this for your name, Xander. We agreed to do it for you."

Xander's eyes burned with tears, and Devon pulled her into a tight embrace.

So much for not crying.

Stupid, wonderful Devon.

Evy broke in and held her close. "Oh, Xander, you are

impossible."

"I'm sorry."

Devon laughed again. "Come on," he said. "Let's go down and see Scraps. I think we all need stitches."

Xander allowed Evy to lead her to the medical bay.

As they walked, Xander found Kale's eyes staring at her.

Such a mixture of anger and grief and relief, and none of it made any sense. But if she'd been feeling that much at one time, her head would have exploded.

Why wouldn't he just talk to her? Instead, he turned and walked down the corridor alone.

Devon's words meant the world, but they would have meant more if Kale had said them.

CHAPTER 30

The kitchen smelled like sausage. Scraps whistled a cheerful tune as he fried eggs and rehydrated oatmeal. Xander set the table like normal.

It had been Jaz who'd realized something was wrong when she didn't see Xander aboard. Marty had repaired the sabotage Ed had done to the engines immediately after Xander had told them about it.

Xander still felt bruised and sore but happy. Really, truly happy. She had friends—friends who had chosen her.

Scraps sang some off-color, off-tune song about a peeping tom in a bar as he dished up oatmeal. The morning routine had become so familiar now, she wondered if she could leave it after they reclaimed the *Destiny*.

Evy sat at the table. "Good morning, Xander."

"Hi, Evy."

"How are you feeling?"

Xander shrugged.

Evy touched her shoulder. "Sure you're all right?"

"Yes, Evy, I'm fine. I'm just—I wanted to keep everyone safe."

"Well, darling," Evy said, "that's not wrong. You just tried to do it all alone." She took Xander's hands and held them tightly. "I owe you an apology."

NAMELESS

"No, Evy, you don't."

"Yes, I do," Evy said. "I was so caught up in my own sorrow, I left you to fend for yourself. As your therapist, it was entirely unprofessional."

"Evy."

"And as your friend, it was immensely self-serving." She smiled. "Forgive me?"

"But you were hurting. I understand."

"Darling? Will you forgive me?"

Xander smiled. "Of course, Evy. I forgive you."

Evy hugged her gently. "Thank you."

Xander leaned against her.

This was friendship. Learning each other. Making allowances for each other. Picking up the pieces and moving forward together. Had she ever had a friend like that? She didn't think so.

"We're in this together, Xander," Evy said. "And that's how we'll finish it. Together."

"Whether I remember or not," Xander said.

"You haven't given up, have you?" Evy held her back a little. "I hope not."

"No," Xander said. "I haven't. But I'm content to just be me for a little while. Maybe I'm trying too hard to remember. Instead of looking for the past, maybe I need to look for right now."

"Wiser words never spoken." Scraps set the pot of oatmeal on the table. "Now, Xander, I need your help again." He gestured to Al who clutched his leg, humming to herself.

Xander laughed, and Scraps held out a cup of green tea to her. "Would you?"

She hesitated. But only a moment.

She and Kale really hadn't spoken since the rescue, but that didn't matter. She would be his friend, like Evy had been hers. She would help him if he wanted it, and she would bring him tea because she could.

She took the tea.

"Good girl." Scraps grinned. "Now, little doctor." He turned to Evy. "Let me serve you some of my fantastic reconstituted oatmeal."

"I can only imagine, Scraps," Evy said, "how dreadful the meals on every other bounty hunter ship must be without you there to provide such culinary excellence."

⊕

Xander found Kale in the loading bay, polishing the *Scimitar* with a cloth. The underside of its wings already gleamed.

He lifted his eyes as she walked in.

Xander's heart skipped, but she didn't hesitate to approach him.

"Good morning," she said.

He quietly set the polishing cloth on top of the wing and took the tea from her hands. "Good morning." He sipped it. "Thanks."

She nodded.

She waited for him to say something else.

He didn't. He just drank the tea.

Great. Great vibe we've got going here. I'm going to stand here and and watch him drink his tea. She frowned. *Almost wish he'd yell at me again so I'd have a reason to leave.*

After an awkward minute, Xander turned and walked toward the corridor. Maybe he didn't want to talk, and that was okay.

It surprised her. But it really was okay. If he didn't want to

NAMELESS

talk now, maybe he would later.

"Why were you on Callisto?"

His voice stopped her in her tracks. She looked over her shoulder at him. He stood, still holding the tea. She couldn't understand the expression in his eyes.

"That's where the *Anastasia* left me. I didn't have a choice." It sounded defensive. She hadn't meant to sound defensive, but she did. "I—waited tables. I worked at the bar. That was it."

He smiled. "Why are you so desperate to make people think you're not a whore?"

She whirled on him. "Well, do you want people to think you're a lousy shot?"

He jerked in surprise, eyes widening.

And then his face brightened in a grin. "But I'm not a lousy shot."

"My point exactly." Xander sagged. "If I walked up to you and told you you couldn't hit the broad side of a barn, how would you feel?"

"I'd think you were an idiot."

She blinked. Well, that was one way to look at it. "Why?"

"Why what?"

"It wouldn't bother you?"

"Not if it isn't true." Kale sipped his tea. "And anyone who's seen me fight knows it isn't." His gaze sharpened.

He didn't have to say the rest. Her face warmed. She didn't have to tell people she wasn't a whore. Anyone who knew her already knew. Anyone who said different was an idiot.

She folded her arms. "Thank you."

He scoffed.

"No, thank you." She stepped closer. "So many people have

379

helped me, and I haven't thanked them soon enough."

He watched her in silence, steam from his tea twisting around his eyes.

"One of the prostitutes in the bar helped me." Xander smiled, images of Sylphie flashing before her eyes. "She gave me the credits to get away."

Kale said nothing and sipped his tea.

"I don't think I'd ever met a prostitute before. And I was scared of her. Because I thought she was a bad person. But, she wasn't. She just made a choice. She was the only person willing to help me."

Kale still said nothing.

So she kept babbling. He probably didn't care, but oh well.

"And then you were willing to help me too. Everyone who I think is bad turns out to be the person I need. Why is that?"

"Because you're screwed up."

She gaped at him. How dare he say something like that! How rude!

And how true.

So very true.

She'd spent so much of her time looking at how wrong everyone around her was. She hadn't spent any time looking at her own heart.

"You're right," she said. "I am."

Kale sipped his tea.

"No matter how hard I try," she said, "I just can't remember. I can't remember anything."

"Except that God crap you told Devon?"

"How did—did he tell you?"

Kale shrugged.

"I didn't think he'd say anything."

"If you remember something, I'd think you'd want to tell people."

"Even if it makes people think I'm from the Sanctum?"

Kale scoffed into the mug. "You're not from the Sanctum."

"How do you know?"

Kale shrugged again. "You're different."

"That's what Devon said."

"You'll believe it from him but not from me?"

She tilted her head. "You say things you don't mean."

Kale blinked in surprise and grinned. "Yeah, I do. But only to my friends."

She'd never seen a real expression in his eyes before. His grin was dashing, heart-stopping. He needed to grin like that more often.

"Scraps says you're a good man," Xander said.

The grin faded to a half-smile. "Scraps says a lot of things."

"Are you?"

"Am I what? A good man?" He shook his head. "No. I don't think so."

"Why does Scraps think so, then?"

"Scraps sees the best in everybody. I'm just me." He held out the mug of tea. "Want some?"

She glanced up at him.

His expression was still guarded, his eyes wary. The openness she'd seen before had vanished.

"It's good." He offered the cup again.

She took the mug from his hand and sipped it.

"It *is* good." She offered it back, but he shook his head.

"Keep it."

"Thanks."

His eyes pierced her. The quiet deafened her. If he didn't speak soon, she had to leave. She couldn't take the intensity. He had more mood swings than she did.

"My mom ran off when I was three."

His abrupt statement startled her. She glanced up into his face and found his eyes studying her.

"My dad died when I was eight."

She held her breath and waited for him to continue.

"Devon's family took me in. Sent me to school. Showed me what it was like to have a home." He shifted. "I spent about a year at a NUUSA university when I was still a teenager, but it wasn't for me. So, I went to Mars. Got in some trouble. Grew up." He shook his head. "Got in over my head with a syndicate—the Dragons."

Xander winced.

He looked at the *Scimitar*.

"That's when I—well—I guess, that's when Devon found me. Told me about Talon, the *Prodigal*, and I signed up."

Xander wanted to move closer but feared to interrupt him.

Kale's life, his story, lay hidden in these layers of words, his dreams, his goals, his identity. And he had chosen to share it with her.

"That's pretty much everything that matters about me," he said.

"I doubt that."

"Well, it's all you're going to hear." He brushed his dirty hands on his pant legs. "Little kid like you doesn't need to be hearing stuff like that."

She frowned. "I'm not a little kid."

"Yeah, you are."

"I'm nineteen years old."

"Oh, wow, nineteen. Getting old—" He stopped. "You're sure about that?"

"Yes, I'm nine—" She paused. "I'm nineteen."

She looked at her hands that held the tea cup. Her hands. Her nineteen-year-old hands on her nineteen-year-old arms, and she began to shake. In a flash, she felt anything was possible. Kale was her friend, and she was 19.

"I'm nineteen." She laughed. "I remember."

She hugged Kale's waist, laughing with joy.

And Kale stiffened on contact.

Xander froze.

She gasped and released him, her heart racing. "I'm—I'm so sorry. I didn't—"

His face was blank, shocked, stunned.

Xander's face burned. How could she have done something so impulsive? He had opened up to her, like a real friend, and she had overstepped the bounds.

Too much too fast, you idiot.

She stepped back, giving him space, but Kale stepped forward and pulled her into his arms.

His heart thrummed in her ear behind the hard muscles of his chest. His giant hands cradled her lower back and shoulder blades, and his cheek rested against the crown of her head. Smelling him this close made her head spin, her own heart beating in time with his.

Kale hugged her. And he hadn't let go yet.

She could get used to this.

"Should I say happy birthday?" His voice rumbled in his chest, and his breath tickled the back of her neck.

"Sure."

Her face burning, she pressed her nose into his chest and stifled a nervous giggle as she slid her hands around his waist, careful not to drop the tea or spill it down his pants. He probably wouldn't appreciate that.

His lean, strong arms held her steady. His heart beat against her ear. The warmth of his body chased the chill of the metal corridors away, and she wanted to snuggle deeper into his embrace.

What would he think about that? If she lifted her face, would he kiss her? She'd dreamed of what his kiss would feel like since Ring-Seven. What were the chances he'd had the same dream?

"Woo-hoo!" Al screamed in the hallway as she raced past. "Woo-hoo! Reconstituted oatmeal! Woo-hoo!"

Kale laughed and released her. Xander stepped back out of his arms and smiled, face still burning. He held her gaze with a smile of his own and turned back to retrieve his polishing cloth.

"Kale?" Xander started.

"Yeah?"

"Are you—are you sure we should keep going after the *Destiny*?"

He stopped and looked at her. "I don't think it's the best idea," he said, "but I do think it's the right thing to do."

"Why?"

"Because it's not theirs. It's yours. It's a part of who you are, and they don't have a right to it." He turned back to his work. "Don't worry, Xander. We'll get it back."

She smiled again and nodded, moving toward the door as though she could fly. Al ran past again, laughing and giggling, scattering daisies all over the ship. They were everywhere.

"Al." Xander laughed. "What are you doing?"

"Flower-flower! Al likes flowers!" She handed a daisy to

Xander.

Xander laughed and smelled it. "Where did you find daisies?"

"On Thebe," Al said. "Al found in awful little stinky building with the awful stinky woman with no teeth-teeth."

"Martha Jean?"

"Martha-Martha-Martha!" Al spun in circles. "Al likes daisies! Happy-happy flower."

"You're right, Al," Xander said. "They are."

Al laughed and ran back down the corridor, scattering more of them as she went and giggling like a fiend. Such a strange little android.

They would have to find out where she came from and who made her. Maybe her creator could explain why she was so strange.

Xander reached the corridor that led to the bridge. Ben descended from the command deck and stopped in the corridor.

Scowling, he held a daisy. Had Al been through the corridor yet, or had Ben picked it up from the floor? He wrinkled his nose and tossed the flower away. He walked toward the galley.

Why would Ben do that? Maybe he just didn't like daisies? The bright white faces of the flowers smiled up at her from the floor panels. How could anyone dislike them?

Laughter echoed from the galley, but she walked up the stairs to the bridge. She passed Captain McLeod's chair and Ben's navigational console and stood in front of the superglass windows protecting the bridge from space.

In the distance, the Jovian moon Io hung in the velvety backdrop of space. Pockmarked with lava pits and speckled with craters, it looked like a pepperoni pizza.

With a smile, Xander set the daisy Al had given her on the

raised seam of the superglass window. The little daisy smiled at the stars.

"I'm called Xander," she said. "I'm nineteen years old, and I am a follower of Christ." She smiled. "That's all I remember for now. And that's all I need to know."

Something brown and sleek skittered across the metallic floor plates of the bridge. A rat?

Yes. A giant rat with long whiskers and beady black eyes glinting like obsidian in the lights from the control panels. Its claws clicked on the metal plates, and its pointed face turned up to her, whiskers twitching. She stared back.

Weren't people scared of rats?

Xander frowned. Sylphie hated rats. She'd screamed every time she'd found one in her room, and the Oasis had been full of them. Actually, all of Callisto had been full of them, all disease-ridden and filthy. And while Xander didn't like them, they weren't scary.

The rat didn't move. It kept staring at her.

Shouldn't she be scared?

Xander held her breath. A memory surfaced at the back of her mind, so dim, so vague she almost thought it couldn't be real.

She stood in a lab and gazed into a wire cage at a big brown rat. It ran in circles in the cage until she gave it a chunk of bread, which it began to nibble. She spoke to it, but she couldn't remember what she said.

Had it been a pet? Why had it been in a lab? Why had *she* been in a lab?

Something crashed. Xander jumped and grabbed the control console to steady herself. Was the *Prodigal* under attack? Had something blown up?

No.

Al stood before her with a wrench, and the rat lay dead on the floor. Al had crushed it.

Al lifted her face, grinning, fiber optic hair shifting from red to a color so black it almost didn't glow at all.

"Rats are bad, Xander-person." Al stepped forward and held out another daisy. "Have a daisy."

Xander took the flower from Al's spindly fingers, and Al turned and walked away, humming her strange little tune. She left the dead rat on the floor.

Xander remembered the rat in the cage. It hadn't been a pet; it had been an experiment. And it had died too.

But how? And why? What did it have to do with her?

She wanted to remember, but dead rats weren't exactly what she'd had in mind. Instead of leaving this daisy on the bridge, Xander tucked it in her shirt pocket.

Captain McLeod wouldn't appreciate a dead rat on the bridge.

She spotted a maintenance cabinet in the corner. She'd clean it up before anyone found out.

What bothered her more, that Al killed a rat or her memory of a dead one?

As she stooped to clean up the mess, she let her gaze rest on the rat's dim eyes, wide with shock at the brutality of its own death. How had the rat from her memory died?

She couldn't remember.

She dumped the rat's dead body in the refuse chute in the corner. Out of sight; out of mind, right? Now she didn't have to think about it anymore.

Xander returned the brush and pan to the maintenance closet

and walked back toward the galley. Time for breakfast. She needed to get back before the crew came looking for her.

Her footsteps echoed on the bulkheads, but the rat from her memory didn't fade. She could still see it, but the image didn't make sense. The dead rat in her mind floated in a wire cage.

Floated? What sense did that make? None. The product of a broken mind with too much stimulation. Dead rats didn't float.

Xander shoved the memory away. She didn't want to think about the rats, the one from her memories or the one that Al had bludgeoned on the bridge.

The crew laughed in the galley.

Yesterday, with its dark, nonsensical memories, didn't matter. And tomorrow wouldn't matter until it arrived. Tomorrow they would attack the *Tempest*. Tomorrow they would regain the *Destiny*. Today, she would eat breakfast with her friends.

Light from the galley washed over her. She focused on the cheerful daisy in her shirt pocket and let the memory of the dead rat slip away.

Coming Soon
from A.C. Williams

Namesake

The Destiny Trilogy

Part Two

For other titles from Crosshair Press,
visit **www.CrosshairPress.com**!

cr✪sshair
press

Discussion Questions

NAMELESS is the first book in the Morningstar Series, designed to challenge what people think about Christianity, the Church, the Bible, and religion in general.

To start the conversation we've given you discussion questions focused on the particularly challenging elements of the story.

Dive in. Don't be afraid to talk about what's really going on in the world or in your lives.

Join the discussion online at
www.MorningstarDestiny.com
or visit the Morningstar Series Facebook page,
www.facebook.com/MorningstarDestiny.

NAMELESS – DISCUSSION QUESTIONS

The Book

- How did you feel when you read *Nameless*? Were you immediately engaged or did it take a few chapters? Describe your emotions.

- Who was your favorite character and why? How did you identify with Xander? With Kale?

- Is this a plot-driven book, a fast-paced page turner? Or is it a character-driven book, unfolding slowly with focus on developing the characters?

- The author uses more than one viewpoint to tell the story. Which viewpoint did you like best and why? Why do you think the author chose to tell the story that way? What difference does it make in the way you experience the story?

- What are the main themes in the story? How many can you identify? Are there sub-themes?

- What symbols does the author use in the story? Symbols can be people, places, or objects with a deeper or hidden meaning. They often represent themes or characters in the story.

- What was your favorite part of the book? Is there any dialogue you particularly liked? Did any passages strike you as profound or insightful? Is there a statement in the book that summarizes the book and its main theme? Is so, what is it?

- Did you like the ending? Why or why not? Would you have the story unfold differently?

- Did this story change you in any way? Did you learn something new, change your mind or gain new perspective on familiar issues?

The Characters

- What does Xander want to accomplish? What motivates her? Do you think Xander is justified in her actions?

- Xander and the Prodigal crew repeatedly ended up in life-threatening situations. Do you agree with how they handled those situations, or are there actions we shouldn't take, even to survive? What are they and why?

- Has someone ever treated you unfairly like Vix treated Xander? Did Xander handle it the right way? What would you have done differently?

- How did Scraps convince Evy to trust him? What caused Evy's change of heart? Have you ever talked to someone you trusted instantly?

- Discuss the differences between Kale and Devon. Why are they such good friends? Do you have a close friend who's very different from you?

- After the fight on Ring-Seven, Devon chose to stand beside Kale despite his dark past. Have you ever had to love and support someone despite their background or past actions? Would you have chosen the same as Devon or decided to walk away? How would either choice affect your life and relationships?

- Discuss the difference between Kale and Mr. Clayton (the man from the Sanctum). Is it better to be rough yet authentic, or respectable but hypocritical? What's a time when you covered up a dirty secret because of what others would think?

NAMELESS – DISCUSSION QUESTIONS

- When Xander first meets the crew of the Prodigal, she sees them as a threat, but she comes to view them as family. Have you ever met someone you didn't like at first, who later became your friend? Did you change or did they?

- When Xander fist walked onto the Prodigal, she thought it looked like a dump, but by the end of the book, it feels like home. Why did that happen?

- Describe the dynamic between Kale and Xander. How has Xander's experience with men shaped her opinion of Kale? How does Kale's past affect how he sees Xander? Can you relate?

- Do you think Xander changes by the end of the book? If so, how? Is it a change for the better?

Let's Get Personal

- Do you identify with Xander in the difficulties of living in a broken world? If so, in what way?

- Do our personal beliefs influence our actions? If so, how?

- How do you identify yourself? What shapes or determines your identity? Does your faith play a role in your identity?

- Can other people help you discover your identity or is it something you have to find for yourself?

- What are common ways people try to find their identity? Does it usually work?

- What happens to your sense of self-worth when the basis for your identity falls apart? How does that affect your interaction with others?

NAMELESS – DISCUSSION QUESTIONS

- Share a time from your life when you felt alone and isolated with people who didn't understand you. How did you feel and what did you do to cope?

- What makes someone a Christian? What make someone a non-Christian? How can you tell the difference?

- Have you ever gone out of your way to help someone, even when your friends mocked you? Did it turn out well, or did you end up hurt?

- Have you ever done something you didn't want to do just because it was the right thing? If so, what happened and how did it affect your life?

- Have people ever found out something ugly about you? How did you respond? How did they react?

- Have you ever done something you regret? How do you move on? Is it important to talk to others?

- As a Christian in a broken world, how do you deal with difficult people? Have you seen someone you admire handle a situation with a difficult person?

- Is it wrong for a Christian to curse? Why or why not? If non-Christians around you are cursing, should you tell them to stop?

- What do you believe about homosexuality? Why? Have you ever had a friend whose sexual preferences differed from your own? How did that affect your friendship?

- How do you love broken people without agreeing with or condoning their lifestyle choices?

NAMELESS – DISCUSSION QUESTIONS

- How do you keep loving someone even when they reject you? How do you show Christ to someone who doesn't believe He exists?

- Do you have a place that feels like home to you? What makes it home to you? Is home a place or is it the people who live there?

- What's the greatest sacrifice you've made for a friend? What makes your friends worth any sacrifice? What wouldn't you do for them?

- Do any of the characters in Nameless remind you of someone you know? How?

CPSIA information can be obtained at www.ICGtesting.com
Printed in the USA
LVOW06s2350020115

421314LV00002B/342/P